The
GIFTED

Books by Ann H. Gabhart

The Scent of Lilacs
Orchard of Hope
Summer of Joy

Angel Sister
Words Spoken True

The Outsider
The Believer
The Seeker
The Blessed
The Gifted

The GIFTED

A NOVEL

ANN H. GABHART

Revell

a division of Baker Publishing Group
Grand Rapids, Michigan

Published by Revell
a division of Baker Publishing Group
P.O. Box 6287, Grand Rapids, MI 49516-6287
www.revellbooks.com

Printed in the United States of America

Library of Congress Cataloging-in-Publication Data
Gabhart, Ann H., 1947–
    The gifted : a novel / Ann H. Gabhart.
      p. cm.
    ISBN 978-0-8007-3455-8 (pbk.)
    I. Title.
    PS3607.A23G54 2012
    813'.6—dc23   2012007167

Scripture quotations are from the King James Version of the Bible.

Page 157—"Come Life, Shaker Life"—*Selection of Hymns and Poems; for the use of Believers*. By Philos Hamoniae, 1833

Pages 158, 405 & 431—"Simple Gifts"—*Manuscript Hymnals*, 1837–47

Page 389—"Search Ye Your Camps"—*New Lebanon Hymns*, 1841

The internet addresses, email addresses, and phone numbers in this book are accurate at the time of publication. They are provided as a resource. Baker Publishing Group does not endorse them or vouch for their content or permanence.

12   13   14   15   16   17   18   7   6   5   4   3   2   1

To my family—
a treasured gift and blessing.

A Note about the Shakers

American Shakerism originated in England in the eighteenth century. Their leader, a charismatic woman named Ann Lee, was believed by her followers to be the second coming of Christ in female form. After being persecuted for those beliefs in England, she and a small band of followers came to America in 1774 to settle in Watervliet, New York, and there established the first community of the United Society of Believers in Christ's Second Appearing, more commonly known as Shakers. By the middle of the nineteenth century, nineteen Shaker communities were spread throughout the New England states and Kentucky, Ohio, and Indiana.

The Shaker doctrines of celibacy, communal living, and the belief that perfection could be attained in this life were all based on revelations their Mother Ann claimed to have divinely received. The name *Shakers* came from the way they worshiped. At times when a member received the "spirit," he or she would begin shaking all over. These "gifts of the spirit," along with other spiritual manifestations, were considered by the Shakers to be confirmation of the same direct communication with God they believed their Mother Ann had experienced.

The Shakers sought a peaceful, simple life by shutting away the "world." They were as self-sufficient as they could be, raising their own food and making their own clothes from cloth they weaved and their shoes from leather they tanned.

One of their best-known sayings was "Hands to work. Hearts to God." They believed work was a very necessary part of worship. So when their communities grew in population and they had many hands to keep busy, they began to sell the products of their enterprise—garden seeds, brooms, hats, potions, and silk kerchiefs, to mention a few. Shaker may be the first commonly known trademark name in America. If it was a Shaker product, it was trusted to be as advertised and a good value for the money. The Shakers were also known to be a peaceful and generous people who never refused help to any in need.

In Kentucky, the Shaker villages of Pleasant Hill and South Union have been restored and attract many visitors curious about the Shaker lifestyle. These historical sites provide a unique look at the austere beauty of the Shakers' craftsmanship. The sect's songs and strange worship echo in the impressive architecture of their buildings. Visitors also learn about the Shakers' innovative ideas in agriculture and industry that improved life not only in their own communities but also in the "world" they were so determined to shut away.

Journal Entry

Harmony Hill Village
Entered on this 11th day of June in the year 1849
by Sister Sophrena Prescott

The Gathering Family sisters picked the last of
the strawberries in the patch behind the barn. Only
got a paltry 8 gallons and Sister Wilma said some of
those were so small they were nigh on impossible
to cap. But the late-picking jam will be sweet in any
case. The sisters have cooked a plenitude of jam. The
brethren will be well supplied for their trading trips.
If those people at White Oak Springs don't buy it all.
They eat well there, I am told. Matters not to us who
eats our excess jam. We have been blessed with a
bountiful harvest of berries and it appears the wild
raspberries are bearing an abundant crop.

Two of the young sisters have gone out into the
woods with buckets to gather the raspberries. The
thought of raspberry pie for dinner is a pleasant one.
But I worry I shouldn't have given Sister Jessamine
permission to go. She will find the berry vines. I have
no doubt of that, but will she be entangled by the
briars and end with her dress and apron ripped and

ruined? Will she remember to bring any berries home in her bucket? Ah, Sister Jessamine, a sweeter little sister one could not have. Yet, she is often the subject of discussion among the elders and eldresses. What will we do with Sister Jessamine?

Eldress Frieda may take me to task for giving the sister permission to go into the woods, but she has diligently kept to her duties for days without mishap. Plus I did send Sister Annie with her. At eighteen, Sister Annie may be younger than Sister Jessamine by a year, but is as sensible as Sister Jessamine is not. Even so, I worry like an old hen that has lost sight of her little chicks and fears the shadow of a hawk passing over. I haven't seen the shadow, but I know our Sister Jessamine only too well. I will be peering out the window all the afternoon and not properly paying mind to my task of penning the labels for the jam jars.

1

"Sister Jessamine, where on earth are you taking us?" Sister Annie asked as she held on to her cap while ducking under a low-hanging branch.

Jessamine didn't slow her walk as she glanced back at Sister Annie. She liked Sister Annie. She really did. But oh, to be alone in the woods and not always encumbered with a sister to slow her down. She wanted to run free. To swing on a vine if she took the notion. To sit and lean back against a tree trunk and dream up stories about the birds above her head. None of that would be considered proper behavior for a Shaker sister, and Sister Annie did so want to be a proper Shaker. She'd be sure to confess anything she thought improper to Sister Sophrena, no matter which of them committed the supposed sin.

"The best berries are up ahead," Jessamine said. "I can smell them."

"You're not smelling raspberries. That isn't possible," Sister Annie said even as she stopped and lifted her nose a bit to sniff the air.

Jessamine bit the inside of her lip to hide her smile. "My granny could smell squirrels in the trees."

Sister Annie's groan plainly carried up to Jessamine in spite of the rustle of last fall's leaves underfoot. "Is there anything your granny could not do?"

"Stay alive." Jessamine muttered the words under her breath. She didn't want Sister Annie to be reporting them.

After all, it had been almost ten years since her granny failed to keep breathing and the old preacher carried Jessamine to the Shaker village. Not bad years. She wouldn't want her Shaker family to think she was ungrateful for the food and shelter they'd given her. Given her druthers, she would have stayed in the cabin in the woods, but a child of ten is rarely given her druthers. Or a girl of near twenty either for that matter. Duties and responsibilities went along with that food on the table and roof over her head.

There were no perfect places this side of heaven. That was something her granny used to tell her, although in Jessamine's mind their cabin in the middle of the woods seemed perfect enough. Of course her granny never said the first thing about the Shakers. She might not have heard about how they aimed to make a perfect place on earth to match the perfection of heaven. A place with no sin of any kind. A place where all lived as brothers and sisters. A place where a girl couldn't run off to the woods on her own to pick a handful of raspberries and pop them every one in her mouth. At least not without feeling a little guilty about how she might be depriving her sisters and brothers back at the village of a tasty pie.

So far she hadn't found that first handful of raspberries to eat or to put in her pail. And she wasn't being exactly truthful saying she could smell raspberries. She only said that so Sister Annie would keep walking deeper into the woods. The girl's flushed face gave every indication she was ready to turn back. A frown was thundering across her forehead and her mouth was screwed up into a knot not much bigger than an acorn. Any minute now she was going to plant her feet on the path and refuse to go a step farther. And they had to be close to White Oak Springs. They had to be. All Jessamine wanted was a glimpse of the place.

One of the new sisters had built such a word picture inside Jessamine's head of the hotel at White Oak Springs that Jessamine thought it must be a palace set down in the middle of a flower-filled oasis. This sister claimed that in the heat of the day beautiful girls walked across grassy yards with fine parasols to keep the sun off their faces while young men from all around the country sought their favor.

The new sister, who was going on seventeen, sighed with longing as she whispered these stories to Jessamine in the dead of the night with no other ears listening. When Jessamine told her it sounded like the fairy tales her granny used to tell her, Sister Abigail insisted these fairy tales were true. Her stories brought up such fanciful images to Jessamine that she had been overcome with the desire to witness this sight herself. To know if such a fairy-tale place could be true. Parasols instead of caps. Hair curled and held up with jeweled combs instead of stuck forever out of sight.

Jessamine touched her cap and had the errant thought to yank it off and fling it up in a tree for a squirrel to line his nest. But she did not. Instead she carefully tucked a loose strand of her honey blonde hair out of sight. She didn't really want to be wayward. She merely wanted to see with her own eyes what Sister Abigail had described. Surely there was no sin in simply looking.

White Oak Springs was real. She knew that. The Shakers sold their products to the people there. Springs of water were reputed to bubble up out of the ground with a foul odor, but those who came to the springs held to the notion that taking the water cured a myriad of ailments and revived the health. Sister Sophrena waved that off as ridiculous when Jessamine asked her if such was actually possible. But Jessamine's curiosity was aroused. She had carried many buckets of water from a spring to her granny's cabin, but the water had been naught but water. Cool and pleasant for a truth with a joyful song as it trickled out of the rocks, but all it had ever seemed to cure was thirst.

Sister Abigail claimed the Springs were to the west or maybe the south. Then she had pointed due north. The sister completely lacked a sense of direction, but Jessamine had teased a few bits of information from other sisters as they fashioned hats and neckerchiefs that might be taken to the Springs to sell. She was sure she and Sister Annie were going in the right direction, but she had no clue as to how far away it might be. Perhaps too far for Sister Annie's patience. Especially with no berries to show for their long walk.

"You're going to get us so lost not even Elder Joseph will be able to find us, Sister Jessamine." Sister Annie stopped walking.

"We're not lost, Sister Annie. I promise." Jessamine looked back at her. "I have a keen sense of direction and will have no problem at all finding our way back to the village."

"I guess you can smell your way." Sister Annie jerked her handkerchief out of her apron pocket to wipe the sweat from her broad forehead. The poor girl's hair was straggling down out of her cap and her face was red, and not all from the heat, as she glared at Jessamine. "I don't know why Sister Sophrena insisted I come with you. She knows I hate traipsing after you in the woods."

"She knows you'll come back." Jessamine reluctantly turned to walk back to Annie.

"Yea, where else would we go? The village is our home, and I think we should begin in that direction right away. It's obvious you have no more idea where a berry patch is than I do." Annie held up her empty pail. "We have yet to pick the first berry. Sister Sophrena will not be pleased to see us return with empty buckets after being gone so many hours."

"A good patch is just up ahead." Jessamine looked back at

the faint trace of a path she'd been following. Through the trees she thought she could catch sight of more light. That had to mean a road or some kind of clearing. Perhaps the grounds of the Springs itself. She imagined the colors of the parasols spinning overtop the pretty girls' heads. Or perhaps they would be bright white just like the caps she and Sister Annie wore. "Only a little farther."

Sister Annie grabbed Jessamine's arm as she started to turn away. "I'm not going another step away from the village. Not one step."

"Then perhaps you can rest here while I go find the berries." Jessamine flashed her best smile at Sister Annie, but it did nothing to make the other girl's frown fade or to get her to loosen her grip on Jessamine's sleeve.

"Nay, we are both turning back. We can find a different path back through the woods and perhaps find a few cups of berries to prove we were using our time wisely instead of doing no more than ruining our dresses."

Jessamine looked behind her. The light through the trees seemed even brighter and more inviting. She could be that close to seeing those parasols and ruffled dresses, to gazing out on a real, live fairy tale. She wasn't exactly yearning to be part of it. She just wanted to see it. The thought of the parasols pulled at her like an invisible thread.

The very word entranced her. *Parasols*. She thought of telling Sister Annie that. Letting the word roll off her tongue and then making up a story about a frog making his home under a parasol caught by the wind and blown into the woods. A beautiful princess would discover the parasol and find the frog. One kiss and they'd live happily ever after. And the princess would love parasols and the frog-turned-prince would nearly croak every time he saw one.

"Whatever are you smiling about, Sister Jessamine? This is no time for smiles and frivolity. We are lost in the woods."

"Nay, Sister Annie. We're not lost." Jessamine swallowed her smile.

"Well, perhaps not, but we aren't where we should be. It could be we have strayed off our Shaker property."

"That could be," Jessamine agreed. The Shakers owned many acres, but they had been walking a good way. "Why don't we go on a little ways? I think there may be a road up ahead where walking will be easier."

"A road!" Sister Annie's eyes flew open wide as she glanced around. "You think we are that near those of the world? Oh, my heavenly days, Sister Jessamine. What possessed you to lead us into the world? What will we do if we meet some worldly man intent on sin?"

"Men in the world can't be that different from the brothers we see each day." Jessamine tried to make her words sound sure. In fact she had no idea what men were like in the world. Before coming to the Shakers, the only man she'd spoken one word to was the old preacher who had shown up now and again at her granny's cabin toting provisions. Sugar, flour, some pieces of cloth and thread, a tin of coffee beans.

"You live in a storybook land, my sister," Sister Annie said. "Men of the world have not the love our brethren back at the village have. Or the peaceful hearts. They see something they want. They take it. You have been long with the Believers and so have an innocent mind, but I have only been here in the peace of the village a short while. I know what those of the world are like. I am not long from their sinful ways."

"Surely not all men are thus," Jessamine said.

"Not all, but who can know which sort of man we might stumble upon here in this wild place with no recourse but flight." Sister Annie's eyes narrowed on Jessamine. "You truly have no idea of how a girl with your looks might tempt the devil to rise in a man. Eyes the blue of cornflowers and straw-colored hair."

Sister Annie's words put warmth in Jessamine's cheeks that the walk had not. "It is not the beauty on the outside that matters, but that on the inside." Even her granny had told her that before she came to live with the Shakers. Now Sister Sophrena told her the same over and over.

"True enough," Sister Annie agreed. "But the outside beauty is what tempts men to sin often as not."

"How do you know so much about men and what makes them sin?"

"I am not the innocent you are, my sister. My father ran a tavern before he passed last year and my mother and I came to join the Believers. Trust me, I know." Sister Annie's mouth tightened. "More than you might want to imagine."

"But I just want a peek out at the world. Sister Abigail told me about this place called White Oak Springs. Have you ever seen a parasol, Sister Annie?"

"A parasol?" The other girl twisted her mouth to the side as her frown was edged off her face by the beginnings of a smile. She shook her head in disbelief. "You have led us on this wild-goose chase for berries because you want to see a parasol? Sister Sophrena will never believe this."

Jessamine smiled a bit hesitantly. "They sound so pretty. Parasols." She let the word roll off her tongue. "Don't you think so?"

Sister Annie laughed out loud as she stepped closer to Jessamine and put her arm around her waist. "Come, my sister. I will draw a picture of one for you when we get back to the village."

"But we aren't allowed to draw pictures unless a spirit directs our hands." Jessamine began walking back down the path. She was so sure the Springs might be just on the other side of those trees, and a picture of a parasol wouldn't be the same as seeing one twirling in the hands of a girl who might be a princess.

"For information purposes, I'm sure Sister Sophrena will allow it."

Jessamine sighed and surrendered her feet to the will of Sister Annie. Her guardian appointed by Sister Sophrena. She peered back over her shoulders. "Is White Oak Springs close?"

"I couldn't say, since I have almost no idea of where we are, but I think it is much farther away. At least another hour's walk. And we are not going there no matter how many raspberries you might smell."

"But the raspberries would make a delicious pie."

"Then smell some back this way. I will not be swayed. We are not going one step farther away from the village and certainly not one step nearer that den of iniquity." Sister Annie's frown returned. "I have heard plenty of stories about that place. Men and women of leisure with nothing to do but court trouble. Worse even than a tavern where men are often intent on wrongdoing. Such is not our way, Sister Jessamine. The Shaker way is to give our hands to work and our hearts to God."

At times, Jessamine was amazed at Sister Annie's acceptance of the Shaker way. She had a much tighter grip on how to be a proper Shaker after only a few months at the village than Jessamine did after years.

"Yea, it is true," Jessamine agreed quietly. "It was foolish of me to want to glimpse such a place of the world. I will confess my wrong thinking to Sister Sophrena."

"Trust me, Sister. The world is not a place for the likes of an innocent lamb like you. We are safe with our sisters and brethren." Sister Annie grasped Jessamine's hand with affection. "Come, let us leave this place of possible dire consequence and go home."

Disappointment welled up inside Jessamine and a tear slid out of the corner of her eye. Thankfully Sister Annie had turned away and didn't note her foolishness. But what dire consequences could possibly come from seeing a parasol bright against the sunshine?

A sudden boom made Jessamine jump. The color drained from Sister Annie's face as she spun around to clutch Jessamine's arm.

"Gunfire! Oh, dear Mother Ann in heaven, keep us safe," Sister Annie cried as something came crashing through the trees.

2

Sister Annie whirled away from Jessamine to take off running but instead tripped over a root and went sprawling. The rattle of brush and crack of broken branches grew louder as whatever was out there kept tearing through the woods toward them.

Jessamine hurried to help Sister Annie up while saying, "We can't run. Best to simply hide out of sight. It's probably only a horse. Or perhaps a bear."

"A bear!" Sister Annie's voice was little more than a squeak. Then she shook herself a little and went on in a calmer voice. "Nay. The Ministry would not let us go into the woods if there were bears." She let Jessamine pull her back behind a large oak tree.

"We shall pray they know. A horse, even one in a state of panic, is not nearly so fearsome as a bear," Jessamine said as she peeked around the tree.

She could see nothing. Her heart was pounding up in her ears, more in anticipation than fear. A bear or even a runaway horse might be as good to see as a parasol. She held her breath and waited for something to emerge from the trees. She tried to feel shame for her eagerness since she could feel

Sister Annie trembling beside her, but she could hardly wait. A person couldn't really know a thing until she witnessed the sight of it with her own eyes.

"Don't give away our hiding spot." Sister Annie grabbed Jessamine's collar as though to keep her from falling out into the open. "While a horse might not be fearsome, the man astride him could be. That was gunfire. Of that I am positive."

"Someone squirrel hunting perhaps," Jessamine offered.

"Nay. Squirrel hunters walk quietly through the woods as they seek their game." She yanked on Jessamine's collar. "Have you no fear, Sister?"

Jessamine paid her no mind as she kept peering around the tree. "It's only a horse. I can see it now. With no rider."

"Is there a saddle?" Sister Annie mashed her back so tightly against the tree trunk that the rough bark had to be digging into her skin even through the sturdy material of her dress. She looked out of the corner of her eyes at Jessamine.

"Yea, I think so."

"Then there was a rider. He will be chasing after his horse."

"Perhaps, but I don't see anyone and the poor animal looks frightened." Jessamine stared at the horse a moment. "He's slowing down. I'll go catch him and then we can look for his rider."

"We're not looking for any rider." Sister Annie grasped Jessamine's collar even tighter. "And you can't catch a horse. You know nothing about horses."

Jessamine patted Sister Annie's hand. "It will be fine. My granny said animals know when a person is trying to help them. Worry not." She uncurled the girl's fingers from her collar and stepped away from the tree.

"If you get hurt, Sister Sophrena will blame me. And what about that gunshot?"

"Engaged in our duty, we have nothing to fear." Jessamine pulled out one of the Shaker sayings.

"This is not our duty."

"Did not Mother Ann tell us it is our duty to help any who are in need of help? To do good to all we meet. We can't run away without seeing if our help is needed."

"I can," Sister Annie said even as she edged around the tree to watch Jessamine.

Jessamine didn't look back again. She kept her eyes on the horse that raised its head and blew air out its nose when it spotted her. But with one of the reins caught in a bush, the horse must have felt tethered.

"Easy, boy." Jessamine spoke softly as she slowly approached the horse. She had no idea if she had addressed the animal correctly.

Sister Annie was right. She knew nothing about horses. But she had once befriended a young raccoon in the woods with the help of her granny. That had taken food of which she had none now. A few berries might have been helpful. Or an apple. Horses liked apples. She did know that much. She clucked her tongue. She'd heard the brothers make that sound when they hitched the horses to the wagons back in the village.

The horse lifted its head high and watched her with dark brown eyes, but its hooves were still. Jessamine took that as a favorable sign. She held her hand out toward its nose the way her granny had taught her to meet any stray dog that showed up at their cabin. Granny liked dogs and always invited the hounds up on the porch to rest awhile before they went on their way. One old dog had come by nearly every week, but Granny hadn't claimed ownership of it. Said a dog should be free to come and go as it pleased.

Horses were different. Especially one with a saddle and dangling reins like this brown beauty with flecks of foam dotting its neck. The horse backed away from her hand and pulled its reins loose from the bush, but Jessamine grabbed them out of the air. The horse immediately calmed when it felt the tug of the reins.

"Were you out here all alone?" Jessamine asked softly. "Or did you unseat your rider?"

"You are forgetting the gunshot." Sister Annie stepped out from behind the tree.

"Nay, I have forgotten nothing. But that could have been far away and nothing to do with this horse."

"And we could be lined up with our sisters to go into the evening meal, but we are not." Sister Annie looked ready to cry. "Oh, but how I wish we were. I'm never going berry picking with you again. I don't care what Sister Sophrena says I must do."

"I'm sorry, Sister Annie." Jessamine took her eyes off the horse long enough to throw a glance back at the other girl. "I truly am. Why don't you go on and start back? I will follow as soon as I make sure no one lies bleeding out in the woods."

Sister Annie hesitated. "But what if someone is lying bleeding? What do you propose to do about it? Let us both go back to the village and get help. That is the only sensible thing to do. You know Sister Sophrena would never forgive me leaving you and letting you face danger alone. You are her favorite."

"Nay, that is not the Shaker way. We are not to raise one brother or sister up over another." She recited the words she'd heard dozens of times.

"Nor are we to run off and get lost in the woods either and yet here we are." Sister Annie's voice was a whisper shout.

The horse nickered and jerked up its head, yanking the reins loose from Jessamine. The horse shied away from her and then, as it seemed to get its bearings, started walking back through the trees. It no longer seemed frightened in the least but moved with purpose.

"Wait here," Jessamine told Sister Annie. She paid no mind to the other girl's protests as she followed after the horse.

23

She had been right about the open space between the trees ahead of them. There was a road, but not a well-traveled one. It was no more than a logging trail perhaps made by some of the brethren from the village as they harvested logs from the forest. Certainly it wasn't a road that would lead to a place like White Oak Springs.

She noted a stump nearly as wide around as a wagon wheel and she looked up, imagining the tree it had once been. A hole had been torn in the forest roof. She shook away the mournful feeling that tried to capture her. The tree had no doubt been turned into a useful building, and nothing or nobody on this earth lived forever. Not this tree. Not her granny. And perhaps not the rider of the horse she was trailing behind.

The horse stopped and nibbled a few blades of grass.

"And so you care no more than that about whoever you lost from your back?" Jessamine spoke aloud as if the horse would understand her words.

The horse lifted its head and looked at her for a moment before turning its attention back to the patch of grass. Jessamine walked past it to search but saw nothing but more trees. The fallen rider must have dusted himself off and gone back to wherever he'd come from, however odd it seemed that he wouldn't search for his horse first.

She was ready to turn back when she caught sight of a boot up ahead of her. A boot that was connected to a man lying in a deep rut. Jessamine hardly dared breathe as she stepped closer to the man, who was lying much too still. Blood oozed from an angry-looking wound on the side of his head, and his right arm was bent in an unnatural angle.

With relief, she noted his closed eyes. That could be a hopeful sign. Much better than open and staring at nothing except the beyond side of death, she decided as she peered at his chest. Yea, he was definitely breathing, but she couldn't see the least bit of flutter to his eyelids.

Jessamine had no idea what to do next. Go for help, she supposed, but how without leaving the man there alone? That seemed wrong. She moved another step closer to him. His felt hat had spilled off and dark brown hair tumbled down over his forehead. He could be a prince. Not one she might see after kissing a frog, but one from somewhere across the sea. Handsome and strong. Or at least strong before the fall from his horse. Now helpless as he lay there with his chest rising and falling but showing no other sign of life.

She should do something. Speak to him. Try to bring him back to consciousness. Then he might tell her how she could help him. And whether he was real or just one of the storybook princes her granny used to make up to entertain her. Maybe she was only imagining him there in front of her the way she'd just imagined the tree lifting to the sky a moment ago.

She shut her eyes and opened them again. He was there. Still as stone, but definitely there. She could see dark whiskers beginning to shadow his clean-shaven cheeks. A dark moustache sprouted below his nose, but he had no beard like so many of the brethren at the village. She stooped down beside him and reached out her hand toward his face. She couldn't remember ever touching a man's face. Her granny had no use for men other than the old preacher and the princes who populated her stories.

"Dream them up," her granny would say as she rocked back and forth in the chair on the porch. "That's the only kind to have truck with, my sweet little Jessamine. You keep that in mind when you get older, child. Don't be settling for just anybody. Wait for your prince. The good Lord will send one."

But after she came to the Shakers, Sister Sophrena told her the Lord had changed his mind about men and women finding one another and having families. He'd revealed as much to Mother Ann. She'd taught her followers that being married caused too much conflict in the world and was a sin a person did well to repent of and set aside. The Shakers tamped down on the normal temptations of the flesh by keeping the sisters and brothers always apart with separate doorways and staircases and eating tables. The Ministry feared even a slight brush against one of the opposite sex might plummet a Believer into sin.

So it could be with her touching this man's cheek. Her hand hovered in the air over him. The warmth of his skin rose up to her and she told herself she should put her hand behind her. What was that Bible verse where the Lord told his followers it was better to chop off one's hand rather than let it pull one into sin? But what was so sinful about a touch? No one would have to know. She wouldn't have to admit her sin of curiosity to Sister Sophrena. While the good sister said unconfessed sin was a burden on the soul, so far Jessamine hadn't felt all that burdened when she kept a lapse of obedience to herself. She rather thought it was a favor to Sister Sophrena not admitting all her wayward thoughts.

For years, the poor woman had tried to get Jessamine to embrace the Shaker way, but Jessamine couldn't stop her wondering. And her wandering too. She wanted to know. She wanted to see beyond the village. She wanted to imagine. She wanted to make up stories about princes. And it would be good to know exactly how a man's face might feel under her hand instead of just imagining it.

"Is he dead?"

Jessamine was so startled by the voice she almost fell on top of the man. She caught her balance and jerked back her hand as she scrambled to her feet. With her hand over her heart and a bit out of breath, she turned to stare at Sister Annie on the road behind her. "You startled me, Sister Annie. I didn't know you followed me."

"I didn't want to. Believe me. But we are sisters and if there's danger, it's my duty to share it with you."

Jessamine turned back to the man on the ground. "I don't think he is a danger to us."

"Perhaps not in his current state, but what about the gunshot? You keep forgetting that there was gunfire." Sister Annie leaned forward to peer around Jessamine toward the man. "Does he have a gun?"

Jessamine let her eyes sweep down the man's slender body. He wore a coat something like the brothers wore to meeting, but of a richer-looking cloth, and his shirt was very white. The coat lay open to reveal a regular belt around the waist of his dark trousers. "No gun that I can see."

"Well, somebody had one. If not him, then somebody else." Sister Annie looked around. Her voice trembled as she went on in almost a whisper. "Somebody who could be watching us right now. May our Eternal Father protect us."

"Do you think he was shot?" Jessamine knelt down beside the man again. She thought of pulling her handkerchief out of her apron pocket to wipe away the blood on the side of his face. That could not be sinful even in Sister Annie's eyes. "We have to help him."

Sister Annie surprised her by agreeing. "Yea, but how?"

"You can go to the village and get help while I wait here with him."

"Nay. I won't leave you alone with a man of the world, and besides, I would get lost a dozen times trying to get back to the village. That would be no help to him or us either. By the time the elders sent out people to search for us, the man might be dead."

Jessamine's heart jumped up in her throat. "We can't let him die."

"God holds the number of our days."

"But I don't want him to die." Jessamine kept her eyes on the man's face.

"You don't even know him, Sister Jessamine. You are only

imagining one of those stories in your head that get you into nothing but troubling fixes." Sister Annie's voice was cross again. "It would be best for you to rein in such thoughts before you fall into sin. This man is not one of the princes in the fairy tales your grandmother told you."

"Yea, Sister Annie. You are right, but even so, we must help him. We must take him back to the village where Brother Benjamin can treat him for his injuries."

"That might be a proper plan, but how?"

"Perhaps on his horse," Jessamine suggested. The horse might still be nearby.

"The man's arm appears to be broken. He could have other bones broken as well. Even if we were strong enough to do so, we might make his injuries worse putting him on a horse."

"Well, if we can't move him and we can't leave him, what can we do?" Jessamine looked at his face with the blood trickling down toward his ear from the angry gash on his head. She did take out her handkerchief then and dabbed it against the wound. She waited to see if Sister Annie would condemn her actions, but when she did not, Jessamine reached out with her other hand to take hold of the handkerchief.

With great care to make her movement look totally unplanned, she gingerly laid her hand down on the man's cheek. The emerging whiskers were prickly under her fingers. She forgot about Sister Annie watching her and ran her fingers up his cheek toward his eye. There his skin was smooth and his lashes soft as downy feathers. Quite without thinking she dropped the handkerchief and touched her own eyelashes with her other hand. His felt much the same as hers.

"Whatever are you doing, Sister Jessamine?"

"Just wiping the blood from the gash on his head," she said quickly.

"I might be more apt to believe that if the handkerchief were in your hand instead of forgotten on the ground."

A flush rose up into Jessamine's cheeks as she snatched up the handkerchief and began dabbing at the bloody gash again. "Forgive me, Sister. But I had never touched a man's face before. I have continually wondered about their whiskers. How they might feel."

"Sister Sophrena often says your curiosity may be the death of you, but whether or not that is true, I am beginning to fear it will be the death of me." Sister Annie let out a long sigh. "And we are not one iota nearer a solution to our dilemma than we were. We have no choice. We must leave him here and go back to the village. Elder Joseph will know what to do."

"I suppose you are right."

Reluctantly Jessamine lifted her hand away from the man's face and started to stand. But before she could get to her feet, the man's eyes popped open and he grabbed her wrist. She sucked in a startled breath as Sister Annie let out a frightened yelp behind her. She jerked to free herself, but the man's grip was strong. She was caught as surely as a rabbit in a snare. So she went still and stared down into eyes the brown of butternut.

After a moment, she said, "Hello." Her voice carried hardly any tremble at all.

3

"An angel." The man's voice was as deep as his eyes were piercing. "I must be dead."

"Nay, assuredly not. Your grip is much too strong for a dead man." Jessamine glanced down at his hand around her arm and then back at his face. Behind her, Sister Annie was breathing fast, as if she had already started running away even though she hadn't moved one toe, but Jessamine's curiosity was conquering any thought of fear. "And I must regretfully admit to being far from an angel."

"Where am I?"

The man tried to raise his head to look around. When he groaned and fell back to the ground, his grip weakened and Jessamine pulled free of his hold.

"Rest easy," she said. She stripped off her apron to wad up and slip under his head. "You are in a woods not far from the Shaker village of Harmony Hill."

"Not far?" Sister Annie sounded incredulous. "Honestly, Sister Jessamine, we have to be miles from the village. Miles."

Jessamine ignored her as the man studied her face before he asked, "What happened?"

"I cannot say for certain, but it appears your horse may have thrown you."

"Don't forget about the gunfire." Sister Annie spoke up again behind her.

"There are two of you? Or perhaps a whole band of angels coming for me. I should be so lucky." There was little humor in his short laugh that turned into another groan as again he raised up to peer past Jessamine toward Sister Annie.

Jessamine gently pushed him back down. "We have no angel wings. Only aprons and caps. We are sisters from the village."

"Sisters. I hear your sister's voice, but see no one. Tell her to come closer so I can see if she is as beautiful as you."

"Her spirit is much purer than mine. That's where true beauty lies."

"It matters not who is beautiful." Sister Annie's voice was strident. "We must return to the village for help before darkness falls. There could be more men of the world in the woods."

They did need to do something and soon. Jessamine started to rise to her feet, but once more the man grabbed her arm and kept her from standing.

"What is your name, little angel?"

"Jessamine and behind me is Sister Annie. We want to help you, but we're not sure how."

"And there is the matter of the gunfire your sister heard."

"Yea."

"Do I have a hole in my chest leaking out my lifeblood as we speak? Is that what makes me so anxious to see angels?" He turned loose of her arm to put his hand to his chest.

"Nay. There is no wound in your chest. You do have a wound on your head that is bleeding, but it does not appear to be too deep. Perhaps you hit a branch when you fell."

"Or perhaps it was that gunfire your sister cannot forget. Are you sure there was gunfire or could it have been thunder?" He sounded almost amused.

"I know gunfire when I hear it," Sister Annie said. "It is a noise like no other. A sound that can signal death for man or animal."

"Your sister Annie knows of what she speaks."

"Do you think someone was shooting at you?" Jessamine looked over her shoulder at the dark shadows under the trees. They suddenly looked menacing instead of inviting.

The man got an odd look on his face. "I don't know."

"Do you know how far you are from your home? It could be we should go there for help instead of all the way back to our village."

The look on his face grew more concerned. "I don't know that either. I seem to not know anything. I do not even know a name to tell you by way of introduction."

"You must know your name," Sister Annie said.

"So one would think."

The man tried to raise himself to a sitting position using both arms. When he pushed against the ground with his injured arm, he let out a cry of pain. Jessamine scrambled to put her arm behind his back to hold him upright. He shut his eyes and took several deep breaths.

"Your arm looks to be broken," she told him. "But the bone isn't protruding through the skin. So that is good."

He opened his eyes and peered down at his arm. "Good. I guess that is one way to look at it." A fine sheen of perspiration covered his face. He leaned away from her arm and managed to sit on his own.

Jessamine picked up her apron. There were bloodstains on the white.

"So now what, little sister? Do we sit here in the middle of the woods and wait for someone to find us or for another gunshot to disturb our peace?"

"We will go get help." Sister Annie spoke the words with decision.

"And leave me to the darkness of the forest and my mind. And the evil that might be lurking in the shadows and waiting to find me alone."

"We won't leave you," Jessamine said. Then she changed it. "I won't leave you."

"And I won't leave you alone with him," Sister Annie said.

"What a quandary." The man frowned. "I do wish I knew my name. It is hard to think of any sort of sensible plan when I can't even come up with my own given name." He patted his coat pockets with his hand. "Empty. No clue to who I am there."

"Your horse might carry something to help," Jessamine said.

"My horse. That is our answer. Help me to my feet."

"You could have other injuries."

"Then it is time we found out about them," he said as he began trying to get up on his knees.

Jessamine stooped by his side and the man put his hand on her shoulder. "Help us, Sister Annie," Jessamine said.

Sister Annie came around behind the man and with great reluctance put her hands under his armpits. It took several attempts, but the man seemed to grow stronger with each attempt until he was finally able to stand. With his broken arm close against his body, he put his other arm around Jessamine's shoulders and leaned so heavily on her she feared she might crumple under his weight. The blood drained from his face until it was as white as her collar.

"Do you feel faint?" Jessamine didn't wait for him to answer. "A foolish question. It's clear you feel faint. Here, see if you can step over to that tree. You can rest against it a moment to gather your strength while we fashion a sling for your arm from my apron."

He did as she said and then stood silent while she and Sister Annie tore strips from her apron to tie around his neck and chest to hold his arm against his body.

She looked into his eyes when they had finished. "I'll get your horse. Then you will have to get on it. We will be unable to lift you."

When she started away, Sister Annie trailed after her. Jessamine stopped her. "You should stay beside him, Sister, to hold him up if dizziness comes upon him. He won't hurt you."

Sister Annie frowned and stood her ground. "I don't know how you could know such a thing. He is a man of the world and not one of our good brothers."

"Worry not, little sister." The corners of the man's mouth turned up in a grim smile. "I promise to only use you as a crutch. Nothing more."

"I can pray it so." Sister Annie took two steps back toward the tree but stayed well out of arm's reach of the man.

"So you believe in prayer, Annie," the man said.

"I do." Sister Annie's voice carried absolute surety. "Don't you?"

"It's hard to say since I know so little else, but I feel no comfort at the thought of prayer. No comfort at all. I must be a lost soul in more ways than one."

Jessamine wanted to turn and offer him some word of assurance, but the truth was that sometimes she wondered about her own prayers. If they might merely be more story words she'd thought up that meant nothing at all. She pushed the blasphemous thought away. She believed. Absolutely she believed. It was just that sometimes she wasn't exactly sure what it was that she did believe.

What she remembered from hearing the Bible stories at her granny's knee and what the Shakers told her was truth seemed too different. Sister Sophrena was always telling her to pray for the truth to be revealed to her. She had silently said that prayer many times, but no clear truths had been planted in her mind. Instead the prayers seemed to open doors to more questions. And more worldly thoughts of the prince her granny said the Lord would send her way. That very thought was sinful and would put her feet on a path her Shaker sisters assured her would lead to naught but sin and sorrow. She had no desire for more sorrow, but she did have the worrisome desire to know more of many things forbidden by the Shakers. Like White Oak Springs and parasols. And how a man's beard felt under her hand.

Her hand tingled as she remembered the prickly feel of the man's cheek. Something like she imagined and yet at the same time totally different. No doubt a long beard like Elder Joseph wore would not feel the same. Perhaps more like the coat of that long-ago pet raccoon.

"Please hurry, Sister Jessamine," Sister Annie called to her.

"Yea," Jessamine answered softly.

Sister Annie was right. It was time she quit dawdling and thinking on things with no bearing on the duty at hand. The horse raised its head and stared at her warily when she walked toward it to once again capture its reins. She moved very quietly, but the horse, seeming to divine her purpose, backed away from her.

"The man says you must talk to the horse." Sister Annie's voice made the horse throw up its head. Whether with curiosity or alarm, Jessamine couldn't determine.

Without looking back at Sister Annie and the man, she began talking softly almost under her breath. "Nice horse. Remember me. I didn't do you any harm before. I only want to catch your reins and take you to a nice barn where one of our kind brothers will pour out grain for you to eat and wipe down your coat. You must be hungry."

She stooped slowly to pluck up a bit of grass growing in a spot of sunshine and then stood to hold it out to the horse. She held her breath while the horse considered the offered grass as if wondering if it was worth the risk of stepping closer to her. And then it did. She let it nibble the grass from the palm of her hand as she caught hold of the reins with her other hand.

The horse followed after her with no hesitation as she led it back toward the man propped against the tree. Sister Annie watched him warily from several feet away. She would have been no help at all to the man if he had started to fall.

"Now what?" Sister Annie's eyes shifted from the man to the horse. "We lifted him from the ground, but we cannot lift him onto the horse."

Jessamine held out the reins to Sister Annie. "You take the horse and I will help our friend mount up."

"Friend. You're letting your imagination run away with you again, my sister." Sister Annie frowned. "He's naught but a man of the world. No friend or prince either. For all we know he might have deserved to have someone shooting at him."

"Shh, Sister Annie." Jessamine matched her sister's frown as she continued to hold the reins out to the other girl. "Your words are unkind."

"But perhaps very true," the man said with a short laugh. "It could be I did deserve the fate of a bullet crease in my head. But if so, I have no recollection at all of why that might be so, and I do promise you that I will restrain any evil impulses that might beset me, at least until after some person of medicine has straightened the bones of my arm. You say there is such a person at your village?"

"He has fixed many a Believer's bones so they could return to their labors in the fields when they healed." Jessamine smiled over at him.

"This man will do no labor in our fields," Sister Annie muttered, the words barely loud enough to hear.

"But it could be I labor in fields somewhere." The man looked down at his hand. "My hand does not look overly soft. I can't imagine that I don't do some kind of work." He let out a long breath. "How very strange not to know any answers."

"Perhaps it is the injury to your head that steals your answers," Jessamine told him. "Brother Benjamin may be able to help with that too. Come, the horse seems to wait upon you patiently."

He pushed away from the tree and wobbled back and forth until Jessamine shoved the reins into Sister Annie's reluctant hands and wrapped her arm around his waist to keep him balanced. "Lean on me."

"I fear crushing you."

"I am stronger than I look," Jessamine said.

He was a head taller than she was and when he slid his good arm around her shoulders, she felt his weight bearing down on her all the way to her heels. He smelled of the woods and sweat, a manly scent she secreted away in her imagination along with the feel of the stubble of whiskers on his cheek and the strength in the hard muscles under his coat.

A completely foreign feeling tickled awake inside her as her heart began beating too fast. Suddenly she knew, without any doubt, that this very feeling of some sort of unmet need was the reason for the Believers' rules that kept the sisters and brothers forever separate. But in spite of the way her cheeks were burning and her stomach was doing some odd flips, it was not altogether an unpleasant feeling.

The horse turned its head to nicker at the man without fright.

"The animal appears to know you." Jessamine hoped the man would think her shortness of breath was due to the way he leaned on her. And in truth it was.

"At least someone does." The man took his arm from around Jessamine's shoulder and grabbed hold of the front edge of the saddle. He put his foot in the stirrup and lifted himself up easily, but then once on the horse he slumped forward.

"This is not going to work. He will fall off before we go ten feet and then be injured worse than ever," Sister Annie said.

The man grasped the horse's mane and raised his head up. "Sensible sister Annie is right. My head won't quit spinning. One of you best ride along with me."

"Have you ever ridden a horse, Sister Annie?" Jessamine asked. "I have not."

Sister Annie looked ready to drop the reins as she backed away from the horse. "You had never caught a horse either. Or touched a man's face or done a dozen other things that you have done today. If one of us must ride, I suggest it be you. I have no desire to wrap my arms around a man of the world."

"Even one as handsome as me?" the man said with a little laugh.

Sister Annie gave him a look through narrowed eyes. "So you know you're handsome, but you don't know your name."

The man put his hand up to his face and felt across his nose and chin. "You have a point there, sensible Annie. As a matter of fact, my words may have been no more than wishful thinking, since I have no idea if my nose sits on my face straight or sideways."

"I will ride with you." Jessamine took the reins from Sister Annie. "But you'll have to hold on until I can walk your horse to a stump to help me climb up behind you."

She had to make two attempts from up on the stump, but at last she managed to throw her leg over the horse that had become quite passive with his master in the saddle. The horse moving under Jessamine's seat felt very odd, and she thought it very likely she would simply slide off over its tail when it took a step forward. She tugged on her dress, but no way could she cover both her ankles with the way her skirt bunched up under her as she sat astride the horse.

Such an exposure of limbs was yet another sin she would have need to confess to Sister Sophrena. Sister Annie had a way of reporting the least thing whenever she accompanied Jessamine on a duty. So it would be best if Jessamine didn't neglect to remember her lack of modesty in her confession of wrongs to Sister Sophrena even though the sturdy Shaker shoes and stockings hid every inch of skin. Oh, for the barefoot freedom of her young years.

"How do you stay on?" she asked as she shifted uneasily on the horse's broad back. The man appeared to be well settled in the saddle in spite of his dizzy head and weakened state.

"Boots in the stirrups help," he said even as he wobbled to the side a bit. She grabbed hold of his waistcoat to steady him, but it was more than obvious that if he continued to fall, she would have to turn him loose or be subject to following him to the ground.

"I think it might work better if you move in front of me," he said. "That way I can hang onto you and conquer the dizziness, and you can hold onto the pommel of the saddle or my good horse's mane. Your sensible sister can lead us along toward your village."

Jessamine slid awkwardly off the horse but managed to land on her feet. It was easier climbing back on with the man helping her with his good arm. He scooted back in the saddle to make room, but there was no air between them. She was the same as sitting in his lap.

Sister Annie looked at her with eyes wide as saucers and a red blush warming her cheeks. "Are you sure you can ride thus, Sister Jessamine?"

Jessamine had no problem reading her thoughts. More sin to confess. "Yea, I think I am too tightly wedged into the saddle to fall off."

"Your falling off was not my chief concern." She raised her eyebrows at Jessamine.

"Yea, but our injured brother falling off is our chief concern. This does seem to be the best way."

"Brother. Am I your brother?" The man wrapped his good arm around Jessamine and leaned against her back.

"All men are our brothers," Jessamine said.

"That sounds like Bible talk. But I think I would much prefer you not be my sister."

Jessamine didn't know what to say to that, so she ignored his words and pointed Sister Annie in the direction of the village. She was relieved when the man said no more. She had enough confusion running through her mind from the feel of his body against her without the addition of words with uncertain meaning. As they made their way slowly through the trees, she told herself she was nothing more than a post the man was clinging to for support.

His body leaned more heavily against hers and she thought he might be losing consciousness. She sat strong and steady even after her shoulders began to ache under his weight. They would soon be in the village where she could give over the burden of the man to the brethren. She would seek out Sister Sophrena and confess the sin of touching the man. But she wouldn't feel remorse even if Sister Sophrena told her she should. And she wouldn't forget. The prince of her imagination had become a man of flesh and muscle and bone.

Then Sister Annie's words from earlier whispered back through Jessamine's mind. *This man of the world is no prince.*

Journal Entry

Harmony Hill Village
Entered on this 12th day of June in the year 1849
by Sister Sophrena Prescott

My fears about allowing Sister Jessamine to go searching for raspberry vines in the woods turned out to be well founded. She and Sister Annie brought no berries home in their buckets. But they did bring back something. At near dark when I had all but given up on them and was ready to seek out Elder Joseph to see what would be best to do to find our lost sisters, they appeared out of the gloaming.

At first I thought it might be no more than a vision brought on by my worry. Sister Annie leading a horse when I know her fear of the large animals and Sister Jessamine astride that very horse with a man of the world wrapped as close to her as the shuck on an ear of corn. He was slumped, his head resting on her shoulder. It was plain to see by her pale face that his weight was a burden she struggled to bear as she leaned a bit forward over the horse's neck to give the man better support. Her skirts were bunched up as she sat astride the horse with no way to maintain any sort of proper modesty.

I went out to meet them. I thought it best to hear at least part of their story before raising the cry for help. Sister Annie's tears began spurting as soon as she saw me. Her cap was sitting askew and words begging forgiveness spilled out of her mouth. I touched her face and bade her be silent as I looked up at Sister Jessamine.

"He is injured," she said. "His head and his arm. We knew naught else to do but bring him here. He cannot remember where he lives. Or even his name."

She wore none of the ready guilt on her face like that showing so clearly on Sister Annie's. Instead her eyes challenged me to find wrong in what she was doing. Not the first time I've seen that look in our sister's eyes. She often stumbles over the tried-and-true rules handed down by the Ministry. Nay, more than stumbles. She does her best to step over them or run around them without consideration of how those very rules are what make our village and every village of Believers veritable paradises on earth.

I took the reins and sent Sister Annie for help as there were no other brothers or sisters on the road or pathways. All were in the upper rooms practicing their worship songs. I could hear the voices drifting down to where we stood on the road. In my worry, I had deliberately chosen to neglect my duty of gathering with my family. As it turned out, my concern for my little sisters was not alleviated by the sight of them coming home. New concerns surfaced.

The man raised his head to peer down at me, but the movement must have made him ill for he began retching. If I had not stepped back quickly,

*my dress would have been quite ruined. Not that
such would matter. Dresses can be laundered. Sister
Jessamine grasped his arm that was about her waist
and somehow they managed to stay on the horse in
spite of his heaves. The man mumbled something I
could not properly hear but that might have been
an apology for his sickness. Sister Jessamine kept her
firm hold on his arm, and he dropped his head back
on her shoulder as if it were a welcome respite.*

*When he seemed settled, I led the horse forward
to a fresh spot on the road. It was a relief to see the
brethren hurrying from the house and then Brother
Benjamin was there directing us to the infirmary in
the Centre House before the brethren tried to lift
the stranger from the horse. Once in front of the
building, the men took him down gently although he
seemed to turn loose of Sister Jessamine with some
reluctance. His left arm was bound to his chest by
strips from her apron that were stained with blood.*

*Her collar too bore the evidence of the man's
blood. So even though I had many questions, I
chose to wait to ask them until this day. I thought
it better to send the young sisters to their rooms to
clean themselves before the retiring bell rang and let
confession of their wrongs wait for the morrow.*

*Sister Annie was waiting for me at first light. She
told me in detail all that happened with no hesitation.
Sister Jessamine will come to me later today to make
her own confessions. She will tell a different story,
but one that will seem as true to her. Her mind thinks
differently. In spite of being with us for so many
years, I fear that inside she remains the child who
ran so free in her natural grandmother's woods and
knew nothing of the real world. All was a lark to her*

until the grandmother's death. She still knows little of the world. For since that time she has lived among us where peace reigns and the evils of the world are shut away. Sometimes I think it might have been better if she had experienced more of the wickedness of the world as our Sister Annie has. Then she might feel more readiness to accept the Shaker way and mash down the curiosity that continually trips her up. We shall see what she has to say for herself.

The man they brought into the village remains a mystery. He claims to not know his name. Brother Benjamin reports that possible with a head injury. It appears he was shot and the bullet grazed the side of his head. Brother Benjamin says the lapse of memory was not caused by the bullet wound, but rather a blow to the back of the head. Brother Benjamin has set the man's arm and dressed his wound, but says only the Eternal Father knows if or when the man might come to his senses. If we are unable to determine from whence he comes, Elder Joseph will send for the town's sheriff. The gunshot wound is a worry. We have no desire to harbor a fugitive from the law.

4

Tristan Cooper had no idea where he was when he opened his eyes to see a wrinkled face peering down at him. Her white cap and collar pulled up a memory of beautiful blue eyes gazing down at him, but whatever beauty might have once shone in this woman's face had long since surrendered to age.

Perhaps he had done no more than dreamed the other face. The very memory seemed to be drifting in the fog of his mind, untethered to any actual happening.

"Hello, young brother. Are you ready to return to the land of the living?" There was kindness in the old woman's voice.

Brother. His lips tried to form the word to speak it aloud, but his mouth was too dry, and the sound he uttered made no sense even to his own ears. But her addressing him as brother brought the memory of the striking blue eyes sharper. It had not been a dream. One with those eyes had found him in the woods. They had ridden his horse to her village. Her name. She told him her name, but it hid in the murkiness of his mind. He could not call it forth.

He wondered if this woman leaning over him now could be her grandmother. Or great-grandmother. She looked ancient, and though the blue of her eyes was faded like the blue of a cloth washed and hung in the sun to dry on too many days, they might have once been the vivid blue of the girl's eyes.

"A few sips of water will lubricate your tongue." When the woman smiled, even more wrinkles appeared in her face. She slid her arm behind him to lift his head so he could drink from the glass she offered him.

When he gulped the water greedily, she pulled the glass away. "It is best to take in the water slower. You don't want to lose it all on your clean bed if it lands too hard in your stomach and rebounds back out."

She put the glass back to his lips, and he did as she said and let the water trickle into his mouth. It was cool and refreshing. This time she held the glass to his mouth until every drop slid down his throat.

"Thank you," he said as she lowered his head back down on the pillow.

"So your voice returns," the woman said as she sat down on a chair pulled up close to the bed. "And what of your name? Has memory of it returned as well?"

"My name?"

"Yea, the young sisters who brought you to the village said you claimed to have no memory of who you are."

He did remember then. More than the beautiful face surrounded by white. He remembered his confusion of thought and the odd feeling of being completely adrift with no memory of who he was or what he was doing. And the sensible sister talking of gunfire.

"Was I shot?" he asked. He lifted a hand to the bandage above his ear. His other arm was bound to a hard, flat piece of wood.

"Yea, it appears so. You have a bullet crease to the side of your head. An inch to the right and you would be talking to your Maker instead of me." She kept smiling as if that idea was no reason for concern.

"Who shot me?"

"That might be something you would have more knowledge of than I." The color of her eyes might be faded and deep wrinkles might be lining her cheeks, but there was no dimming of the mind of the woman staring at him. When he made no answer, she went on. "Our young sisters heard the shot but saw no one but you in the woods. They were quite brave to offer you help."

"Or foolish," Tristan said.

"Yea, foolishness is a trait of one of the sisters, but you might be indebted to her foolishness on this occasion. The section of the woods where they found you was far from any sign of civilization. You might have long laid in the woods without their intercession on your behalf."

"And whoever shot me might have come back to finish the job."

"So you know someone was trying to harm you?" She leaned forward in her chair as though to better hear him. "That it was not an accident?"

"I remember nothing about it, mistress . . ." He hesitated. "If you've told me your name, I don't remember that either."

"Or your own?" She fixed her eyes on him again as she awaited his answer.

"Or my own," he said easily. It had been true out in the woods when he said the same to the sister with the beautiful eyes. His confusion then was real enough. He'd been floating in an unknown sea. But now while his thoughts remained jumbled, he did know his name. Tristan Cooper. But it seemed the better part of wisdom to not claim clarity of mind until he knew more about where he was and what had happened to land him there.

"There was nothing on your person to reveal your name or where you are from," the old woman said.

"Do you think I could have been set upon by robbers?"

"That is a possibility," she conceded. "It is wrong of me to question you when you are in such a weakened state. You are in need of nourishment now that you have returned to a conscious state. And Brother Benjamin will want to examine you."

She pushed herself up from the chair. She wore a white apron over a dark gray dress with a white collar lapped across the front. The same type of collar had covered the bodices of the dresses of the two young women who had brought him here from the woods. He didn't remember much about the ride once the young woman had managed to clamber up on the horse in front of him. He remembered even less about this place. Nothing but a vision of a large white building that made him wonder about heaven again and then grim men in black who had him more concerned with being carried into the underworld.

It wasn't the first time he'd had that concern. Such dark dreams tormented him when the fever had overtaken him while he was fighting in Mexico. The army doctor said he expected him to die then. Men on every side of him did surrender to death from the same cause. Not bullets or artillery fire, but fever burning away their lives.

He reached out to grasp the woman's apron skirt before she could move away from the bed. "Have you forgotten your name too?"

She laughed then. A pleasant sound even with the rumble of age in it. "Nay, I have forgotten little in my lifetime. I am Sister Lettie. For many years, I was the closest person they had to a doctor here in the village, but then Brother Benjamin came among us. An answer to prayer, since age was stealing my stamina to properly tend to the ill among us. Now I watch his healing and sit with the sick as I finish out my time of usefulness."

"What is this place?" Tristan asked. "You wear the same type dress as the girls who found me in the woods and they called each other sister as well. While I can imagine the two of them sisters, you appear too old to be a sister to them."

"We are all sisters and brothers here. You are in the village of Harmony Hill. Have you heard of the Believers in the Second Appearing of Christ, more commonly called the Shakers among those of the world?"

"Shakers?" Tristan tried to think.

"You might have seen our seeds or used our potions. Our trading brothers carry our products far and wide."

"I guess I haven't had much need of seeds. Or potions up until now." Tristan put his hand up to his head. It was beginning to ache and he had to fight the desire to close his eyes and sink back down on the pillow instead of seeking answers.

"If the Shaker name does not bring forth some memory, then I daresay you are not from any of the parts nearby."

"I could have simply been riding through."

"That could be," Sister Lettie agreed with a smile. "If so, you have been forced into a delay of your trip, but have no fear. Elder Joseph will send word to the sheriff that you are here. He will know if your people are searching for you. We were simply waiting for you to come to consciousness to see if you remembered who you were."

"And now I don't."

"Now you don't, but your memory will no doubt return," Sister Lettie said. "You are young and in fine health. That will work in your favor."

"How long have I been here?"

"This is the second day. Brother Benjamin determined sleep would best serve you. His draughts gave you healing rest."

"Two days." He tried to remember, but there was nothing after the vision of the white building rising before his eyes and the men coming for him. Only a black void. "Was I out of my head the whole time?"

"Not exactly out of your head. More in a state of sleep. Brought on by Brother Benjamin's medicine. Fear not. He will explain more when he comes to examine you."

"Why do you think I am fearful?"

"The way you hold to me." She glanced down at his hand gripping her apron.

He turned loose as he murmured, "Forgive me. I do feel odd. I wouldn't say exactly afraid. More unsettled not knowing where I am."

"Or who you are?" She raised her eyebrows at him.

"Or who I am," he agreed. He had the feeling she knew he wasn't being truthful. To take her mind from that, he asked, "Can I see the young sisters who brought me here?"

"Nay, that would not be allowed. They did their duty in helping one in need, but the Ministry would not give permission for them to have improper intercourse with one of the world. Such might lead to sinful thinking."

"I'm talking to you."

She laughed again. "But I am old. And a person of medical abilities. The Ministry doesn't concern themselves with requiring me to follow all the rules to the letter. In the infirmary we must attend to the needs of our patients. That is the first rule. To heal."

"I only wanted to thank them."

"I will convey your thanks by the proper channels to Sisters Jessamine and Annie."

"Yes, Jessamine." With the name, her face floated in front of his eyes again. "Was she as beautiful as I remember?"

"Our Sister Jessamine is very fair of face. Another perfectly sound reason to not put either of you in temptation's pathway. She is learning to be a proper Believer and you will recover your memory and be on about your life. Unless you decide to listen to the true way of the Believers and throw your lot in with us."

He put his hand to his head. "I know nothing about your ways."

"True enough, and I have let you talk much too long. I can see that your head is thumping again." She refilled the glass with water from a pitcher and stirred in some powders. "This will help."

He drank without protest. She left him alone then. He heard the door shut behind her. He heard no lock turn and thought to follow her out of the room to see the place he was in. But when he tried to sit up, the room began spinning. So instead he lay back on the pillow and wondered how long he could manage to hide here.

He didn't know who had shot at him or why. Had it been done in calculated anger or by chance? He forced himself to concentrate on what might have happened in the woods but accomplished nothing more than making his head pound even more fiercely. Whatever memory he had of that had been wiped away by the path of the bullet or perhaps the bang to the head. He gingerly felt the back of his head and winced when he touched a swelling there.

He'd seen men in the war in Mexico lose rational thought with the guns blazing around them. He had not. Instead everything had been clearer and emblazoned on his memory with the prospect of death stalking him with each boom of the artillery or gunfire, but he was no longer on a battlefield. Nor did he have any reason to think someone had a desire to shoot him. It was surely no more than an accident or the random misfortune of being set upon by a highwayman robber. As far as he knew, he had no avowed enemies anxious to waylay him in the woods.

Even so, until he knew that for a certainty, it might be best to take advantage of these Shaker people's kindness. Besides, the fact he had a bullet crease in his head wasn't the only reason he hadn't admitted to his name. Laura Cleveland. She was the reason. She and his mother.

His mother had met Laura the summer before at one of the popular Kentucky springs where the waters were touted to cure everything from rheumatism to melancholy. Or spinsterhood.

Not that Laura had much chance of turning into a spinster. She was a lovely girl from a fine family. As Tristan's mother continually reminded him, Laura would make someone a wonderful wife, but so far Tristan had no desire for that someone to be him. She had a way of twisting her mouth into an unflattering bow, and something about her eyes bothered him.

When he made the mistake of sharing those thoughts with his mother, she got that look he spent most of his childhood trying to avoid.

"There is nothing at all wrong with Laura Cleveland's eyes," she said and, after a moment's hesitation to recall the color, added, "A refreshing pale blue, aren't they?"

"Very pale. More gray than blue," Tristan said. The gray of an overcast sky in the winter.

His mother's brown eyes had darkened and flashed with anger. "You are in no position to reject such a favorable match as Laura Cleveland because of the color of her eyes."

Tristan hadn't backed down. Not then. "It's not the color of her eyes. It's the lack of interest I see in them. I do not make her pulse quicken. Nor does she mine."

Her mouth turned up in a grim smile. "Good heavens, Tristan, I would have thought your time with the army would have divested you of such youthful romantic ideas."

"I have no wish to tie myself to someone I don't love or who doesn't love me."

"Love." His mother waved her hand through the air as though dismissing the word. "The kind you're talking about is no more than a whisper in the wind that passes through and leaves behind nothing of real worth. Best to look straight at the reality of one's prospects."

"Is that what you did with Father? Made a coldhearted decision to wed and bear him children without the first consideration of love?"

The flicker of pain that crossed her face made Tristan sorry he had allowed her to goad him into unkind words. His father had gone to war with him and carried home to Georgia the fever that had nearly killed Tristan. His father had not been strong enough to fight it off. He'd been dead nearly a year.

Her voice softened as she answered him. "Love can grow between two people if they go into a union with a proper attitude. Our parents favored our marriage and it was advantageous to both of us. For one, you were a result of that union." She reached over and put her hand on his cheek with affection. "You and Laura will make a lovely couple."

"I don't think—"

"I don't want to hear it." Every trace of softness left her face as she cut off his words. "Sometimes you think too much, Tristan. But if you want to think, then think on this. Your father neglected his business when he went off to fight the Mexicans and came home too ill to have any thought of the future. We are in danger of losing everything." She stared up at him to be sure he understood her words. "Everything. Do you understand that? Our home. Our position in Atlanta society. Everything."

He wanted to tell her he cared nothing about any of that, but she was his mother. As her only son, it was his duty to take care of her. She had lost so much in the last two years. Her husband. Her daughter to childbirth fever and the highly anticipated grandchild with her. There had been a few times since he'd returned home that he feared she might be losing her sanity. And other times he thought it likely he might lose his if he didn't get away from her demands. Or give in to them.

And so he had agreed to spend the month at White Oak Springs. Courting Laura Cleveland. Perhaps that would give him time to find another way or to become more appreciative of Laura's charms and she of his.

He did push a warning at his mother. "You should be aware that Miss Cleveland has given absolutely no indication that my court is welcome. She may already have a beau."

"Nonsense," his mother said. "She is quite unattached and I know for a fact her father likes you and will advance your cause to his daughter, who appears to dote upon him. Besides, you will have the entire summer season at White Oak Springs to convince Laura to be interested in you. You're very charming when you set your mind to it, Tristan."

He had been at White Oak Springs paying court to Laura Cleveland for a whole week. The place was lovely and swarming with beautiful belles. Several of them had sought his attention and that had seemed to pique Laura's interest. She had walked with him along the tree-lined paths. She had written his name on her dance card with a flourish. They had shared a picnic on the grounds with strands of music floating over to their spot on the grass. At the Springs, music was ever in the air, turning thoughts toward romance, and Laura appeared to be looking more favorably on a romance with him.

The attack in the woods from whatever assailant for whatever cause couldn't have come at a better time. A few days hidden among these odd people would give him time to think. Time to come up with a way to escape his mother's plans. Whether she said he should be or not, he wasn't ready to give up on the idea of meeting a girl to love. A girl who fired his imagination and the mere vision of her face caused his palms to sweat. A girl like the sister with the beautiful blue eyes. That was the kind of girl he wanted to court. Someone real and not simply a cardboard cutout of all the things a Southern belle should be.

He wasn't being fair, he thought, as he stared at the white ceiling over his narrow bed. He couldn't spot even a trace of lamp soot or smoke on the ceiling or the walls that were the same clean white. The whole room was bright with light from a wide window directly across from his bed. Another bed was beside his, but its white cotton spread was undisturbed. A narrow blue board with pegs wrapped around the walls. A candleholder hung from the peg nearest the door. Oddly enough, a chair identical to the one beside his bed was hung upside down on two pegs next to the candle. No curtains filtered the light through the window. No rug was thrown on the floor to add color to the room. He saw nothing in the room to give it the look of home. But then this was a sickroom. His sickroom.

He settled his head into the pillow as the pain began to ebb away from him. Brother Benjamin's potions were good.

No, he definitely wasn't being fair to Laura Cleveland. She was more than a cardboard cutout. She was every inch a charming woman with the clout of a rich father who did, as Tristan's mother had said, like him. Robert Cleveland was new rich, which explained his eagerness to have Tristan court his daughter. Money could buy a lot, but not a welcome place in the established circle of Atlanta society. Tristan was already established there even with the misfortune that had hit the Cooper family in the last few months. Name was important in Atlanta. Much more important than money. Mr. Cleveland hoped to have an abundance of both by arranging a suitably advantageous marriage for his only daughter.

At twenty she had already given her father reason for despair by refusing suitors, or so Tristan's mother told him. Mr. Cleveland wouldn't look fondly on a suitor turning the tables on his daughter. Perhaps that was why Tristan was in the woods. Perhaps he was running away.

5

"But Sister Sophrena, aren't we instructed to help those in need?" Jessamine looked across the small desk at the older sister and hurried out more words before she could answer. "Do all the good we can all the time we can."

Sister Sophrena peered at Jessamine over round spectacles perched on her nose. She didn't look exactly angry. Sister Sophrena was never brought low by unreasonable anger, but she did look distinctly perturbed. Although Jessamine had grown quite familiar with that look over the years, she nevertheless had to call up a considerable amount of self-control to keep from shifting uneasily in her chair.

She wasn't afraid of Sister Sophrena. She would do Jessamine no harm. She loved her. Jessamine knew that, but what made her want to squirm under the sister's steady stare was the feeling that she wasn't measuring up. She wasn't being a proper Shaker sister. She was disappointing Sister Sophrena. Yet again.

Jessamine wanted to blurt out that she was sorry, but it was as much a sin to lie as it was to be disobedient. She wasn't sorry she had led Sister Annie so far into the woods on the pretense of finding berries. She wasn't sorry she had helped the man. She wasn't even sorry she had let her hand explore the feel of his cheek. Her own cheeks warmed at the thought and she hoped Sister Sophrena would think it was shame reddening her face.

"I assume you are meaning to say do all the good you can in all the ways you can, as often as you can to all the people you can." Sister Sophrena breathed out a small sigh as she removed her spectacles and pinched the bridge of her nose. "It's best to repeat Mother Ann's precepts with accuracy."

"Yea, you are right. It would be wrong to allow someone to get a wrong idea because of my careless memory." Jessamine seized on this to move away from the worrisome topic of her sins. "I can recall many of those I learned in school from Sister Josephine word for word. Like this one. None preaches better than the ant and it says nothing."

Sister Sophrena twisted her mouth to the side but was unable to hide the smile sneaking into her eyes. "Are you trying to tell me something, Sister Jessamine? Would you prefer I said nothing?"

"Nay, Sister Sophrena." Now Jessamine's face burned even redder. She had a way of continually speaking the wrong thing to land her in an even bigger hole. "I am ever ready to listen to your instruction."

Sister Sophrena's smile disappeared as she held the spectacle handles in her hand and tapped the frames against the table. "But are you ready to heed it, my little sister? That is the question."

"I am ready to try," Jessamine said in a small voice.

"As you have been ready to try so many times before."

"Yea." Jessamine stared down at her hands clutched together in her lap. She did try. Really, she did, but then something would happen to send her down a wayward path. Like Sister Abigail's tales of parasols. Jessamine hadn't mentioned that to Sister Sophrena, but Sister Annie would have told of how Jessamine's desire to see parasols had led them on a wild-goose chase through the woods. But perhaps it was as God intended. Perhaps angels had led them to that place solely for the purpose of helping that poor man.

She peeked up at Sister Sophrena, who had her eyes shut and was now pinching her lower lip instead of the bridge of her nose. It was not a good sign. She was waiting for something more from Jessamine. In her mind, Jessamine flipped back through the sins she'd confessed. Disobedience. Willfulness. Lack of proper consideration of her sisters and brothers, especially of Sister Annie. Deception in leading Sister Annie so far into the woods with no proper concern of fulfilling her assigned duty to pick raspberries.

"Have you confessed all your sins, Sister? The unburdening of your sins is necessary in order to live the pure life of a Believer and to find favor from the Eternal Father and our Mother Ann. Unconfessed sin in your heart is like a worm inside an apple. On the outside the apple may appear fine, but inside there is ruin. Don't let sin eat away at the insides of your heart."

"Nay, I'll pray not to let such happen." Jessamine put her hand over her bosom. She frowned slightly. "Did Sister Annie tell you some sin I may have forgotten? If so, I will gladly repent of it."

"Repentance isn't merely lip service to me. It's a changing of your will. More even than that. A surrendering of your will to that of the Lord's will for your life."

"But if I can't recognize an action as a sin, how can I know to repent of it?" It seemed a reasonable question to Jessamine, but she knew she should not have voiced it when a frown flickered across Sister Sophrena's face.

"The rules of a committed Believer's behavior are drawn out in the Millennial Laws passed down from the Ministry in New Lebanon. You have but to read and apply those rules to your behavior. Obedience to the way is much to be desired if you wish to sign the Covenant when you turn twenty-one."

Jessamine turned her mind away from the thought of the Covenant. For months Sister Sophrena had been talking of her committing to the Shaker way when she reached twenty-one. Not just for this day, this month, but for forever. To sign a document promising to be a good and faithful Believer and never look for love other than the perfect love of the Lord and her sisters and brothers. To put behind her all thoughts of improbable fairy tales and childish stories. To set her feet on the Shaker path and look forward to years of peace and service with the reward of true salvation.

She did want salvation. When her granny first told her about the Lord's great love years ago, she had opened her heart to that love. And she'd been ready to do as her granny's worn Bible said she must and love God in return and her neighbor as herself. Since, at that time, Jessamine knew no person other than her granny and the old preacher who brought them supplies, obeying that commandment had seemed as easy as breathing.

After she'd come among the Believers, Sister Sophrena said Jessamine's granny was right to teach about the need to love God and her neighbor, but that more was required. Proper behavior and obedience to the Ministry rules was as necessary as love and would not be burdensome once one firmly set her feet on the Shaker path.

"I do try to be obedient and remember the rules," Jessamine said now. "I never fail to step up on the stairs with the proper foot and kneel on the right knee to say my prayers as a dutiful Believer before and after each meal and all the other times too. I labor the songs and dance and whirl with fervor."

Sister Sophrena leaned across the table toward her. "But, my sister, is the fervor of your whirl because the spirit takes hold of you or merely for the joy of whirling?"

Jessamine looked down at her hands clasped in her lap as she tried to come up with an answer that would not cause her sister increased concern while remaining truthful. She could almost feel Sister Sophrena's eyes probing the top of her cap as she waited for an answer. Jessamine's feet suddenly felt itchy and she considered standing up and whirling right out of the room. But that would be heeding the call of the wrong spirits.

The truth was, she had never felt the spirit other Believers claimed made them whirl and dance and sometimes bray like donkeys. Jessamine loved meetings. She loved the singing and dancing and was always ready to join in when others of the Believers pantomimed picking and giving out imaginary fruit or a gift of sweeping fell over the assembly. She could pretend to sweep out evil with every bit as much fervor as the others in the building. She listened enraptured when one of the brothers or sisters was taken over by a spirit from the beyond and spoke in tongues or sang words that had no meaning. She was ever ready to whirl, but it was never because of the spirit falling on her or rising within her. Sister Sophrena knew that.

After a long moment, when the only noise was that of the bird in a tree outside the open window and a horse passing by on the road, Sister Sophrena spoke again. "It is easier to talk to you, Sister Jessamine, if you do not hide your eyes from me. Or your thoughts."

Jessamine looked up into the sister's plain face. There was nothing remarkable about her looks, but she did have the perfect Believer's face. One that offered love and kindness while at the same time insisting on obedience and truth. Sister Sophrena was very dear to her. She had guided Jessamine through those first months at the village when the loss of her granny was a raw wound inside her. Sister Sophrena wasn't old the way her granny had been. Not young. Not old. In her middle years and at the peak of her ability to put her hands to work for the Lord. That's how the Believers judged age. By one's working ability and maturity.

By that standard, Sister Annie was much nearer the age to sign the Covenant than Jessamine would ever be in spite of being a year younger. In fact she had told Jessamine she would sign the Covenant with gladness to leave the wickedness of the world behind if they would allow the document to be signed by one younger than twenty-one. But they would not. That too was written in the Believers' rules.

"Is not joy in the whirling enough?" Jessamine said.

Sister Sophrena sat back in her chair. "I don't know, Sister. That is something you have to determine on your own. Whether the joy comes from the spirit or not."

"Where else would it come from?" Jessamine asked. When Sister Sophrena didn't answer right away, she noticed the song of the mockingbird in the tree outside the window again. "Like the mockingbird. Do you not think he sings for joy because his eggs will soon be hatching into baby birds?"

Sister Sophrena listened for a moment. "Yea, there is joy in his song." Her eyes softened on Jessamine. "And in yours. But you must decide not to sing the wrong songs or walk the wrong paths."

"But the man might have lain in the woods long without help. Even died there. Could it be that the Lord directed my steps there in order to help him? That it was providence instead of happenstance?"

"Did you hear a voice leading you into the woods?"

"Nay," Jessamine admitted.

"Were there angels beckoning you to follow that path?"

"Nay."

"It is good that you are truthful. For Sister Annie has already told me that your lust for knowledge of worldly things is what led you down that path."

Jessamine felt a new rush of color in her cheeks, a true

flush of shame this time. It was often so when she made confession to Sister Sophrena. She fell so short of the mark of a dutiful Shaker sister. "But good came of it when we were able to help the man."

When Sister Sophrena didn't answer right away, Jessamine went on. "Didn't it? We were able to bring him to Brother Benjamin to fix his arm and help him. I know it looked sinful to you the way he was leaning on me when we came into the village, but that was the only way he could stay on the horse. It meant nothing in the worldly way."

"And you felt nothing worldly while you were so near him?" Sister Sophrena's eyes pierced her.

Jessamine's cheeks burned brighter. "I felt very unsettled. Unsure of every feeling that ran through me. Aware of my very toes. I didn't know whether I was falling in sin or being lifted to paradise." She wished those last words back when Sister Sophrena tightened her lips and shook her head slightly as though weary of listening to Jessamine. "I guess thinking that means I surely was falling into sin. But was it a normal feeling? One that people of the world don't turn from?"

"Why do you think I can answer such questions?" A furrow formed between Sister Sophrena's dark eyebrows.

"You told me once that you were married when you came into the Believers. That you had to rid yourself of the sin of matrimony." The frown on Sister Sophrena's face was growing darker, but Jessamine ignored it and plunged on. "I know that was many years ago, but before you came here, you must have experienced those feelings. Worldly love."

"My former husband and I had a different relationship. A marriage encouraged by my father with little consideration of love as the world knows it or as we here at Harmony Hill embrace it. Many marriages of the world are such. Naught but reason for despair." Sister Sophrena pushed her lips together into a grim line as if she was fighting that despair even yet.

Then her voice softened as she reached across the small writing desk to touch Jessamine's cheek. "You, my dear sister, will never have to know that despair. You have been spared the temptations of worldly love. And the sorrows. Trust me. It is better so."

Jessamine knew she should be quiet. That she should accept what Sister Sophrena was telling her. But the words tumbled out of her mouth anyway. "But what about children? Did you never want to have children?" Jessamine stopped and her eyes widened. "Or perhaps you did and they became your little sisters and brothers as happens to others who come among us."

"Nay. I had no children. The Lord intended for my path to the Shakers to be an easy one. Like yours. You came so young with more innocence than most your age because of the way you lived separated from the world with your grandmother. Life here was not a lot different for you except with more people to love as you loved your granny."

"I do love my sisters." Jessamine paused a moment. "And my brothers too, but—"

Sister Sophrena cut her off. "Do not pick at this the way you might a scabbed over sore. The love we have here is pure and not selfish. It encompasses all your family of Believers and brings peace to your heart and mind. We serve one another in love. You did a good deed for the fallen young man and in the process had feelings stirred within you that you had not felt before. You can stomp out those feelings the same as any wickedness the devil tries to put into your mind. Put them behind you and continue on the right and perfect way. The young man will recover and return to his world."

"Yea, Sister Sophrena." She lowered her eyes to her hands again and then peeked up again. "Is he well now then? Has he remembered who he is and where he was going?"

"Sister Lettie reports that he spends much time in sleep.

Brother Benjamin has given him potions to give his mind rest in hopes that will help him recover his thinking powers."

"He seemed to think fine. He just didn't know his name or his reason for being in the woods."

Sister Sophrena's frown began slipping back between her eyes. "Don't allow your curiosity to lead you into more sin, Sister Jessamine. Concentrate on your duties and abandon these wayward thoughts. Think not on the man's name or anything about him."

"Yea, Sister Sophrena," Jessamine said again. "I will reflect on my duty to the Lord and Mother Ann and my sisters and brothers."

"Such an attitude will serve you well."

Jessamine meant the words when she spoke them to Sister Sophrena. She would never intentionally defy Sister Sophrena, but at the same time she very much wanted to see the young man again. She couldn't seem to rid her mind of the thought of letting her eyes linger on him. Perhaps even letting her hand touch him again to see if those strange feelings that rose inside her were merely from the excitement of the moment or something more. Wayward thoughts were not so easy to abandon.

Journal Entry

Harmony Hill Village
Entered on this 14th day of June in the year 1849
by Sister Sophrena Prescott

The sisters are busy gathering rose petals for our rosewater. It is much in demand by those of the world as perfumed water and as a refreshing agent for the hands and face. Our own use is more for flavoring our cakes and teas or for treating ailments of the eye. We need not soak our bodies in perfume to make them sweet smelling for our Lord and Mother Ann. The aroma produced by dedicated work and the love rising up from our meetinghouse when we go forth to exercise our songs in worship—that is what pleases the Spirit.

On instruction from the Ministry, I am watching Sister Jessamine with a careful eye since her return from the woods with the man from the world. I trust she tells me the truth when she claims no desire to stray upon wayward paths, but her imaginings of the world are a stumbling block in her path toward living as a true Believer. It is evident she has curiosity about the stranger she brought into our midst. Not the simple curiosity some of the other brethren and sisters might feel as to who the man is and how he came to be in the woods. Nay, her curiosity is the more dangerous kind. The kind that will plummet her into sin if she allows it to grow and wrap tendrils of temptation around her.

There is no sin in curiosity in its innocent state. Such is good, for it is the spark that leads to new discoveries resulting in good for all in our community. When a Believer is performing a task and becomes curious about how better to accomplish said task by improving the tools necessary or the process, then that is a gift. Such curiosity has led to the addition of rollers on our bed legs that give us ease in cleaning the dust from under them and to the carving of slots in our large spoons that makes serving up vegetables so much more efficient. Many innovations we use in our tasks every day were brought about by appropriate curiosity and attention to duty and not to things of the world.

It is my prayer that our sister doesn't succumb to her sinful curiosity and that the man of the world will soon be well enough to be gone from our village. Sister Lettie reports the bone in his arm will knit back together in time and that his confusion seems to be lifting although he has yet to remember his name. That seems odd to me. I have difficulty believing a man could forget his name, but Brother Benjamin does not feel the same suspicions that want to linger in my mind. Perhaps it is no more than my desire to have him away from here, taking his worldly temptations with him. We have shut away the world to keep such sin from us. I fear it can only be the devil sneaking it back among us with trickery.

*Eldress Frieda says I must not think uncharitably,
and she is right. I have confessed my lack of trust in
the watchcare of the Ministry and our Mother Ann.
At the same time, the eldress has instructed me not to
let Sister Jessamine stray from the village. But it is my
opinion that the danger to our sister is no longer only
among the trees. It resides in our midst.*

*There too is the letter. An appropriate time will
have to be determined to give it to Sister Jessamine.
It had been thought to wait until she neared twenty-
one and spiritual maturity, but now I wonder. How
can we set an age or time when a person is mature
enough to look into her past at the truth of her
beginnings? If that is what it tells. I do not know, for
I did not break the seal of the inner envelope before
giving it to the Ministry.*

*But I do fear—whatever the letter says—that it
might only further confound our young sister's mind.
For what purpose? Who knows if whoever penned
the letter even still breathes? No other letter has ever
come for her. None at all. She seems greatly alone in
the world except for the Believers here who embrace
her as a beloved sister. A very beloved sister, even if
at times she can be our exasperating sister as well.*

6

The morning after Jessamine made her confession and promises to Sister Sophrena, she had resolutely determined to completely shut from her mind any wayward thoughts or sinful desires as she paid mind to her duties in the rose gardens. She concentrated on snipping the rose blooms off the bushes and stripping the petals from the stems to fill her basket.

The blossoms spread a beautiful fragrant blanket across the field and made this duty a thousand times more pleasing than being stuck in the hot washhouse or in the kitchen peeling mounds of potatoes and onions. Each duty was valuable and to be performed with dedication and care. Sister Sophrena often reminded her of that truth if she noted the slightest look of dismay when she told Jessamine her duties for the week. And no sister was continually assigned to an odious duty. A week was not forever, although there were times it seemed it might be when stuck in the upper room ironing endless piles of shirts and dresses. So in the spring and early summer, Jessamine was thankful many hands were needed in the rose gardens.

Sister Abigail stepped up beside Jessamine and softly touched one of the roses. "It seems such a pity to not place so much as one rosebud into a vase to brighten our retiring room."

Jessamine smiled at the young sister and pretended not to notice the frown Sister Annie leveled toward them from the next row. Sister Annie had doubts that Sister Abigail desired to learn the Shaker ways. Even something as simple as the Shaker way to gather rose petals.

"She longs for the world and has no eye for the Shaker path," Sister Annie told Jessamine after their first day in the rose gardens a week ago.

"You are patient with me, Sister Annie. Why not with Sister Abigail who is so new to our ways?" Jessamine had asked.

"She does not want my patience. She wants only things of the world and her talk of such is bringing disharmony to our sleeping room." Sister Annie narrowed her eyes on Jessamine. "To you. Can you deny she has you thinking of the world?"

"I cannot blame Sister Abigail for that. I ever have curiosity of the world. You know how often I have need to confess that fault to Sister Sophrena."

"Yea, but Sister Abigail does not think it a fault. She thinks the ways we show her are what is faulty."

There was truth in what Sister Annie said. Jessamine did like hearing Sister Abigail talk of the world. About parasols and other frivolities that Jessamine knew nothing about. But now, Jessamine tried to keep her mind on her Shaker duties as she had promised Sister Sophrena she would do. Part of that duty on this day was guiding Sister Abigail in how to efficiently pluck the rose petals.

Although little expertise was required and Jessamine had shown the young sister the quickest method to strip the petals time and again, the girl kept dawdling instead of bending to her task. Now she clipped a rose, then lifted the bloom up to sniff it before she began slowly pulling the petals loose two or three at a time to let them drift down in her basket.

Jessamine smiled at her with no censure. One of Mother Ann's most oft repeated sayings was to do their work as if they had a thousand years to live, or as if they might die on the morrow. Sister Abigail must be thinking on the thousand years to live, for the way she was working, it might take her that long to fill her basket. Jessamine thought of telling her that, but instead she only said, "The roses are grown not for their beauty but for their usefulness."

"How can a rose be grown without some eye seeing its beauty? It appears to me that if the Lord gave the rose such beauty, he surely meant for us to use our eyes and our noses to enjoy it in every way and not for rosewater only." She clipped another bloom and lifted it to her nose to breathe in its beauty.

"It is not necessary for us to test the fragrance of every bloom. We can trust that the Lord has filled them all with a pleasing and useful scent," Jessamine said.

The girl gave Jessamine a little smile, then picked another rose to hold to her nose as well.

When she carried the fourth rose to her nose, Sister Annie looked over at her and completely lost her patience. "We are not to be indulging in a rose-sniffing frolic, Sister Abigail," Sister Annie told her with a frown. "It is our duty to fill our baskets with the petals. Not our noses with fragrance."

"But the fragrance is there for the free taking, Sister. I have stolen nothing from the petals by breathing of their fragrance." She took another sniff of the bloom she held before she pulled off the petals and spread them out evenly in the bottom of her basket. "You know what those of the world do with your rosewater, don't you?"

"We shut away such wondering and keep the sins of the world away from our borders." Sister Annie sounded cross as she snipped off a lush bloom and stripped the petals with one firm twist. She stepped forward toward another bloom as if eager to leave Sister Abigail and her foolish talk behind.

"I did not say they sinned in any way in the use of the Shaker rosewater." Sister Abigail's hazel eyes suddenly looked watery with tears. She had a great desire to be liked. Not simply loved by the sisters around her but liked with smiles and attentive ears to her stories.

Sister Annie stormed on up the row with nary a glance back. Jessamine snipped off the blooms Sister Annie had passed by in her haste to get away from Sister Abigail's stories of the world and resumed her duty of training the younger sister in the proper Shaker way.

"Sister Annie is right." Jessamine raised her voice a little in hopes her words might carry across the roses to Sister Annie's ears. "We can pick much faster without giving each rose a trip to our nose. The fragrance is in the air. Breathe the scent there and strip the petals for your basket."

Sister Abigail let out a small sigh. "It would be far better to be one of the pampered young ladies at White Oak Springs bathing in the rosewater." She peeked up at Jessamine to see if her words had awakened her curiosity.

"Bathing in it?" Jessamine let the rose petals drift from her hand down into the basket.

"Yea," Sister Abigail said.

Jessamine offered Sister Abigail an approving smile for remembering to use the Shaker word for agreement. That was a welcome step along the Shaker path, even if the girl couldn't keep her mind on harvesting the rose petals. "No wonder we have to pick so many rose petals. Rosewater baths. I can hardly imagine."

Actually she could only imagine too well and she hungered for more details to add to her imagining. Sister Annie was far up the row and no other sisters were near, so what could it hurt to listen to Sister Abigail tell of how those of the world used the rosewater? Jessamine could pick just as quickly with words in her ears as not.

Sister Abigail smiled. "When I worked there last summer, the ladies would often ask me to pour as much as half a bottle of the fragrant water into their baths and then sprinkle great handfuls of fresh rose petals on top of the water. Believe me, I found much occasion to dip my hands in the baths when I brought them extra hot water so they could soak among the rose petals longer."

Jessamine ran her fingers through the rose petals in her basket. She wondered how it would feel to lay back in a warm bath with the fragrance of roses rising around her while someone carried water to the tub. Not a proper Shaker thought. Color rose in her cheeks as she looked around to see if any of the sisters had somehow divined her slip into vanity.

She had promised Sister Sophrena she wouldn't let her thoughts stray down wayward paths and here she was letting them do that very thing.

"That would not be the Shaker way," Jessamine said. "It would be good to keep our minds on our tasks and put our hands to work. It's unwise to tempt our thoughts with worldly ways."

"But wouldn't it be wonderful to be one of those young ladies who never have anything to do but listen to music and dance in the moonlight?" Sister Abigail lightly stroked her cheek with one of the roses.

"We have music and dancing." Jessamine tried to block Sister Abigail's words from her imagination, but dancing in moonlight wormed into her mind.

"Not the way they do. Being held in handsome young men's arms. Kissing in the shadows."

"It's not fitting to allow our minds to dwell on sinful things of the world." Jessamine pushed an echo of Sister Annie's firmness in her voice.

It was one thing to be curious about parasols and rosewater baths. It was quite another to let her mind chase after the thought of kissing. Her grandmother had kissed her, dry lips touching her cheek as she pulled the quilt up over Jessamine each night. Right after she'd ended one of her fairy-tale stories. The prince and princess always kissed before they went back to the castle to live happily ever after. In Jessamine's mind, sparkles of happiness had flashed at the first mention of the kiss. Like the glittering dust from a shooting star drifting down around them.

Sister Abigail did turn back to the roses and wasted no time in stripping off the petals as if she'd been harvesting roses every bit as long as Jessamine. But she wasn't silenced by Jessamine's firm words as she lowered her voice to ask, "Have you never thought of how it might feel to be kissed, Sister Jessamine?" She didn't wait for an answer. Instead she smiled slightly as she peered over the roses at Jessamine. "It will do no good for you to deny that you have. The stain of truth is on your cheeks."

"I know nothing about kissing." Jessamine barely spoke the words above a whisper. It would not do for Sister Annie or any of the other sisters to hear them speaking of kisses. "A Believer doesn't allow such worldly thoughts to distract her from her duties."

"Perhaps a Believer like Sister Annie." Sister Abigail looked up the row at the other sister and lowered her voice even more. "A staid and common Believer. One who has no imagination for romance."

Jessamine tried to rein in her imagination. She had promised Sister Sophrena. "Mother Ann teaches us that our thoughts are character molds. They shape language and action. So it is best if we think on things of the spirit or our duties. Idle imagining of worldly things such as kissing can do nothing but sink us into trouble."

Sister Abigail laughed softly. "You certainly speak the truth there. Many a girl has been brought low by kissing when she allowed the wrong man too many kisses. Trust me. I saw much when I was working at the Springs last summer. Some good things. Some not. I even admit to letting myself be pulled back into the shadows a few times myself."

"Sister Abigail!" Jessamine stared at her.

"You don't have to sound so shocked. No harm came from it. He was only a year or so older than me. He worked with the horses and would often wait for me beside the pathways to the springs." Sister Abigail sighed as she lifted one of the rose blossoms to her nose again. "His lips were very soft."

"Why did you come among the Believers?" Jessamine peered over at the girl. She seemed so resistant to everything Shaker.

"It wasn't a happy choice," Sister Abigail said. "My father has ever been the kind to run after this or that idea. My mother and I and my little brother and sister had no choice but to follow him. Although if I could have found Jimmy to see if his kisses meant anything, I might even now be a married woman with roses in a vase on my kitchen table."

"But here you have row upon row of roses." Jessamine waved her hand at the roses.

"Roses that it is a sin to enjoy. How can it be a sin to enjoy a gift of the Lord?" Sister Abigail ran her hand over the rose blooms and then touched her lips. "Kissing is a gift too. The Lord put such desires in our hearts."

"While you are among us, it might be better to not dwell on such gifts. To think more on the gifts of the spirit and the gift of work." Jessamine turned her eyes back to the roses and tried to concentrate on her work. It was not good to think how one's lips felt every bit as soft as the petals. It was not good to wonder if a man's lips might feel the same. To think that she could know exactly how a man's lips might feel if she'd allowed her hand to stray from the cheek of the man in the woods to his lips. An image of his face popped in front of her eyes.

She shook her head to keep from thinking on how his lips had looked. When she spoke again, it was as much for herself as Sister Abigail. "It is better to spend less energy on talk and more on our duties."

"Yea, I can't seem to keep my tongue still as I've been told is the better way. Sister Annie says I am the serpent in the garden." Sister Abigail smiled with no outward sign of being the least bit upset by Sister Annie's accusation. "Perhaps she is right. For I look at you and I see someone who would like to taste of the fruit of the tree of the world. To know of things that the sisters here want to keep from you."

"I am often too curious about wrong things," Jessamine admitted.

"Like the man you and Sister Annie found in the woods. I have heard he is very handsome. Did you find him so?" Sister Abigail looked at Jessamine. "Or would you think it a sin to admit you admired his looks?"

Jessamine looked up the row to where Sister Annie was clipping roses with such fervor it was easy to see irritation building in her to the point of sinful anger. At the other end of the garden, Sister Edna stood with her hands on her hips staring at Jessamine and Sister Abigail. Jessamine did not need to be near to know the look of displeasure that would be on her face. Displeasure that would surely grow darker if she knew their overabundance of chatter was about kissing. Sister Edna believed in following the rules. All the rules without exception. Without the possibility of excuses. Excuses had no place on a faithful Shaker's tongue.

At times, Jessamine thought the only pleasure the woman had was in catching one of her sisters in wrong. Jessamine smiled grimly as she pulled off two more roses. If that was true, she had without doubt given the woman much pleasure. She suspected Sister Edna often owned the eyes that peered out from the hiding places to be sure none of the brothers and sisters engaged in improper behavior. Clandestine meetings in the shadows along the pathways of Harmony Hill were strictly forbidden. Certainly there could be no kissing. If a wayward sister or brother tried any such thing, watchful eyes would see and report such sinfulness to the Ministry.

"It matters not how one looks on the outside." Jessamine heard the echo of her words to the man in the woods.

"Perhaps not here in this place where these people have turned the normal ways of life upside down," Sister Abigail said. "But how one looks can matter a great deal at a place like White Oak Springs. The beautiful girls always have a dancing partner, and if a girl lacks in beauty, she'd best hope her father has money in order to make a favorable match."

"You make it sound so, so . . ." Jessamine couldn't come up with the right word.

"Common?" Sister Abigail looked over at Jessamine with her eyebrows lifted. "It is common. Men and women marry. Some for love as you want to imagine in your storybook romances. Some for convenience. Some for family standing. Some for a lark."

"Not here in Harmony Hill. Here we walk a purer path. A path without sin."

Sister Abigail laughed. "All paths have pebbles of sin that rise up to trip a person. Especially when the pebble is more like a stone dropped into your lap, Sister Jessamine." Again she lifted her eyebrows at Jessamine, but this time with a grin that Jessamine had come to recognize meant she was going to say something she knew to be outside the Shaker way. "I hear you sat in the unknown man's lap on your way back to the village from the woods. And how did that make you feel with him being so handsome and all?"

"I confessed my sinful feelings to Sister Sophrena," Jessamine said.

"It is not a sin to think a man is good-looking in the world."

"We are not in the world."

"But don't you desire to see him again?" Sister Abigail didn't wait for Jessamine to answer. "I saw him in the doctor's garden early this morning as I hastened to the privy before the morning meal. He looked very pale, but it is true that he is quite handsome."

"Outside so early in the morn?" Jessamine didn't know whether to be glad the man was well enough to be in the garden or worried that he might be so well he'd be leaving before she caught sight of him again.

"He was. Perhaps at doctor's orders. I've heard some believe the sun can be a powerful healer. The same as some believe the water from the springs rising out of the ground at White Oak Springs has healing powers." Sister Abigail turned back to her roses.

And just in time. Sister Edna was stalking up the row toward them.

"Dear sisters," she said in a tone that negated every bit of the meaning of the word dear. "It is a dereliction of our duty to do naught but flap our lips. We are here to pick the rose petals." She frowned over at the bare layer of petals in the bottom of Sister Abigail's basket. "This is not a difficult task, Sister Abigail, if one keeps her mind on what she is to do, but it appears you are allowing Sister Jessamine to pick all the roses while you are content to stand and talk."

"She is only just learning the Shaker ways." Jessamine spoke up as she kept her eyes on the red petals filling her own basket. She should have dropped some of her petals into the younger sister's basket.

"Excuses are of the devil," Sister Edna said. "And the devil has no welcome in our rose gardens. It would be best if Sister Abigail goes to pick roses with Sister Annie for the remainder of our duty here."

"Yea," Sister Jessamine said meekly with hopes that Sister Abigail would also lower her head and respond with meekness.

"Yea, Sister Edna, if you think that best," Sister Abigail said. "But we were only speaking of the good benefits of sunshine. That is surely what brings the abundant blooms here, is it not? And it can also cause the blooming of love in our hearts." The girl smiled winsomely at the older woman and went on quickly. "Sisterly love, of course."

Sister Edna's eyes narrowed on Sister Abigail as she seemed to be searching for fault in the girl's words. At last she said, "A glib tongue is not the best tongue. Silence is much to be desired, Sister Abigail, and a gift you should prayerfully seek." She turned her eyes on Jessamine. "And you too, Sister Jessamine. It is a danger to one's soul to lead a young sister astray."

"To do so would bring me sorrow," Jessamine said. "I will mend my ways and pray for more wisdom in my conduct."

Sister Edna's face didn't soften even though she spoke words of acceptance. "Very well, sisters. Let us continue our duty with no more lagging."

She put her hand under Sister Abigail's elbow to propel her up the row to where Sister Annie continued to strip the rose blooms with the energy driven by anger. It promised to be a long day for both Sister Annie and Sister Abigail.

But Sister Abigail's spirit wasn't bothered. She waited until Sister Edna looked away to flash Jessamine a smile over her shoulder and whisper, "Love the sunlight."

"What are you whispering about, Sister Abigail?" Sister Edna gripped the girl's arm harder and gave her a jerk forward.

"Just being thankful for the warming gift of the sun. And wanting to share that gift with my sisters," Sister Abigail said with an innocent smile. "Is it not proper to share gifts with our sisters?"

"Not gifts of mischief. I don't know why Eldress Frieda

ever thought the two of you could work together. I will be informing her of your slack work here in the gardens."

"Will I be denied the evening meal?" Sister Abigail asked as she moved up the row toward Sister Annie. "Like a naughty child?"

"Nay. You know little of our Shaker way," Sister Edna said. "Wrong actions and thoughts bring their own punishment and steal the peace that can be yours. We deny no one the food necessary for health."

Jessamine sighed as she watched them move away. She did not intend to be forever in trouble. She rose each morning with the intent to walk the Shaker path with obedience, but something was continually tripping her up.

As she began clipping off the roses and stripping the petals, she tried to think only of the silky feel of them on her fingertips, but that brought to mind Sister Abigail's words about kissing. And that brought to mind the man from the woods. She did have the desire to see him again before he left the village, but she knew Sister Sophrena would never allow that. But what if she did happen to walk past Brother Benjamin's medicinal garden? With the sun rising in the east. Or perhaps sinking in the west. The doctor's garden received sunlight morning and evening.

Journal Entry

Harmony Hill Village
Entered on this 15th day of June in the year 1849
by Sister Sophrena Prescott

Sister Edna reports a lack of dutiful mindfulness to
their task of picking rose petals by Sister Jessamine
and Sister Abigail. Sister Edna is gifted with an
observant eye when it comes to seeing lapses and
faults. Such gifts are sometimes a help in maintaining
proper discipline in our village, but I must say I am
glad I do not share that gift. Even listening to our
sister relate the wrongs she sees makes me weary.
I often find it hard to sit silent as the list goes on and
on. Small sins, but as Sister Edna insists and correctly
so, sins nevertheless.

I do have to admit to feeling a heavy sigh build up
in me as she continued on about Sister Jessamine's
improper attitude. Sister Jessamine seemed so ready
to work to recover the proper peace of a Believer,
but wrong thoughts tempted her yet again. She is
so young. Even younger inwardly than outwardly, I
believe. Her mind is much too easily entranced by
fanciful ideas. She confessed that her worldly desire

to see parasols was the reason she led Sister Annie on that wild-goose chase through the woods—a caper ending with the two of them perilously close to danger. Parasols of all things. It quite makes my head ache. I despair of ever teaching the girl proper discipline unless she can rein in her curiosity about such trivial things.

Perhaps it would be wise to move Sister Abigail to a different retiring room. Sister Edna reports the two have been heard whispering during the time for sleep. I do have to agree with Sister Edna in regard to that young sister. Sister Abigail has little desire to be among us. Her natural father forced his family to come among us. Such sisters—those compelled to come into the village rather than coming of their own free will—have much more of a struggle believing in the truth of the Shaker way. I have spoken to Sister Abigail many times, encouraging her to confess her sins, to seek the truth, to pick up her cross and live a life of belief and duty. She smiles. She speaks words of confession empty of meaning.

That doesn't mean she won't change. Many do. I think of myself when I came to the village. I too carried doubts and worries and the desire to look over my shoulder back toward the world. But I found love here. Such feelings as I had never experienced either at my childhood home or in my sinful marital union. Those same feelings of love are available in abundance to Sister Abigail and have been known by Sister Jessamine for nigh on ten years here among us.

But I fear our Sister Jessamine is experiencing some new feelings not as pleasant or to be desired as the feeling of love between our sisters. Feelings brought on by her encounter with the man of the world.

I cannot keep from hoping he will soon recover his senses and be on his way and take his worldly temptation with him. I have to confess a sinful hope that Sister Lettie is wrong when she says he is showing interest in our way of life here and may linger among us to explore the Believer's way. It is wrong of me to harbor the desire to deny him that blessing, but I do worry about Sister Jessamine.

That is certainly nothing new.

I should leave my worries behind and sweep them out of my mind. The devil puts such concerns in our thoughts to spoil our peace. It would behoove me to consider my proper duty as a journal keeper. I err by dwelling on such worries instead of reporting our progress here in our village. I must marshal my thoughts in proper directions.

We are harvesting an abundance of rose petals. There will be much rosewater to sell to the world. The brethren planted a late crop of corn and our East Family sisters have begun to pick the first bearing of green beans for our tables. The peaches are swelling on the trees. Thankfully, the late frost did not do the damage we feared. The cherry trees are heavy with fruit. The pickers will go out today to harvest the sweet fruit before the birds can steal them. My mouth waters at the thought of the pies we will enjoy from our trees.

Sunday we will go forth to labor our worship songs. We are allowing people of the world to come to our Sunday morning meetings again. I wonder if it might not have been wiser to continue to bar them from our services. Most only come to ridicule our ways. In my time here at the village—going on fourteen years now—I have only known of three to convert to our ways from witnessing our worship times. But then Eldress Frieda would remind me to offer praises for those three.

Would that I have reason to offer praise for the injured stranger. May he set his feet upon the way to salvation among us. Meanwhile I shall endeavor to keep Sister Jessamine busy with so many tasks she will have no time to wonder about the world.

7

Tristan didn't know why he said Philip. The name just flew out of his mouth when the Shaker doctor asked if his memory had returned. He knew a Philip in the army. Philip Jeffries. A slight young man with no chance at all of fighting off the fever. He died right next to Tristan without making a whimper of protest. Tristan hadn't even realized Philip was dead until they carried his body away.

It didn't seem right to die so quietly before one even reached the age of twenty-five. Better to go out fighting. To die on the battlefield dispatched in a moment of glory, although Tristan hadn't witnessed many of those. He'd seen plenty of dying, but little glory. His father told him the battlefield charges would seem more glorious after a few years dulled the memory of the blood and fear. Tristan supposed enough years hadn't passed for him as yet. He doubted they ever would. He remembered sand and the burning sun and the tormenting flies along with the boom of artillery fire and the stench of spilled blood and putrid flesh.

While Tristan willingly volunteered to fight the Mexicans, he wasn't a soldier. His father was the soldier in the family, ready to jump into the fray at the first clash of sabers.

Tristan joined the Georgia militia in an attempt to offer up the Cooper blood so his father could stay home. But the old soldier refused to pass up the chance to fight for his country and had paid for it with his life. Not killed in any of those glorious charges on artillery positions but by an insidious disease he'd carried home to Georgia.

Tristan's father had not been well enough to begin the final assault on Mexico City. Instead of boarding the ships for the embarkation, he'd been discharged and sent home. The fever caught up with Tristan before the army reached Mexico City. Whether it was the one that afflicted his father or that caused Philip Jeffries to stop breathing hardly mattered. Fever in a sick camp was fever. The Grim Reaper cared not what label man put on death. So when they carried away the body of young Philip Jeffries, Tristan had every reason to expect he might soon join the man in the mass graves outside the camp. But he determined his would not be a silent surrender of his last breath. He'd go out warring against the devil himself if need be.

That's what these strange people called Shakers claimed to do. War against the devil in search of a perfect life. One devoid of sin of any kind. Toward that end they kept the men and women strictly separated. Even to having two front doors in every building that might be entered by both men and women. One door for the sisters and one for the brethren. Sister Lettie assured him it was a good way. One that kept sin from their thresholds.

He had doubts sin was so easy to bar from their houses. Every preacher he'd ever known had expounded at length about the sinfulness of man. Not that Tristan had worried that much about his sinful nature in the last few years. He'd left church behind even before the war. Any remnants of faith he'd carried with him to Mexico were lost on the battlefields. Others beside him had called out to God. Vainly. The shells kept exploding. Men fell and bled out their lives on foreign soil just the same, whether they were faithful believers or the worst rabble-rouser. It mattered not. Nor did prayers keep the fever from felling those standing at the end of the battles. There was no mercy.

He didn't tell all that to Brother Benjamin, although the man might have listened with patience. The doctor was a big man, thick through the chest and broad across the shoulders, but his hands had the gentleness of a woman as he treated Tristan's wound.

"It is good that your memory is coming back." The doctor paused in applying the ointment to Tristan's head to study his face after he came out with the name. "Philip. Is that a surname or your given name?"

"My given name," Tristan said and then had no idea what last name to speak. It didn't seem right to steal poor dead Jeffries entire name.

Brother Benjamin waited a moment before he said, "Has your memory only yielded up the one name?"

Tristan could hear no censure in the Shaker man's words, but he noted a flicker of distrust in his eyes. Tristan spotted a bottle labeled rosewater behind the doctor's head and quickly said, "Rose. Philip Rose."

Brother Benjamin nodded with a smile. "A name is a valuable memory. What else have you remembered?"

"How can I know what I might have forgotten?" Tristan asked.

"You knew you'd forgotten your name."

"Only because I thought to tell it to the young sisters who rescued me and nothing was there to say."

"That makes a measure of sense. So perhaps I should ask questions to test your memory for answers." The doctor leaned forward to finish bandaging Tristan's head. "You are healing well."

"That wasn't much more than a scratch. The arm is the problem." Tristan held up his splinted arm.

"Temporary only." Brother Benjamin lifted a chair down from the pegs. "The bones will knit back together soon enough and give you little more trouble."

Brother Benjamin set the chair next to Tristan's bed and blew out an easy breath as he settled in it as if Tristan were his only patient. Tristan had no idea whether that was true or not. He'd only been out of the room once after the old sister encouraged him to step out into the doctor's garden early yesterday morning to fill his lungs with fresh air.

It had been good to be on his feet again and nice to walk through the garden that abounded with all sorts of plants. Some with flowers. Some without. In front of the building a few Shaker people had hurried along the paths through the early morning air with purpose in their steps. The women all wore white collars and aprons over plain dresses the same as Sister Lettie and the young sisters who'd found him in the woods. The men also had their uniform of light-colored shirts and dark pants held up by suspenders. The women's faces were partially hidden by their bonnets and the men's eyes shaded by their straw hats.

The people walked singly and without conversation, seemingly intent only on their destinations. They didn't exactly move past him with haste but with more of a determined, even pace like that of a person setting out on a long journey. While he had stared without polite restraint at them, only one of the Shakers passing the few feet from where he stood gave him more than a bare glance.

That one had been a young girl. For a moment, he thought it might be the young sister from the woods, but when the girl paused on the path to look directly toward him, it was not. A pretty girl, but not the vision of beauty he remembered seeing when he opened his eyes in the woods.

The Shaker girl eyed him so boldly that he raised his hand and called a greeting to her. Her face exploded into a smile as she took a step off the path toward the doctor's garden. But whatever she was opening her mouth to say was swept away by an older woman rushing forward to put her arm around the girl's waist and hustle her on along the pathway. Tristan couldn't hear the woman's words, but it was plain she was berating the girl.

Sister Lettie informed him later in the day that it would be best if he did not attempt to speak to any of the Shaker sisters. Such contact would be an unnecessary distraction from the sisters' assigned duties.

Tristan needed a distraction now to turn Brother Benjamin's piercing eyes away from him before he saw through Tristan's lies. He wasn't even sure why he'd pulled the fake name out of the air. Why not admit his real name and where he was from? Why did the idea of the Shakers calling in the county sheriff worry him? He had no reason to fear the law.

Tristan reached up to touch the bandage around his head. Somebody had shot him. He should want to see the sheriff, to bring the culprit to justice. But he had no idea who the culprit was or why anybody would shoot at him. Just thinking about it made his head ache. Had someone really intended to kill him? And if they had, were they simply waiting for him to show his face again to take better aim the next time? But why? That was what he needed to figure out.

Nothing about that returned to his memory. His name came back. He remembered his mother's plans and Laura offering him her cheek for a lukewarm kiss after the dance on Saturday. He shifted on the hard, narrow bed and met Brother Benjamin's steady gaze. Lying about his name wasn't doing the kind Shakers any harm. Tristan simply wanted to hide here among these peaceful people a few days while he got things straight in his mind. Even if the wound turned out to be from a random bullet, he still had a dilemma. Propose to a woman he didn't love or run away and desert his mother with nothing except a ledger full of debts?

If he joined the Shakers, that dilemma would disappear. No marrying allowed in this village, or so the old sister told him. Perhaps that's what he should do. Just become Philip Rose, a new brother in the village. His mother could even join him here and then all their problems would be solved. At the thought of his mother wearing the somber dresses with a bonnet covering her elaborately coiffed hair, he almost laughed. Simple living was not his mother's style.

Nor his. Before Mexico, his life was one big round of socials and parties in between university sessions where he was simply marking time before going to work in the family business. His Grandfather Whitley had made a fortune in the buggy business, and just as his father had taken over for his father-in-law, Tristan was expected to step into his father's shoes to keep the company going. Business was good. The Whitley buggy could be spotted on most any city street in the south. Selling buggies wasn't the problem. The problem was selling enough buggies to make up for the speculative investing his father had done in various friends' shaky endeavors. That lost capital had endangered the family's fortune to the point Tristan's mother was ready to barter her son for a fresh influx of security.

Not exactly how he might wish his future. But some things a person couldn't escape. Duty to family was one of those things. It was his duty to step up to save the honor of the family name. To become a gentleman businessman. To pass the family wealth down to the next generation. He could not give in to the desire to do something more exciting than making deals to sell more buggies while smoking cigars in a gentleman's club. Something more than charming the richest girl to accept his proposal and maintain his mother's social standing.

He didn't know exactly what that would be. Prior to the war, he'd been happy enough to drift along waiting for his purpose in life to find him. The war had changed that. Made him want to grab hold of life and get good out of every minute.

Before his mother sent him news of his father's death, he was considering going west to be part of the new frontier in California. Nothing his grandparents and parents had done in Georgia would matter. He'd be judged solely on his own merits. It might be good to see the spoils of the war. To explore and wonder and build.

But those thoughts were no more than a dream that would never come true. A man in his position had responsibilities. His mother told him as much. His father's lawyers told him as much. Laura's father would tell him as much. A man could not play at exploring all his days. There came a time of reckoning and it would be well for him to remember that.

Unless he became a Shaker like the man quietly waiting for Tristan to admit to his past. Even thinking that as a joke was crazy, but then as he stared at Brother Benjamin, it suddenly didn't seem all that much worse than the future waiting for him back at White Oak Springs.

Tristan didn't want to think about that. So instead of waiting for the doctor to voice his questions, he asked one of him. "Were you a doctor before you came here?"

"Yea. I have only been in the village five years." Brother Benjamin didn't seem to mind the question. He sat straight in the chair with his hands spread out flat on his knees. A portrait of calm.

Tristan wondered if he could come up with any question that could upset that calm. "What made you decide to come live here?"

"I originally joined with a village in the east. But they had need for a doctor here at Harmony Hill, and I wanted to use my healing gifts where they were most needed. So when the Ministry asked me to come west, I was pleased to comply with their directive."

"Did you have family in the east?" It sounded very desirable to simply leave family and responsibilities behind, but at the same time, difficult to actually do.

"My worldly wife came into the Society with me. We embraced our new life fully. She with as much zeal as I. Our fondness for one another easily changed into the filial love that is so strong amongst all the Believers. The last time I heard news of Sister Eleanor, she was settled and peacefully so with the New Lebanon Society."

"What about your children? Did they join up as well?"

"Our children were of the age to make their own decisions. Two followed us into the Society, but one of those did not endure. He left for the tribulations of the world." A frown flickered across the doctor's face, but could not seem to make enough of an impression in the man's peaceful demeanor to linger there. "I continue to hope for him to see the error of his ways and seek salvation again, but not all are suited to the Shaker way."

"Do you think I would be? Suited to your ways?" Tristan asked, even though he had no serious interest in withdrawing so completely from the world. At least not forever.

The doctor smiled. "That is something each person must determine for himself. Those who have interest in learning more about our ways are always welcome to come live among us for a time."

"You don't have to sign any papers? Pay for your keep? You can just come?"

"I thought I was to ask questions of you and now here you are the one with questions spilling out. Sister Lettie has told me of your inquiring mind. So let me try to explain." Brother Benjamin paused as though to marshal his thoughts. "Those who choose to stay among us do sign a Covenant of Belief, but not until they are sure of their course. The Covenant is simply an agreement to abide by the rules established by the Ministry that helps our communities maintain peace and unity of purpose. Those who join our Society agree to turn over their property to the ownership of all, confess their sins, and embrace celibacy."

"Why?"

"Why?" Brother Benjamin's smile disappeared. "That is a question that has bedeviled man for centuries. A question doctors such as myself have been trying to answer in a thousand different ways. Why do fevers carry off one person and hardly bother another? Why does the heavenly Father let us discover the cure for some diseases and hide the cure for others? Why is man so intent on the destruction of peace even to the sacrifice of life? Why are there so many ways to die?"

Tristan stared at the doctor, not sure what to say.

The man's smile returned. "But none of those are the question you asked, are they? I'm thinking you simply want to know why marriage is forbidden in our midst."

"I used to go to church. I never heard any preacher speak against getting married. Most seemed taken with the idea of joining people in holy matrimony."

"Our Mother Ann received a different vision. God revealed a new plan for peace and right living to her. Individual families carry too much of a burden and cause stress that pulls one away from worship of the Lord. Christ did not marry. We are to allow the Christ spirit to dwell within us and to love all with equal caring and not focus our love on the few who might share a similar name."

"But . . ."

Brother Benjamin reached over and touched Tristan's arms.

"Perhaps that idea disturbs you because you have a wife in the world worried about what has happened to you."

"No," Tristan said quickly and then backed from his fast denial. "At least I'm fairly certain I do not. I think that is something I would remember."

"So is your name." The doctor sat back in his chair and studied him. "Do you remember where you're from?"

"Texas." He didn't know why he lied about that. Georgia would have been just as distant to this little village.

Brother Benjamin lifted his eyebrows a bit in surprise. "A ways from home then. Why are you in Kentucky? Relatives here? Business?"

Tristan frowned and shut his eyes as though concentrating on remembering. He had no idea what reason to give. That was the trouble with lies. One kept leading to another. He wasn't a good liar. Had never been good at inventing the truth. Although if his situation with Laura Cleveland was any indication, he was getting more practiced at it. His every attention to her had been a lie.

"I don't know," Tristan finally said. It wasn't totally a lie. He didn't know why he'd been riding through the woods. Everything about that day before he saw those beautiful blue eyes staring down at him were a dark cauldron of forgetfulness.

"You have made a good beginning. Let your mind rest again now." Brother Benjamin leaned forward to pat Tristan's arm before he stood up. "And if you do decide to learn more about our ways, you will be welcome among us, Brother Philip. The way of salvation is open to all who will accept it."

"I am curious about your ways. Your quest for peace and harmony among your brothers and sisters." Tristan felt guilty about lying to this good man, but he wouldn't be among them for long. A few days of lies. Harmless lies. He pushed himself up off the bed. "Is it all right if I go walk in your garden again? Sister Lettie said the good air might help clear my head."

"There are those who claim poisons ride in the air ready to slay us with sickness, but Sister Lettie is right about the air in a garden. It surely carries as much healing power as any of the roots I grind." He hung his chair upside down on the wall pegs. "We will talk more on the morrow."

It was good to feel the strength returning to his legs as he walked through the doctor's garden. Sister Lettie had told him that each plant there had a healing purpose. But as the sun began to sink toward the western horizon, Tristan thought their healing purpose was more than the roots and berries or leaves. He remembered their backyard garden in Atlanta with the vibrant azalea blooms in the spring to the fragrant camellias in November. But he'd never dug the hole for the first planting in it. They had servants for that.

This garden was different. Subdued in comparison to the ones he'd known in the south or even to those at White Oak Springs. Here, some of the blooms were hardly to be noticed and instead, the greenery was lush and full. Yet it was orderly. Even the rose gardens he could see in a field behind the white stone house were orderly. Rows upon rows stretching away but with few blooms. Sister Lettie said that was because the petals were picked for the rosewater that had loaned him his name.

Tristan pulled a small dark-green leaf off a bush and rubbed it between his fingers, releasing its minty scent. He wondered if the mint healed anything or perhaps it was only used to soften the bitter taste of some of the doctor's tonics. He had no doubt it had a purpose.

Everything in this village seemed to have a purpose. Everything but him. He'd thought to find a purpose when he went to war, but the battles did no more than demonstrate there was no purpose to life if it could be given up so easily and for so little gain. While he had made it through the battles and fought off the fever, his survival seemed due merely to chance, nothing more.

His mother would say he had a purpose. To keep her in rubies and feathers. To marry Laura Cleveland and produce the next generation of Coopers who might have no purpose except to do the same. Tristan wanted more. He wanted to have a reason to step out on the paths of life and walk with determined step like the odd Shaker people passing by the doctor's garden with eyes downcast, thinking only of their purpose.

What had Sister Lettie told him? That they worshiped through their work. Tristan didn't know about the worshiping. But purposeful work—something to do that mattered—that sounded worth pursuing. Even if it was nothing more than making a better buggy the way his grandfather Whitley had done. Doing something besides dancing attendance on a woman he didn't love to satisfy a woman he'd never been able to please.

Perhaps he could eventually find the purpose in that, but what about love? Was his mother right that he was being a foolish romantic to hope for love? But then she hadn't stared death in the face only a few months ago the way he had. That had sharpened his vision, made breath more dear, love more to be desired. Life should matter. Life did matter. And what one did with that life had to matter too.

A bell began to toll on top of the stone house. He'd heard the bells often in the few days he'd been in the village. Early and late. Signals for the beginnings and endings of the day. Times for eating and working according to Sister Lettie. The paths began to fill up with more of the Shaker faithful as, summoned by the bell, they hurried to their next purpose.

He stood in the shadow of the building and watched them. He tried to guess by their walk if they were young or old. He wondered if the girl who had wanted to speak to him the day before would be back, but when a young Shaker woman stopped on the path to look up toward the garden, it wasn't the girl from yesterday. It was the beautiful girl from the woods.

He'd promised Sister Lettie not to bother any of the Shaker sisters. But how could it be wrong for him to thank this girl who had saved his life? He stepped out of the shadows and down to the path before she could turn and hurry away.

8

Jessamine had absolutely no reason to be on the pathway leading past the doctor's garden. It wasn't on her way from the rose gardens to the Gathering Family House where she was supposed to be going for the time of rest and contemplation before the evening meal. Once she got to her retiring room, she'd have plenty to contemplate, including the way Sister Sophrena's brow would darken when Jessamine confessed her wrong actions. She would have to confess them. Some sins could be brushed off like lint from her blue dress, but others were more like the beggar's-lice that clung to her skirt tail after she'd been in the woods. Something that had to be picked off one at a time with meticulous care.

But Sister Abigail's words about seeing the stranger in the garden had tempted Jessamine's feet to step out on this wayward path. Thoughts of the stranger had haunted her all through the day even without Sister Abigail's teasing comments to bring him to mind. Sister Edna had made sure Jessamine and Sister Abigail filled their baskets in different areas of the rose garden on this day.

Jessamine should have shut the door on her wrong thoughts as she had promised Sister Sophrena she would do. She should have let her mind dwell on sisterly love and nature's gifts. But what if that unsettled feeling the man's touch had awakened in Jessamine was a gift of nature? Her granny had talked of love in her stories, but Sister Sophrena was ever ready to remind Jessamine that those stories were merely fairy tales with no seed of truth in them. Not something that could ever actually happen.

A thousand kisses could never turn a frog into a prince. Sliding one's feet into glass slippers didn't make a charwoman a princess. Such were only silly flights of imagination. Naught but stories. Even her granny had made sure she knew that. But she'd also told her to wait for her prince. That had to mean her granny believed a few princes were out there somewhere and that one might find Jessamine someday. She'd had no way of knowing Jessamine would be taken in by the Believers where the princes were all brothers and any thought of the romance her granny had woven into her stories was a temptation of the devil to be stomped out of one's thoughts.

Jessamine had done many stomping exercises since she'd been with the Shakers. Some poor sister or brother was always being bedeviled by this temptation or that and calling out for help to keep evil from his or her heart's doorstep. Jessamine liked the stomping dances where all the moves were free-spirited even though the noise could be deafening. But that was more exciting than the solemn back and forth shuffling marches and circles where one foot out of the way might throw everybody out of step. Even though she diligently practiced the steps of the dances, she still had to watch for the marking pegs inserted flush with the floorboards to keep from taking a wrong step. The whirling and sweeping and stomping exercises were so much easier. All she had to do was watch and not step on people felled by the spirit.

That afternoon in the rose garden she'd tried doing a little stomping. Nothing any of the other sisters who worked alongside her might notice. But each time she thought of the stranger from the woods, she stomped her foot down firmly and gave it a twist as if to rid the rose garden of an aphid before it could suck the life out of a rose stem. Her aphid was curiosity about the man and the way memory of his very touch caused her cheeks to warm and heart to leap.

She mashed down her unsettled feelings, but they kept creeping back into her mind. They were not entirely unpleasant feelings. In fact the more she tried to stomp down on them, the more they seemed to scatter and bring up new reasons for wonder. She remembered once stepping on an anthill and causing a storm of ants to swarm all over her foot. No matter how hard she shook her foot, a few of the ants clung to her shoes and stockings.

That was the way her wonderings were. She couldn't seem to promise them away. She couldn't stomp them away. They kept crawling all through her mind. The touch of his face with the bristle of whiskers under her fingertips. The strength in his grip when he'd grabbed her arm. The odor of his sweat. The way he'd leaned on her as they rode back to the village. The feel of his body against her back. So foreign from her own.

She had dozens of Shaker brothers. She'd danced beside them in meeting. She'd seen them working and sometimes lifting heavy loads. She'd noted the strength in Brother Samuel's arms when he was handling a team of horses. She knew her brothers were strong, but she had never imagined how different the muscles in their arms and chests would feel. She had such a curiosity about so many things, but she hadn't even known to be curious about that.

Sister Annie said she was an innocent. That Jessamine's sheltered life made it impossible for her to even imagine how wicked the world was. Sister Sophrena wanted to shield her from that world and preserve her innocence. She claimed such innocence was a gift. Sister Edna said the world was a pit of destruction that would swallow Jessamine whole if she strayed out into it. Sister Abigail longed for that forbidden world and had little use for anything Shaker.

Jessamine didn't agree about that. She loved her Shaker sisters. She admired the quiet strength and faith of her brothers. She didn't have the desire to be part of the world the way Sister Abigail did. She simply wanted to peek across the way at it. To imagine what her life might have been like if her grandmother hadn't died. To imagine what might have happened if her granny's promised prince had found her. Even more, she wanted to let her imagination roam free and dream up fanciful stories.

Sometimes she thought if she could only have a blank journal and a pen, she would be the happiest Shaker sister at Harmony Hill. Words gathered inside her and pushed against her heart. She had to continually fight the desire to write them down the way she had done for her grandmother. As soon as she learned to form her letters, she'd let the words spill out of her on any bit of paper she could find. She'd written whole stories in the margins of other books.

The first time her grandmother caught her writing on the end pages of one of her books, Jessamine had been sure she was in for a switching. But her grandmother had read aloud Jessamine's story of a creek stone wishing it could drift out into the world like the sticks and leaves that swirled past it and laughed.

Then her smile faded as she laid her hand roughened by age and chores on Jessamine's cheek. She'd looked almost sad as she said, "I suppose it's in your blood."

"What's in my blood?" Jessamine had looked down at her hands where she could see the faint tracings of blue veins under her skin. Where her blood flowed.

"Storytelling." Her granny shook her head a little. "The same as in his."

"His?" Jessamine looked around as if expecting to see somebody in the house with them. But no one was there. "Who?"

The sad lines on her granny's face deepened. "The prince who loved your mother."

Jessamine hardly dared breathe as she focused on her grandmother's words. She rarely talked about Jessamine's mother, who had died when Jessamine was born, and had never once mentioned a father. From the look on her granny's face, Jessamine was afraid to ask anything more, but her granny was always able to read her thoughts.

"Oh, my sweet Jessamine." Old as she was, she lowered herself right down on the floor beside Jessamine and drew her close to her side. "There are times when if it weren't for the sight of you in front of my eyes, I'd wonder if the prince was any more than a figment of my imagination and I was the storyteller."

"But you knew my mother."

Granny stroked Jessamine's arm for a moment before she answered. "I never knew your mother, only the prince who loved her."

"But you had to know her."

"I do know her now. I see her eyes in your face and hear her song in your voice. He told me what she looked like. He wanted you to look like her, and as best I recollect his description of her, you do. But the storytelling comes from him." She paused a moment as she looked into Jessamine's eyes. "And from me."

Jessamine stared at the dear face of her grandmother. "But I don't understand."

"It is a long story with much sadness and some joy."

"Tell it to me," Jessamine pleaded.

"Let me think if you're old enough. How many years are you?" Her granny didn't wait for Jessamine to answer. "Seven, if I haven't misplaced a year."

"I'm almost eight. That's old enough, isn't it?"

"Yes, for some stories, but other stories need more years to understand. For now let it be enough for me to tell you that your beautiful mother loved you and would have lived for you if not for the fever that stole her after your birth. And that the prince who loved her, loved you too. So much that he brought you to me where he knew I would love you and fiercely watch over you and teach you. And what I couldn't teach you, you would learn on your own in this wooded paradise." Her arms had tightened around Jessamine as her lips brushed against her hair. "Sometimes giving up something shows more love than trying to hold onto it."

"But when will I be old enough to know the whole story?"

"When you're twelve," her granny answered without hesitation. "Then you'll be on the brink of womanhood and better able to understand the mysterious powers of love."

"But—"

"No more questions now." Her granny put a finger over Jessamine's lips to stop her words. "When you're twelve, you can ask every question and I will listen and answer those I can."

"But I have to know . . ." Jessamine spoke around the finger pressing against her lips.

Her granny relented and took her finger away. "All right. One question now. But only one, so think well on what you want to ask."

Jessamine didn't hesitate. She knew what she wanted to know. "Will he ever come back?"

"You ask the question I cannot answer. Perhaps he will. If he can. And if he can't, then we will find a way to go to him. When you are twelve."

It was a promise Jessamine had clung to. One that she had believed. But one that death had ripped from her heart. Now Jessamine didn't even know the name of her father or mother. She knew her own name—Jessamine Brady. But her granny's last name wasn't Brady. It was Kendall. The name was written on the inside of the front cover of her grandmother's Bible. Ida Kendall. But there were no other names. No mention of marriage or children. Only that name written in the front. The old preacher had known Jessamine's name, but he claimed to know nothing more when Jessamine questioned him.

"She was your grandmother. That I know. Great-grandmother I'm thinking," the old man said as he waited with her for the men he'd brought with him to finish digging her grandmother's grave out behind the cabin. "And your name is Brady. Jessamine Brady, but I never heard her say the first word about your parents. I'm sorry, child, but your grandmother didn't talk about what she didn't want to talk about. She was a fine woman, but she never entrusted her story to me. Nor yours."

"She said my mother died when I was a baby," Jessamine told the preacher. "But I have a father. I'll stay here and wait for him to come." She sat up straight in her grandmother's favorite chair and crossed her arms over her chest.

She was ten. It seemed possible to her. She could fish in the stream. She could dig up and plant the garden. She could find fallen branches in the woods for the stove. But the old preacher told her she couldn't stay at the cabin. That she'd have to go to the Shaker village.

Now she knew he was right. She had been too young to stay in the woods alone. But at the same time she sometimes wondered if the prince who had loved her mother had come back to her grandmother's cabin and found her gone. The one who had passed the storytelling blood down to her.

But made-up stories had no purpose in a Shaker village. Such books were forbidden as a frivolous waste of time. One could read the Bible and books that told Mother Ann's story. The Millennial laws were read at least once a year and bits of stories from newspapers were read aloud during some meetings in the family houses. How Jessamine longed to have the newspapers in her hands, to let her eyes explore every story on the pages and not only the stories deemed suitable for her ears by the Ministry. She wished for a pen to write her words in the white borders of the pages.

A couple of years ago, after Jessamine confessed her desire to write down the words of a story, Sister Sophrena instructed her to write songs instead. Songs were a way of letting the words out of her heart that would bless her brethren and sisters. Jessamine took the paper and pen Sister Sophrena gave her with every intention to do as she was told. She planned to sit quietly and allow Mother Ann to gift her with a worship song, but when no song words rose in her mind, the blank page became too big a temptation. Words spilled from her pen, writing about a boy finding a bird with a broken wing. He gathered seeds and berries to feed the plain brown bird and carried it in his pocket to protect the injured bird from the hawks and foxes. At last the bird could fly again and the boy opened his hands to let the bird go.

Jessamine had paused in her writing to ponder whether to end her story there or to turn the bird into a magical creature ready to grant the boy his fondest wishes. All might have been well if Sister Edna had not come into the retiring room and caught Jessamine.

When the woman demanded to see what she was doing, Jessamine had handed over the paper with great reluctance. Sister Edna could not have possibly read more than three lines when she squawked like a goose having its feathers plucked for a pillow. Without reading another word, the woman ripped the paper to shreds, taking no care to keep the pieces from falling all over the floor.

After she dropped the last of the paper bits, she brushed the palms of her hands together as though pleased to be finished with the task. "Thinking on pretend stories is a sinful wasting of one's time. You need to concentrate on noble things of the spirit. Think on Mother Ann and her precepts."

"But we pretend in worship. We fill invisible baskets with pomegranates. We pretend to catch balls of love thrown down from heaven by Mother Ann. We even listen with raptness when one of the brethren claims to be an Indian chief and starts speaking in a language none of us knows."

Her words brought forth another squawk from Sister Edna. "You surely can't mean to compare your scribbled words with those true and perfect gifts of the spirit sent to us from Mother Ann." The woman's eyebrows almost met over her eyes as she glowered at Jessamine. "Be careful, Sister Jessamine, that you do not step into a bog of sin that will swallow you up. The gifts of worship are real and true and to be embraced with joy. The spirit will not be mocked."

"But—"

"Not one more word," Sister Edna said as she turned to leave the room. Her whirling skirt sent the bits of paper flying under the beds and all about the room. The woman paused at the doorway to look back at Jessamine. "Pick up every piece and throw each sinful word into the stove where the fire will devour them. Then it would be well for you to be prayerful that your sinful thoughts will not hold your feet too closely to fires of retribution for such wrong behavior."

After she was gone, Jessamine looked down at the scraps of paper scattered across the floor like flakes of snow and mourned her lost story. Slowly she picked up every piece, but she didn't throw them in the fire as ordered. She was alone in the room. There was no one to see her tie her handkerchief around the bits of paper and secrete the story in her apron pocket.

For days she'd carried the story around, carefully concealing it each time she changed clothes. The story built in her mind until it was almost as if the bird she imagined had come to life and was actually confined within her handkerchief. Then one day while in the woods with a group of sisters in search of ginseng roots, she lagged behind the others until she could only faintly hear their voices. Stepping behind a large oak tree, she pulled the knotted cloth from her apron pocket and gingerly opened it. The bits of paper were crumpled and mashed with hardly any piece large enough to hold a recognizable word, but in her hand they were a bird. She opened her fingers and surrendered the papers to the breeze. They fluttered in the air a moment and then drifted down to the ground. She thought of the rains melting the paper holding her words into the earth and smiled.

She never confessed her disobedience of Sister Edna's order to burn the papers. It didn't seem necessary even though Sister Sophrena claimed confession of even the smallest sin freed one's spirit and drew one closer to the perfection of the Lord. But Jessamine felt no guilt. The story of the bird by itself wasn't important, but the way stories boiled up inside her was. The prince who loved her mother had passed that gift down to her.

Besides, in spite of what Sister Edna told her, Jessamine couldn't see how made-up stories were that much different from the spirit drawings and songs given to others among the Believers. Such were much celebrated during the Era of Manifestations. Jessamine had witnessed the elder sisters surrounding a young sister's bed as they waited in the glow of lamplight ready to write down the words the child uttered while asleep and then singing those words at next meeting.

To Jessamine, a story seemed to be just as much a gift of the spirit rather than a sin she might need to confess. Her granny had never thought it wrong and she had been every bit as much of a believing woman as Sister Sophrena, praying with Jessamine every night and telling her wonderful stories from the Bible.

But while Jessamine didn't think of her stories as sins, that didn't mean she didn't recognize other times when she did willfully sin. She could tell herself she was doing no wrong to take a bit of a detour toward the Gathering Family House at the end of the day to see if she could spot the stranger in Brother Benjamin's garden. She could even think of stepping off the path into the garden to pull out a weed from among the doctor's medicinal plants. How could there be sin in ridding the garden of a weed? But she could almost hear Sister Sophrena telling her to be more attentive to the weeds wanting to sprout in her heart.

Whether letting her feet carry her past the doctor's garden and not keeping her eyes on the path in front of her was sinful or not, she knew without a doubt that wishing for some glimpse of the stranger was a breach of her promise to Sister Sophrena. And she knew just as surely that the man stepping out of the shadows and taking hold of her arm was exactly what she had hoped would happen.

9

The girl pulled in a quick breath and her eyes flew open wide when Tristan stepped in front of her. He hurried out words of apology. "Forgive me. It wasn't my intent to startle you, Jessamine."

She didn't speak. Instead she seemed poised to turn and run away, so he put his hand lightly on her arm to keep her beside him for a moment. That was all he wanted. A moment. He smiled at her as he went on. "That is your name, isn't it?"

"I can't talk to you," the girl said.

"I promise to do you no harm." She was every bit as beautiful as he remembered, with eyes even bluer than his memory of them. But perhaps her worry was darkening them. "Are you afraid of me?"

"It's against the rules."

"You talked to me in the woods," he said.

"That was different. You were in need then. And we were away from . . ." She hesitated.

"Away from the rules?"

"Nay, the rules should always be with us, but in the trees, there was no one to see."

He took his eyes off her face to glance around. Where

moments ago the paths had been busy, now they were empty. Summoned by the bell, the Shakers had all gone into the houses. "There's no one about now."

"Someone is always watching."

"You mean your God?" He looked back at her. Her chin was lifted, but she wasn't casting her eyes about. Instead she was standing very still like a deer in the forest that had hopes, however vain, that it had not been seen by the hunter it feared was in the woods.

"Nay. The Lord is ever with us," she said quietly. "There is no way to escape his eyes. Nor that of the watchers." At last she took a quick look over her shoulder.

"Are you afraid of them?"

Her eyes flew back to his. "My brothers and sisters? Oh, nay. They love me. Even when I do wrong." She turned her eyes to the ground as color rose in her cheeks.

He thought he detected a tremble in her arm. He tightened his hand on her as a strange feeling pushed through him. He wanted to protect her and bring a smile to her lips instead of a tremble. "Then I must be what you fear, but I assure you that you have no reason to be afraid. You can trust my promise to do you no harm."

"Nor do I fear you," she said softly before she looked up. "My granny used to tell me that our greatest fears always come from within. And that the only way to conquer such feelings is to look honestly and without pretense at them."

Her face changed, lost any hint of fearfulness, and instead took on a look of determination that impossibly deepened the blue of her eyes even more. If a man wasn't careful to keep his wits about him, he could be swallowed whole by those eyes. She pulled her arm free from his hand only to take hold of his sleeve to tug him off the path and into the deepening shadows next to the stone house.

He gave her no resistance. He was quite willing to stand

there through the dark of the night if she wanted him to. He told himself he owed her at least that much after she'd obviously risked her reputation by bringing him here to her village for help, but he was glad of the daylight. He didn't think he'd ever seen a lovelier girl even with her bonnet covering all but a few strands of blonde hair and with no ruffles or flounces on her dress to enhance her looks. As different from Laura as day from night.

Once in the shadows, she dropped her hand away from his sleeve but kept looking straight at him. A smile trickled out on her face. "I'm glad you are recovering from your injuries. Have you remembered your name?"

"Yes," he said, then hesitated. While it hadn't bothered him all that much to lie to the Shaker doctor, he found it hard to do the same to this girl. But he had no other choice. The lie already told could not easily be taken back now. "Philip."

"Philip."

She tried out his name and he could not keep from wishing it was his real name falling from her lips instead of the lie. But he continued with the farce. "Philip Rose."

"It's good the memory of who you are has returned, Philip. It is a sorrowful thing to not know who you are."

Her smile faded away, but she was just as beautiful, smiling or not. Tristan decided it was more than the shape of her features and the blue eyes, lovely as they were. It was the light from within those eyes and the innocence radiating from her face. He wanted to ask how old she was, but bit back the question. It wasn't proper to ask a lady her age once she was no longer a child, and even though this girl might have the innocence of a child, she was every bit a woman.

"Now if I could just figure out some other things." Tristan touched the bandage on his head. "I don't remember anything about being in the woods before you and your sensible sister found me. Is she all right now?"

"Yea, Sister Annie will always be all right. She is prone to follow the rules and live the perfect life."

"Unlike you?" He raised his eyebrows a bit.

"I have many lapses in proper behavior to confess."

"Like this? Talking to me?"

"Yea." Again the color rose in her face, but this time she didn't look away from him.

"Sister Lettie has told me that the men and women are forever separate here."

"Yea. Mother Ann deemed it right and the Ministry has established rules to follow her edicts."

"Where is she? This Mother Ann. Is she the one you think might be watching?"

"Nay. She has stepped across the divide into the next realm, but she often sends back messages." He must have looked puzzled because she went on. "Spirit messages and gifts of love straight from heaven."

"Gifts of love," he repeated after her. "I could use one of those."

"As can we all," she said. "Although right now Sister Sophrena who tries to guide me along the proper Believer's path would be more apt to wish a gift of obedience down on me. She will be very grieved with me when I tell her that I stepped into the shadows to speak to you." Her smile disappeared.

"So why did you?"

"I don't know." A frown chased across her face before she pushed out a little breath of air. "Nay, now I'm adding untruth to my list of sins. I do know. I have great curiosity about the world that lies outside our village, but that too is a sin that causes me to forget the rules. Nay, not forget, but to ignore. That is much worse than forgetting."

"You look the picture of innocence to me. A beautiful picture of innocence." Without thinking about what he was doing, Tristan stepped closer to her. "And you smell of roses."

"I suppose when one is in a rose garden all day, it is only natural to carry away the sweet scent."

"You were in a rose garden all day?"

"Picking the petals for our rosewater." She sniffed her fingers and then held her hand up to his nose. "Next week I may smell of lye soap from the washhouse or perhaps onions from the gardens."

She laughed, her worries of a moment ago apparently forgotten. The sound wound around him like a silken thread that he didn't want to break.

When she started to pull her hand away, he caught it and sniffed her fingers once more. "On you those might be as fragrant as roses." Her hand in his was small but sturdy, her nails cut bluntly across and scratches from the roses marking her fingers.

"Oh my," she whispered, but she didn't try to pull her hand from his. "Sister Sophrena was right."

"About what?" He looked straight into her blue eyes.

"About how wondering about worldly things can be like stepping into the middle of a whirlwind. It can make your head spin."

"What worldly thing are you wondering about that has your head spinning?" He turned loose of her hand and brushed his fingers against her cheek. Her skin was enticingly soft.

Her eyes opened wide at his touch, but she didn't step away. She moistened her lips before she answered, "It is too sinful to speak aloud."

"Are you wondering about how it would feel to be kissed?" He let his finger stray down to her lips. His own lips tingled with the desire to pull her close and drop his mouth down to hers. He could almost taste the rose sweetness of her.

"I know nothing of kissing." Her words were a bare whisper of breath as she stared up at him.

"But you want to know."

She made no answer, but she didn't move away. He let his hand drift down to her shoulder and was pulling her closer to him when the bell on top of the house began to toll. As though awakening from a trance, she pulled in a sharp breath and jerked away from him.

"Nay," she said softly, and then a little harsher. "Nay."

She whirled away from him and ran out of the garden.

"Wait." He took a step after her, but when she didn't look back at him, he stopped. Even if his legs weren't still trembling and weak, he couldn't chase her down the pathway. Not in this village where she was not even allowed to speak to him. Instead he watched until she was out of sight before stepping back into the shadows to lean against the stone wall of the building. The stone was cool against his back as he stared at the empty pathway and hated the clang of the bell that had sent her flying away from him. Then again, perhaps none of this was really happening. Perhaps he was still in the woods and dreaming this strange village with the beautiful sister. If so, he wasn't sure he wanted to wake up.

As Jessamine hurried along the pathway toward the Gathering Family House, she felt eyes staring down at her from every high window in the Centre Family House and the meetinghouse too. How could she have acted so wantonly? Actually pulling the man into the shadows to talk to him. And then a mere breath away from tiptoeing up to offer her lips to his.

She touched her lips with her fingers. His fingertip tracing her bottom lip had felt so different and had set off feelings inside her she'd never known or imagined. He was right. She had been wondering about kissing. Thinking sinful thoughts of his lips touching hers. Imagining how that would feel. Even now her lips felt strangely bereft as though missing something needful. The kiss of a prince.

He's no prince. Sister Annie's prudent warning ran through her mind. Words Jessamine knew were true. He wasn't a prince. He was an ordinary man named Philip Rose who would ride away from their village and never be seen again. Jessamine pressed her knuckles hard against her lips to stop the tingling desire that lingered there. It was good the bell had rung to save her from her own folly. Wasn't that what Sister Sophrena was always telling her? That her reckless lack of self-control was what kept getting her into trouble.

And now it had made her miss her supper. Late to the eating room was not acceptable. Plus, she would be missed. She would have a great deal of explaining to do even if eyes hadn't noted her sin of standing in the shadows with the man from the world. But it wasn't the missed meal she was regretting. Not if she was honest with herself. It was the missed kiss.

What was it her granny had told her? That it did little good to tiptoe through a creek. That a body might as well step on into the water and get a firm footing, since on tiptoes or not, a body's feet were going to be wet. Maybe it was the same with sin. Sister Sophrena was going to tell her that she'd fallen into sin by giving in to the temptation to pass by the doctor's garden. She'd stepped in a little deeper when she hadn't run away from the man. If she was going to do so much tiptoeing in sin, she might as well have plunged in with both feet. Grabbed the kiss while she could. Satisfied her curiosity.

But there was a difference between stepping through a creek on firm footing and falling down in the water on purpose and wallowing in it. Even her granny hadn't suggested that. At least not unless it was on a hot summer day when it was unlikely to do her health any damage. Who knew what sort of damage offering up her lips to a man from the world out of naught but curiosity would do?

In her granny's stories, the kiss always came right before the happily-ever-after ending. A kiss to seal the bonds of love. Her father had surely kissed her mother before she died. Vowing love forevermore through eternity. A prince who loved a girl could vow no less.

Jessamine could imagine such love without effort. She could feel it in the breeze that showered down apple blossoms in the spring, hear it in the birds' songs outside her sleeping room window, and see it in the velvet depths of a rose. It lifted her heart, made her feet feel like dancing.

Sister Sophrena would tell her that wasn't romantic love. That such was God's love, the love he showered down on those who obeyed his commands. The selfish love celebrated by those of the world wasn't deemed worthy by committed Believers. The love that swelled a Shaker believer's heart was a purer love. A virtuous love.

And yet, the Bible spoke of the love a man had for a woman. Jacob worked fourteen years for the love of Rachel. Even the Christ had spoken of a man leaving his parents and cleaving to his wife. A holy union, or so it had seemed when her granny had read aloud the words of her Bible to Jessamine. And told her about the prince who loved her mother.

If only her granny had lived long enough to tell Jessamine the rest of the story. Then maybe she would understand about love. She wouldn't have the terrible curiosity that billowed out inside her and made her want to know about such forbidden things. She could settle into her life as a Shaker sister and work with her hands and live the life of purity Sister Sophrena promised would bring her happiness.

Then maybe she wouldn't wonder what she might have felt if the bell hadn't rung and she had let the man from the world touch her lips with his. She moistened her lips and shut her eyes there on the walkway in front of the Gathering House. Her imagination took wing and heat flooded her cheeks at her wayward thoughts. She could not possibly climb the steps and go into the house. Sister Sophrena would want to know why Jessamine had not been in her place at the eating table, and she had no words to tell her yet. So instead she walked on past the Gathering House toward the barns.

When she saw the apple orchard, she veered off the path and, without thought, picked up her skirts and began to run. She loved the orchard. Among the trees, she was her granny's sweet Jessamine again, a blossom of the woman she would someday be with no limits on the things she could imagine.

How could one stop imagining? Why would anyone even want to stop imagining? Who put imagination inside a person if not the Lord?

One of the Shaker sayings came to Jessamine's mind. *Man is a harp with a thousand strings. Touch the spiritual chord of his heart, and lo, with what inspiration he sings!*

Spiritual chord, Jessamine reminded herself. Not the harp strings of the world. Not the desires for worldly kisses and ways. She should stomp out the temptation of the devil and tamp down her imagination. That would be what Sister Sophrena would tell her.

But she didn't feel like stomping. Not at all. Instead she began whirling through the trees. Her feet felt almost as if they were floating above the ground. She'd seen many sisters whirl the same in meeting and claim they were dancing with angels. But Jessamine saw no angels whirling with her. She saw only the man from the world and felt his fingertip tracing her lips. She didn't know what there was about him that so enchanted her, but she could not deny the enchantment. She did not want to deny the enchantment.

Journal Entry

Harmony Hill Village
Entered on this 16th day of June in the year 1849
by Sister Sophrena Prescott

Whatever will we do with Sister Jessamine? She
has given in to the temptation of sinful desires yet
again. To make matters worse, she delayed confessing
the lapses in right behavior to me until after I heard
the reports from Eldress Frieda who was alerted
by the Ministry. The eldress was much grieved by the
reports as am I. We are both very fond of our young
sister, but there are behavior mores we must abide
by if we are to live peaceably in our community one
with another without sin.

It is thoughts of the man of the world that are
leading Sister Jessamine off the proper paths of love
and obedience. With heavy heart, I listened to her
halting confession. She knew not that I had already
heard of her wrongs, although it is certainly likely she
suspected as much. She is aware there are those who
watch to be sure proper behavior is maintained on
the pathways around the village. Such is a necessary
duty if temptations of the flesh are to be avoided.

She did her best to appear penitent as she detailed her wrongs. It was evident she knew I would be displeased and was sorrowful for that reason. How could I not be displeased? She purposefully walked out of her way to go past Brother Benjamin's garden with the knowledge told to her by Sister Abigail that the man of the world might be taking air among the good doctor's medicinal plantings. Oh, my dear little sister. She has no conception at all of the possible consequences of her impulsive actions. To her credit, the watcher did say the man of the world accosted her. To her detriment, she did not flee the temptation. The watcher reported that though the man laid his hand upon her arm, there seemed no force implied in his actions.

Sister Lettie does report the man is aware of the rules and had been plainly told not to bother the sisters. However, most men of the world seem unable to understand our ways and see no harm in speaking with one of the sisters if the opportunity presents itself. Such men have no desire to exercise the dutiful diligence to the rules necessary to overcome the customs of the world and abide by the Shaker way.

But our Sister Jessamine has been with us many years. She knows the rules. She simply chose to chase after knowledge of the world. She admitted as much to me with a contrite look that I fear had more to do with her knowing she had disappointed me than anything to do with her wrong actions. The watcher reports it looked as if Sister Jessamine was the one to pull the man of the world into the shadows of the garden where the watcher was no longer able to clearly see the actions of the two of them.

When I asked her about what happened in the

*shadows, Sister Jessamine said they talked of the rose
gardens and of how the man had remembered his
name. She claims nothing any more sinful than her
wanting to speak to him happened. But I wonder,
since her cheeks fairly flamed as she spoke. I did ask
her if the man touched her. This Philip Rose.*

*She kept her eyes on her hands folded upon her
apron while she told of how he touched her cheek
with the tips of his fingers. When I remained quiet,
she pushed out more words to fill the air between us
and claimed his touch was like fire on her cheek.*

*I asked her if she found that a bad feeling.
A painful one. But I had little hope it would be so.
She has ever been one to throw herself after wayward
thoughts.*

*Her whispered nay was so softly uttered I more
saw it than heard it.*

*There are times when I wish Sister Jessamine was
not so truthful. For now what is there to do but see
that she is not alone to succumb to temptation again
while the man of the world is among us. That is
what the Ministry sees as the only possible answer.
They have been patient with Sister Jessamine on
many occasions, but this is a very serious infraction.
We cannot have such rules of conduct ignored so
blatantly. For her own good they have handed down
the order for constant supervision at least until Sister
Jessamine can prove herself worthy of trust again.*

*I cannot argue against their verdict. I offered
up Sister Annie as the one to stay ever with Sister
Jessamine, but Eldress Frieda reminded me that it
must be one of the Covenant-signed sisters who has a
willing obedience to the Millennial rules. She is right,
as always, and it would be a difficult task, at any*

rate, for Sister Annie who is often unable to stand up against Sister Jessamine's enthusiasms as evidenced by their escapade in the woods on Monday.

Nay, Eldress Frieda says it must be Sister Edna. When I heard her name, I suggested I be the one charged with watching Sister Jessamine myself, but it is evident the Ministry has determined that I am too closely connected with my young sister. As I am. I shall endeavor to not put Sister Jessamine higher than any of the other young sisters in my estimation. She is a lovely girl with a spirit of joy that is a gift to her sisters, but there are many other young sisters around me with gifts just as lovely. I must view each of them with kindness and humility and equal love.

Eldress Frieda was not taking me to task. She was quite plain in lauding my love of the young sisters and my watch care over them all. And she assured me she does not hold me at fault for giving this sister with her loving smile and troubling lapses so much attention and care. But she says now we must allow the Ministry to guide our actions. Our sister must learn the discipline to control her impulses before she is of the age to sign the Covenant.

I felt it my duty then to remind Eldress Frieda of the letter that lies in wait for Sister Jessamine.

Eldress Frieda looked very concerned as she voiced her worry that the letter might confuse our sister's steps even more. While I knew she spoke true words, I felt it necessary to speak up for Sister Jessamine's relation who left the sealed missive for her and remind the eldress of how long we have already held the letter from our young sister. While we did not do so with intent, but merely from neglect of memory concerning it, now that it has been

*remembered, it did not seem truthful to pretend it did
not exist.*

*I know dear Eldress Frieda had no intention of
suggesting any sort of untruth. She was merely
showing her deep concern for our young sister's
future here among us. She fears a letter from the
world might push Sister Jessamine to make grievous
decisions and cause her to choose a pathway leading
to naught but sorrow for her.*

*I too can summon up no confidence in the
decisions our young sister might eventually make in
regard to her future. Oh, how I wish I could decide
for her, but our novitiates have the freedom to choose
their own paths, rightly or wrongly.*

*After much consideration, Eldress Frieda decided
to ask the Ministry to open and read the letter before
determining the best course to take. There seems
little need in sharing something painful with our
sister when she is already surrounded by doubtful
thinking. Meanwhile I am to inform Sister Edna of her
new duty and Sister Jessamine of her opportunity to
begin a better walk with her family of Believers. Sister
Edna will not be resistant of the duty, but I fear Sister
Jessamine will be downhearted to know she has lost
the trust of those who love her. I will pray she will
quickly conform her thoughts and actions to such
ways considered proper for one of our sisters.*

*It is good that tomorrow we will meet together
to exercise the songs and dances to bring our
spirits back into harmony. It will be good to labor a
sweeping dance to cleanse us from the wrongs of the
week and bring purity to our bodies and minds so
we can receive the gifts of the spirit from our loving
mother. Good spirits will not abide where there is*

dirt. That includes the natural dirt of the world carried into our buildings on our shoes as well as the filth of sinful desires besmirching our thoughts. Such dirt needs to be swept from the corners and crevices where it is wont to hide—whether that be the hard to reach corners of our abodes or the equally hard to reach recesses of our hearts.

10

Tristan couldn't get the young sister out of his mind. Even as he promised Brother Benjamin he wouldn't forget the Shakers' rules for the remainder of the time he was in their village, he knew if he had the chance to speak to Jessamine again, he would break his word without hesitation or remorse. He was already lying about his name. That seemed to make other lies easier to say.

When the doctor asked how he was feeling, Tristan pretended more weakness than he felt. His dizziness was gone, and while his arm was far from healed, that would not keep him from mounting his horse and riding back to White Oak Springs. He would have to go back. He couldn't desert his mother forever, and he had no real reason to hide out in the Shaker village.

The more he thought about the gunshot in the woods, the more he had to believe he had simply been accosted by a thief seizing the opportunity to steal whatever coin Tristan had in his pockets. As for his horse, the animal could have escaped the thief, who in turn must have been frightened off by the voices of the two women. Luckily enough for Tristan.

It was the only thing that made sense. The only thing that explained his empty pockets and the bullet wound to his head.

His mother would be frantic by now. Not due to worry for his safety. She probably had few worries about that. She would think he had merely ridden away with no regard to her needs or state of mind. Perhaps he had. It was certainly true he was resting on the Shaker bed when he was not that far distant from the bed at White Oak Springs. His mother had sold one of her jeweled brooches to finance their time there. A few weeks that was to assure their future. And negate his dreams of adventure.

His mother didn't want to hear about his yen for adventure any more than she had wanted to listen to his pleas for love. But where she might have been somewhat moved regarding his wish for love, she had absolutely no sympathy for his need to seek excitement in his life.

"Adventure!" She looked up at him from the list she was making of things they'd need in Kentucky as if he'd spoken a word not fit for her ears. "People who set off on adventures generally find nothing but a bad end. Think of your father and his eagerness to go fight the Mexicans. You well know the sad end of that thinking." She dabbed at her eyes with her handkerchief.

"Now, now, Mother." Tristan spoke up quickly in hopes of keeping her from dissolving into a puddle of tears as she was wont to do since his father's death. "You know Father would have never been happy again if he hadn't stepped up to do his part in defense of our country."

"Oh yes, your dear father was quite ready to charge off down the trail of glory. His problem was reining in his impulses and tending to business at home. Now here you are. Wanting to follow in his footsteps." Her tears dried up in an instant as she rose from her desk to poke his chest with her finger. "Let me assure you that glory will not keep a roof over our heads. Nor will you chasing after adventure. Think about what happened when you took off for Mexico with those ideas in your head. Your father in his grave and us left with very few resources."

"I didn't start the war, Mother, and there was little glorious about any of it."

"Exactly. Now you're beginning to talk sense. Your father—wonderful man that he was—had a serious lack of good sense about many things. I have ever hoped you will be more turned like me and able to focus on the practical issues of life. Such as how we mean to survive."

"Our company is still operating. Whitley buggies are in as much demand as ever."

"So they are, but what seems to be escaping your attention is that your father did much speculative investing without proper consideration of the risks. Mr. Ridenour has been going through our affairs and has regretfully informed me that your father took from the company's till to speculate on land deals that have not delivered income. That, indeed, may have never been properly documented by your father. The company my father and his father before him built up with dedication and sound business acumen is in danger of failing if those funds are not restored."

"Is this Mr. Ridenour accusing Father of taking money illegally? And who is he anyway?" Tristan asked.

"Mr. Ridenour is an associate with the firm that has long looked after my family's legal business needs. Barton and Fister. You are familiar with those names, I would hope." She raised her eyebrows and waited for his assenting nod before she went on. "As for Mr. Ridenour, he is a very nice man and there's not the least need in you trying to make him the villain of the piece. He has regretted deeply having the unpleasant duty of making me aware of the dismal facts of our situation. He has not accused your father or anyone of malfeasance. Merely incompetence, but that is enough. That is certainly enough."

"So we need money."

"Indeed. If you want to state it so crudely." His mother put her hand to her forehead as if having to think of money pained her. "Never in my life did I think I'd have to concern myself with such vulgar necessities. I don't know what William could have been thinking when he so endangered our livelihood." Her voice carried the tremble of tears as she sank back down on her chair. "He was always looking for something better, something more. He had a way of waving away worries and charging ahead, sure there would be a way. Perhaps if he had lived, he would have found that way, but now it's up to us to make our own way."

"Men are getting rich in the goldfields of California. You've read about that in the papers." Tristan had made no decisions on what he actually wanted to do. The idea of adventure, of leaving behind all that he knew, all that was expected of him, pulled at him. To make a fortune on his own and not simply ride along on his father's or his grandfather's coattails. That could happen in California. It was happening for other men there.

She sprang out of her chair again, grabbed his coat lapels, and gave him a little shake as she tiptoed up to glare into his face. "More men will die there than get rich. You survived Mexico. There's no need in tempting fate further. You need to mine the goldfields closer to home."

"And what goldfields are you suggesting, Mother?" Tristan asked, even though he already knew the answer. "The Cleveland fortune?"

"Perhaps my words were a bit brash. The stress of our situation has me quite beside myself." She turned loose of his coat and smoothed down the lapels. "I had no intent of suggesting that dear Laura was merely an object to be pursued for our financial security. She's a lovely young woman. Worry can make one say the most dreadful things. Although our financial security is something that must be considered. And it is true that her father has already spoken to Mr. Ridenour about perhaps investing in our company, but that possible investment does not come without strings."

"And I'm the string."

"We've been through this a dozen times, Tristan. You have to marry someone and I know Laura will make you very happy. Think of the children you will have." She looked away from him out the window as if she could see something he could not. "Sons named Cleveland and Whitley. Can't you almost see them out on the lawn, climbing trees, carrying on the proud Cooper name?"

He turned and let his eyes follow her gaze through the double windows to the green lawn spreading away from the house. But he wasn't seeing children. He was seeing the road leading away. A road he could not take. He was all his mother had left. A man could not disavow his family, and so he had accompanied his mother to White Oak Springs. To mine the Cleveland family gold.

Yet here he was, sequestered in this Shaker village, pretending to be someone he was not while innocent blue eyes haunted his thoughts.

The rising bell pulled him from sleep before dawn on Sunday. The Shakers were early risers. Sister Lettie had told him there was much work to be done in the village and no time to waste in accomplishing the necessary tasks set before them. Time was something to be treasured and used wisely. That was something he had not always done before he joined the army and was so plainly confronted with the possibility of time coming to an end for him. Now he could see the wisdom of the old sister's words. So when the bell rang, he sat up and faced the day himself even if he had no necessary tasks. At least none in this village.

He put on the plain, sturdy clothes the Shakers had given him. Sister Lettie had split the sleeve of the shirt so he could pull it over his injured arm. It was awkward but he managed. The arm ached but the pain was not unbearable. He flexed his fingers. They felt stiff and swollen, but at least they moved. At least he could still move. He had another day, even if he didn't know what the day might bring.

His stomach growled, but he ignored its complaints. If this day was like the others he'd been in the village, it would be awhile before Sister Lettie brought him breakfast. She said every villager had duties to perform before the morning meal so that those in the kitchens were not working while others lolled in bed. All were servants in the community. None to be served, but all to serve.

In time, there would be breakfast and good food if the meal followed the way of the previous days. Nothing like the food they'd had in the army. Hardtack and whatever could be gathered from the countryside. The land ravaged by war and picked clean by too many hungry men yielded up little. A scrawny jackrabbit. A rattlesnake at times.

The dawning light filtered through the window and pulled him out into the garden to lean against the wall where he'd talked to Jessamine. Away from the pathways, it was unlikely he'd be noticed in the gray morning light. He didn't want to cause more problems. While he might like to stand in the shadows with Jessamine once more, it would not be wise to bother her. Not only because he'd be breaking the Shaker rules, but because the memory of her eyes was so unsettling to him.

The sky began to lighten and blush pink before fingers of golden light brightened the day. As the sun reached down toward him, Tristan decided to be Philip Rose one more day. Sister Lettie had said they opened their meetinghouse doors to those of the world on Sunday mornings.

"It is hoped that our spiritual labor will convince those of the world who come with curiosity of our worship to choose the way of salvation and seek the gift of simple purity among us," she explained. That was before he had broken the rules by stepping out of the garden to talk to the beautiful Jessamine. He didn't know what she might be ready to say to him now.

But later, when she brought his morning meal, she seemed no different. Even so, Tristan felt the need to make an apology.

"Forgive me for ignoring your rules," Tristan told her as she arranged his breakfast on the table beside his bed. "It didn't seem that wrong to thank the young sister for helping me in the woods. To my way of thinking, it seemed more wrong not to do so. As you told me, I might have died without the help of her and the other sister."

"Were you seeking Sister Annie out to thank her as well?" Sister Lettie fixed her eyes on him.

"I didn't see her passing by the garden."

Sister Lettie's smile set off a whole new set of wrinkles. "I hear truth in your words, Brother Philip. Our Sister Annie would not set her feet on a wayward path that would lead her past the good doctor's garden. Sister Jessamine did allow her feet to stray and now must pay the cost."

"Cost?" Tristan peered up from his eggs at Sister Lettie. "I did not mean to cause trouble for her."

"You did not. She found the trouble on her own. That is true with every person, all the way back to the Garden of Eden. As much as we try to shift the blame to another as Adam and Eve did, the choice always ends up to be our own. We can give in to our sinful nature or walk a purer path and overcome the temptation strewn in our way."

Tristan stared at his food with a sudden lack of appetite. "What will be done to her?"

"You needn't look so worried, my brother. We do not

mistreat our brothers and sisters. She will merely be encouraged with loving attention to pay closer mind to the rules."

"How?" He couldn't imagine what punishments these people might use. Would she be locked away to give her time to consider her wrongs? Or set to some unpleasant chore to castigate her straying feet?

"She will be watched. That is all. Until such a time as she can earn back the trust of her brethren and sisters. Obedience to the rules is necessary as you will find if you stay among us."

"Watched? That doesn't sound too bad," he said with some relief.

In the shadows the day before, Jessamine had told him someone was always watching. So her situation wouldn't be that much different now. Come morning, he'd be gone. She could go back to her life, and he would go back to his. That was as it had to be, but he couldn't help wishing the bell on top of the house had held off ringing for another moment when they had stood in the shadows together. A kiss would have been a sweet memory to carry away with him.

Perhaps it was better that it hadn't happened. Better that he could only imagine her lips yielding to his. To even speak to him was sin here in her world. To even think of her was impossible in his world. His future was tied to Laura Cleveland. He had no future with a beautiful Shaker girl.

"It is not allowed to let good food go to waste." Sister Lettie's words brought him away from his thoughts. "Your strength will return much faster if you feed your body."

"I will never be able to repay your kindness." He finished off the eggs and biscuit on his plate.

"Kindness levies no fees. Believers are to do all the good they can to everyone they meet. You were in need of help. We were able to give aid to you out of the blessings the Eternal Father has given us. Our Mother Ann passed down the sure truth that we must ever depend on the giver of every good gift." She took his plate but continued to watch him. "It is our duty to use whatever gifts we're given to be of service."

"Your gift of healing?"

"Yea. And my gift to listen without judgment. Not all can do that." Her eyes probed his. "What of you, my brother? Have you ever thought to use your gifts for the good of your brethren and the Lord?"

"I have no such gifts." Tristan looked away from her. A tutor once told him he had a gift for drawing, but his father was uncomfortable with the idea of an artist son. Even one who liked most to draw buildings or outlandish inventions. His father sent the man on his way and threw out the sketching pens. Days later, Tristan had a new tutor and his first gun with orders to learn to shoot. He'd become an expert marksman. His father said he was gifted with steady hands and a good eye.

When he looked up, Sister Lettie was still watching him, so he added, "Nothing the Lord would want to use at any rate." There was no gift in killing.

"How very wrong you are. All are given abilities and gifts. To use one's hands in work is a gift to be treasured, and who among us can't do some kind of work? As long as it is honest labor, then the Lord is honored by the performance of such. No labor is more to be admired than another, for God is in all our work."

She set the plate aside and came back to run her hands up and down his fractured arm. "Brother Benjamin says you are ready for a new wrapping. We can talk of work while I do that necessary task." She scooted the small table he'd just been eating from closer to Tristan and positioned his arm on it before she took a small pair of scissors from her pocket. After she snipped through the ties, she began to unwrap the bandages on his arm, with great care. She looked up at him for a moment as she said, "I would think a man of your age would have done some work."

"Only schoolwork before the army. Training for war does not seem a proper gift to offer to the Lord."

"We can agree to that." Sister Lettie turned her attention back to removing the bandages from his arm. "We as Believers do not hold with war except the war against sin. Our testimony is for peace now and always. No Christian can use carnal weapons or fight. We oppose wars of households and wars of nations."

Tristan frowned a little as he thought about her words. "But what if someone comes into your village to do you harm or to steal from you? How do you defend yourselves?"

"We depend on God and Mother Ann to defend us. It is not our way to resort to violence." She kept her eyes on the bandages she was removing as she explained. "If something is taken from us, then we will pray for the person who had such pressing need for it that he would break one of God's commandments to take it. When we finish our prayers, we go to work to replace it."

"But what if they threaten to physically harm you? A man should be able to defend himself against injury." Tristan couldn't imagine anyone thinking differently.

"Yea, that is the thinking of the world. And some of our brothers on their trading trips have been set upon by thieves intent on harm at times."

"As I was in the woods." Tristan grimaced as the sister lifted his arm, not so much because of the pain but because of the way the bone grated inside his arm. An unnatural, unpleasant sound that attacked his wholeness.

Sister Lettie glanced up at him. "Do you need one of the doctor's draughts?"

"No, that might make me sleepy. I wouldn't want to sleep through your time of worship."

"Are you a churchgoer in the world?" she asked as she turned back to her work.

"I was before I went to the war. That changed everything."

"It may have changed you, but the Eternal Father and his truths never change." Her voice held no hint of doubt, nor did her eyes when she looked up at him.

"You say that, but other men of God preach different messages." He hesitated, but Sister Lettie never seemed upset by anything he said. So he went on. "You Shaker people here have a different belief than any I've ever heard before."

"Yea. The truth shown to our Mother Ann through many visions and dreams." Her words were as sure as her hands as she positioned her scissors between Tristan's skin and the bandage to make another snip.

"But other preachers say they have been shown the truth as well through the Word of God and prayer."

"So they do. That is why we each must pick up whatever cross we're given and follow with faith. Each must decide his or her own way."

Sister Lettie pulled the last of the bandage away from his skin and carefully lowered his arm to the table before feeling along the bone. He did his best not to flinch.

As she gently washed his arm that was black with bruises, she said, "It is good to see how the young can begin to heal so quickly. You will be as strong as ever in a few weeks, but now let us be sure to keep your arm straight. A crooked arm can be a burden."

"The bone feels like it's moving."

"Yea, you will need to keep it immobile for several more weeks, but the wrappings I will put on today will make it easier for you to move around and care for yourself." She stood up and began mixing a whitish powder into some water in the basin. She looked over her shoulder. "Perhaps even join in the exercise of our songs. We will trust you to abide by the rules and not accost any of the sisters. Not even those you think are in need of your gratitude."

"Do you dance, Sister Lettie?"

"I have danced and whirled." She raised one hand up and did a half turn before she picked up the bowl and a roll of bandage strips to come back to the table. "But now I am old and must be content to watch most of the exercises. I can still stomp out the devil and labor the sweeping song to rid my life of sin."

"I can't imagine you having sin."

"All sin, my brother. All." She pushed some of the cloth strips down into the thick mixture in the bowl. When they were soaked, she lifted them out and deftly began wrapping the cloth pieces around his arm. "Our choice is whether to confess that sin and begin to strive toward the goal of a purer life. One where the gifts we have been given, those that do honor to the Eternal Father, rise within us and spill out to the good of our brethren and sisters." She pointed toward him. "And you do have useful gifts. The simple gifts are the best. Those of dedicated labor and love. I look at you and I see potential."

"Potential for what?" he asked.

"Ah, that is what you must discover. With prayer and meditation. I see your confusion. The way you hide the truth not only from me but from yourself. But you must know that nothing can be hidden from the Lord."

"The Lord is the one who seems hidden to me." Tristan saw no reason not to be truthful.

"Nay, my brother. The Lord does not hide from us. He is ever there. Now and forever." She stared at him a long moment before she went on. "Nay, he is not the one hiding." She laid thin strips of wood on each side of his arm and wrapped more of the cloth soaked in her potion around his arm to hold the splints in place.

He thought to tell her that she had not seen the things that he had seen. That she hadn't heard the sick and dying crying out for mercy and finding none. But then what did he know of what she had seen? It was certain she was seeing him too clearly. Much too clearly. But after this day, he wouldn't be hiding any longer. At least not from what must be done.

11

Jessamine didn't know what she had expected. She had not only willfully disobeyed the rules, she had done so in the very center of the village directly across from the meeting-house. While the meetinghouse was generally empty except on Sundays, the rooms above it were not. Those chosen to the Ministry, two elders and two eldresses, lived there in seclusion in order to fairly perform their duty to watch and judge, to steer the village with rules and directives.

When the Believers went forth to exercise their worship, it was the Ministry's eyes peering through the specially made peek holes on the stairway walls to be sure no wrong actions took place. But they did not only watch on Sundays. They watched every day from their windows or gave the duty to others to watch from appointed places.

Jessamine knew their names. Elder Horace and Elder James. Eldress Sue and Eldress Joanna. She had seen them on occasion walking back and forth between the meetinghouse and the Ministry's workshop behind it. Quiet shadows with heads bent studying the ground. Prayerful always, according to Sister Sophrena.

But surely prayerfulness did not necessarily keep one from looking upward at clouds skipping across a blue sky or to the explosion of blooms in the orchard nearby. Nature patiently offered her gifts. It seemed wrong to refuse those gifts by not noticing. It seemed doubly wrong to ignore such beauty while being ever watchful for some evidence of sinful actions.

She had known they would be watching. Not the Ministry perhaps, but someone. Someone was always watching. And she had never intended to keep her lapse of proper behavior completely secret from Sister Sophrena. Part of it for a certainty. Jessamine saw not the least need in admitting her desire to kiss the man from the world as they stood in the shadows. Such knowledge would only distress Sister Sophrena, who would perhaps think she should shoulder some of the blame for Jessamine's shameful disregard of the rules. She would fear she hadn't taught Jessamine well enough.

That wouldn't be true. It wasn't the lack of knowledge of what was and what wasn't allowed that tripped Jessamine up, but simply her desire to know and experience those things she wondered about. Things of the world like the touch of the man's finger on her cheek. At least she hadn't lied about that to Sister Sophrena, even if her answer had brought the look Jessamine so dreaded into the sister's eyes. Not anger. Sister Sophrena never got angry with her. Sometimes Jessamine thought she might like it better if Sister Sophrena did yell at her or even strike her. That would be easier than the look of disappointment. A mingling of sadness and concern over Jessamine's unrepentant spirit.

Jessamine always did her best to look remorseful and to say repentant words. She was always sorry to fall short of Sister Sophrena's mark. But she never truly regretted the curiosity that generally led her into wrongdoing. Nor did she sincerely regret the minutes she'd spent in the shadows with the man from the world. If she was honest with herself, she had to admit what she truly regretted was jerking away before he touched his lips to hers.

The night before, she had whirled in and out among the apple trees until she was too dizzy to stand. Then she had embraced one of the trees with the bark digging into her arms while her head stopped spinning, but her thoughts had continued to spin with her wondering about the kiss that almost was. She kissed the back of her hand. She picked up a smooth stone and kissed its cool surface. She even thought of running on to the barns to find a horse to kiss. At least that would be something living and breathing.

But she had tamped down on her foolishness and made her way back to the Gathering House. She adjusted her cap before she eased open the door into her sleeping room and slipped quietly inside as though just returning from a necessary trip to the privy. It was the time of reflection and rest before the evening meeting in the upper room where they would practice the proper steps of their laboring dances for the next day's worship.

Several of the sisters were so deep in reflection they didn't even look up when she stepped into the room, although Jessamine could feel the rush of outdoor air that came with her. Sister Abigail flashed a grin at her as though she knew what caused the flush on Jessamine's cheeks before she covered her mouth with her hand and looked down at the book she was holding. Even from across the room, Jessamine could see that it was a book of Mother Ann's precepts. She herself had been set to studying the very same book often enough by Sister Sophrena after some lapse in behavior.

Sister Annie stood up and patted down the broad white collar over her bosom. Jessamine quickly smoothed down her own collar but that did nothing to forestall Sister Edna's annoyance. A piece of tree bark fell from the folds of Jessamine's collar. She deftly caught it before it hit the floor and dropped it into her apron pocket.

Sister Edna swooped across the room toward her like a

hawk diving down to sink its talons into a rabbit that had strayed too far from cover. "Are you hiding something, Sister Jessamine?" she demanded.

"Nay," Jessamine answered, while thinking she was indeed hiding a great deal. A great deal that she would never wish to reveal to Sister Edna. The sister in front of her had little patience for wayward thinking.

Sister Edna held out her hand, palm up, toward Jessamine. "If you've brought something sinful into our sleeping rooms, it is my duty to know what it is." When Jessamine hesitated, the woman went on. "It is more than obvious that you have been straying from the proper path. You missed the evening meal and now you come sneaking in with your collar askew and smudged with black. Whatever have you been doing?"

"Forgive me, Sister Edna." Jessamine hung her head down in an effort to appease the woman. "I did not come promptly enough when the bell rang to signal the meal. I regret my tardiness."

"That hardly explains the black on your collar."

The room was very quiet as the other sisters waited to see what story Jessamine would concoct to explain her absence. She had been told—out of Sister Edna's hearing—that her excuses were often very entertaining. She thought her sisters might truly have been very entertained if she told about the man of the world touching her cheek. The thought of it was entertaining to her own senses, but she hardly dared tell Sister Edna that much of the truth.

"Nay, you are right. As you know, I was in the rose gardens throughout the day. I must have soiled my hands and then my collar as I straightened it."

"I worked in the same rose gardens. I managed not to soil my apron and collar. Besides, I have yet to see any black roses in our gardens." She thrust her hand, palm up, toward Jessamine. "Let me see what you hid in your pocket."

"It is but a piece of bark." Jessamine pulled the bark from her pocket and placed it in Sister Edna's hand. "When I missed the evening meal, I thought it would cause no harm if I took a walk through the apple orchard. The sight of the apples swelling on the branches lifts my spirits with the seen evidence of the good Lord blessing our family with abundant fruit. The thought of such blessing made my feet itch until I felt the need to whirl among the trees."

"Perhaps you were dancing with angels," one of the young sisters spoke up. Sister Wileena was always hoping to see angels.

Sister Edna turned to glare at her as if the poor girl shared in Jessamine's guilt. "The angels have stopped coming down to dance with us. You have been told that many times, Sister Wileena."

Sister Wileena looked down at her hands. "Yea, Sister Edna. But why? When I first came among the Believers three years ago, there was much talk of angels speaking through chosen instruments and bringing messages from the other side. Why have they stopped coming?"

"The Era of Manifestations is past. The leaders at New Lebanon have told us as much. We must now tend to the duties handed down to us from the Ministry and worship with appropriate discipline and commitment." Sister Edna turned her eyes back to Jessamine. "Discipline that some of our sisters struggle to practice."

"Yea, Sister Edna," Jessamine said. "I will go wash my hands and put on a clean collar before our gathering time."

"A clean spirit might be more to be desired. You should pray for such and not keep entertaining wrong thoughts that might lead you into sin."

Sister Abigail stood up and stepped closer to Sister Edna to peer at the bark in the woman's hand. "Oh my, look at that! Sister Jessamine has brought us in a worm."

Sister Edna shrieked and slung her hand, sending the bark

flying across the room to bounce off the wall and hit on her bed. "Get that off my bed. At once."

Sister Abigail's smile was wide as she turned away, but Jessamine didn't dare let her lips show any amusement as she snatched the bark off the bed. If there had ever been a worm on it, there was none now. She ran her hand over the bedcover and found nothing. Nor was there anything on the floor or any evidence of it meeting its demise smashed against the wall. Without doubt, Abigail had lied to upset Sister Edna. A very successful lie.

"Are you sure there was a worm, Sister Abigail?" Jessamine asked as she lifted the cover to shake it a bit.

"Oh yea." Abigail took a step back as though worried the worm was too near her, but Jessamine saw the girl's mischief as she goaded the older sister. "A very plump one with strange hairy horns and many legs."

Sister Edna shrieked again and lifted up her skirts to show her sturdy shoes. A couple of the sisters giggled and Jessamine bit the inside of her lip to keep from smiling. Then she sighed. She had not the least trouble imagining the worm right along with Abigail, but how could she convince Sister Edna the worm was in her hand on the way back outside? She would be worm searching all night or perhaps be appointed to stand beside Sister Edna's bed at ready to catch the creature when it crawled out of hiding.

The bell sounded, summoning them to the upper room for the time of practice, and gave Jessamine an escape.

She looked over at Sister Edna tiptoeing backward toward the door with her skirts still hiked. "With your permission, Sister Edna, I will get the broom and sweep every inch of the floor in order to find the worm and carry it out of our house. That way we can all sleep easier this night."

"I can stay and help her since I saw it so well," Abigail spoke up. "With its many legs."

Again a couple of the sisters tittered behind their hands as they began to line up at the door. It was evident everybody but Sister Edna was aware the worm was a figment of Sister Abigail's imagination. Something even Sister Edna must have been beginning to suspect as her eyes narrowed on Abigail.

"Nay, Sister Abigail. You are in need of practice to learn the songs for our meeting. Sister Jessamine will find the creature after your apt description." Sister Edna dropped her skirts and led the way out of the room.

Abigail reluctantly followed after her with a glance back at Jessamine. When Sister Annie passed Jessamine, she gave her shoulder a sympathetic touch. Jessamine tried to look sorry to be missing the practice, but in truth, she was not. She was glad not to have to do the marches up and back and sing the same verses over and over again until the very words seemed to be pounded into her head. Why the leaders favored songs with so few words or songs with no recognizable words at all, simply repetitions of sounds with no meanings, was a mystery to her.

Jessamine loved words and could see no reason not to use them with abandon to tell about the love of God and the blessings a Believer could know by living the simple life. But when she said as much to Sister Sophrena once, the sister had gently reminded her that it was the simple life she was forgetting. A Believer was to ever strive to seek the gift to be simple in all things, even in song.

But things weren't always so simple. Even an imaginary worm. Or an imagined kiss. Or knowing what to believe. Or even who she was. If only she could ask her granny. Her granny knew the answers to at least some of her questions. But those answers were lost to Jessamine forever. Sister Sophrena told her not to worry about what she could not know, but to accept what she did know. That the Lord loved her and her sisters loved her and the simple life was best.

But was it? That was always the question that tickled the back of Jessamine's mind. How could she be sure of that? She knew so little of the world and she had so many questions. Questions she could have asked her granny but that would surely upset Sister Sophrena and could never even be voiced in the hearing of a sister like Sister Edna.

With great care, Jessamine swept the floor and under the beds and every corner as she had promised Sister Edna. There was no worm, but the more she swept, the more real the worm became to her. A worm that would someday fly. How could a worm whose very belly dragged against the ground or was anchored to a tree trunk every minute of its life imagine someday flying?

Jessamine held out her hand as if the worm was crawling upon it. She could almost feel it moving across her skin, each inch forward a laborious journey. But someday that would change. Someday it would float through the air so changed that unless one witnessed the change, it would never be believed. Perhaps she was that way too. Inching along in one life and not able to imagine what might happen if she shed her Shaker cap and apron and stepped out into the world. Could she fly? Did she want to fly?

With her empty hand held out, she walked to the window and gently nudged the pretend worm from her hand to the windowsill. There, in her imagination, it transformed into a beautiful black and gold butterfly to lift off into the air to continue its life journey. She knew it would not happen that quickly. She knew that a real worm would have to spend time in a cocoon before it had wings and that not all butterflies were so colorful. She'd worked with the silkworms. She'd seen the cocoons. She knew, but that didn't mean she couldn't imagine.

She leaned out the window and breathed in deeply. The sun had set, but its light was lingering as though reluctant to surrender the day. When she leaned to the left, she could see the rose garden with new buds lifting up to spread open with the sunshine on the morrow. Her eyes drifted from the roses to the center of the village.

The oak and maple trees didn't hide the white stone of the Centre Family House, but the doctor's garden was out of sight on the far side of the house. It didn't matter. Philip wouldn't still be outside. That didn't mean she couldn't pull his face up in her memory. She put her hand on her cheek where his finger had traced a line down to her lips.

Above her, she heard the shuffling sounds of her sisters and brothers practicing the dances. Back and forth. In and out. She knew the steps so well she could do them in her sleep. Then the music of the voices drifted down through the open windows to her. She heard Sister Annie, who always sang with great spirit even in the practices while Jessamine generally tried to hide her voice under the other voices. Joining in but not standing out.

Again she was glad for Sister Abigail's invisible worm that let her escape the singing practice and gave her mind time to take flight. To remember her moments with Philip in the garden. To think on the imagined kiss that had sent her into such a spinning turmoil among the apple trees. She couldn't believe her turmoil would have been any greater if the kiss had actually happened. Then at least her wondering would have been satisfied and she would have only had to feel shame.

Shame she had quite readily admitted to Sister Sophrena the next day. But it was too late for easy escape then. Sister Sophrena looked sorrowful when she came to her Sunday morning before they marched out to the meetinghouse, but the decision had been handed down. Jessamine could no longer be trusted to keep her promises of penitence. She would not be allowed a moment alone to stray from the proper paths of behavior. Sister Edna would be ever with her to be sure she did not surrender to willful temptations.

"Forever?" Jessamine asked.

"Nay, my sister." Sister Sophrena had lightly touched Jessamine's arm. "Not forever. Only until you have shown you can control your impetuous spirit that has at times led you dangerously near pits of sinful destruction. You knew you should not seek out the man of the world and yet you did so. Willfully, with no regard for the rules of behavior that serve us so well here in our village."

"But Sister Edna does not even like me." Jessamine could not keep back her words. "Each day will be a trial for both of us."

Sister Sophrena breathed out a sigh so soft Jessamine only heard it because of the profound silence that had fallen over them in the sleeping room. All the other sisters were in the hallway ready to march out to the meetinghouse. "And what of you? Do you not love Sister Edna as you should?"

Jessamine looked down at the floor. While she did not want to tell Sister Sophrena a lie, it was also wrong to admit to having ill feelings toward a sister. After a moment she said, "Her thoughts and mine are very different."

"But she does know the rules well and faithfully abides by them. The Ministry feels she will be a good example for you during this time when you must willingly conform your thoughts and actions to those acceptable for a Believer. Even though you are yet too young to sign the Covenant of Belief, you have been with us many years, Sister Jessamine."

"I have." Jessamine's throat felt tight as she remembered imagining the worm turning into a butterfly the night before. But she could not fly away from the Shaker village. She had nowhere to fly. And no desire to leave her family. The very thought of not being near Sister Sophrena made her almost unable to swallow.

Sister Sophrena's voice was gentle as she put her hand on Jessamine's shoulder. "Are you having doubts that this pathway is where your feet belong?"

"Nay." She blinked to keep back tears. "I have nowhere else to go."

"There are always different paths. Few are who can walk the narrow pathway."

Jessamine looked up at her and was surprised to see tears threatening to spill out of Sister Sophrena's eyes the same as they were her own. "The pathway to heaven?"

"The very one."

"Is there only one way, Sister?"

"Yea, my child. The way of love. You must give your heart to God and your hands to work." Sister Sophrena reached out to squeeze Jessamine's hand. "A way you have chosen. Do not give up on loving the Lord and your brothers and sisters now. Cling to that love with all your might."

"I will," Jessamine whispered as she slipped to her knees beside the bed. "But can't I be watched by you?"

"Nay." Sister Sophrena tightened her hand around Jessamine's for a moment before she turned loose. "The elders and eldresses of the Ministry have appointed that task to Sister Edna. It is my hope and prayer you will profit from her guidance. And that you will make right decisions when temptations beset you."

"Yea." Jessamine bent her head in submission. What choice did she have? For whether she wished for butterfly wings or not, she had none. She could not even imagine flying away from this place. This was her home. These were her family.

Her granny's words whispered through her mind. *Someday your prince will come.* The man of the world's face flashed in her mind as her face tingled where he had touched her. But Sister Annie was right. He wasn't a prince. And even if he was, he would be riding away from the village. Or if he did stay, then he would be a brother. A forbidden prince.

"Good." Sister Sophrena stood and reached down to pull Jessamine up off her knees to stand beside her. She studied

Jessamine's face a moment without smiling. "Sister Edna waits outside the door to walk beside you to meeting. Trust me, my sister. Everything will be the same. You will labor the songs and rejoice in the spirit and soon will earn back the trust of the Ministry if that is what you wish to do."

"Yea, I do so wish."

"We shall see in the days ahead. We shall see. The devil has a way of throwing stumbling blocks in our paths at times."

"I will stomp out his temptations." Jessamine spoke the words with vehemence.

"Perhaps you will, my little sister. And I will be ready to stomp them down with you." She gave Jessamine's arm a gentle squeeze. Outside the sisters and brothers began to sing the gathering song. "But come, we must hurry and not be late for meeting. There we can exercise our labors of love and welcome the spirit that will fill us with joy."

Jessamine followed her out of the room where Sister Edna waited, her face stern and unsmiling as she stepped up beside Jessamine. She would do her best to allow no joy to sneak past her to lighten Jessamine's punishment. But then did not joy rise from the spirit inside? Perhaps Jessamine was in a cocoon now—a dark time of stillness. But the wings would grow. Sister Edna could not block that joy. She could not stop Jessamine's spirit from singing or her imagination from soaring.

12

The Shakers marching into their church house looked much the same in their like clothing. The women wore blue dresses with the broad white collars lapping over their bosoms and caps covering their hair. The men had on brown or black breeches and coats. They swept off their hats as they came through the door and hung them on the pegs around the room. Tristan could have stood up and fallen into line with the men and appeared to be one with them in his borrowed Shaker clothes.

The people of the world sitting on the benches along the wall probably thought he was one of them. He'd felt their curious eyes on him when they were allowed to file in and fill the benches around the wall, but Tristan kept his head down almost as though in prayer. Another reason they might think he was one of them.

Brother Benjamin had escorted him across the road to the white frame building more than an hour ago. To get him settled before the worship hour, he'd said. The meetinghouse had little of the look of a church. No steeples or bell towers. The bell was on top of the stone house they'd come from.

Tristan had been surprised to see so many carriages and buggies sitting along the road as though pausing in their journey through the village. Some people still sat in the buggies while others had climbed down to gather in groups to talk the way Tristan had often seen church members do at his own church in Atlanta. But these men and women weren't dressed as the Shakers he'd seen.

"Are they members who don't live in your village?" Tristan asked Brother Benjamin as he gestured toward the waiting people.

"Nay. They come from the world to watch us labor our songs."

Tristan looked back at the people gathering in the road. More buggies were coming and some men on horseback. "Sister Lettie told me people came, but so many?"

Brother Benjamin smiled. "Yea, when the weather is good as it is today with the sun blessing us, we have a good number of visitors from the world. Our worship exercises seem to be a Sunday amusement to them. Some make it a holiday outing and come to rest in our shade with their baskets of food. It is not a bad thing if we bring a time of peace and contemplation into the lives of those burdened by the worries of the world."

"Sister Lettie said your leaders hope those who watch might decide to join you."

"My sister surely also told you that very few actually do make that decision. But it is a good thing to offer salvation to all who will come." Brother Benjamin settled his eyes on Tristan. "You, Brother Philip, would do well to consider our way."

Tristan met his look and spoke with honesty. "Your way seems very odd to me, Brother Benjamin."

The brother didn't seem to mind Tristan's plain words. "As it does to many. That is why they gather to watch. But we do not mind those who come with curious minds. We are happy to welcome such thinkers into our family, for it is those with minds forever searching for better ways to work who bring the most benefit to our community." He paused at the bottom of the steps into the meetinghouse. "I sense that kind of curious mind in you, Brother Philip. A mind that wonders and seeks. Such is a gift."

"Sister Lettie told me about how your leader, Mother Ann, talked about gifts. That is the right name, isn't it? Mother Ann." When the doctor inclined his head in agreement, Tristan went on. "But Sister Lettie also says this Mother Ann treasured the gift to be simple over all others. That doesn't sound like somebody with curiosity but someone who follows."

Brother Benjamin laughed softly. "See, your curious mind is stirring up questions already. Yea, Mother Ann did prize the gift to be simple. As do all true Believers. Those of the world have never taken the time to seek a core of inner peace and therefore don't realize how the gifts of simple thinking, obedience, brotherly love can make a mind unfurl like a flower in the sunshine. An open mind is a mind free to see and feel God and his purpose for one's life. And then he supplies the gifts that we need. Those are the gifts our curious minds seek."

The doctor turned away from Tristan and led the way up the four steps and through the east door. The men's door. The inside of the building held no more clues that this was a place of worship than did the outside. The whole building was one big open space where thankfully the windows on each side were raised to allow the early morning air to cool the room. No pulpit was anywhere in sight. No pews either, unless the narrow backless benches lined up on opposite ends of the room counted as pews. More benches flush against the walls circled the room.

Tristan's and the doctor's footsteps echoed on the wooden floor as they walked across the empty room.

"Where is everyone?" Tristan didn't intend to whisper, but his voice came out hushed.

"We will gather after the bell signals time for worship," Brother Benjamin said. "I thought it best to find you a place before the strangers from the world begin jostling for seats on our visitor benches. Sometimes the benches overflow. Then those from the world must listen and watch from the outside. They have no problem hearing. We have been told that when the air is right, the sound of our songs carries to the town miles away."

"Miles?" Tristan couldn't hide his skepticism. He'd heard a lot of hymns sung, some with enthusiasm, but never any that he thought could be heard much past the churchyard.

"So we're told." Brother Benjamin smiled. "I cannot speak of the truth of it since I am here making the music instead of there listening to it, but I have no reason to doubt the word of those who say they've heard the sound of our songs. It could be the spirit gathers up our notes to carry them on the wind." Brother Benjamin put his hand to his mouth and then threw out his arm as though flinging his words into the air.

Tristan didn't know whether the doctor was making light of the idea of the spirit carrying the music so far or if he was serious. The man was smiling, but it was a different smile as if just being in his meetinghouse had settled some spiritual air on him. Some of that same spiritual air seemed to want to whisper against Tristan. A little shiver of expectation crawled up his back. It was not entirely a good feeling. Something was getting ready to happen in this building, and he wasn't sure he wanted to have any part in it. But he kept following the Shaker doctor across the open floor even while he had the strange sensation of being watched.

What was it the beautiful sister had told him in the shadows? That someone was always watching. He shrugged the thought aside. Preachers had been telling their people that since before Christ walked on the earth. *Be good. The Lord is watching. Listen to his word and he will take care of you.* Tristan had believed that might be so once. Years ago. Before the war had knocked those childish thoughts out of him.

Now he didn't know what he believed. It was easier not to think about it. Easier to play a part and not expect too much from the Lord. He wasn't ready to deny there might be a God, but he was ready to do some serious doubting about whether that God cared whether he lived or died, or what he did each day of his life.

But what about Jessamine and that other sister, the sensible one, finding you in the woods? The thought whispered through his mind. Put there perhaps by the expectant spirit in this Shaker church house. Tristan pushed aside the thought. Happenstance. Fortunate perhaps, but nothing but mere happenstance.

Brother Benjamin was talking again. "It would be best for you to sit on these stairs here in the corner." He was pointing toward a set of three steps leading up to a closed door. "That way there will be little chance you will be squeezed in too tightly or bumped by those of the world on the benches. You need to protect your arm while Sister Lettie's bandages harden. She told you as much, didn't she?"

"She did." Tristan held up his arm ensconced in the sling Sister Lettie had fashioned for him after she had finished wrapping the dampened bandages around his arm. She'd told him the concoction on the rag strips was merely starch. The same starch the sisters used to keep their collars crisp on their shoulders except thickened until it was near to solid. But she'd warned it would take awhile to dry and harden. Until then he was to be careful not to knock his arm against anything or else they might have to start fresh, pulling the bone back in line.

Brother Benjamin watched Tristan sit down on the steps and then went back across the floor and out the door. His steps echoed in the still room. Tristan's feet itched to stand up and follow him. It seemed too odd sitting there on the steps in the empty building.

And entirely too silent. He didn't know the last time he'd been in such profound silence. He imagined he would even be able to hear a bug crawling over the threshold or one of the Shaker spirits floating past. Hadn't Sister Lettie talked about spirits coming down to their meetings? Maybe they were coming early.

A chill walked up his back. Again he had the feeling of being watched. Perhaps the spirits were eyeing him, wondering about this interloper. This liar. But it wasn't only the spirits watching. Behind him he heard a creak of wood. Someone was coming down the stairs. He scooted over against the wall to make room for the person to open the door and come into the meeting room.

But the door didn't open and the silence fell again. A silence far from empty. It awakened apprehension in his mind, and even with his back to the wall, he had the sensation someone was sneaking up on him. On the field of battle, that had not been an uncommon feeling. Those soldiers with undisciplined trigger fingers were often ready to fire at the wind or a bush rustling even though the captains cautioned against being spooked into firing too soon. Better to save one's ammunition for when the enemy was more than a rattle in the brush, but a clear danger.

Tristan had no reason to feel spooked now. He was far from the field of battle and quite safe in this Shaker church house. But the feeling of being watched grew stronger until he could almost hear the in and out breaths of the watcher. He looked at each and every window, but no one was peeking in from outside. He stared at the door on the opposite side of the room to see if perhaps it had opened a crack. Eyes peered back at him from a small opening above the door. A square only large enough for eyes to look out into the room.

Slowly he shifted to look up above the door behind him. The same kind of opening was there. He couldn't see if anyone was looking through it from where he was sitting directly below the peephole, but he didn't have to see the eyes to know they were there. Someone was on the steps on the other side of the door. Right behind him. Standing there silent and waiting. But for what? What did the watchers hope to see him do?

He thought about standing up and walking out the door. He had no real reason to stay and watch their worship. Nothing but the curiosity that Brother Benjamin had said was his gift. And to see the beautiful sister once more before he rode away from here forever. One more look before he pushed her away from his thoughts and returned to his world. And Laura Cleveland.

Marriage to Laura wouldn't be so awful. He could work in the buggy company. Maybe his curious mind could come up with an even better buggy than his great-grandfather's design. He could draw plans for his and Laura's own house. Or build tree houses for his sons and daughters. He wouldn't have to quit living because he married Laura. It would, as his mother kept telling him, simply open up paths into a new life.

But first he'd feast his eyes on Jessamine one more time. Talk to her if he had the opportunity. He didn't care if eyes were watching or not. He wanted to stand up and tell them so. But instead he ignored the eyes. In Mexico, he had withstood much worse than eyes pinning him to this step. If he could charge into artillery fire, he could surely bear up under the scrutiny of a preacher person or two.

Even so, he was glad when the bell began tolling the hour, and outside he heard the sound of singing as the Shaker believers began marching toward the meetinghouse. He could see one line of them coming down from the east of the village through the open windows. The visitors from the world hurried into the building ahead of the Shakers to jockey for the best seats. Tristan could almost feel the peephole eyes shifting from him to the new disturbances in the building, even as the visitors were settling their eyes on him.

Tristan kept his head down and watched the people out of the corners of his eyes. He had no reason to worry anyone there would know who he was. He had only been at White Oak Springs a short week before whatever had happened in the woods landed him in the Shaker village. Hardly enough time to make acquaintances with anyone in the area.

Nevertheless, he was relieved when the Shaker men and women streaming into the meetinghouse doors grabbed the attention of the onlookers. Outside the singing continued, but each Shaker fell silent as they stepped into the building. Anticipation charged the air as the men marched to the benches on the side of the room where Tristan sat and the women filed to the benches on the other side. They stood until every Shaker had come into the building. Then at a signal Tristan did not catch, they all sat at the same exact time and waited in silence for perhaps another signal to begin their worship.

The world visitors must have been cautioned to remain quiet, because they made no noise either, other than a shuffle here and there as this or that person shifted to get a better view. The onlookers in the building were mostly men, but through the windows, Tristan could see families settling on blankets with their baskets of food just as Brother Benjamin had said. A day for picnics. Those at White Oak Springs would be doing the same.

He and Laura had shared a picnic the Sunday before as they sat by the spring pool and listened to the White Oak band play and sing love songs. It was to have been a romantic time, a time when Tristan was supposed to begin making his affection for Laura known. In actuality the ants had invaded their food and a bee so determinedly buzzed Laura's head that they deserted their blanket and food and retreated to the hotel porch. There Laura claimed a headache and retired to her room before he could offer up the first affectionate word. Much to the dismay of Tristan's mother.

Tristan let his eyes slide to the beautiful Jessamine. Ants and bees wouldn't spoil a picnic with her. His eyes had been drawn to her the instant she stepped through the door. As if she felt the same draw, she'd looked toward him and then quickly away. An older woman beside her frowned and nudged her toward the benches. Now Jessamine was studying her hands folded in her lap, but he had the feeling she was only too aware of his eyes on her. The sister beside her didn't have the same timidity. She sent him such a forbidding look he almost expected her to stand and demand he be removed from the gathering.

He didn't want that so he looked down at his uninjured hand resting in his own lap. But after a few seconds he sneaked another peek over at Jessamine and caught her eyes on him. She looked worried, the fresh joy in her face when they'd met in the garden gone or at least cloaked. How could he feel such an unspoken connection to a girl he barely knew? He ran his thumb over the tips of his fingers and remembered how her lips had felt as he'd traced them. Soft and ready, even if forbidden. Across the room, she moistened her lips with her tongue and a blush rose in her cheeks as if she were divining his thoughts.

She bent her head as one of the Shaker men stood and stepped into the open area between the benches and introduced himself as Elder Joseph. The same quiet dignity that hovered around Brother Benjamin seemed to wrap around the elder as he spoke words of welcome to the visitors. To Tristan's relief, he made no mention of him. After instructing the visitors not to interfere with the worship dances, he invited all to watch and listen with eyes and ears receptive to the spirit that would come down from heaven when they labored their songs.

The anticipation in the room increased until the air fairly tingled as though lightning was playing through the room. The lightning of the spirit. Tristan took another look toward

Jessamine, but she was watching the elder, as were all the Shakers. Quiet, waiting, ready. The old brother stepped to the side of the room, and again moving as one, the Shaker men and women stood and began lifting the benches to carry them out of the way. A hush fell over them as the men and women lined up across from one another. Even the visitors on the benches seemed to be holding their breath in expectation.

A woman's voice rang out, pure and true, singing about Shaker life. Other voices joined in and the men and women began marching toward one another as the song filled the air.

> Come life, Shaker life! Come life eternal!
> Shake, shake out of me all that is carnal.
> I'll take nimble steps, I'll be a David,
> I'll show Michael twice how he behaved!
> I'll take nimble steps, I'll be a David,
> I'll show Michael twice how he behaved!

"See, I told you," one of the visitors whispered loudly. "They're going to dance together."

But the Shakers didn't touch or join hands. They passed in lines, walking briskly. Then they sang the song over again and this time they stood still and began shaking their hands. For some among them, it was as if shaking their hands set free the shaking motion to climb through their arms to their shoulders and heads and then it sank down through them until every inch of their bodies was quivering. The singing got livelier and louder, and just when the same words repeated over and over had worn a groove in Tristan's mind, the tune changed and so did the steps. A new burst of energy showered down on the dancers. Rows of the men and women marched in and out and even formed circles. But so practiced were their moves that no bad steps ruined the symmetry of their dance.

All at once like well-trained parade horses, the Shakers stopped moving and stomped down their feet. The noise startled many among the visitors, and one lady let out a frightened squeal before she clapped her hand over her mouth.

The order of the dance seemed to be completely lost as the men and women began stomping and pushing down with their hands as they shouted about chasing away the devil. Some began whirling. Some raised their hands to the heavens and began jabbering nonsense. Some continued to sing, but the sounds weren't words Tristan could understand. He didn't know what to think as he stared at them in wonder.

Brother Benjamin was stomping like all the rest. Sister Lettie stood with her hands lifted and a serene look on her face in the midst of the bedlam. Beautiful Jessamine whirled past him. But she was not lost in the spirit, for when she got close to him, she smiled. Directly at him. He wondered what the Shakers would do if he stood up from his appointed place and went out on the dancing floor to follow after the girl. He could almost feel his hand in hers as she led him through the dance. He could imagine her laughter. His feet itched to make his imagining true, but he stayed where he was and only followed her with his eyes. He'd promised Sister Lettie and Brother Benjamin not to interfere with their worship.

As suddenly as the free-spirited dancing began, it stopped, and one of the singers began a new song.

> 'Tis the gift to be simple, 'tis the gift to be free.
> 'Tis the gift to come down where we ought to be,
> And when we find ourselves in the place just right,
> 'Twill be in the valley of love and delight.
> When true simplicity is gain'd,
> To bow and to bend we shan't be asham'd.
> To turn, turn will be our delight.
> 'Till by turning, turning we come round right.

Again the dancers began their measured steps interspersed with turns and bows as the singers sang. Tristan kept his eyes on Jessamine as she wound through the lines of dancers, her feet light, her movements in time to the melody. There was a freedom about her, a grace that seemed different from the others. As though she were dancing for the joy of the movement and not necessarily in fervent pursuit of the spirit. Or perhaps he just imagined that because he didn't want her to be one with these odd people.

More songs and dances followed. They swept with imaginary brooms and sang songs in childish babble. Suddenly they all dropped to their knees and lifted their hands toward the heavens as they sang a prayerful song. Then once the prayer words were sung, they bowed their heads to the ground and stared at the floor while silence filled the room. Here and there a visitor shuffled his feet or coughed, but absolutely no sound came from the assembled Shakers as they continued to stare down at the floor.

Something powerful about the silence sent a chill down Tristan's back. It was the feeling on the battlefield right before the charge was sounded. That moment when a man was facing his mortality, seeking courage, wanting to extend the moment and at the same time to hear the charge order and simply get it over with. He wondered what the Shakers were thinking as they knelt together. Was it some sort of peaceful serenity? Gratitude for the perfect life they aimed to find? Perhaps sorrow for their wrongs? Or for what they'd given up to live a life of worship with no freedom to reach for love as the world knew it?

But then some in the world didn't have that freedom either. Love had to be sacrificed for practical purposes. It was good when a man and woman married for convenience and discovered love in the process the way his mother and father had, but love wasn't always so easily ordered to suit a family's needs. In fact sometimes love wasn't ordered at all. It just happened.

Tristan's eyes settled on Jessamine. Her head was bent like all the others, a position of silent repose. Prayerful. Committed. Dedicated. Even if there was no Laura, he had no future with the beautiful sister. She was one with these odd people. A people who believed romantic love and marriage a sin.

He shifted uneasily on the steps as the silence continued. He wanted to go pull her up to stare into her eyes and ask what she believed. But that was foolish. He barely knew the girl. Love didn't happen in a flash. At least not lasting love. That kind of love needed time to grow like a fruit tree pushing down roots and reaching branches to the sun until it could bear fruit.

Then as suddenly as the Shakers had fallen to their knees in silence, they rose to their feet and began forming lines to leave the meetinghouse. Tristan also stood. He didn't know if he was supposed to follow them out, but he couldn't bear another minute inside the building. Let the onlookers think he was one of them. He didn't care.

He lagged a little behind the Shaker men as they silently exited the building. He was outside and down the steps when one of the visitors chased after him, calling out, "Tristan Cooper!"

Tristan made the mistake of letting his step hesitate at the sound of his name. He should have kept walking, pretended no recognition.

The man grabbed his good arm and swung him around. "I thought that was you. What in the name of all that's holy are you doing here?"

13

Jessamine lagged behind the other sisters on the way out of the meetinghouse in spite of Sister Edna's annoyed looks her way. Sister Edna couldn't tell her to hurry because the spirits had ended the meeting with silence. When that happened, the Believers were to continue in silence as they returned to their houses. There, they would contemplate the spiritual gifts of the meeting before the bell rang for the midday meal. The food would be simple, prepared in advance, and eaten in yet more silence.

But Jessamine wasn't in any hurry to get to her room. Instead she moved as slowly as possible while peering around at the people from the world. She wanted to see how they were dressed and what foods they spread on their blankets as they sat under the shade trees and attuned their ears to the Believers' songs.

It wasn't only her wondering about those from the world outside the meetinghouse that made her steps lag. She greatly desired to catch yet another sight of Philip Rose. He had been in the meetinghouse, taking in all that happened from where he was seated directly below one set of the watching eyes. She had never before seen anyone allowed to sit on those steps to the door to the Ministry's rooms. Never. That had to mean the Ministry favored this man more than most from the world. Had they given him this special vantage point in hopes he would see and note the spirit falling so abundantly down on the Believers? Perhaps even open up to it? Not that Jessamine had ever been overtaken by the spirit the way many of her brothers and sisters were each and every time they went forth to labor the songs.

Once when she expressed concern over this lack, Sister Sophrena had assured Jessamine she had no need to worry. "Many very committed Believers have never felt the first quiver of shaking or heard even a whisper of an angel's message from above."

"But shouldn't they?" Jessamine asked. "If they truly believe in a good and proper way?"

"Oh no, my sister. While you with your human eyes might see that as a lack in one who believes, our Lord and Mother Ann look with holy eyes. They know all our thoughts and our gifts since the Eternal Father is the one who planted those gifts within us. A gift of weaving or cooking is surely as worthy in holy eyes and as valuable to our family as one of whirling in a burst of abundant spiritual joy."

"But what of the gift of imagination? Of words?"

"Each gift within us can be useful, but such must be properly channeled for the good of the Society and not simply for our own amusement." When Sister Sophrena noted the disappointment on Jessamine's face, she had offered more words of encouragement. "You will learn to use your gifts to our good. I know the pull of words to you, so write them in your journal. Record the events of your day. Write of the work we do, for such is a testament of our love for the Lord and our Mother. Such written records confirm our faithfulness and industry and are much to be desired."

But she hadn't wanted to write truth. At least not the truth of ordinary daily events and chores. She wanted to capture the truth in the stories that bubbled up in her imagination from she knew not where. Stories of princes and magical kingdoms. Stories of eagles or ladybugs. She felt little joy in writing down the number of dresses she had ironed or the packets she had filled with an exact number or measure of seeds. Not unless the dress began to sparkle and have ribbons festooned across it like the dress Cinderella wore to the prince's ball or the seeds in those packets grew beanstalks high into the air where she could climb into a different world. That's what her imaginings did. Helped her climb into a world where amazing things could happen. A world where a prince might ride into her life as her granny had once promised.

That wasn't the world she was in. She was a Believer or near to one. Only a little more than a year away from signing the Covenant. Perhaps when that happened, when she actually made the written promise to abide by the rules forever, then she would be ready to use her gifts in a more proper and fitting way. She would write down the events of the day without the desire to embellish them. She would know the pure love of the Believer and not wonder about the forbidden love of the world. She would not think of how a man's lips might feel on hers or have trouble keeping her promises to Sister Sophrena. She would be able to withstand the temptations that had her feet lagging to catch sight of Philip Rose before Sister Edna pulled her away from the meetinghouse.

The man from the world had fastened probing eyes on Jessamine as soon as she'd entered the meetinghouse. In spite of her promises of obedience only moments before, Jessamine had not kept her eyes away from him. Instead she had sneaked many looks his way and once smiled quite brazenly at him while whirling with pretense of being filled with the spirit. She could only hope the watching eyes would believe her smile prompted by her spiritual fervor.

They would not. Any more than Sister Edna had as her bony fingers pinched Jessamine's arm each time the sister even imagined Jessamine was allowing her gaze to stray toward the stairs. Jessamine had kept her face turned away from Sister Edna, but she had chanced a couple of peeks up at the eyes in the peepholes. She was never able to read those eyes—whether they were angry or loving or full of the spirit.

But now as she pretended exhaustion from laboring the dances and stepped up the pathway slowly, she had no trouble at all reading Sister Edna's eyes. Or Sister Sophrena's. The good sister was not frowning at her like Sister Edna, but instead wore a look of weariness. Jessamine remembered the tears in her dear sister's eyes while they talked in the sleeping room before marching out to meeting. Tears put there by Jessamine's own wayward spirit.

It seemed no matter how she vowed to correct her behavior, she could not resist the pull of her wondering imagination. She was going to have to work to change her ways, or she might never be free of the scowling Sister Edna beside her.

Out of the corner of her eye, she saw Philip Rose follow the brethren out their door as if he wanted to join in their line but feared he would not be allowed. Jessamine didn't know whether to hope that he might be drawn to the way of the Believers or to dread the thought. She should wish to see him set his feet on the road to salvation, but the thought of him being her brother gave her no joy.

When Sister Edna grabbed her elbow and jerked her forward, Jessamine stumbled just to be contrary. Another sin for which she would have to beg forgiveness. But that was why she was still close enough to see the onlooker from the world rush out of the meetinghouse door behind Philip.

She heard the name the man spoke as plainly as if he had spoken the words directly to her. "Tristan Cooper."

She saw Philip hesitate as though the man had roped him

with the name and pulled the loop tight. At last Sister Edna's curiosity was aroused too, and she stopped goading Jessamine to continue on toward the house. Instead she bent her ears toward Philip and the other man as did many of the Believers around them. The man wasn't very tall but his midsection bulged out roundly. Not a man on friendly terms with much physical labor.

"Tristan Cooper," the man repeated. "I thought that was you. What in the name of all that's holy are you doing here?" The man was smiling, but it wasn't a particularly pleasant smile. More the kind Sister Edna bestowed on Jessamine when she caught her in some wrong. Such occasions seemed to give the sister an odd pleasure.

Without a hint of an answering smile, Philip turned to face the man. Brother Benjamin stepped out of the line of Believers to go to his side. Another brother, Simon, moved over beside the onlooker from the world. Brother Simon's face showed naught but serene peace, but he was sturdy and broad across the shoulders—a wall against the threats of the world. The onlooker paid the Shaker brothers no mind. His eyes were tight on Philip.

Other people from the world filed out of the meetinghouse to cluster behind the two men. The Believers stood on one side waiting to hear Philip speak some sort of answer to the man while the world people on the other side appeared to be pleased to have an added attraction to their morning's amusement. A few of those under the trees got to their feet and edged closer to better see what might be happening.

"Do I know you?" Philip said.

The man wasn't put off by Philip's question. "I think you should. We ate at the same dining table over at White Oak Springs last Sunday. Lenwood Patrick's my name." The man started to extend his hand toward Philip, but seemed to think better of it and dropped his arm back to his side. "Then again, it could be your eyes were so full of that beautiful Cleveland lass, you weren't seeing anybody but her that day." The man's smile spread wider.

White Oak Springs. Philip was from White Oak Springs. Perhaps Sister Annie was wrong. Perhaps he was a prince. A prince by a different name than the one he claimed. What had the man called him? Tristan Cooper.

Brother Benjamin spoke up. "You must have Mr. Rose confused with someone else."

"Mr. Rose? Somebody's confused, but not me. I never forget a face." The man's smile became more of a scowl as he looked at Brother Benjamin. "And I have plenty of others who can vouch that this is the man I supped with last Sunday. Tristan Cooper. Including his own mother. The poor woman has been quite beside herself." He looked back at Philip, eyeing the sling holding his arm and the bandage on his head. "What happened to you anyway?"

"I fell off my horse." Philip lifted his arm in the sling away from his body toward the man. "Broke my arm. These good people have been doctoring me."

"Well, it's a known fact these Shaker folk know their medicine potions, so I'm guessing there are worse places you could have landed. I've swallowed a few of their elixirs over at the Springs from time to time myself." He stared at Philip a long second before he went on. "None of them ever had me forgetting who I was though."

Philip simply stared back at the man without speaking. Would a knock on the head make him forget his name and then remember it as something it wasn't? Such seemed doubtful, but the thought that Philip Rose might be a concocted name didn't upset Jessamine. In fact, if Sister Edna hadn't been so close to her that the woman's breath was almost warming Jessamine's ear, she would have laughed. She supposed she shouldn't celebrate falsehood if indeed Philip was merely lying and not delusional because of the wound to his head. Whatever the reason, he had chosen to be someone else. Something Jessamine often considered. That worm into a butterfly. A stranger into a prince.

Perhaps he was as unsure of his identity as she was of hers. But no. The short round man had said Philip had a mother worried about him. Or she supposed it was Tristan who had the mother worried about him. Philip had deserted his identity. And not only his identity but also his family and the beautiful girl who waited for him at White Oak Springs. He had no doubt stood in the White Oak Springs shadows and traced that girl's lips. Probably had done more than trace them. No bell would have spoiled their moments.

An unknown feeling crawled through Jessamine. She wasn't exactly angry or sad but something in between. Not a pleasant feeling but rather one that poked her and made her uneasy. She stared at the man she and Sister Annie had rescued in the woods and waited for what he might say next. But it wasn't his words that were upsetting her peace. It was the thought of that other girl in the shadows with him. That girl would know what a kiss was like.

Tristan stared at the man in front of him and tried to hide his dismay. A liar was always found out. His father had told him that many times. Right before he told him that if a man lied, it should be for a reasonable cause. His father respected the truth—unless telling it might not be useful in obtaining his ends. While Tristan had never known his father to lie outright to him or his mother, he had no doubt the man bent the truth when it suited his purposes. Was that what Tristan had been doing? Bending the truth for his own purposes? But using a false name was more than bending the truth. Now he had been found out in a most public way.

He'd planned to ride away with the good doctor and Sister Lettie none the wiser about his subterfuge. He didn't like seeing the grim set of Brother Benjamin's mouth as he waited for Tristan to say something. Tristan didn't know why it mattered what these odd people thought of him. He'd likely never see any of them again. Even the beautiful Jessamine.

The week among the Shakers had been interesting, but nothing that was going to change his life. He might wish he could raise his hands toward the ceiling and call down something spiritual to embrace as they did, but he couldn't imagine whirling and marching back and forth with visions of worship. His turns and whirls on a dance floor would be with a partner. His time in churches an expected duty in order to set the proper example for his children. Children he must have to carry on the Cooper name.

A name he might as well admit to there in the midst of the Shakers, but he did not. Instead he looked at the short, round man in front of him and held his hand out toward him. "Mr. Patrick, it's good to meet you, but I regret to say you must have me confused with another." What was one more lie even if everyone in hearing distance knew the words he spoke carried no truth. It seemed easier to carry on the farce than to own up to his name.

Lenwood Patrick hesitantly took Tristan's hand with a look of consternation. Tristan did remember the man from their shared dinner. He was a northerner who talked nonstop of his many triumphs in business. Tristan had paid little attention to his chatter other than being amused at how the man seemed so intent on impressing his mother. Something that bragging of his riches had certainly not done. In Tristan's mother's eyes, a man of means had no reason to flaunt those means. Back in her room she had lifted her nose and disdainfully called the man a Yankee. That was the very worst thing his mother could ever say about any man.

Now the man's grip on Tristan's hand tightened until Tristan wondered if he was trying to physically pull the truth from him. "I'm not the one confused."

Tristan stared the Yankee in the eye with not the least sign of recognition and smiled. "I've heard it said that every man has a double somewhere. You must have met mine." He pulled his hand free.

The man peered at Tristan through narrowed eyes that were not much more than slits in his fleshy face. "You can pretend what you want. But we both know who you are. Your mother will be quite relieved to hear that you are safe. And so nearby. Rumors were floating about that perhaps you had headed out to the goldfields in California."

"You should be careful not to spread rumors on your own," Tristan said softly. "Good day, Mr. Patrick." He turned and began walking away with Brother Benjamin matching his every step. The other Shakers also began moving away. Tristan chanced a glance toward Jessamine. What would she think of a liar? She looked a bit mystified, but he saw none of the condemnation on her face that was so evident on the frowning face of the sister beside her.

"Your lovely Laura Cleveland has not been happy," Patrick called after him. "But there is no shortage of gentlemen ready to step up to help her forget her tears."

Tristan kept walking. He doubted seriously if Laura had shed one tear over his disappearance unless it was simply as an act to gain sympathy. Tristan almost smiled. Perhaps this escapade of his would be the last straw for Laura and she would throw him over with not a second's thought. He could hope so at any rate. It would be good to be free of his mother's expectations. Free to actually chase off after California gold if he wanted. Free to find love.

He let his eyes slide back over to Jessamine. The pinched-faced older sister had a grip on the young woman's arm that looked tight enough to leave bruises. Yet the young sister was paying her no mind as she stared straight at him. The mystified look was gone, replaced by a worried, almost sad look as if she knew this might be the last time their eyes ever met. He had the incredible feeling that if he held his hand out toward her, she would jerk away from the woman beside her and come to him. His hand tingled with the desire to reach out to her.

He clamped down on the foolish thought. He barely knew the girl. She was beautiful. There was no denying that. Her spirit almost sparkled. Nor could he deny that something about her spoke to him. Had done so since his first sight of her in the woods when he thought he might be dead and looking at an angel. But he couldn't love her. Not so quickly. Not without more time. Time they didn't have.

He flexed his hand and kept it at his side. The older sister leaned close to whisper something in Jessamine's ear that made the girl look down immediately and turn away. Tristan kept walking beside Brother Benjamin, who said not a word until they climbed the stairs and returned to the sickroom.

Then he looked straight at Tristan and said, "The man from the world spoke truth."

Tristan didn't shy away from Brother Benjamin's eyes. "He did. My name is Tristan Cooper. Not Philip Rose."

Brother Benjamin was silent a moment as he considered Tristan's words. He looked more disappointed than angry. The silence built until it was nearly as profound as the silence that had fallen over the Shaker worshipers at the end of their meeting. Tristan stood up under the doctor's searching look even as he fished around for words to beg forgiveness for his lies. But nothing he thought of seemed right to say.

"What was the reason for your lie?" Brother Benjamin finally asked with a perplexed frown. "We cared not what your name might be."

"I don't know," Tristan said.

The doctor's voice was calm as he said, "I sense that is another lie, my brother. That is the way with lies. One leads to another until truth is lost in the high grass of so many untruths."

"It's not entirely a lie." Tristan let out a long breath. "I honestly didn't know who I was when the two sisters found me in the woods and then when I found out I was shot, I had no idea why or who might have done that. I feared going back to my other life until I could remember what might have happened in the woods."

"And have you remembered now?"

"No. That day is lost to me, but other memories are not." Tristan paused and wondered just how honest to be with the doctor. "I think I was hiding from my future."

"Is it a future you fear?" Brother Benjamin sounded more kindly with each question.

"I'm not sure fear is the right word, but it is one that I move toward with some reluctance. I thought perhaps a few days in your peaceful village would help me see things more clearly."

"Sister Lettie supposed you were struggling with some demon. She knew not whether it was something without that threatened you or something within. She has offered many prayers for you."

Sister Lettie had known he lied all along, but had treated him with great kindness. Had even prayed for him. A lump jumped up in his throat. He swallowed hard and told himself it was foolish to feel tears pushing at his eyes. Sister Lettie probably prayed for everybody she came in contact with. It was what these people did. Danced and shook and prayed.

Brother Benjamin touched Tristan's shoulder. "While we respect the truth, we don't condemn those who stumble. With confession, you can come around right and find the peace you lack if you stay here with us."

Tristan looked at the brother's face and was tempted. Another week among these kind people. Another week of peace. More chances to see the beautiful Jessamine. But that would be another week of lies and he had lied enough to those who had cared for him without any real reason to do so.

"I have to go back," he said.

"The world can be a wicked place." The doctor squeezed Tristan's shoulder before taking his hand away. "But each man must make his own choices. For right or for wrong."

Tristan wanted to tell him that was the problem. He wasn't able to make his own choices. All his life, someone else had been choosing for him. His father's choice had led him down a soldier's path. His mother's choice was pushing him toward a marriage altar. Even if he could have stayed there among the Shakers, he wouldn't have the choices he wanted. He would turn into hands and feet in service to their beliefs. That was no choice at all.

He looked at the doctor with a good bit of regret as he said, "I will miss you and Sister Lettie. You will thank her for me, won't you?"

"Yea, but thanks are unnecessary. She did naught but her duty in caring for you. I will have a brother bring your clothes and your horse. The bandages should be sufficiently hardened now so your arm will be properly protected as long as you keep your seat on the horse."

Tristan touched his arm and was surprised at how stiff the rag binding had become. "I am indebted to you."

"Nay, our mercies are freely given." Brother Benjamin waved his hand in dismissal before he turned to leave. He stopped at the door to look back at Tristan. "You will always have a place among us if you decide to turn from the ways of the world and seek the path to salvation. Perhaps that is the journey you fear to begin. Some men resist their need for the Lord."

He didn't wait for Tristan to answer, but went on out the door. That was just as well, for Tristan had no answer.

It felt right putting on his own clothes again, even though he had to rip open the seam of his shirtsleeve in order to slip it over his bandaged arm. It felt right pulling on his boots with his good hand. It felt right mounting his horse. The animal nickered when he put his hand on the horse's muzzle. That too felt right.

What didn't feel right was riding away from the village without telling the beautiful Jessamine goodbye. Without satisfying his desire to touch his lips to hers at least one time.

He turned his horse in the direction that would take him to White Oak Springs. He hoped it would be a long ride. He did not look forward to facing his mother. Her joy at his return would not overshadow her anger. He was sure of that.

He had no thought of Laura at all.

Journal Entry

Harmony Hill Village
Entered on this 18th day of June in the year 1849
by Sister Sophrena Prescott

*Monday. I have ever loved Mondays. A day to
step into service with renewed vigor while Sunday's
meeting echoes in one's spirit. Even before I came
to Harmony Hill, I welcomed Mondays, although
Sunday then did not echo so beautifully within my
soul. While each Sabbath should have been a time
for rejoicing, instead the days more often were spent
by those around me dwelling on unmet expectations
and even recriminations. I never seemed able to
please anyone. Certainly not the man with whom
I entered into the sinful state of matrimony and
perhaps not even my Lord with my halfhearted
worship. I sang but never with joy. I bowed my head
but more in fear than devotion.*

*But the Lord had mercy on me and nudged
my former husband, Brother Jerome, toward the
Believer's path. I would have never come on my own.
The idea of the shaking and dancing worship seemed
too odd to me then with my spirit trapped and frozen*

within me. Oh, but the joy of loosing those restraints.
Of accepting the love Mother Ann throws down to
us with such wondrous abandon. Of understanding
one's place at last. Accepting that place. Rejoicing in
that place. Hands to work. Hearts to God. Both bring
me such joy now when before there was no joy, only
tiresome duty.

Duty here among my brethren and sisters is not
burdensome. Many hands make the work easy.
Our good mother told us to work as if we had a
thousand years to accomplish our tasks or as if we
had knowledge of our death on the morrow. Here
at Harmony Hill the labor of our hands is surely as
much an act of worship as any song we might go
forth to exercise.

That, at least, is a truth Sister Jessamine has
embraced. She has ever been willing to work
faithfully and obediently at whatever duties assigned
to her. She loves her sisters and brothers. I have no
doubt of that. But. Oh, why is there always that word
when I think of dear Sister Jessamine? I have no
such thoughts when I consider Sister Annie or Sister
Wileena or even Sister Abigail. That sister will not
long be with us unless she has a change of heart.

But our Sister Jessamine has a pure heart. I see it
in her eyes. She is eager to do her duty. And yet she
often stumbles along the pathway of proper behavior.
I fear her stumbles may increase with Sister Edna her
constant companion.

I should cross out those last words. The Ministry
knows best. Perhaps Sister Edna's stern guidance
will be exactly what Sister Jessamine needs to bring
peace back to her spirit, but I worry that will not
prove true. I saw the look in Sister Jessamine's eyes as

she followed Sister Edna out to their duty of planting late beans this day. It was a look I had not seen there before. A weary look. A sad look.

A look that may have more to do with the incident following our meeting yesterday than with her duty in the gardens. The man from the world was proven to be deceiving us and has left. Good riddance, I say! I noted him watching Sister Jessamine in the meeting. It was not the look of one considering the Believer's path. Nor was her look back at him one that should be exchanged between a brother and a sister. It is a good thing—a providential gift—that he is gone from us with his lies and temptations. Without the upheaval of his presence, Sister Jessamine will have the opportunity to settle back into the way of a proper Believer.

There is still the letter. Eldress Frieda has not shared with me the decision of the Ministry in that regard. That is not my concern. Nor my duty. I am to weave bonnets this week. A good duty to begin on a Monday. Making something useful with my hands. But I could be just as content pulling weeds from the spice gardens.

Or there is always the laundry. A good and fitting duty for a Monday. There is something satisfying about scrubbing clothes. Even in my worldly life, I took to Mondays because it was washday. Then I had to make many trips to the spring for water that had to be heated in iron kettles, but I never minded the chore. I counted it a blessing to be outside with the sky for a ceiling and the trees for companions.

Laundry here in our village is not a bit burdensome with many sisters taking their turns in the washhouse. We have no need to make tiring *treks to the springs, for pipes bring the water to the washhouse. And scrubbing time is much shortened by the machines one of the Believers in the north invented. That is the way with our Society. We continually search for a better way and share that way with all. The work of our hands is a gift and Mondays a time to treasure as we begin a new week of honoring God with our labor.*

I have been blessed with many Mondays here at Harmony Hill in the fourteen years since I came to join with them. I had just turned twenty-three when we came on a Monday. Is it any wonder I have such affectionate feelings toward Mondays?

14

Tristan pretended not to notice when Laura's cheek muscles tightened as she suppressed a yawn. Tristan bit the inside of his lip in an effort to hide his own yawn. His apology was boring the both of them. But they kept walking together, kept doing their best to keep up the smiling pretense of courtship.

She had not seemed at all surprised to see him back at White Oak Springs or particularly pleased. He'd heard absence made the heart fonder, but a week apart had done little to warm either of their hearts if their walk around the lake was any indication. Two acquaintances thrown together with little to say to one another of any import.

She paused in their walk to look out at the ducks on the lake. A gaggle of the fowls began racing across the water toward them in hopes of bread crumbs. The owner of White Oak, Jefferson Hargrove, liked to goad the ladies who took such pleasure in feeding the birds by claiming how good the fattened ducks would taste at the end of the season. He could say anything to the ladies with that indulgent laugh of his and they would flutter their fans and think he was merely teasing them. But Tristan had no doubt roast duck would be on the man's table before the snow started flying here in winter.

Hargrove was a wiry bundle of energy and charm who had trained as a doctor and served as a soldier in every war in the current century. He was reputed to be able to outshoot any man in the country and enjoyed proving his abilities at his resort's shooting club. Even as Tristan and Laura stood by the lake and looked out over the water sparkling in the sun, they could hear the booms of other men target practicing not so far away. He looked down at his arm still in the sling Sister Lettie had fashioned for him and wondered if he could shoot with any kind of accuracy with his left hand.

It was strange, but he had found everything more difficult to do when he got back to White Oak Springs. While at the Shaker village he hardly noticed the inconvenience of his injured arm. Perhaps because there no one expected anything of him. He could lie in the bed or walk about the doctor's gardens. He could step into the shadows with the beautiful sister where he'd had not the least problem caressing her cheek with his left hand.

"Oh, I do wish we had some bread for them," Laura was saying. The ducks were right at their feet, making guttural sounds of demand.

"I could go to the kitchen and fetch some," Tristan offered. Anything to please. Anything to make the afternoon pass.

"Would you? Oh, that would be lovely." Laura turned the full shine of her smile on him.

Her light brown hair was caught up in an elaborate twist on the back of her head with a few curling tendrils carefully pulled loose to frame her face. Tristan had no doubt her maid had spent much of the morning combing and pinning the curls and helping Laura into her corsets and frothy white dress. She carried a matching white parasol unfurled over her shoulder to protect her pale skin from the sun. Her hand on the parasol handle was very white and slim and soft. He doubted she'd ever done so much as pick up her own handkerchief.

He remembered the beautiful sister's hands with the briar scratches from her day spent harvesting rose petals. Her cap had hidden all but a few blonde wisps of hair that held out the promise of spun gold. Her dress had been of a simple, almost coarse material and covered with that bulky collar and an apron, but her feminine shape had not been completely hidden. Vaguely he could remember clinging to that shape as he rode to the village with her. That was a memory he wished he could bring into clearer focus.

"Whatever are you thinking about, Tristan?" Laura waved a lacy hankie in front of his face. "You seem a hundred miles away."

"Forgive me, Laura. I fear the knock to my head has dulled my thinking." He forced a smile as he regretfully let his memory of the beautiful Jessamine slide back into the shadows of his mind.

"That will improve, won't it?" The hint of blue in her gray eyes faded as alarm flooded her face.

"The doctor at the Shaker village seemed to think it was but a temporary problem."

"Yes, but are you sure you shouldn't seek out other treatment? Do you truly think anyone there in that village would know about medical issues? Being sequestered the way they are."

"They seemed very knowledgeable about many things." When he saw her look of doubt, he continued. "The Shaker doctor had practiced as a physician before he became one of them."

"If that's true, why ever would he join with those people?"

"I suppose he believes in their way."

"You mean shaking and dancing and claiming such behavior is worship?" Her smile returned as she twirled her parasol. "Last summer while I was here at White Oak, they took an excursion to the village as an amusement. I was a bit under the weather that day so was unable to go." Laura touched her forehead lightly as if remembering the distress of her illness even now. "But my friends regaled me with many stories upon their return. I found some of them hard to believe. Julia Byrd claimed one of the men fell rigid right at her feet. Stiff as a board with his eyes wide and staring. She was quite sure he was dead and said it was enough to make her swoon. That she might have done just that, except she worried they might drag her away and do their best to turn her into one of those plain women."

When Laura laughed, Tristan politely smiled along with her, but she must have sensed his lack of enthusiasm. "Oh well, when Julia tells it, it is quite amusing." With a small sigh, she turned back to stare at the ducks now losing hope of bread crumbs and drifting back out to the center of the lake.

It was a beautiful lake. A beautiful place. It was rumored Dr. Hargrove had invested a veritable fortune in the four-story brick hotel that was the center point of the resort. Between June and September the Springs was a swirl of balls and other social entertainments. Courtships abounded. Of course many did actually come for the medicinal properties of the mineral spring waters reputed to cure everything from ague to rheumatism to dropsy.

The doctor also touted the benefits of fresh air and healthy food. Tristan wondered if the man had once been a Shaker. His ideas sounded very like something Sister Lettie would advance. The thought of Jefferson Hargrove a Shaker made Tristan smile with genuine amusement. Too bad his smile came too late to impress Laura with his enjoyment of her story.

But the man he'd met the week before when Tristan and his mother had arrived at the Springs was unlikely to exclude himself from the company of women no matter what stress they might engender. It was rumored Dr. Hargrove was on the hunt for a new wife and had his eyes on a lady less than half his age. He'd been heard to claim that then they might be equally vigorous. Now in his sixties, the man boasted he had already outlasted two wives. Nothing Shaker-like about any of that.

When another small sigh escaped Laura, Tristan remembered his promise of bread crumbs. "Do you want to wait here while I get bread for the ducks or perhaps you'd be more comfortable on one of the benches?" Tristan pointed toward a well-shaded group of benches between the lake and the hotel.

"Never mind, Tristan. The ducks appear to have lost interest." She turned without actually looking at him to begin walking along the lakeside path again. It was obvious it wasn't only the ducks that had lost interest.

They strolled along in silence. At least they seemed to be able to match their strides. Perhaps with time they might be able to match a few thoughts and feelings as well. They'd only met a couple of weeks ago. A plant didn't germinate and bear fruit overnight. Love could take awhile to flower.

But what of attraction—the seed of love? The sight of a beautiful girl could plant that seed in an instant. He knew it was possible because it had happened in an instant for him with the beautiful Jessamine.

He clamped down on the thought. He couldn't allow himself to dwell on memories of Jessamine. In all likelihood, he would never see her again. She would become a devout Shaker sister. He would become a devout husband and father.

That would not be such a trial. Laura was lovely. When his sons arrived and grew into little men, he could plan adventures with them just as his father had planned adventures for Tristan. He wouldn't plan sending his sons to war. He hoped never again to hear the bugle call to war. But there would be mountains to climb. Wilderness places to explore. Perhaps in time, they could even go west and see the wonders there.

Marrying Laura would not be hardship. Rather a beginning. His mother had assured him of that last evening after her long tirade taking him to task for not sending word of his whereabouts. He claimed the loss of memory, but she was not as believing as the Shakers. She knew him too well. When at long last her anger had vented, she once again slipped on her comfortable Southern lady charm that pretended helplessness while hiding an iron will that made sure things happened as she wanted.

It had worked well on Tristan's father. And he supposed it was working on him. Wasn't he here walking with Laura Cleveland? Hadn't he promised his mother the night before to be so charming that Laura's gray eyes would begin to warm when she gazed at him instead of reminding him of the cold wall of a cave? Not the blue of a warm summer sky.

He shut his eye, disgusted with himself for allowing Jessamine to sneak back into his thoughts again. Charming. That was what he had promised to be. And if that didn't work, then direct. He'd just go down on a knee and ask Laura to marry him. She'd say yes. It didn't matter that she seemed to be having as much problem exercising her charms on him as he was on her. She had to answer to her father the same as he did his mother. The two of them had plotted and decided what was to happen. Now they were impatiently waiting for their children to dance to the music they'd written.

Dancing. Would every thought he had bring forth the Shakers? And Jessamine. Dancing and whirling. Smiling at him.

He looked toward Laura at his side, but her parasol hid her face. "Why don't we go sit in the shade, Laura?" He pushed the sound of a smile into his voice as he put his hand under her elbow and guided her off the path to one of the benches placed strategically to rest the walkers. "I'm anxious to hear what happened while I was gone last week."

And I will laugh and smile at all your little anecdotes. He spoke that promise silently, but he intended to keep it.

Laura looked at the bench and hesitated. Tristan whipped out his handkerchief with his good hand and managed to spread it on the bench to protect her pristine white skirt.

"Thank you," she murmured as she perched on the bench without leaning against the back. She folded the parasol and placed it beside the bench before carefully arranging her skirts to hide any hint of ankle.

Being a lady had its definite disadvantages, Tristan decided. Jessamine would have surely taken a seat on the bench without the first worry of her dress the same as she'd straddled his horse with no visible concern over her exposed shoes and stockings. He tried to recall the turn of her ankle, but all that happened in the woods was little more than a blur. He remembered nothing at all before he awoke to the sound of the two sisters wondering what to do with him. That time was erased as if it had never happened, but the still angry-looking wound on his head and his encased arm were proof enough it had.

Tristan sat down next to Laura. The white froth of her skirts spilled over against his legs. "You look lovely," Tristan said. And she did.

Her eyes widened a bit as though the last thing she expected to hear from him was a compliment. But she must have heard the same from many admirers. She had been surrounded by several eager men when he'd come down to the hotel lobby to meet her. As his mother reminded him at least ten times a day, he was not the only man at White Oak Springs hoping to find favor in Laura Cleveland's eyes.

She looked demurely down at her hands, ungloved as a

concession to the heat and the casual setting. "It's so kind of you to notice."

An uncomfortable tick of silence fell over them then before Tristan reminded her to tell him all the events he had missed in the past week.

"Let's see." She looked up and away for a moment before she went on. "We had the midweek ball. Quite the event. And the men had a shooting tournament on Thursday. A few of the ladies played lawn bowls and the men got out their bats and balls and horseshoes. Dr. Hargrove even suggested some of us ladies might enjoy trying to pitch the horseshoes. A few accepted his challenge and tossed a few. The men had great fun over that."

"Did you give the horseshoes a try?"

"Oh no." Laura let out a trill of laughter. "I was quite content to watch and save my energy for the evening dances. And my nails." She held her hands out toward him as though to prove her good sense. "I rather fear Sally Jenkins will be unable to go without her gloves for weeks."

It would have been the perfect opportunity to take one of her hands. She was practically offering them to him, but the realization came to him too late. "It sounds like a fun week," he said lamely as she dropped her hands back into her lap. The knock on his head must have made him forget how to be charming.

"Yes, the people here at the Springs intend for their patrons to have plenty to do." She stared down at her hands, once more folded demurely on the frothy white material of her skirt. Perhaps realizing she might sound uncaring, she hurried on. "It goes without saying that everyone was quite concerned about you all through the week. Your poor mother was beside herself with worry." Again she rushed on to claim worry of her own. "As we all were."

"What did everyone think?"

She didn't quite meet his eyes. "We didn't know what to think since we had only so recently made your acquaintance. Your mother said it was quite unlike you to simply disappear without a word to her and from what she had told us about you when she was here last season, that did seem true." She glanced up at him. "You did know she brought your father here to take the waters in hopes of restoring his health after he returned from the fighting in Mexico, didn't you?"

"Yes, she wrote me about how Father was feeling better at the time. Then the next news I got was of his death after they returned to Georgia."

"Such a trial for you both." She looked genuinely sad. "So when you didn't return last week, we were very concerned for her and hoping she would not have to face more sorrow."

"How kind of you." Tristan's words came out drier than he intended, and her eyes flew up to his face to see if he was mocking her. He pushed a smile across his face in an attempt to assure her of his sincerity.

"Yes, well." She managed a practiced smile in return of his. "We did our best since we had no way to guess at what might have befallen you. We even had prayer with your mother. One of my dear friends here, Flodella, she's the granddaughter of a preacher. I think you met her at the ball last week. Anyway, at first your mother was sure you would be back any minute but after two days passed and then three, we—my friends and I—surrounded your mother in a prayerful circle and Flodella spoke the most devout prayer for your safety and return."

"I'll have to thank her." From the Shaker prayers to Laura's and her friends' prayers, he seemed to have been surrounded by prayers. "Thank all of you."

"That's hardly necessary." She waved a hand in dismissal. "We're just overjoyed our prayers were answered."

Somehow he wasn't feeling that joy radiating from her. A

moment of silence fell over them before he asked, "So, was the consensus of the ladies that I had ridden away with no regard to my dear mother or that I had perhaps come to a bad end with my body floating in the river?" He was sorry for the words as soon as they came out of his mouth. A lady's sensibilities were to be respected and talking of bodies floating in the river could easily spin a gently bred lady into the vapors. He had no wish to deal with a fainting woman.

He was getting ready to offer a profuse apology for his callousness or be ready to fetch smelling salts when he heard what sounded like a giggle. Maybe he was hearing wrong and it was a sob. But no, she pushed her hand over her mouth and faked a cough. He didn't know whether to pretend he was offended or make a pretense of not being aware of her amusement. What would a charming man do? Perhaps the thought of his body floating in the river was not so distressing to her sensibilities as he'd imagined. A smile worked its way out on his lips.

She peeked up at him, her hand still over her mouth but with the smile evident in her eyes. "I do apologize, Tristan. It is quite unseemly for me to smile at your question when in fact you were obviously set upon by unsavory characters and in some danger of your life. Might have possibly even come to the end you indicated."

"Smile? I think laugh is a more accurate word." He leaned back on the bench, not upset at all. He looked at her with new eyes. "So I'm guessing there was some conjecture about what might have happened to me. Wagering even, perhaps?"

"I heard a bit about that possibility among the gentlemen. Certainly not among us ladies." She fanned her blushing cheeks with her handkerchief.

"But you did talk about it?" Tristan said.

"Oh indeed. Talk is, after all, our main pastime."

"And what were the winning suppositions?"

"A few had you going back to Texas. Julia did so want you to have a pining heart for a señorita there. But most were of the mind that you had escaped to the goldfields."

"Escaped?" Tristan raised his eyebrows at her. "Escaped what?"

"Me, of course." Laura laughed again. This time she didn't bother trying to hide her merriment.

"A man would be extremely foolish to attempt to escape a lady as lovely as you." It appeared he hadn't forgotten all his charm while with the simple Shakers.

"So some might think." Laura's smile faded as she looked directly at him.

He met her gaze and thought he should just go down on one knee right there in front of the bench and offer his devotion and his name. Get it over with. But though their shared laughter had helped him see her as a real person rather than an obligation, he still felt no desire at all to reach out to touch her cheek or feel her lips under the tips of his fingers as he had with the beautiful Jessamine. Nor did she appear to be entertaining the thought of him stealing a kiss. At least with any kind of pleasure. Instead the laughter had given way to a certain grimness, a look that made him wonder if she had even more desire to escape him than he did her. For a moment, he almost considered asking her that.

But what if he was wrong? What if she was waiting for words of love? Then again, perhaps she'd rather hear he was floating in the river. He had the strange urge to reach up and touch the wound on his head.

The moment of truth passed as she looked away from him with a reminder of the time. They stood and walked back toward the hotel to prepare for the evening festivities.

He told himself it was good he hadn't offered her words of love with no truth in them. Not while the beautiful Jessamine continued to haunt his thoughts. Another few days here with Laura, more strolls around the lake, more smiles, more dances in the moonlight, and perhaps an attraction would flicker to life between them. His memories of Jessamine would fade. Then everything would be fine. His mother would be happy. Laura's father would be happy. He looked over at Laura. Perhaps even Laura would be happy. Happiness would abound.

15

Jessamine did not have a good Monday. Normally she embraced the duty of working in the gardens because it seemed good to be part of the miracle of seeds bursting and pushing tendrils up toward the sun. God's gift to his children, her granny used to tell her when they planted their garden plot. At least those children willing to put their hands to the plow.

Her granny was akin to the Shakers in that way. She believed the Lord intended a person to work, but not every minute of the day. "The good Lord gave us hands to work, but he also gave us eyes to behold his wonders. I'm thinking he expects us to take the time to ponder on those wonders."

Jessamine had always thought Sister Sophrena might lean toward her granny's way of thinking even if she never came out and said she admired the scent of roses in the air or the busy buzz of bees working through the apple blossoms brightening the orchards. But Jessamine had seen her pause on the paths. She'd seen the look on her face sometimes when she was writing in her journal. Jessamine had peeked at a few lines from that journal from time to time and recognized the thread of joy in the words. Not that the sister would ever speak against the Believers' way of simple plainness and only

190

seeing beauty in the usefulness of the roses for rosewater or the dance of the bees amid the blossoms because it resulted in honey and apples for the Believers' tables. She would not. The Believers' way was her way.

It was Jessamine's way too. The village was home. Her roots had grown down into the Shaker soil as surely as the beans she was dropping into the rows would germinate and reach down into the garden soil. She had nowhere else to go. She didn't even know the name of the prince who had loved her mother and been her natural father. She knew Sister Sophrena's name. She knew her love.

It hadn't been Sister Sophrena's choice for Jessamine to be shackled in constant supervision punishment with Sister Edna. The Ministry had so ruled. All had to abide by the rules. That had become clear at the end of the Era of Mother's Work when so many of the young people had neglected their duties to run after angels and visions of all sorts.

When Jessamine first came among the Believers, it was not at all unusual for some of the young sisters to leap from their chairs in the schoolroom and whirl without restraint. Jessamine often leapt up to join them even though nothing in her spirit commanded her to do so as the other girls claimed. Jessamine simply had itchy feet while they had gifts of the spirit.

Jessamine had anticipated receiving like gifts. When the gifts didn't fall from the heavens over her and she was merely beset with tears for the loss of her granny's voice in her ear, she'd had to fight the ugly stain of envy in her heart for those who did receive the gifts like Sister Betty. A year younger than Jessamine, Sister Betty was so continually gifted with spiritual messages in her dreams that the older sisters often clustered about her bed with lamps and writing instruments to record whatever she might say in her sleep.

On those nights, Jessamine lay awake watching with great curiosity and that worm of envy. But it wasn't only Sister

Betty who was gifted with special manifestations. Sister Connie, who never seemed the least interested in anything spiritual and could not even form her letters with ease, had sometimes been impelled to take paper and pen and draw elaborate lines and circles.

So much had been happening then. Every week in meeting, Jessamine was treated to the wildest imaginings as she waited anxiously for her own gifts of the spirit. But she'd never felt the first twinge of a vision. No spirit commanded whirling. None compelled drawing. She heard no gifts of song or angels whispering to her even in her dreams.

She couldn't understand it. It seemed to her that she, able to build castles in the air or dream up talking birds, should be the one chosen for visions. Yet the Shaker gifts of spirit were denied her and given to others who—when they weren't being beset with visions—could not imagine the first turret on a castle.

Even so, it had not been a bad time for a child prone to letting her imagination take wing to come among the Believers. While the Shakers never credited any part of their visions to imagination, the continual presence of angels with their strange requests gave Jessamine a ready excuse for any lapse in obedience to the rules. One that Sister Sophrena sometimes doubted, but ever accepted while forgiving Jessamine's shortcomings.

But then the messages from beyond became less and less joyful and more and more upsetting. Accusations of impropriety. Of inadequate love. When the instruments of the spirits began voicing upsetting revelations about the elders and eldresses and questioning the Ministry, the leaders began to doubt the revelations were truly from Mother Ann. After a time of unease and questioning, the New Lebanon ministry proclaimed the Era of Manifestations over.

The spirit drawings were hidden away. The holy mounts covered up and abandoned. All were advised to concentrate on being simple and walking with obedience. Without discipline, the Society could not survive. So Jessamine understood the reason for Sister Edna dogging her every step. She had broken the rules. What the Ministry ordained could not be changed. But that didn't mean she had to like it or that it wasn't spoiling her garden duty.

While Jessamine normally took pleasure in plunging her hands into the silky smoothness of the seeds in her planting bag and drawing them out to drop into the rows, this day it just seemed a chore that caused sweat to run into her eyes and her back to ache. It was almost as if instead of following two steps behind Jessamine, Sister Edna had crawled up on her back to weight her down.

She warred against the weariness. She thought of the bean vines that would grow. She thought of her granny and how she would pray over the garden before they planted the first seed and after every row was seeded and tamped down.

She missed her granny even if she had been gone so many years that her face was becoming fuzzy in Jessamine's memory. She missed the angels even though she had never seen the first one. She missed the man from the world. Tristan Cooper. She longed to say the name aloud, to try it on her tongue, even if only in a whisper, but Sister Edna would hear. Her sharp eyes would probably see if Jessamine so much as silently mouthed the man's name.

"Whatever is the matter with you, Sister Jessamine?" Sister Edna said crossly as she stopped covering over the seeds with her hoe and leaned down to pick a bean seed out of the row. "That is the second time in this row you have dropped three beans instead of two as is proper."

"Forgive me, Sister Edna. I will try to be more careful."

"Your mind is not on your tasks this day, Sister." Sister Edna straightened and handed Jessamine the bean she'd retrieved from the dirt. "I daresay it is instead drifting to sinful thoughts of that man you brought among us. He proved himself to love the world and to be with no honor, did he not?"

"Perhaps his mind was confused as he said." Jessamine studied the bean in her hand.

"Confused about his name? I think that unlikely."

"He gave every appearance of truthfulness when he claimed not to remember the day Sister Annie and I came upon him in the woods." Jessamine dropped the bean into the row and reached into her seed bag for another to add to it.

"I have doubts you are the best judge of truthfulness when it appears you have only a passing acquaintance with the truth yourself at times." Sister Edna's voice carried scorn. "You and Sister Abigail as well. Pretending a worm upon your collar."

"That was not my pretense," Jessamine said quietly as she continued to place the bean seeds in the row. She was careful to do it properly.

"I wouldn't be a bit surprised if the two of you hatched the plan to cause me concern."

"Nay, I would not want to cause you distress, Sister Edna."

"Well, you've certainly caused poor Sister Sophrena enough problems." Sister Edna tamped down the dirt with extra vigor. "Promising obedience and then running straight to make cow eyes at that liar. And don't think I didn't see you sneaking looks at him during meeting. Did you think the Ministry would not be watching? They always watch."

"Yea." Jessamine knew nothing but to agree with her. Everything the woman said held truth. She felt more and more pressed down until she wondered that her feet weren't sinking to her ankles in the soft dirt. "Yea, you are right. I have much reason to repent."

"It is good that you understand your need to change. You should count your blessings that the Ministry has given you this opportunity to mend your ways and step back from the miry pits of sin that trap so many of the world."

Jessamine turned to look at Sister Edna as she efficiently pulled the dirt over the seeds and tamped it down. "Have you never wondered about the world, Sister Edna? What their way is like?" She knew she shouldn't ask, but she could not seem to hold her words back.

"Nay." The woman's brows tightened in a frown. "I have breathed of the rotten air of the world and care not to do so ever again."

"Were you brought here as a child like I was?"

Jessamine was suddenly curious about this sister who seemed more concerned with faultfinding than lifting up. One of Mother Ann's precepts came to mind about how it was as much a duty to commend a person for doing well as to reprove that person for doing ill. That was certainly not something she was going to quote to Sister Edna nor was it something Sister Edna gave any indication of practicing. Kind words rarely tumbled from her mouth. Gladness didn't appear to be one of Sister Edna's gifts.

"Nay. I was not so blessed. I was already past the time of childhood. The same as Sister Sophrena when she came."

"Yea," Jessamine said as she turned to begin dropping the seeds in the row again. "She has told me that she had the sin of matrimony to overcome."

"Many among us walked the sinful path of marriage in the world. It is expected of one there."

"You?" Jessamine looked back at her. "You were once married? In love as the world loves?"

"The sinful state of marriage has little to do with love. Even the kind of love those of the world are ever chasing after. Those feelings bring more sorrow than joy even in the way of the world's thinking." Sister Edna leaned on the handle of her hoe as her eyes narrowed on Jessamine. "It seems odd to me that your mind is so filled with the romantic nonsense of the world when you have so long been surrounded by the pure love embraced here among our family of Believers. I fear you have been letting your ears be filled with the sinful talk of some of our novitiates more recently from the world."

"Nay. My sinful curiosity rises from within," Jessamine said quickly. She had no desire to bring disapproval down on Sister Abigail. Even if the sister's whispered stories in the night had awakened Jessamine's desire to see White Oak Springs, Jessamine's own feet carried her on that willful trek through the woods. Her own hand had reached out to touch the cheek of the man of the world. She had stepped willingly into the shadows with him. Indeed had pulled him into the shadows herself and thus steepened her plummeting fall into sin. No fault for that could be laid upon Sister Abigail.

"You do seem beset with a sinful nature." Sister Edna sounded almost pleased with her pronouncement.

"My head has always been full of wonderings and stories." Jessamine pushed the pretense of sorrow into her voice.

"You should ponder on the stories of Mother Ann's life or those in the Bible." Sister Edna looked down. "Or while in the garden, think only on placing the seeds in the row."

"Yea." Jessamine carefully dropped several seeds into the row before she let her curiosity override her good sense. She looked up at Sister Edna and asked, "Did you come in with a husband of the world? Children who became your sisters or brethren?"

Each question darkened Sister Edna's frown. "You ask too many things that have no bearing on our lives as Believers. I have left the stress of such worldly things behind and set my feet on the way to salvation. My children were blessed to be given the gift of a perfect life. It is not a fault that can be laid to me that two of them chose to reject that gift before they were of the age to join in our family of Believers."

"They went back to the world?" Jessamine's eyes softened on Sister Edna. "That must have been a sorrow for you."

The woman's face hardened even more. "I am sorrowed any time one of my sisters or brethren falls into sin. Here in our Society, we do not favor one sister or brother over any other. Sister Sophrena has surely impressed that truth upon you."

"Yea." Jessamine had often been told that was the Shaker way, but she had never seen how it would be possible to love every one of her sisters exactly the same. Nor had she believed many among them were able to manage such except the eldresses with their years of devoted practice in proper sisterly love. And perhaps Sister Sophrena. She didn't believe it was true for Sister Edna. Jessamine was seeing her in a new light and not as simply one of the watchers always ready to catch someone straying from the assigned way.

With that new light shining down on the unsmiling sister, she wanted to see even more. "Was it hard to surrender your worldly love for your husband? For your children? I have seen some who come among us struggle mightily with turning from the world's way."

"Those struggle who are reluctant to pick up their cross and carry it. Only those. And you, Sister Jessamine, you ask questions that should not enter your thoughts, much less cross your tongue." Sister Edna's eyes were stern. "I should not like to have to report your troublesome thinking and lack of diligence in carrying out your duty for the day to the Ministry."

Jessamine had some doubt of the sister's reluctance in that regard. The very idea of reporting Jessamine's contrariness brought a measure of cheer to Sister Edna's eyes. She didn't smile, but her frown vanished.

"I will aim for more diligence." Jessamine didn't want trouble with Sister Edna. She would tamp down her curiosity.

"And more silence," Sister Edna said. "Remember, none preaches better than the ant, and it says nothing."

"Yea, Sister Edna."

Jessamine leaned over and dropped seeds into the row. She did not mind silence. She and her granny had shared much silence. Comfortable silence. Silence where thoughts could grow and entertain. Silence at times broken by her granny's singing the words of a favorite hymn. At times the hymn's words had seemed not to actually break the silence but to add to it. Silence among the Believers was sometimes the same. A time when holiness could fall down over them all. She wasn't feeling that kind of silence now.

The cessation of talk between her and Sister Edna had no peace in it. Only the sound of uneasy truce. Jessamine could not keep from sneaking looks at Sister Edna and wondering which of the brothers might have once been joined with her. A devout brother. One who did not often let a smile slip onto his face. She could not imagine the sister married to a man who embraced happiness as a gift of peace. She had often had the same wondering thoughts about Sister Sophrena until the sister told her that her former husband had journeyed to a village in the east. But Sister Sophrena had no children to set on the Shaker road the way Sister Edna obviously had.

Jessamine had seen many mothers and children parted among the Shakers. She'd noted the tears, the struggles. Sister Edna might have once suffered such tears even if she denied it now. How could a mother not suffer some feeling of loss with the surrendering of her young? How could a father? But it happened. Fathers brought their children and left them. Mothers brought their children and left them.

Jessamine's own father had taken her into the woods to Granny and left her. And never returned. The prince who loved her mother. An ache opened up inside her heart and she felt terribly alone even with Sister Edna close enough behind her to touch and more sisters spread out across the garden, planting beans with the same movements. A planting dance.

She was never outwardly alone, but inwardly she sometimes

felt ever alone with no one who loved her as she really was. Sister Sophrena loved the sister she wished Jessamine could be. Sister Annie loved her because that is what she had been told to do. Love your sisters. Sister Edna loved no one if her scowl was any indication. Her granny had loved her without reservations, but her granny was gone.

God was not gone. God loved her. God loved everybody. At least those who kept his commandments, or was that the way she was to show her love for him? Yes, that was it. The verse she'd been taught came to her mind. *If you love me, keep my commandments.*

Mother Ann threw down bushels of love on her followers. Those who obeyed the Shaker way. It was Jessamine who was out of step. She was the one stepping out of union with her sisters. She was the one yearning for a different kind of love. The wrong kind of love. Worldly love.

Tristan Cooper. She let his name whisper through her thoughts as she remembered his fingers tracing her lips. It was his leaving that was making her feel so alone on this day. So unloved. So forlornly and forever unloved. She'd never see him again. She'd continue down the Shaker way, planting seeds that would bring forth food, sweeping dirt from every corner, lifting her voice in song and exercising the dances.

She would not always feel so alone. She would keep the commandments. She would be loved by her family of Believers. She was loved by the Lord. The Bible promised as much. *For God so loved the world.* Whether she was here in the village or part of the world, God so loved.

Journal Entry

Harmony Hill Village
Entered on this 18th day of June in the year 1849
by Sister Sophrena Prescott

Monday is drawing to a close. The retiring bell will soon sound to signal the time to blow out the candle and put away my journal. The week has had a good beginning. My fingers are sore from the weaving of the straw into bonnets, but with the diligence of our sisters continuing through the week, we will have many bonnets for the brethren to carry with them on their trading trips. It is good to make something useful that benefits those of the world the same as it does us here in our village.

Sister Edna reports that Sister Jessamine did not shirk her duties in the garden this day, and other than voicing a few questions with no place in the mind of a Believer, she submitted to the constant supervision without showing distress. I asked Sister Edna what questions concerned our young sister, but she said they were worldly questions that did not bear repeating. She assured me she had impressed on Sister Jessamine the need to keep her thoughts on the task at hand. Sister Edna has embraced her duty of seeing Sister Jessamine through this difficult time. She is ready to diligently watch and make sure our sister's feet come back to the proper path of obedience.

I did not speak with Sister Jessamine. In fact, I did not see her speak a word to anyone as she kept her eyes downcast during our family meeting in the upper room. I admit to feeling some sorrow not to have her words in my ears and her eyes smiling my way, but perhaps it is for the best. She is under Sister Edna's guard now. As much as I love my young sister, I failed in leading her in the proper way. I feel that failure acutely with her not so far from the age when she could sign the Covenant of Belief. And I worry for her now.

I have seen young sisters leave for the world rather than submit to constant supervision, but most of those were sisters who had already planted their feet firmly on the pathway to sin by improper words or secret meetings with one of the brothers. Or at least what they thought were secret meetings. Few things are hidden for long from the watchers. But all are given a chance to turn from their sins and come back to the Shaker way. Just as Sister Jessamine has been given. I do not think she will slip away in the night. The man who tempted her is gone from here to where we do not know. Nor care.

But now there is the letter. Eldress Frieda says the Ministry has decided to allow Sister Jessamine to see it unless she refuses. I do not know what the letter says or even who it is from. All I know is that it has been here for many years, almost as long as Sister Jessamine herself. So once more, I worry.

Worry is wrong. I know that. Even before I came

among the Believers, I knew that. The Christ told
us so in the gospels. "Take therefore no thought for
the morrow: for the morrow shall take thought for
the things of itself. Sufficient unto the day is the evil
thereof." That verse often circled in my mind in those
days when I despaired of ever knowing another
day of peace while shackled to a man in sinful
matrimony. Even in the world's eyes, our union had
no good to it. I am thankful every day for Brother
Jerome's decision to join with the Believers. The
Eternal Father poured down grace and gave me the
joy of many days of peace here with my sisters. So
I will not think of the trouble of the morrow. I will
rejoice in the peace of the day.

If the letter has words in it that will tear our sister
from our bosom of love, then the morrow will be
soon enough to face that sorrow. Tonight I will
put away my writing tools, blow out my candle,
and enjoy the rest due a laborer who has faithfully
worked with her hands and given her heart to God.
Each Believer must do that for himself or herself. No
one could have ever done so for me and I can never
do so for any of my sisters. Not even Sister Jessamine,
whom I do love.

A prayer for her. That is what I can do as I kneel
by my bed before my time of rest. A prayer for all
my sisters.

16

Tristan considered claiming his arm was aching too much for him to go down to the dining room that evening, but one look at his mother's face let him know he could not escape the evening. Even if he had been in real pain. Which he was not. Laura might not trust the skill of the Shaker doctor, but Brother Benjamin had done his work well. Even Dr. Hargrove hadn't argued that.

The owner of the Springs had caught Tristan in the lobby after he and Laura came back from their afternoon stroll. With great interest, he grilled Tristan on every aspect of Brother Benjamin's treatments.

"And you say he gave you sleeping powders?" Dr. Hargrove peered at Tristan intently as if expecting him to reveal something of great import. The man was half a head shorter than Tristan but every inch of him vibrated energy. Even standing there studying Tristan's arm, Tristan had the impression that any second he was going to shoot away to talk to someone else.

"I don't really remember much about the first day or two," Tristan said. "But the old sister who nursed me said the doctor thought it best if I slept while the swelling on my head receded."

"Interesting. Is the knot still there?" Without waiting for an answer or permission, the man reached up to probe the back of Tristan's head with his long fingers. "Ah yes, there it is. That must have been some goose egg. You're fortunate the swelling popped out instead of in or you might not be standing here now."

"I had much fortune that day after my misfortune of being set upon by a highwayman."

"You think that's what happened then? That someone attacked you to take your money." A frown settled on his face as Dr. Hargrove dropped his hand away from Tristan's head.

"When I came to, I had nothing in my pockets and the track of a bullet on my head."

"But were you not in a remote wooded area?"

"That's what I am told."

"You don't remember why you were in that part of the woods?" The man studied him as if trying to make sense of what Tristan was telling him before he went on. "I have to admit parts of your story bring questions to mind. It doesn't seem reasonable that thieves would be lying in wait in a place where very few if anyone would be traveling."

"It does seem an unlikely chance, but then I was shot."

"True." Dr. Hargrove's forehead wrinkled in thought. "Are you sure you weren't on your way to meet someone? Or that someone didn't follow you?"

"I have no idea. I remember being here at the Springs the day before. The dancing and music. Nothing at all about the day in question."

"Nothing? Not why you were out riding? Nothing?" Dr. Hargrove looked disbelieving.

"Nothing until I was found by two Shaker sisters out hunting raspberries. That was truly fortunate."

"Huh! For you or for them? Out for berries and back with a man." Dr. Hargrove laughed as though that was the funniest thing he'd ever said. Several in the lobby looked over at the man and smiled indulgently. He appeared to lose interest completely in who had shot Tristan as he switched his thinking to the Shakers. "Quite an adventure for those girls. An ugly bunch. Never saw one of those women over there who didn't hurt your eyes."

Tristan smiled. "You must not have seen Jessamine."

"Jessamine, eh?" The man lifted his wiry gray eyebrows at Tristan. "Sounds like you might have gotten to know the sister a little better than a brother might. No wonder you were in no hurry to find your way back over here."

Tristan held up his hand to stop the man's wrong thinking. "No, nothing like that, but she was lovely."

"Even in a bonnet, you say? And that hideous collar crafted to hide the very fact you might be looking at a woman. One good thing, I'm thinking the way they make them work that at least they don't bother with those ruinations of female health—corsets. Give me a woman who can take a deep breath any day."

He didn't seem to expect an answer and Tristan gave none. Instead the doctor poked his finger on the stiff bandage around Tristan's arms. "I do hope they aligned that bone right. If not, you might never be able to shoot straight again." Dr. Hargrove looked up from studying Tristan's arm with a smile splitting his face. "Not that those people over there would worry about your shooting arm. They're pacifists, you know. Don't believe in war. What that really boils down to is they sit back there on their rich acres and let the rest of us keep the country safe for them."

"They were kind to take me in."

"Oh, they take everybody in. The better to increase their land holdings. You do know that everything a man owns goes directly into their coffers if a person is fool enough to join up with them, don't you?" Dr. Hargrove shook his head as if he couldn't believe anybody would be that foolish. "And the more they can get to sign up with them, the more hands they've got to make their brooms and hats and grow their pumpkin seed. Those old preachers have it made, if you ask me. Tell their troops what to do and don't allow any free thinking. And some of those preachers are women or so I'm told. Pulling the strings and making grown men jump to their orders. Can't imagine what kind of man would want to live that way."

When he paused for breath, Tristan said, "I didn't meet any of the preachers. Just the doctor and his nurse."

"And the beautiful Jessamine." Dr. Hargrove grinned. "If you weren't deluded by whatever that Shaker doctor gave you and she truly was a sight for sore eyes, then that seems a sorrowful waste. What with that celibacy thing they have going over there. That's another thing that makes you wonder about what kind of man is willing to throw in his lot with them. Celibacy! Not something I'd recommend for a young sapling like you. Or for an old codger like me either." The doctor clapped Tristan on the shoulder and laughed again, this time louder than the time before. Then he was off like a hunting dog losing interest in one scent and working to find a new trail.

But the questions the doctor had raised settled in Tristan's mind as he struggled to change for dinner. There was no way he could get a dinner jacket over his bandaged arm. Finally he allowed his mother's maid to fashion a new sling from one of his mother's silk sashes and just draped his coat over his shoulder. It would be unhandy but he had no other choice. Not if he wanted to shoot straight ever again. The one thing his father thought Tristan did well. Shoot. The one thing he never cared if he ever did again.

Just the sound of the shooting club that afternoon as he'd walked with Laura had brought back too many images he wanted to block forever from his thoughts. Shooting targets wasn't the same as what he'd done in Mexico. And even if he had escaped Laura as she'd surmised and gone to the California goldfields, he would have certainly needed to be armed in that wild country. It could be he should have been armed in the woods only a few miles from this Mecca of society and ease.

Perhaps he had been. The night before when he returned to the Springs, he searched his room for his father's pistol without success. While he couldn't remember carrying it into the woods, he did know he brought it to the Springs from Georgia. His mother had insisted because of the shooting club. Perhaps the gun was lost to the thief the same as whatever else might have been in his pockets. Had he been carrying his father's gold watch? He hadn't even thought about the watch or the gun while he'd been at the Shaker village. Neither seemed important there.

Tristan looked around the elaborately decorated room with its large soft bed carefully fluffed and draped in a dark green coverlet by unseen servants who returned the room to pristine condition every day. Fresh water filled the pitcher and bowl to splash on his face upon arising in the morning. A rag rug of a rainbow of colors covered the wooden floor by the bed. Another rug spread more cheer in front of a chair near a window. A fairly recent issue of *Harper's Weekly* was beside the lamp on the table. Tonight when he returned to the room after whatever entertainments were scheduled, the lamp would be lit and waiting. A wardrobe sat against the wall with large doors that revealed drawers on one side and a place to hang his suits on the other. A long mirror on the wardrobe door reflected back Tristan's image. His mother's room that adjoined his was similar except with a dressing table and an extra sitting chair and plenty of ruffles and flounces on the bedcover and curtains to appeal to the ladies.

None of it was a thing like the narrow cot in the sparsely furnished room at the Shaker village. The only decorations there were the chairs and lamps hanging from blue pegs all around the room. Out of the way but in reach if needed. Everything plain and simple. And yet, he almost wished he were still sleeping there on this night. Still being Philip Rose. Still listening to old Sister Lettie's wisdom. Still hoping to catch sight of the beautiful Jessamine.

He stared at himself in the mirror. He would not think of the young Shaker woman again. He had his duty as a Cooper. His lips flattened in a determined line. He was not in Mexico. He was not poor Philip Jeffries in a grave. He was in a veritable paradise paying court to a lovely woman who knew how to laugh. That was not a bad thing.

So what if he'd lost a day or two of memory and a few treasured possessions, if indeed his father's gun and watch were missing? So what if he'd lost his heart to the beautiful Jessamine? He had never expected to fall in love with Laura. Security generally trumped love in the game of life. Love was a poor man's card of choice. A man who had nothing could easily throw that to the wind and pursue love. A man with a house, an estate, a failing business, a mother depending on him, could not so easily do the same.

That mother tapped on his door. "We must not be late, Tristan. We are sitting with the Clevelands this evening and Robert expects promptness. As do I."

Tristan pasted a smile on his face before he opened the door. "I'm quite ready, Mother."

She gave him an up and down look. "We can only hope. You met Laura's mother last week. Dear sweet Viola. I do hope you're able to recall that." She raised her eyebrows at him as she went on. "A mouse of a woman with not much to say. I daresay she's often afraid to open her mouth around Robert. He arrived here two days ago. Thank goodness, you saw fit to recover your memory and return forthwith. Another day and you might have ruined your chances forever."

"It would seem to me that Laura's approval is what I need. Not his."

"That's because your head is full of romantic nonsense." His mother let out an exaggerated sigh. "Trust me on this, Tristan. Men like Robert Cleveland run the world. And their families. If he wants Laura to marry you—and he has given me every indication in our previous meetings that he does want you to be the father of his grandchildren—then you can be assured yes will be on Laura's lips when you go down on your knee to propose to her."

He opened his mouth, but his mother spoke before he could. "And don't even consider pretending you might decide not to make that proposal. We have no other choice."

"What were you going to do if I didn't return?"

"I don't know." A worried look flashed across her face and she looked ten years older before she said, "I honestly do not know."

Instantly sorry he'd goaded her, he touched her arm and spoke softly. "It's all right, Mother. I did come back. I wouldn't desert you."

Sadness settled on her face for a moment. "Promises are easy to make. Your father made plenty of his own with the same heartfelt intentions and then he went off to catch the fever."

"The war is over, and I don't make promises I don't intend to keep."

"That's good to hear in my ears, but those are words you need to say in Laura's ears." Her voice hardened a bit. "The sooner the better."

"Why the rush? We're going to be here for another month at least, are we not?"

"Open your eyes, Tristan." She poked a finger into his chest. "This place is full of bachelors intent on marriage and there is no more attractive candidate for their attentions than our lovely Laura. I've even heard rumors that Laura came to the Springs expecting to hear a proposal. And not one from you."

"Then from whom?" Tristan asked. "Has she a secret love?"

"So the rumors go, but you know I don't put much credence in gossip. I do know one thing. She has no serious suitor her father approves. It is Robert Cleveland you must win over. Starting this very evening." She straightened the collar of his coat and smoothed down the silky sling. Her voice softened as she went on. "Any man should be glad to welcome you into his family."

"I'll do my best to make you proud, Mother."

"Yes, well, the less you say about your supposed loss of memory and stay among those strange Shaker people, the better." The softness fled from her face as she turned to collect her reticule. "The man does not suffer fools lightly. He demands attention and right thinking."

"Right thinking in what way?"

"Whatever way he's thinking, obviously." She waited for him to open the door and then proceeded through it, lifting her head high as she assumed her public persona. A person had to remember one's station in life and keep up appearances, come what may.

Tristan followed her, bracing himself for the evening ahead. Would he too have to turn into someone different? Someone ready to bow and scrape to win the approval of Robert Cleveland. He thought of Brother Benjamin then and his air of confident peace. There was no pretense to him. Just a man who knew his path and was glad for the simple life. A life without the stress of marriage. A man who knew what he believed and was giving his life to it.

Maybe that was Tristan's problem. He didn't believe anything. The war had emptied him of belief. He didn't deny God existed. He simply didn't think he cared one whit what happened to Tristan. But then the beautiful Jessamine had found him in the woods. That thought whispered through his mind again. And now he couldn't forget her eyes.

What was it Sister Lettie had told him? That the Lord gave gifts to all his children. Providential care could be considered a gift. If it had been another sister like the cautious Sister Annie, he might have been left in the woods while they went for help. He might have been beset by wild animals or by the return of whoever had shot him. He might even now have deserted his mother in spite of his promise not to.

An inner smile lightened his thinking as he thought about his meeting with Jessamine being providential. If it was and the Lord up in his heavens had deemed them a match, then surely he would bring them back together. It would have to be soon, because before the week was out, his mother would see to it that the expected proposal words were spoken to Laura.

17

Tristan and his mother arrived at their assigned table at the same time as Laura and her parents. After pleasantries were exchanged, they settled in their seats. The table sat eight. One chair was empty and the other two were occupied by a Mr. and Mrs. Floyd. Tristan had had the misfortune to meet them the week before. A blustery man and a vacuous woman come to the Springs for the water in an attempt to rid themselves of the aches of rheumatism. Tristan gave them a bland smile he hoped wouldn't encourage the man to begin the long-winded description of his every ache and pain that Tristan had been treated to on their last meeting.

Robert Cleveland stared across the table at Tristan. He wasn't a young man. Tristan guessed him in his sixties already, at least ten years older than his wife, maybe more. He was a big man, but not soft. His broad, meaty hands had obviously once been well acquainted with physical labor, and the hint of boom in his voice made Tristan think of sergeants ordering their companies forward. When he spoke, he would expect people to listen. But after the first greetings, he was quiet while the ladies chattered about the lovely day they'd had. Tristan pretended not to be aware of the man studying him the way one might size up a new stallion. Instead he gave his full attention to Laura next to him.

She met his look with a smile reminiscent of the one she'd shared with him as they sat by the lake. "Not off to find any gold this evening, Mr. Cooper?"

"I'm told it takes two good hands to pan for the gold, Miss Cleveland." Tristan returned her smile.

"Gold? What's this about gold?" Mr. Floyd leaned toward them. He was a fleshy man and beads of sweat ran down the side of his face. He pulled out a handkerchief and caught some of the rivulets before they could drip on the table. "Confound it! They should have servants in here with fans."

"It is quite warm," Tristan's mother said. Her face had gone pale at the mention of gold and now she did her best to turn the conversation. "Perhaps a drink will cool you."

Mr. Floyd wouldn't be distracted. "I heard you were off to the goldfields, Cooper. Any truth to that?"

"Goldfields?" Robert Cleveland frowned first at Floyd and then Tristan.

Tristan met his look without flinching, even as out of the corner of his eyes he noted Laura's smile. She obviously was enjoying stirring up a bit of trouble for him. "I've heard men can get rich there," he said noncommittally.

"A scattered few might strike it rich panning gold." Cleveland waved his hand dismissively. "But take my word for it, the only real riches to be made would be in selling the pick axes or sluice pans. Outfit the idiots thinking they'll find their fortunes sifting through pebbles in a creek. That's where a man could make some money."

"What's this about goldfields?" A man stepped up behind the empty chair on the other side of Laura. "Forgive me for being late. I was in the middle of a story."

Laura looked up at him, her smile warm and welcoming. "How delightful, Sheldon. I can't wait to read it. Please join us." Then as if she remembered she was supposed to be giving her attention to Tristan, she turned back to him. "Tristan, I don't think you've met Sheldon Brady, a dear family friend." She turned back to Sheldon Brady as he sat down. "This is Tristan Cooper. And you know his mother, Wyneta, and Mr. and Mrs. Floyd."

Sheldon Brady leaned forward to smile past Laura toward Tristan. "We'll shake hands on the introduction later, my good man. It's been a pleasure this week getting acquainted with your charming mother." The man turned his smile toward Tristan's mother and a flattering splash of color bloomed in her cheeks.

The man was probably near to Tristan's mother's age if the liberal sprinkling of gray among the black hair on his temples was any indication. He was tall, maybe even taller than Tristan, with broad shoulders and the easy air of a man used to admiring glances from the ladies. He wore his cravat carelessly tied and his hair a bit long and unkempt, which gave him a rakish look. After a sip from his water glass, he looked first at Robert Cleveland and then at Tristan. "And so are you both considering being off to the goldfields? One to pan and the other to charge exorbitant prices for that pan?"

"Tristan is not off to the goldfields." His mother hurried her words out.

Laura laughed a little, a delightful trill of pure enjoyment. "No, no, of course he isn't. It was just a little joke between us."

"Perhaps you should share the joke, my dear," her father said.

"Oh, Father, you don't have to know everything."

Tristan had the feeling Laura was doing her best to upset her father. It was certainly a fact she was upsetting his mother who appeared ready to faint.

He shot a reassuring look toward his mother before he explained. "I went for a ride last week and ended up the victim of a highwayman intent on relieving me of my possessions and perhaps even my life. For a while, it seemed possible I might find some gold. Those streets of gold." Tristan smiled as he looked around the table. "To make a long story short, I was rescued by some Shakers and nursed back to life. Forgot who I was for a day or two. So while I was missing, the rumor started that I had ridden off to the goldfields in California to seek my fortune."

His mother was valiantly keeping her lips turned up, but she wasn't happy with his attempt at levity. Laura on the other hand appeared to be very amused if her broad smile was any indication. Mrs. Floyd giggled into her handkerchief while Mrs. Cleveland looked down and began folding her napkin into an ever smaller square. Whether that was to hide her amusement or boredom, Tristan wasn't sure. He was sure Robert Cleveland was not amused as he stared across the table at Tristan.

The new man smiled politely as he shook his napkin open to spread in his lap. "Shakers. Interesting people. There are several colonies of them in the East, one not far from where I once spent a few years in New York."

Like a drowning person grabbing for air, Tristan's mother seized on his words as a way to shift away from Tristan's time with the Shakers. She smiled across the table at Tristan. "Mr. Brady is a writer. Quite well-known for his books of fiction."

"Obviously not so well-known if you have to fill your son in on who I am, madam." The man laughed.

Laura lightly jabbed Brady's arm with her fingertips. "Oh, Sheldon, those of us who love romantic stories certainly would need no introductions once we heard your name. You have readers spread far and wide."

"So, Mr. Brady, what have you written?" Tristan asked as servants set bowls heaped with fresh lettuce on the table.

"What hasn't he written?" Laura jumped in with the answer

before the man could speak. "He's had numerous novels published. My favorite is *Tomorrow's Promise*." Laura put her hands together under her chin and sighed. "Such a tragic shipboard romance between two indentured servants coming to America. It was so sad when they were forced to part."

"Romantic drivel," Robert Cleveland muttered as he attacked his salad.

With no sign of taking offense, Brady laughed again before he said, "But it pays well, Robert. Extremely well. And the ladies enjoy their romance. You should try a little in your life. I'm sure our sweet Viola would enjoy a rose laid on her pillow at night. Dr. Hargrove would gladly surrender a few blooms from his beautiful gardens for the purpose of romance."

"Viola can pick her own rose if she wants one." Cleveland finished off his salad and grabbed a roll.

"You don't have a romantic bone in your body, do you, Robert?" Brady said.

Mr. Floyd, who had been busily tending to his salad, looked up then and shoved the conversation right back in a direction sure to grieve Tristan's mother. "Then I guess you'd fit right in with those Shaker people that our boy here was with last week, Robert. I hear they don't believe in marrying, hard as that is to believe." He looked toward Tristan. "Is that the truth of it, Tristan?"

"That's what I was told." Tristan stuffed half a roll in his mouth so the man wouldn't expect him to say any more. While he didn't mind talking about the Shakers, he did have to return to their rooms with his mother later. Besides, it was definitely better if he didn't let Jessamine's beautiful eyes surface in his thoughts. Not while he was supposed to be winning over Laura with his charm.

But Mr. Floyd was more than happy to expound on the oddness of the Shakers without Tristan's encouragement. "I've been over there. Seen their houses with their separate doorways for the men and women. Stairways too. Claim to live like brothers and sisters, but I'm wondering." He waggled his eyebrows up and down. "If you catch my drift."

Mrs. Floyd giggled again, but then noted Wyneta's pained expression and put her hand on her husband's arm. "Now, James, maybe you shouldn't be talking that way with ladies present."

"I'm not talking any way. Just telling the truth of it. Isn't that right, boy?" The man pointed his fork toward Tristan but didn't give Tristan time to respond. "They dance too. Crazy up and back and whirligig dancing. But there weren't any of those Shaker women I would be asking to dance. That's for sure. Plain as a spoon bowl in their caps and aprons." He held up his spoon to show them before he began stirring sugar into his coffee. "You saw them, Tristan. I'm betting you can vouch for what I'm saying." This time he pointed his spoon toward Tristan. It dripped coffee on the white tablecloth, but the man either didn't notice or didn't care.

Dr. Hargrove saved Tristan from having to come up with an answer. He swooped down on their table to stand behind Tristan. "Did I hear somebody here mention our Shaker neighbors?" He smiled at Mr. Floyd.

The man turned his pointing spoon up toward Dr. Hargrove. "I was just telling them here how none of those Shaker women set my feet to tapping. Ugly as homemade sin."

Dr. Hargrove smiled. "Now, Jim, whatever else you might say about them, they did fix up our friend here and send him on back to us." The doctor clapped Tristan on the shoulder. "And if he wasn't deluded by their potions, he has a different opinion of some of the Shaker sisters, don't you, son? Perhaps you should tell them about the beautiful Jessamine." Dr. Hargrove laughed heartily before he winked toward Laura and went on. "Then again, sitting here beside you, my dear lady, I'm sure he has quite forgotten her beauty."

Then without waiting for any of them to respond, he was spinning off to entertain another table. Or to make trouble. Tristan's mother was looking faint once again. Laura kept her eyes on her plate whether to hide a blush of anger or amusement, he had no idea. Mr. Floyd preened a bit from the notice of the Springs' owner and Mrs. Floyd giggled yet again. An irritating sound coming from a grown woman. The man beside Laura, the famous writer, paused in buttering his roll to look over at Tristan. Robert Cleveland was staring across the table at him too. That was nothing new, but the furrows between his eyes were deeper than before.

"Who is this Jessamine?" Cleveland demanded in his army voice.

Tristan folded his napkin and placed it by his plate. He began to understand why Mrs. Cleveland kept folding and unfolding her napkin as she held down the chair by her husband.

He met Cleveland's glare without flinching as he answered, "Jessamine was one of the young sisters who happened to be out in the woods searching for wild raspberries. They heard the gunshot and, fortunately for me, were curious enough to investigate."

"I would have thought they would have run the other direction," Mrs. Floyd said. "That's what I would have done. Wouldn't you, Wyneta? Viola?"

"It would seem to be the sensible thing," Tristan's mother murmured as she picked up her coffee and took a sip. "I wonder what our main course will be this evening. They have such delightful food here. I've heard that Dr. Hargrove brought a chef over from France."

Her attempt to steer the conversation away from the Shakers failed. Everybody else at the table was suddenly fascinated by the thought of an attractive Shaker sister. Even the writer had put down his fork and was sitting very still as though he wanted to be sure not to miss a word.

"That was very brave of them," Laura said. She didn't sound the least upset or worried about the beautiful Jessamine. She knew her own worth and beauty.

"Or very foolish," Tristan's mother said shortly.

Tristan smiled at her. "That's what the second sister thought. Sister Annie was her name. She wanted to leave me to my chances in the woods."

"Surely she wanted to help you," Laura said.

"In a more acceptable way."

"Acceptable?" Robert Cleveland echoed. "What in heaven's name does that mean?"

"Acceptable to her community. Apparently, it was quite daring for them to offer help to a stranger of the opposite sex. And against their Shaker rules for them to even be near me. The sister Annie wanted to go fetch some of their brethren, but the one named Jessamine refused to leave me alone since I was injured. They had come a long way through the woods in search of berries, and she said it would be full dark before they made it back to the village. Without a doubt I would have been wandering around lost all through the night since I didn't even know my name when I came to. The blow to my head when I fell, I suppose. Anyway, the young sister Jessamine caught my horse even though she claimed to have no previous experience with horses."

"Sounds like an unusual girl," Sheldon Brady said.

"And beautiful besides." Laura smiled at Tristan. "With such a lovely name too. Jessamine."

"What was her last name?" the writer asked. The main course had come. Thick slabs of roast beef with roasted potatoes and carrots. But the man seemed unaware of the food. Instead he was watching Tristan as though his answer had great import.

"I don't know. Everybody over there was Sister this and Brother that. First names only. They wanted to know my full name once I remembered it, but I never thought to ask theirs." Tristan smiled at Brady. "I wasn't thinking too clearly anyway. In a fog from their potions as Dr. Hargrove said."

The others at the table tired of the subject and let their eyes drift away from Tristan. Tristan's mother managed to strike up a conversation with the reticent Viola about a volume of poetry they'd both read. Robert Cleveland finally stopped staring at Tristan and attacked his meal with vigor, as did the Floyds. The Shaker curiosity now seemed limited to Sheldon Brady, with Laura paying polite attention since she was seated between the two of them.

"But Jessamine, that is a rather unusual name. Do you know any Jessamines, Laura dear?" Sheldon Brady picked up his knife and fork to cut a bite of meat, but he didn't put it in his mouth.

Laura took a tiny nibble of her potato as she considered his question. "There was a Jasmine at the finishing school in South Carolina. A lovely girl. She married last year, I believe."

"Well, I hope," Brady said as he finally took a bite.

"That is the only way to wed, I'm told." Laura peeked across the table at her father, who continued to give all his attention to his meal.

Brady smiled at her and her smile in return looked very genuine and not the polite turn up of lips she often sent Tristan's way. But then this man was an old friend of the family and famous enough—in spite of the fact Tristan had never heard of him—that she seemed a bit star struck.

Brady turned his smile on Tristan. "And I am absolutely certain our lovely Laura is making the memory of this Jessamine dim in your memory, Tristan, but what did she look like? If you don't mind sharing."

Tristan felt his mother's eyes poking him from across the table. But the man asked and Dr. Hargrove had already spilled the beans about him thinking the girl was pretty. Not pretty.

Beautiful. He could see no choice except to answer. With a smile toward Laura first. "She looked nothing like our lovely Laura. Her hair was very blonde. At least what I could see peeking out from her cap. The women there keep their hair covered. And her eyes were blue."

"There are many shades of blue," Brady said.

"Blue is blue," Robert Cleveland said without looking up from cutting his meat.

"Oh no, Robert. Not if you are writing romantic stories. There's midnight blue and then the faded blue of a garment washed a hundred times."

"And the blue of a summer sky," Laura put in. "Or those flowers that grow in the wild along the pathways."

"Cornflowers," Mrs. Cleveland spoke up.

"Yes, Mother. Those are the very ones I was trying to remember. Thank you." Laura smiled sweetly across the table toward her mother. The woman's face softened with affection before she turned her attention back to Tristan's mother and Mrs. Floyd, who were making plans for the following day.

Sheldon Brady's smile disappeared as he put down his fork and stared off toward the far wall of the dining area as though seeing something in the air none of the rest of them could see. "I once knew a girl like that."

"Why, Mr. Brady, you sound decidedly pensive," Laura said. "Who was this girl who makes you forget your meal and your table companions as well?"

"Her name was Issandra and she was very beautiful. With cornflower blue eyes."

Mrs. Floyd put her fingers over her lips as another of her grating giggles escaped her mouth. "He must have been in love with her," she said in a stage whisper.

Brady's eyes came back to the table. "I was, Mrs. Floyd. I most definitely was. She was my wife."

"I didn't know you'd ever been married." Laura looked surprised.

"That was the only time. For one year and three months. She died of fever after the birth of our daughter." He bent his head as though the memory of his wife's death still filled him with sorrow.

"How tragic to lose your wife and daughter that way." His mother's voice was so sad Tristan knew she was remembering his sister's death in childbirth.

"I didn't lose the daughter. At least not to death." He looked up then as he explained. "Her name was Jessamine. A romantic name that called forth the memory of the South Carolina garden where I met her mother. The yellow jessamine was filling the air with its intoxicating scent that evening. Her mother spoke her name before she died. And even as I held my tiny infant daughter, I could see the imprint of her mother on her face."

"Didn't know you were a father, Sheldon," Robert Cleveland said before he sopped up the last of the beef juices with his bread.

"I don't suppose I was much of one. It was all so long ago."

"Where is she now?" Laura asked.

"I don't know. If she still lives, she would be twenty this year. I've heard nothing from her for years." He sounded more resigned than sad.

Tristan looked at the man. Could the young Shaker sister actually be this man's long lost daughter? He tried, but he could see no family resemblance to the beautiful Jessamine in Brady's face.

Silence fell over their table as if no one knew what to say next. Then Viola Cleveland surprised Tristan by being the one to lean forward toward Brady and speak as though they were the only two at the table. "Did you never try to go back? To see her?"

"I gave that choice to her in a letter before I left her with my grandmother. She promised to give Jessamine the letter when she turned twelve and let her make the decision as to whether she wanted me to ride back into her life. I thought she would be old enough to go with me then on whatever journeys my wanderlust took me. When I didn't hear from her the year she would have turned twelve, I assumed she had no desire to change her life."

"How very sad." Mrs. Floyd sniffed and touched a handkerchief to her eyes.

"Not really, madam. It was my daughter's choice."

"But didn't you want to see her, to know she was well?" Mrs. Cleveland was still leaning toward him. "A child is the dearest blessing a person can receive. It seems wrong to reject it out of hand."

Brady looked back at her as though her words were stones she had thrown at him. "I don't think I did that. I saw that she was cared for. I loved her. I do love her."

Mrs. Cleveland sat back in her chair and touched her napkin to her lips. "Then you should find her."

"Perhaps I should," the writer said. "Perhaps I should."

"And how serendipitous." Laura was smiling but not with the same abandon as earlier. "You have a blue-eyed daughter named Jessamine whom you suddenly have an urge to find and Tristan is rescued by such a girl only miles from where we're sitting."

"Perhaps not merely serendipitous, my dear," Mrs. Cleveland said. "Perhaps providential."

Providential. The word echoed in Tristan's head. He remembered his thoughts as he was following his mother down to the dining room. That if the Lord meant for him and Jessamine to be a match, he would bring them back together. And now it could very well be he was sitting at the same table as her father.

"Probably no connection at all," Laura's father boomed. He shot a look toward his wife. "Viola is just being a meddling fool. Pay her no mind, Sheldon."

"No, no, Viola is speaking from the heart. She knows about loving a daughter." Brady smiled at Mrs. Cleveland, who went back to folding her napkin after her husband's blast. Then he looked back at Cleveland and laughed a little. "But you're no doubt right, Robert, about there being no connection between our new friend's unanticipated encounter with a Jessamine and my own Jessamine. Even so, there are times when serendipity—not to mention providence—can be the friend of a man who earns his coin penning stories." He turned his eyes back to the ladies across the table from him. "It would make a heartrending story, don't you ladies think? Long lost daughter or, perhaps more accurately put, long lost father is found."

"A waste of time. Chasing the past. It won't do anything but bite you if you catch it." Cleveland looked up and around before he tapped on his cup with his spoon. "Where are those waiters? Hargrove needs to get a better bunch of servants."

Tristan's mother began to chatter innocuously about the delicious ribbon cake for dessert. Nobody mentioned the Shakers or Jessamine again, but thoughts of her so lingered in Tristan's mind that he couldn't concentrate on what was being said around the table. He wasn't the only one. The writer seemed preoccupied as well. Between them, Laura also had little to say. Mr. Floyd took advantage of their silence to begin the litany of his aches and pains. Sister Lettie had told Tristan the Shakers forbade talk during their meals. Perhaps they were on to something.

18

When the rising bell sounded, Jessamine sat up and put her feet on the floor as she had every morning for years. The planks felt cool on her bare feet, and from outside the open window she heard the cheery trill of a mockingbird even though dawn was barely breaking. For a minute with that sound of joy in her ears and the lingering wispy remnants of a blissful dream tickling her mind, she forgot her day would not be as it might have been before Sunday.

That unpleasant truth slammed into her waking brain when her eyes caught on Sister Edna rising from the bed next to hers. Her watcher. Already the woman's eyes were pinned on Jessamine. Waiting to catch her in some wrong. Waiting to squeeze the very joy out of the day. Jessamine dropped to her knees beside her bed as did all the sisters in the room. A Believer knelt to pray upon rising every morning. A silent appeal for an industrious day and right attitudes before they went out to their duties.

Jessamine let the familiar words whisper through her mind. *Dear Father in heaven. Help me to work with willing hands at the tasks thou hast set for me this day. Let my heart rejoice in serving you.* She kept her head bent and her eyes closed as she waited for more prayer words to surface in her mind.

Words of love for her sisters and praise for the blessing gifts of the day. But she did not feel loved. She did not feel blessed. She felt burdened. And sorrowful. The same kind of sorrow she'd felt when her granny passed on.

But no one had died now. She was surrounded by her sisters. Surrounded by their love for her. And yet the sorrow mashed down heavy on her soul as though someone had dropped a heavy sack of troubles across her shoulders.

She kept her eyes tight shut while the sisters around her began rising to their feet. Prayer time was over. She knew that without peeking through her eyelids and yet she stayed on her knees hoping for a prayer to come to mind. A prayer that would help her endure Sister Edna by her side every moment of the day to come. She could almost feel the sister moving toward her to give Jessamine's shoulder a shake and demand she conclude her morning prayer. She would remind Jessamine of Mother Ann's admonition that time was wasting and they had none to waste.

Her words would be true. Wasting time was not the Shaker way. Duties called. But prayers weren't wasted times. She thought of the song "Come down, Shaker life, come life eternal." She wanted the prayers to come down, give her peace eternal, show her the way. She didn't want to simply come up with the words she'd been told the Eternal Father wanted to hear. She wanted the words to be true prayer words from her heart. Besides, she had no way to imagine any words of her own on this morning. Her imagination felt flat as a flapjack stepped on by one of the brothers. One of the fleshier brothers.

"Sister Jessamine, it is time to be about our day."

Sister Edna's words wormed into Jessamine's ears even though she pretended she did not hear as she continued in a pose of prayer.

Sister Edna spoke louder, more stridently. "Sister Jessamine!"

As if the sharply spoken words released something inside Jessamine, a prayer slid through her mind with the ease of a snake slithering off a hot rock to hide beneath that same rock until danger passed him by. *Watch over the man from the woods. Tristan. Tristan Cooper. Let me see him again. If it be thy will. And oh please, let it be thy will.*

"Whatever are you praying for so many minutes, Sister Jessamine?" Sister Edna was standing directly beside her, tapping her toe impatiently. She was already dressed with a crisp, white apron tied around her waist, ready to begin the day's duties and very cross that Jessamine still wore her white cotton sleeping shift.

"I was praying for the day, Sister Edna," Jessamine answered softly as she scrambled to her feet. "As I do every morn."

"Seemed to be taking you somewhat longer on this morning."

"I was praying the Lord might make the day joyful."

"Work well done and done promptly, that is the reason for joyfulness." Sister Edna's eyes were narrow slits peering out of her frowning face. "That is what pleasures our Mother Ann."

"Yea, Sister Edna. I will hasten to dress so that we may begin our cleaning."

Jessamine looked around the room as she got to her feet. There were five beds on each side of the room. Sister Edna had moved her things to the bed against the inside wall next to Jessamine's. She wanted to be sure Jessamine made no midnight escapes. Such a thought had never occurred to Jessamine in the years she'd been among the Shakers. At times she had used the excuse of a trip to the privy to go out into the night and take joy in the sky full of stars. On other nights in the midst of summer, she often slipped outside to escape the gathered heat in the sleeping rooms, but she had never thought to sneak out of the retiring room simply to escape her sisters.

At least not until now. The night before as she lay straight and still on her narrow bed waiting for sleep to come, the velvety night had called to her with its promise of moonlight and stars. Her feet had itched to run out into the night and let the sound of the whippoorwills and tree frogs fill her ears with nature's music. She wanted to find a place in a garden and see the lightning bugs rise from the grass to disappear in the gloaming of the gathering night. Things she had done while living with Granny. Things she had nearly forgotten. Things that for some reason now pulled at her.

Perhaps it was Sister Edna forever frowning by her side that was making Jessamine feel the backward pull toward the freedom of her early years when her granny let her rise or sleep when she chose. She taught Jessamine when she was ready to learn and told her stories when she was ready to dream. But Jessamine was no longer a child. No longer a free spirit of the woods. She was a Shaker sister with responsibilities and penance to pay and the willingness to pay it in order to return to peaceful communion with her sisters.

And yet things were not the same. Even before Sister Edna was tied to her in constant supervision, things had not been the same for her in the Shaker village. She knew exactly when they had changed. The stranger in the woods. It was the touch of his face, so different under her fingers, that had begun the unsettling of her life. Merely the sight of his warm brown eyes staring at her had unleashed strange new feelings inside her. Then when he traced her lips with the tip of his finger, her granny's stories of princes and love began dancing through her thoughts in a new way as a yearning awakened inside her for things that could not be.

That was why it had been hard to come up with the proper words of prayer as she knelt by her bed. In the back of her mind she kept hearing the echo of her granny's words. "Love will find you, my sweet Jessamine. Never fear. Someday love will find you."

"But how will I know it's true love, Granny?" The memory of her child's voice sounded in her head.

"The stars in the sky will be brighter. The sunshine in the spring will be warmer. The scent of the roses will be sweeter. Your toes will want to dance and your heart will want to sing."

"Were you ever in love?"

Even now Jessamine remembered the look on her granny's face as she answered. "Oh yes, my sweet child. Oh yes. It is something not to be missed. No matter the cost, it is something not to be missed."

"I haven't missed it. I love you." Jessamine had grabbed her granny around the middle and hugged her tightly.

Her granny had laughed and hugged Jessamine back every bit as tightly. "And I love you, my child. That too is a love I wouldn't have wanted to miss. But the love I speak of is the love between a man and a woman. A love given by the good Lord above that is rewarded with beautiful children like you. Someday you will know that kind of love. When your prince comes."

Jessamine wished she could ask her granny some more questions. Like did love make a person feel like ants were crawling around inside one's skin? Did it make a girl ready to forget every rule over her life? And what did a girl do when the prince came and then left? If that happened, then Jessamine was surely only imagining the stranger from the woods to be her prince. In her granny's stories, the prince never rode away without the princess. He fought dragons and witches and all manner of evil, but the happily-ever-after kiss always happened at the end.

There could be no happily-ever-after ending for Jessamine with the stranger from the woods. Not with the man she now knew was Tristan Cooper. He was no prince. He had ridden away without even seeking her out to say goodbye. She had merely allowed her imagination to gallop away with her without reining it in, as Sister Sophrena so often told her she must.

Perhaps that should have been her prayer while on her knees before the start of the day, for truly the words she'd let slide through her mind begging the Lord for another sight of the stranger from the woods were wrong prayer words. Even sinful words and none the Lord or Mother Ann would bend ears down to hear. Instead they had surely clapped their hands over their ears to block out her prayer. And yet, she could not deny the yearning was there.

She should confess such feelings, for they were a stumbling block in her path. She could do so to Sister Sophrena, but never to Sister Edna. Jessamine had no idea who was to hear her confessions now that Sister Edna had been instructed to keep her under constant surveillance.

Once dressed and with Sister Edna by her side, the morning chores were tiresome but familiar as Jessamine gathered dirty linens and clothing and emptied and cleaned chamber pots. Sister Edna considered watching Jessamine to be her duty and did naught else as she followed after Jessamine at the ready to point out the slightest lack in Jessamine's work. It was a great relief to go into the morning meal where Sister Edna's voice could not be droning in Jessamine's ears for at least the length of time they ate their meal in silence.

Unfortunately she could not hope for the same during the day as they worked in the gardens. It would be more of the same chiding words. More fault-finding. More spirit crushing. She almost wished they were assigned to the washhouse—a duty she abhorred. There the noise of the washing machines and sloshing clothes made conversation almost impossible. But the good planting weather was holding, and since it was already past the middle of June, there was some urgency to get the seed of the late crop cucumbers and beans into the ground. All available hands would be in the fields this day while the sun shone and the rains held off. Once the seeds were planted would be the time of prayer for rain.

"Sisters, please wait. I have need to talk to Sister Jessamine," Sister Sophrena called after them as they left the house to go to the gardens.

Jessamine stopped at the bottom of the stone steps down from the door, glad to see Sister Sophrena rushing after them. A smile lifted the corners of her mouth for the first time since she'd left her dreams behind that morning.

There was no similar lift to Sister Edna's mouth. Instead she frowned as she muttered, "Keep in mind we have no time to engage in empty chatter."

Sister Sophrena's hearing was sharp, and she fastened stern eyes on Sister Edna as she said, "I have not chased after you with any sort of chatter, my sister. Only a message from the Ministry for our sister."

Hope fluttered up inside Jessamine. Perhaps the Ministry had decided her penitent attitude was sincere and were going to lift the constant supervision.

"Yea, forgive me, Sister Sophrena. I was only warning our young sister that there is much work awaiting us in the gardens. Good and useful work to profit our Society much in the coming weeks and months." Sister Edna glanced over at Jessamine. "Our sister has a tendency to dawdle at times."

Jessamine had to bite the inside of her lip to keep from refuting Sister Edna's words as she shot a look at the woman next to her. She had not dawdled at all in the two days they had worked together. Except for that morning in prayer. She supposed she had prayed a dawdling prayer. A sinful prayer. Jessamine lowered her eyes to the ground. She wouldn't want either sister to guess the real reason for the blush rising in her cheeks.

"Nay, Sister Edna, you are not being fair. Our young sister

has always been competent and dutiful in accomplishing any tasks assigned to her," Sister Sophrena said. "But as I said, this has naught to do with the work duties for the day. The garden will await after our sister receives the message from those who know best for our community."

"What message is that? She has only been under supervision a short time. As yet she is not ready to be trusted to withstand the temptations that plague her." Sister Edna sounded worried her time of importance might be so soon at an end.

"There is a letter they wish her to read," Sister Sophrena said softly.

"A letter? To me?" Jessamine's eyes flew up to Sister Sophrena's face. "From someone in the world?" Could the Lord be answering her prayer of the morning with a letter? From the stranger? From the man named Tristan Cooper?

"Yea," Sister Sophrena said.

She was ready to say more, but Jessamine jumped in front of her words. "But I know no one from the world. How could I receive a letter?"

"Calm yourself, my little sister. The letter has been here since shortly after you came among us. We were instructed to keep it until such time as you were old enough to read and understand its message." Sister Sophrena hesitated a moment. "The leaders realize you are going through a time of turmoil, but it is well-known that such can lead to spiritual growth and to clearer eyes to make the right choices. Words on a letter will not change the truth of your place among us, and so it has been decided that it would not be right to keep the letter from you any longer."

"What does the letter say?"

"Yea, Sister Sophrena," Sister Edna put in. "What does this letter say?"

Sister Sophrena spared a quick glance toward Sister Edna before directing her full gaze at Jessamine. "That I cannot say.

I have not seen the words within it. In truth, I had all but forgotten there even was a letter as yet unopened until recently."

A tremble began to take root in Jessamine's midsection and grow until tendrils were pushing through every inch of her being. She had a letter from the prince who loved her mother. It had to be. No one else from the world had any reason to send her a letter via the Shakers. But how would he have known she was at Harmony Hill? Perhaps he had come seeking her at her granny's cabin and found them gone. The old preacher could have told him where she was. But then why had he not come for her? So many questions without answers. And now there was a letter.

Sister Sophrena's voice came to her as if through a long tunnel. "Sister Jessamine, are you all right? You appear faint." She reached out to clasp Jessamine's arms. "Take a deep breath and then let it out very slowly. You will be fine."

"She overresponds to everything," Sister Edna said with no charity in her voice.

"Nay, I have never found that so," Sister Sophrena said.

Jessamine pulled in a deep breath as Sister Sophrena ordered. She had felt faint for a moment, but the air filling her lungs made everything come back into focus. Sister Sophrena was still talking. "You can go on to the gardens and begin your assigned duty, Sister Edna."

"My duty is Sister Jessamine," Sister Edna said stoutly. "I was instructed not to leave her alone for any reason."

"She will not be alone." Sister Sophrena turned unsmiling eyes toward Sister Edna. "When we have finished carrying out the orders of the Ministry, I will escort her back to your side."

"But—" Sister Edna started to protest again.

"Your duties in the gardens await, Sister Edna. I'm sure you will be rewarded for your eager diligence to your work."

"Yea." Sister Edna bowed her head in submission to Sister Sophrena's words. "I will await Sister Jessamine in the gardens." She looked up at Jessamine. "Do not tarry once you have viewed the letter Sister Sophrena has for you. We have many seeds to plant."

It was strange, but instead of tarrying toward the garden as Sister Edna thought she might, Jessamine's feet were wont to tarry as she followed Sister Sophrena up the steps and back into the Gathering Family House. She could not imagine what words the letter might hold. For years she had wondered about her beginnings, about the prince who loved her mother, but now that she might be minutes from knowing the truth, she felt fearful.

She had captured stories out of the air with only bits and pieces of the truth and planted them in the rich fertile soil of her imagination. From those seeds, stories had sprouted up that she had twisted and turned as though training a tender tree sapling to grow toward the sun.

What if the stories she'd treasured through the years, the ones buried in her mind with the solidity of truth, what if those stories had no truth? She pulled in another deep breath. It was foolish to worry about something so unknown. Best to square her shoulders and run toward the truth. Sister Sophrena had often told her one never had reason to fear the truth. But on the other hand she did not deny that the truth could bring one sorrow.

It was hard to know what Sister Sophrena was thinking now as she led Jessamine into the small room she used as an office. She shut the door behind Jessamine and then stepped behind the small writing desk to study Jessamine without one glance toward the envelope in the middle of the desk. Jessamine, on the other hand, had difficulty looking at anything else.

19

Without a word, Sister Sophrena picked up the letter and handed it to Jessamine. The envelope was yellowed with age. *Jessamine Brady, Harmony Hill Shaker Village* was scrawled across the front in wavering script. The handwriting of an old man.

The prince who loved her mother wouldn't be aged. Jessamine held the letter gingerly as if weighing its worth. Maybe it would be better if she didn't even look inside the envelope. She didn't have to. The Ministry hadn't commanded her to read the letter. They were merely allowing her to do so if that was what she wanted. If only she knew what she did want.

She turned the envelope over in her hand. The flap was torn. It had been opened. But that was to be expected. The Ministry would have read the words inside to be sure they were acceptable. That was their duty. To protect those in the Society from wrongs and temptations whether such sprang to life within their borders or without.

Sister Sophrena peered across the table at her for a moment before she asked, "Do you fear the words that might be inside?"

"I don't know why I hesitate," Jessamine answered honestly.

"But perhaps you are right. Perhaps I do fear the truth that may await me there."

"What truth is that, my sister?"

"The truth of my being."

Sister Sophrena frowned a little. "Why would you fear that? It little matters now at any rate since you are part of our community. A person's real beginning is when she embraces the Shaker way and steps on this path once and for all. Whatever this piece of paper is ready to tell you cannot compare to that moment of being assured of salvation forevermore."

The older sister didn't understand. She couldn't understand. Jessamine's granny might have understood if she had still been alive to see Jessamine's worry. She would have known how Jessamine had built up a fairy-tale story in her mind about the prince who loved her mother. And now all that could come crashing down according to what words awaited her. Words that had obviously been waiting somewhere in the village for years.

When Jessamine continued to hesitate, Sister Sophrena went on. "You don't have to read it, Sister Jessamine. I can give it back to the Ministry to dispose of as they deem appropriate."

"Nay." Jessamine's fingers tightened on the envelope.

"Then read it so that we can be about our duties." Sister Sophrena's voice wasn't exactly cross, but it did carry the tinge of irritation.

"Yea." Jessamine pulled back the envelope flap with fingers that trembled. She suddenly wished she were alone. She loved Sister Sophrena, but some things should be private. What if there was need for tears?

Inside the first envelope was another envelope. Here the ink hadn't faded and her name was written with a steady hand and a certain flourish that delighted Jessamine's eye on sight. Underneath her name was more of the same wavering writing that was on the outside of the envelope.

This letter was given to me by Jessamine Brady's great-grandmother, Ida Kendall, with instructions to present it to the child when she reached the age of 12. Since I am in failing health, I have grave doubts I will live long enough to keep my promise, so I am sending it to you to give to her when you see fit. I know not the words it holds.

Reverend Garfield Jacobs

Why hadn't the old preacher given her the letter before he brought her to the Shakers? She would have been near enough to twelve. She stared down at his words and muttered, "I am much past twelve now."

"What is that you are saying?" Sister Sophrena asked.

Jessamine looked up at her. "The writing here indicates I was to be given the letter when I was twelve. I am much past twelve."

"Yea, so you are."

"Has the letter been here all these years unopened?"

"Nay, the outer envelope was opened when it was received shortly after you came among us. It was laid aside as you weren't twelve at that time and then I regret to say, it was quite forgotten." A flush of guilt crossed Sister Sophrena's face. "I am at fault there. The Ministry instructed me to keep it in a safe place and so I put it in one of my journals. When that journal was filled, I turned it over to those who keep record of all our journals without remembering the letter hidden inside. Out of sight. Out of mind. I have no excuse for my mindlessness."

She looked so concerned that Jessamine couldn't hold any hard feelings toward her. Not against Sister Sophrena who had taken her under her wing and loved her in spite of her many lapses of correct behavior.

"Perhaps it was as it was meant to be," Jessamine said. "And not the proper time."

Relief lightened Sister Sophrena's face. "Yea, it could have been providential forgetfulness. You were doing so well and settling in so nicely by the time you were twelve. The letter with words to pull your mind back toward the world might have upset that."

"If you think that a possibility, why am I being given the letter now? If it has upsetting words, they will even now be upsetting still." Jessamine glanced down at her name written in such bold script. The handwriting of the prince who loved her mother. The handwriting of her father.

"We were honor bound to deliver the letter once it was found and remembered. We delayed, thinking it might be best to wait until you were of the age to sign the Covenant of Belief."

"That's more than a year away."

"Yea, a day to look forward to with joy, my sister, and not so long from now. A year passes quickly." Sister Sophrena hesitated as if waiting for Jessamine to say something. When she did not, the older sister looked suddenly very solemn as she went on. "If you feel you are ready. No one is forced to sign the Covenant. It has to be a decision of free will and loving commitment."

"Yea," Jessamine said. "So you have often told me."

"It is good to remember what you are told, but better to know what you believe." Sister Sophrena studied her a moment before she let out a small sigh. "I have noted a warring spirit within you in the last few days."

"I have felt much confusion and little joy," Jessamine admitted. "And now I fear this letter will confuse me even more."

"Read it, my sister." Sister Sophrena reached over and touched her arm softly. "You are not the bewildered child you were when you came among us. You will be able to determine the truth or untruth of the words in the letter. I will pray it so while you read and I will also pray your current confusion clears like the sky after a storm."

A storm. That was what Jessamine felt like she was in. A storm of contradictory feelings. She loved her sisters, but she wanted to know a different love. She perhaps held in her hand the answers to questions that had long bedeviled her, yet she hesitated to read those answers. Why had she suddenly latched onto a spirit of fear? She had always before run after answers. She wanted to find out about each new thing she stumbled over. But those had been simple things. Like parasols. Or bullfrogs. Nothing to do with forbidden love or words that might turn the prince who loved her mother into a man like any other.

Sister Sophrena turned away from her and knelt by the chair behind the small writing desk. Jessamine stared at the letter as beads of sweat rolled down her side beneath the loose folds of her dress. The small room felt too warm even though the window behind Sister Sophrena had been lifted to allow the air to circulate. Jessamine drew in a deep breath. It was time to take courage in hand and pull free the letter. Already she had delayed too long. Sister Edna and the garden seeds awaited.

She unfolded the yellowed paper carefully. The page was filled with the same elegant script as her name on the outside of the inner envelope.

> *My dearest Jessamine, my beautiful baby*
> *girl, I love you. I do so desire those words*
> *to be the first that you ever read written by*
> *my hand. I do love you more than you can*
> *possibly imagine. More than even I could*
> *imagine before I held you in my arms. As much*
> *as your dear mother loved you from the first*

moment she knew you were growing inside her. She would have died for you at that moment without a single glance back. She did die for you, a complication of birthing you, but there were regretful glances back, for she mourned the years she would not be able to hold you and love you here on earth. I have not the slightest doubt she looks down on you with much love from her angelic perch in heaven, but she wished more time here with you. As did I. More time for her and more time for me.

You may not be able to understand why I could not give you that time. Time that by rights and nature should be yours. I look into your sweet, innocent face and wonder the same. Yet, I know I have no way to care for a tiny infant. I must follow my muse and write my stories. They torment my soul and demand my mind. So I have given you to your granny. She is also my granny, but my time with her when I was a child was very short. My father did not like the wilderness and saw no need in us finding our way back to the wild place where Granny has ever lived. While I did have my mother long enough to enduringly store her kind face and voice in my memory, she, like your own, died and left me to the harshness of the world much too soon. I want to spare that for you. You will have nothing but love from Granny and freedom for your imagination to take wing. She knows stories and if you turn out to follow our footsteps into a world of story making, then these early years with her will be a gift beyond price.

But today you are twelve and today Granny will tell you about me and give you this letter. Then if you so desire or perhaps I should say when you might so desire, I will return and you can come with me as I travel my writing path. By then, I can only hope my stories will be well received and there will be sufficient funds to supply your needs and that of our granny too if she decides to come with us. That I cannot imagine happening, for she loves her solitude there in her trees. But it could be she will love you more. And me. Enough to agree to journey with us at least for a little while.

Happy birthday, my beautiful Jessamine. I can hardly imagine you as a young girl with long legs and freckles across your baby nose. I can already see that you will have your mother's amazingly blue eyes, but your hair is yet a mystery. Perhaps it will grow in dark and wavy like mine or light as the sunlight like your mother's. She was the most beautiful woman I ever saw or ever hope to see. But you, my sweet little girl child, are every bit as beautiful in your baby way.

You are lying on a blanket here on the bed beside me while I pen these words. You have discovered your hands and look at them with great wonder. So many discoveries are ahead of you. So many wonders. My heart, already full of sadness at the loss of your mother, grows even heavier at the thought of leaving you behind. But what must be done must be done. I will finish these words and fold this page and put it inside the envelope for your eyes in twelve years. Then I will pick you up and hold you

close to my heart and breathe in your precious
baby scent to carry away with me. Tears will
trace paths down my cheeks as I ride away.
Our granny will pray for me and for you. And
someday I will return.

> *Your loving and*
> *devoted father,*
> *Sheldon Brady*

Jessamine read the letter all the way through without stopping, her eyes gobbling up the words as if they were candied plums. Then hardly aware of Sister Sophrena still on her knees praying beside the writing desk, she started at the beginning again. But this time she lingered over some of the words. The words of love that were like fresh-drawn water from the well to a parched throat.

The prince who loved her mother also loved her. She had not realized how much she needed those words until they were settling in her mind. Her father of the world had not deserted her completely. He had planned to return for her. Perhaps he had returned for her, but found the cabin deserted and the old preacher dead and no one to ask what became of his baby girl. What became of her.

She stared at the words on the page until the ink ran together in a dark blur. She didn't know whether to laugh or cry. To shout or fall on her knees in silent prayer. She considered raising her hands and singing a praise song. Something joyful. Something that might make her feet spin. But Sister Sophrena was praying. It didn't seem right to spin while she was kneeling so solemnly. So instead Jessamine read through the words again. Her father of the world thought their imagination a gift, a blessing. Her father of the world had planned to show Jessamine that world. His world.

Sister Sophrena looked up at Jessamine then and slowly rose to her feet. "The words of the letter have put joy on your face, Sister Jessamine."

"Yea. They were written by my natural father while I was yet a baby. Before he left me with Granny. He loved me."

"Yet he did leave you and not return."

The sister's words wormed into Jessamine's joy, spoiling its completeness. "He planned to come back for me. When I was twelve."

"Yea," Sister Sophrena said thoughtfully. "I suppose the reason for the age requirement written by the preacher who brought you to us."

"My granny promised to answer all my questions when I was twelve," Jessamine said.

"All your questions?" Sister Sophrena's voice sounded stiff, as if displeased with Jessamine. "Only the Eternal Father can answer all questions."

"Yea, Sister Sophrena, I spoke without proper thought as I often do," Jessamine lowered her eyes from Sister Sophrena's face. She did not want to disappoint her sister, but at the same time surely there could be truth between them. "I meant questions about my parents of the world. Do you not think it natural for a child to wonder about her beginnings?"

An uneasy silence fell over the small room as Jessamine stared at the floor and waited for Sister Sophrena to answer. Seconds, then minutes dragged by. The hallway outside the room was silent. All the other sisters and brethren had left for their duties. From deep within the house, the clatter of pans rose to her ears as those on duty in the kitchen prepared the midday meal. Jessamine wondered if she would still be standing in the small room awaiting Sister Sophrena's answer when the bell sounded to signal the time of eating. It had not seemed such a difficult question.

At last Sister Sophrena spoke. "Look at me, Sister Jessamine. Reveal your eyes and hide not your spirit. You know the eyes are windows into our souls."

"Yea." Jessamine raised her head with some trepidation, for although she heard no anger in Sister Sophrena's voice, it was not natural for her to stay silent for so long. Her question must have in some ways angered her sister. But Sister Sophrena did not look angry, only weary as though she were having to labor to come up with a proper answer.

Sister Sophrena settled her eyes on Jessamine's face. Jessamine saw no condemnation in her eyes, only concern. A sad smile settled on her lips as she said, "Your spirit has been pummeled with temptations in these last days, my sister. Perhaps the spirits are testing you to see your strength, to harden your convictions so that you will know what you believe. Satan may have his hand in this, for it pleases Old Scratch greatly to lead our young people away from us toward the temptations of the world."

"I will war against such evil thinking." Jessamine said the expected words.

Again Sister Sophrena was silent for a long moment, but Jessamine kept her eyes up. She didn't want her beloved sister to think she was hiding anything from her. Sister Sophrena's face grew even sadder and she shut her eyes for a long moment as though it was necessary to contain her emotions. When at last she opened her eyes again, she said, "Yea, it is good to war against those things that you realize are evil. The recognition of such is what one must learn."

Jessamine started to say something, but Sister Sophrena waved away her words. "The question you ask, the one about whether your curiosity about your beginnings is a natural one, that question is a worldly question. One that should not trouble a Believer. Your worldly mother and father should not matter so much to you. It is your spiritual father and mother you need let your mind dwell upon."

"But . . ."

Sister Sophrena held her palm out toward Jessamine and did not let her speak. Every line of her face drooped with sadness. "I have ever known your curiosity for the world, but until the last week, I thought it only a passing fancy of youth. Now I worry that I am wrong. I worry that the draw of the world is pulling you away from us."

"Nay," Jessamine said quickly. "Nay, Sister Sophrena. You are my family."

"But your mind reaches toward the world. You imagine the pleasures thereof and think not of the dangers for one such as yourself."

Jessamine's face bloomed red, but she could not deny the words.

Sister Sophrena went on gently. "You have ever been tempted by your imagination."

"But is it not good to have an imagination to wonder about things? To come up with new and better ways? To welcome the spirits in meeting? Is not such a gift as good and true as the gift of song or industrious fingers?"

"Properly constrained, such ability to imagine can be a gift, but I fear you have no desire for such constraints. You want no rules over what is proper to imagine. And now you are imagining much about the world outside our borders."

"Yea, you speak truth. I like to imagine freely as though I am clinging to the tail feathers of a giant bird and flying through wondrous worlds. I want to see everything, to know how things came to be, to understand about the love my granny told me my father had for my mother." Jessamine held up the letter. "The love that is in this letter. Did you know such love before you became a Believer?"

"The love of the world betrayed me, left me broken. The love here among the Believers, that love is the pure love. The love that will never destroy your spirit or cause you sorrow."

"But I feel sorrow now," Jessamine said softly.

Sister Sophrena let out a weary sigh. "Yea, I know it is so, my sister. Some quandaries cannot be easily solved. You must make your own choices. It is not one I can make for you, but if you can bear the constant supervision yet a little longer, I feel confident your peace will return and you will once more see your path clearly here in our village."

"I am praying that it will be so, Sister," Jessamine said with meekness. "I will try to stoically bear my punishment for my wayward thinking."

"And what of the letter?" Sister Sophrena said.

Jessamine looked down at the page full of words in her hand. "I am treasuring these words in my heart. It is good to know my father and mother of the world loved me so completely and that they considered me a gift." She paused and felt a moment of sadness. "But the letter is almost twenty years old. There is no hint of where my father might be now or even if he still lives. It changes nothing about my home being here at Harmony Hill."

Sister Sophrena smiled and touched Jessamine's cheek. "That is good to hear, my sister. I will pray for your continued strength as you attempt to pick up your cross and carry it among us. Now the sun is rising high in the sky. It is time we both went out to our duties."

Jessamine thought to slip the letter under her apron in hopes Sister Sophrena would forget she held it, but she did not. She could not. She had to abide by the rules. "Should I carry the letter in the pocket of my apron?" she asked while a prayer flew up inside her that this would be allowed.

A prayer that was not answered. "Nay, my sister." Sister Sophrena held out her hand for the letter. "I think it better if you allow me to hold it for you. At least while you are struggling with worldly thoughts and working to get back into proper harmony with your fellow believers."

Jessamine did her best to hide her reluctance as she surrendered the letter to Sister Sophrena. She told herself it didn't matter. The words were engraved on her heart and she would be able to bring them up into her mind whenever she wanted while she worked beside Sister Edna through the day. But her eyes longed to trace the lines of the letters her father had formed with his own hand. She wanted to imagine his hand writing the words and then stroking her baby cheek.

She pulled up the image as she went out of the Gathering Family House to the garden plot where Sister Edna awaited with much frowning and many questions. What was the letter? Who had written her? Had she no awareness of worldly sin? Did she need to confess wrong thinking? Why was she so quiet?

Jessamine answered each question with as few words as possible while she let the words of her father's letter run through her mind like the repeating choruses of a Shaker song. Over and over. The prince who loved her mother also loved her, and while she did not have his dark wavy hair, she had been gifted with imagination to match his. An imagination that for him led to stories he wrote down just as he had written the letter. Oh, how she hungered to see one of those books with his name on the front. Written by Sheldon Brady. Could there be a more wonderful gift than the ability to take pen to paper?

So she planted the beans and she dreamed. She answered Sister Edna's demands and she dreamed. She ate her evening meal in silence and kept dreaming. They went up into the upper room and practiced laboring the dances. She counted her steps and dreamed of what might have been if her granny had not died.

She stretched out on her narrow Shaker bed and shut her eyes to sleep and wished the dreams to follow her into the night. At first, she was not sure she wasn't still dreaming when she heard her name whispered in her ear.

"Jessamine. Sister Jessamine, wake up."

The whispered voice was insistent and finally pulled Jessamine away from her dreams. She opened her eyes, expecting to see the morning dawning, but the night was still heavy on them. She started to speak an answer, but a hand clamped over her mouth.

"Shh! You'll wake the sister witch."

Jessamine came awake then and knew it was Sister Abigail stooped beside her bed, whispering into her ear. She nodded a little and Sister Abigail removed her hand. It wasn't the first time Sister Abigail had whispered her awake in the deep of the night. Those other times, before Jessamine was being watched, they had sneaked out on the front steps in the moonlight to talk of forbidden things of the world.

Jessamine rose up a little off her pillow to peer over toward Sister Edna. She was a sound sleeper and even now she was snoring as she enjoyed the deserved rest of the faithful Shaker. Jessamine's eyes began adjusting to the night and she could see Sister Abigail was not wearing a night shift but instead her Shaker dress without the white collar or apron.

"What are you doing, Sister Abigail?" Jessamine whispered.

"Leaving." Determination was plain in Sister Abigail's softly whispered word. "I had my hand on the door when I felt compelled to come back to your bed. You should come with me. The world calls to you."

"Nay, I cannot leave my family." Jessamine whispered the words quickly, even as a finger of temptation poked her. She could leave. She could go in search of her father. Her path might cross that of the man from the world again. She might find Tristan Cooper.

"This family has no love for you. Not the way they've tied you to evil Edna. They merely want to make us into slaves to do their bidding."

"Beloved sisters, not slaves," Jessamine insisted.

"You are fooling yourself, Jessamine. We are no more than hands and feet and broad backs to do their labor. Come away with me and experience the freedom of the world."

"Nay, I cannot."

Sister Edna's snore cut off as she shifted in her bed. Jessamine held her breath as Abigail sank down lower beside the bed. But the woman did not awaken as she began to snore evenly once more.

"I must go." Abigail silently stood. Then she leaned back down toward Jessamine. "You will regret not coming with me, but I will pray for your escape."

She slipped like a shadow away from Jessamine toward the door. She looked back once before she silently pulled the door shut behind her.

"And I will pray for you." Jessamine mouthed the words without making a whisper of noise. Then she stared into the dark of the night and tried to keep her feet still. They itched with the desire to follow Abigail out the door. The regret the young sister had promised began rising dark within Jessamine.

Journal Entry

Harmony Hill Village
Entered on this 20th day of June in the year 1849
by Sister Sophrena Prescott

There is upset among our novitiates. Upon
rising this morn, one of the beds was found to
be unoccupied. The young sister named Abigail
has chosen to run back to the world. Sister Edna
reported the news to Eldress Frieda after the rising
bell during the time of early chores. I was with the
eldress when Sister Edna made her report. Both of
us were much disturbed by the folly of the young
sister and the sorrow-burdened life she has no
doubt run toward. A life with none of the blessings
and gifts she could have enjoyed so abundantly here
among us.

The sister never settled into our ways. From the
first day among us she resisted our teachings. While
we all hoped her will would bend and she would see
the error of her ways, I don't think any of us were
overly hopeful of that happening.

I do have to admit I was greatly relieved to see
Sister Jessamine obediently following after Sister

*Edna, for she too had to come when Sister Edna
made the report due to her condition of constant
supervision. I was very uncertain of what temptations
might beset her after she read the letter from her
natural father of the world. She has not tried to
deny her confusion of thought, and when I heard
upon rising that a sister had slipped away during
the night, I could not help but be concerned for our
Sister Jessamine. That was why I was seeking out the
eldress. So I could relieve my worries in her regard.*

*I must confess I did succumb to the temptation
to read the letter that lay in wait for our sister so
many years. Nigh on twenty. Since she was a tiny
baby. I intended to do no more than stuff it back in
the envelope and return it to the Ministry to keep or
destroy as they saw fit, but the words reached for my
eyes. I told myself knowing what the letter said would
better equip me to help my sister in her confusion,
but it is a truth that our minds can very often come
up with what we tell ourselves are valid reasons to
do the things that tempt us. To stray from the simple
path of obedience.*

*The words I read did not cause me to doubt my
life here among my brethren and sisters. I am content
here. It is my life. My work. My worship. But the
words of Sister Jessamine's natural father did bring
tears to my eyes. As Sister Jessamine told me after
she had finished reading through the letter—he loved
her. A worldly love to be sure, but expressed with
such sincerity I could not help being moved by his
words. So it is no wonder our young sister felt some
confusion in her heart.*

*I never knew feelings like that. Never really felt
loved until I came into the Society where I am ever*

surrounded with love. My natural father thought
me no more than a burden. A female plain of face.
He cared not that I showed an affinity for words.
He wanted sons to work with him in the fields and
ride after him to the hunt. My mother, worn brittle
by the cares of the world, only wanted me grown
and settled. The two of them pushed me into a sinful
union of wedlock. Oh, what a blessing it would have
been for me to be carried to the village here at a
young age as Sister Jessamine was. And yet, she does
not recognize the gift she was given. She only wants
to look over her shoulder to the past or into the
beyond and wonder.

I do not have to wonder. I have seen many
troubles of the world. I heard my mother crying in
the night and understood her tears after my own
unhappy marriage. I experienced the stress and sin
brought about by individual family ties just as Mother
Ann warned would happen. But here at Harmony
Hill we have established a heaven on earth, a
paradise of love.

I am content. Sister Jessamine may find such
contentment in time, but for now, it eludes her.
Instead, the letter's words dance in her mind, enticing
her, making her wonder even more about the things
of the world. I know this is true even though she
might deny it every bit.

Eldress Frieda tells me I must stop clinging to our
young sister and allow her to come to belief on her
own. For while we can be a bridge to help someone
along on their journey, we cannot make the journey
for another. Those who come to us must open their
eyes to the truth and embrace it on their own.
We must allow them to step out on the Believers'

pathway and affix their signatures to the Covenant of Belief without unseemly duress.

We can pray. We can labor dances and sing down love from Mother Ann. We can shake carnal thoughts from us. But only if that is our desire. Would that Sister Jessamine's desires will bring her back into communion with her sisters and brothers and not entice her into the world. Into sin.

20

At White Oak Springs the days were for relaxing and taking the waters, but the nights were for socializing and dancing. The Springs threw open the doors to the ballroom at least three times every week. Sometimes more. People came to the Springs to be entertained and the owner aimed to please.

Wednesday night was the first dance after Tristan came back from the Shaker village. He thought of simply staying in his room in order to avoid the awkward attempt to dance with one arm still swathed in a sling, but his mother turned pale and began breathing too rapidly as she sank down on the chair in her dressing room. Her maid, Louise, had to pull out the smelling salts.

His mother had always been prone to swoons if things didn't go her way, and the very thought of him not at least signing Laura Cleveland's dance card this one night was enough to make her doubt her chances for a happy life. So he sighed and agreed to do as she wanted. That had been his path ever since his father died. Do as Mother says.

In the past, before he'd gone off to fight in the war, Tristan had enjoyed the flirtatious atmosphere of such dances. He liked bringing blushes to the faces of the girls as he spun them around the dance floor. It had been a game he wanted to play. But now it simply seemed too warm in the ballroom, too crowded on the dance floor, too noisy with the talk. And not a word that mattered.

He looked toward the double doors that led into a rose garden with longing and thought of escape. But he didn't want to just escape for a few moments of fresher air and rest for his ears. He wanted to escape the whole situation.

He and Laura had walked around the lake again that afternoon, but this time he'd been forward thinking enough to secure bread crumbs. Laura delighted in feeding the ducks, laughing at their noisy demands and greedy beaks. He laughed with her, and once again, the same as the day when they had spoken so honestly with one another about his disappearance, he told himself marriage to Laura would be far from odious.

Laura was lovely. And wealthy. And liked to laugh. So what if her eyes were more gray than blue and showed little warmth when she looked his way. He should count that a challenge and woo her until she did look on him with love. She was a girl any man would be proud to court. In fact, at that very moment on the other side of the ballroom, she was surrounded by several hopeful gentlemen trying to bring warmth to her eyes. She was definitely the most popular belle at White Oak Springs.

He should count it his good fortune she was appearing to favor his attention over the others. He should be there in the circle around her now, paying court. He'd already noted his mother's pointed looks toward him from where she sat next to Mrs. Cleveland. She was courting the family with the same diligence she expected him to attend Laura. He had already lost a week while with the Shakers. He could ill afford to drag his feet now with the other suitors so determined.

In fact, he once more intended to say the words that

afternoon, but when the bread crumbs were gone, Laura had held her hand to her head and claimed a headache. So they had no quiet moments on a bench by the pathways where he could speak words of love. Or if not love, then at least commitment. As though she knew his intent, she had almost run back toward the hotel, claiming the need of a few hours of quiet rest in her room before the evening, but later he'd seen her on the porches. It occurred to Tristan that he might be the reason for her headache instead of the garrulous ducks.

He would pull up his determination and cross the room when the song ended. His name was on her dance card, but one dance would not be enough to please his mother. She expected him to dance attendance on the girl throughout the evening as Laura's other hopeful suitors were doing. He would do his mother's bidding. At least enough to keep her happy so she wouldn't begin to cast around for another candidate for his affections. Several less attractive possibilities were in that very room.

His eyes touched on Thelma Jackson with her strident voice that hurt his ears. Then he quickly passed his glance by Marian Williams whose eyes reminded him of an unhappy weasel and whose face and neck bloomed with red splotches whenever he spoke to her. Both had successful fathers. Rich fathers. Not fathers who forgot to mind to business and went off to war only to carry home a deadly illness. Patriotic and heroic, but heroism didn't pay off debts.

Looks weren't everything, he reminded himself. A good woman with intelligence and grace, that was what he needed. That was what it appeared Laura Cleveland was. All that along with a pretty face and stylish bearing. And the money. He could never forget the money. Perhaps that was his problem. The feeling he was being bought. Then again, perhaps not bought. Sold might be the better word. Sold by his mother to maintain their lifestyle. A lifestyle he no longer cared about.

Still, he could not imagine his mother anywhere but their house situated on one of the best streets in Atlanta. Even the thought of her doing her own housework or laundry was ludicrous. She needed servants. She needed new hats and social events. He could hardly expect her to become a governess or a shopkeeper. The very idea was enough to make a laugh work up inside him as he looked across the room toward her. She had never wanted for anything in her lifetime. Born to money, reared in money, and married in money. At least that had been her intent. She'd had no way of knowing her husband would have a careless view toward their fortune.

Tristan doubted if she'd ever even given any thought to the possibility the money well might run dry. Now that it had, he had a duty to his mother. Not only that, but his father's debts had become his debts. Debts that kept increasing with each passing day like storm clouds piling in on storm clouds. He'd seen the papers from the lawyers. His mother was right. He needed to marry Laura Cleveland.

What he did not need to do was keep recalling cornflower blue eyes and blonde wisps of hair sneaking out of a bonnet. One day could not change his whole life. A day he couldn't even remember. But he did remember the blue-eyed sister. Jessamine.

Jessamine. A flower in the south. Yellow blooms that released their fragrance in the cool of the evening. A heady fragrance that had surely led to many a man going down on his knee in a garden to promise his undying love. Perhaps he needed to be in that southern garden with Laura instead of thinking on the flower he had left at the Shaker village.

"She's the belle of the ball." Sheldon Brady stepped up beside him and followed Tristan's gaze across the floor to Laura. "I think she's already heard three proposals in the three weeks she's been here."

"Three?" Tristan looked toward the man to see if he was trying to fool him.

Brady smiled. "Three. Laura tells me that is nowhere near last summer's pace, but then last summer was play for her. This summer her father is expecting her to seriously consider some of the propositions." The man's smile disappeared as he leveled his eyes on Tristan. "At least one of them."

Tristan veered away from talk of proposals by asking, "Have you known the Clevelands long?"

The man's smile returned, polite, revealing nothing. "Only a couple of years. I did a reading at Laura's finishing school in the East. She so enjoyed my essay that she invited me to visit their home in Boston."

"Boston? I thought they lived near Atlanta."

"The Boston house was her mother's childhood home. Viola much prefers the north, and remains an avid supporter of the arts in that city. And while it would be preferable to not have to depend on such, the social rounds are an important part of my work. The funding part. The ladies buy more books when they know me."

"That's right. You write romantic novels."

"That's how I manage to stay out of the poorhouse, but as Robert says, romantic drivel. Someday I will write the novel I am intended to write. Poetic and sweeping in scope." He said the words in such a way that Tristan wasn't sure if he was serious or simply making fun of himself. "But write I must, whether it is drivel or literature worthy of kings. The paper calls to me and demands my ink."

"Laura seemed quite impressed at dinner on Tuesday."

"Oh yes, Laura." His voice softened a bit as his eyes went back to Laura. "A lovely girl with discriminating taste. At least that's the reason she gives her father for spurning so many promising proposals. I think Robert fears she will be an old maid and Viola fears she won't. Dear Viola has suffrage leanings." Brady's eyes slid over to Viola Cleveland and Tristan's mother and then drifted back to settle on Laura. "Rumor has it you are Robert's favored candidate at present."

"Rumors fly here at the Springs." Tristan kept his voice light.

"They do, but often a spark of truth sets off the rumor. Old rich is fashionable in the south and Robert does want his little girl to have every advantage."

"Most fathers would surely feel the same." Too late Tristan remembered Sheldon Brady had claimed a daughter. The one he left as a baby with his grandmother. The lines on the man's face deepened and Tristan tried to soften his words. "I mean I assume they would. I am not a father."

"But I am and you are right. I did want her to have every advantage. I had so many plans for her. A good school. Journeys to the ocean and hikes into the mountains. Dances such as this when she came of age." He kept his eyes on the dancers spinning past them as he went on. "I suppose I built up a father and daughter fairy tale in my mind to assuage my guilt for leaving her behind. I should have gone back for her whether she answered my letter or not."

"Why didn't you?"

"Why didn't I? An excellent question. But I can only come up with excuses, not a valid answer. The years have held many ups and downs for me. More downs than ups and sometimes I barely eked out enough with my writing to supply my own needs, small as they were. It's only lately that I have found a measure of success that now allows me sojourns in places like this." He waved his hand out toward the dance floor before he looked straight at Tristan. "You are young. You have yet to experience many of the trials of life."

"I fought in Mexico. I thought I might die in Mexico."

"Forgive me, I didn't mean to suggest that fighting in the war and the grief of your father's death were not trials. They surely were," the man said quietly. "But there are trials over which we have little control and times when we simply end up clinging to the boat sides, praying for the best as we traverse the rough waters of life. Then there are those other types of trials where our hand is on the tiller. We are guiding our course with our decisions. We make choices. Those are the trials that can continually haunt us, for we have to wonder if we traversed the right stretch of the river of our lives or if our hand was clumsy on the tiller."

"Do you think the Shaker girl who rescued me in the woods could be your daughter?"

"I don't know. I have done little but wonder about that the past two days as I made a pretense of writing."

"Would your grandmother have joined with them? With the Shakers."

The writer smiled. "That I know without the first doubt did not happen. Ida Kendall was not one to give up her freedom. She would have never left the woods. She had lived there so long she was as one with the trees."

"Perhaps she got sick."

"I think that may be what happened. I don't know why I didn't worry about that when I left my child with her, but Granny seemed ageless to me. My thinking was faulty, for her age was advanced." He paused a moment before he went on. "I did go back to the cabin once, the year Jessamine would have been fifteen. The cabin roof had fallen in and a family of raccoons had taken up residence. In behind the house, I found several graves with no markings other than fieldstones, so I had no way of knowing who lay in those graves. People I had never met or perhaps my grandmother or my daughter or both. The area had seen a cholera outbreak not so many years before I returned."

"So you thought her dead. Your daughter, I mean." Tristan watched the man. They both had forgotten the swirl of dancers in front of them and even Laura surrounded by her flock of admirers as she sipped her drink and took a break from the dance floor.

"I didn't know what to think. I inquired in the nearest town, but no one knew anything about Ida Kendall or Jessamine Brady. That did not surprise me. My grandmother was a recluse who cared not if any living, breathing people inhabited her world. She is the one who passed down to me the desire to create fictional worlds. She lived in her story lands there in the woods. My mother had a little of the fey in her as well, but she gave it up when she married my father. It was ever a grief to her to be compelled to live so completely in a world where make-believe was not allowed. My father was very stern and thought the use of one's imagination was not only foolishness but verging on a sinful waste of one's energy and time."

"That obviously didn't stop you."

Brady laughed. "A child with an imagination can figure out ways to hide his dreaming. I could no more give up stories than cease breathing."

The music stopped and the dancers all changed partners. Laura moved out on the floor with a man named Calvin Green. He looked as if he'd won the prize as the band struck up a new song and he slid his arm around her waist. She, on the other hand, appeared to be as bored with his attentions as she had looked that afternoon with Tristan's once the ducks had finished off the bread.

The couple glided toward Tristan on the dance floor, but when Green noticed him there, he frowned as if fearing Tristan might steal her attention from him even while she was allowing him the dance. Tristan pushed a smile out on his face when Laura looked his way, but she stared back at him with the same cool smile she was giving Green. Then her smile warmed as she noticed the writer beside him.

When Tristan looked at Brady, he shrugged his shoulders a bit. "She likes my foolish stories of love. Many young women do."

"And do you take advantage of their admiration?"

"Only in sales of my stories, my dear man," Brady said with a slight laugh. "As much as I hate to admit it, I'm old enough to be the father of most of my young fans." He looked out to where the dancers were making a kaleidoscope of color as they whirled to the music.

Tristan didn't say anything as he looked back out at Green, now peering down at Laura and speaking intently. Perhaps making his proposal. If so, she gave no appearance of welcoming such.

Beside him, Brady went on. "Isn't it odd how people come to different conclusions? Here the young people whirl to the music to find romance while the Shakers dance to their own music in order to keep out romance. In the village I visited in the northeast, they whirled with fervor to stay spiritually pure and deny any sort of lustful thoughts. Is that how you found it?"

"I saw them dancing. They did whirl and stomp with enthusiasm, and the sexes stayed apart."

"It takes much enthusiasm to banish man's natural inclinations toward romance. Toward love." The man sounded almost pensive as he continued to watch the dancers. After a few seconds he said, "And did the sister you met named Jessamine, the one I wonder might be my daughter, did she dance?"

"She did."

The man turned his gaze toward Tristan. "With fervor?"

Tristan smiled as he remembered the young woman. "I think perhaps Sister Jessamine does everything with fervor and enthusiasm."

"And belief in their ways?"

"That I have no way to answer."

"Tell me again what she looked like. This Jessamine. Now, without Laura listening to water down your description." He watched Tristan intently as he waited for his answer.

"She was beautiful even in her plain dress and with the bonnet. Her eyes were striking, so blue one wondered if they could be true."

"Yes," Brady murmured as if seeing those eyes. "What else?"

"The blonde hair looked promising, but it was mostly hidden. But it wasn't really the way her features and eyes looked so much as the light that radiated from her face. Like the world was waiting for her and she was eager to run to meet it."

"But the world is blocked from the Shaker villages," Brady said.

"So they told me. In fact the girl got into trouble for talking to me in one of the gardens."

"Trouble?" Brady raised his eyebrows at Tristan. "How so?"

"I was told she would be watched to be sure she would not be tempted by things of the world as she was tempted when she spoke to me." Tristan regretted yet again the ringing of the bell that had sent her flying away from him.

"I have heard they take their rules very seriously." A frown darkened Brady's face.

"The devout among them seemed very kind." Tristan tried to reassure him. "If the sister they called Jessamine is your daughter, she won't be ill treated."

"But in my eyes, it is ill treatment to withhold freedom of choice in love. In life."

"What are you going to do then? Will you go offer her that freedom?" Tristan asked. "If she turns out to be your daughter."

"How can I do less?" Brady said. "Whatever the price to my own freedom."

"Freedom can be difficult to hold onto," Tristan said as the music of the dance ended.

"So it can," Brady agreed. "And it looks as if our friend Laura is desirous of gaining her freedom from Mr. Green. Shall you go rescue her or shall I?"

"I think my name is on her dance card next, although dancing with this bent wing is awkward." Tristan raised his broken arm up a little.

"Would you like me to take your place?" The man sounded more than eager to do so.

Tristan looked at him, a little surprised, and Brady added, "Laura is a lovely dancer, but it's no doubt best for you to fulfill your spot on her dance card. Robert and your determined mother must be appeased, don't you think?"

As Tristan made his way across the room to claim his dance, he wondered if he was the only man in the ballroom not enchanted by Laura's charms. It appeared as though even the writer was ready to be her champion.

With a glower toward Tristan, Green surrendered his spot next to Laura, but before he turned away he sent a smiling appeal toward Laura. "I do hope you will seriously consider my words, dear Laura."

Laura kept her lips turned up but there was little smile in her eyes even after Tristan led her back out toward the dance floor when the band began again.

"Another proposal?"

She breathed out a sigh. "Young men are so trying." Then as if she realized what she had said, she went on. "Oh, do forgive my honesty, Tristan. I meant no insult to you."

"I'm young. I'm a man, but I'm not Calvin Green."

"Thank the heavens." Laura breathed out a slight sigh. "At least Father is sensible enough to know there are some available men I cannot abide."

"And could you abide me?" Tristan thought that surely had to be the very worst proposal any man had ever made.

But it made Laura smile fully and completely as she looked

up at him. "I think the two of us can come up with an ami-
cable arrangement, Tristan." She put her hand in his and
then looked at his broken arm. "But I have to admit I don't
know how we are going to manage this dance."

"Neither do I," Tristan admitted. "Sheldon Brady offered
to stand in for me if you'd like."

Her eyes lit up. "Would you mind? Sheldon is a wonderful
dancer and I did quite let my card be filled without saving
him a dance."

She didn't wait for Tristan to answer but looked straight
toward Brady, who was still standing where he and Tristan
had been talking. As if he knew what they were saying, he
stepped through the other couples already moving to the
music. Tristan gave over her hand to Brady and stepped off
the dance floor. Laura was right. The man was a smooth
dancer. The two moved past Tristan in perfect step.

21

Crashing thunder woke Jessamine Thursday before the rising bell rang. Other sisters stirred at the noise of the storm, and across from Jessamine, Sister Annie sat straight up in her bed. When a flash of lightning lit up the room, followed closely by another loud rumble of thunder, Sister Annie put her hands over her ears. Rain began dashing down and Jessamine jumped up to close the sleeping room window. After she glanced back to make sure Sister Edna was sleeping on undisturbed by the storm, Jessamine lingered at the window to watch the lightning run races across the sky.

When she was very small, storms had frightened her. At every clap of thunder, she would scream, put her hands over her ears, and run to hide her face in her granny's apron. Each time Granny would lead her over to peer out a window as Jessamine was doing now.

She would let Jessamine scrunch up close to her while she talked with awe about the lightning flashes and thunder booms. "The might of nature by God's design," she had told Jessamine. "Think on the storm in the Bible out there on the Sea of Galilee that scared the disciples and had them thinking they were going to drown. And what was the Lord doing?"

"Sleeping," Jessamine answered with a peek out at the lightning streaking across the sky close to the horizon. "But I don't see how."

"He knew who was in control. That's why he wasn't afraid. That's why he could sleep. But because the disciples were afraid, he got up and in the Scriptures, it says he rebuked the winds and the wind ceased and there was a great calm."

"But it doesn't say anything about the lightning," she insisted.

Her granny had hugged her close to her side and laughed a little. "A storm is a storm. And a person is going to be in a few while living her life. The thing to remember, my sweet Jessamine, is that the good Lord will be beside you through those storms. He'll get you through."

Jessamine had known even then her granny wasn't talking only about the lightning storms, but she was too young to understand about the storms of life that might be lying in wait for her. She simply trusted her granny to keep her safe.

"You should get away from the window." Sister Annie came up behind Jessamine to whisper in her ear. "It's not safe."

"There's nothing to fear. The lightning won't come into the house." She turned toward Sister Annie. Though it was surely almost dawn, the storm clouds were swallowing any beginning light of the day. Then the lightning flashed again, and it was easy to see the unease on her sister's face.

"My father knew a man struck by lightning once. Killed him on the spot." Sister Annie stepped back as thunder rolled after the lightning. "That's reason enough to fear."

"I suppose you're right, but under roof I think we are safe." Jessamine allowed the other sister to pull her back, but she kept her eyes on the window. It was dangerous. She knew that, but at the same time she wanted to be outside with the thunder in her ears and the rain dashing against her face. She wanted to challenge the storm. She wanted to be free.

"You think." Sister Annie's hand on Jessamine's arm was trembling. "It is better to know."

A flash of searing light filled the room as almost simultaneously thunder shook the windows. Sister Annie let out a little shriek and clutched Jessamine's arms.

The sister in the bed nearest them, Sister Bonnie, raised up to stare at them. "That was close," she whispered.

"But we are not touched. Go back to sleep." Jessamine whispered back. "Our strong house and Mother Ann will protect us."

"Yea." The sister yawned and sank back down on her pillow.

Jessamine led Sister Annie back toward her bed. She was beginning to think she might have to peel the girl's hands off her arms, but with the thunder rumbling away from them, Sister Annie turned loose when they reached her bed.

She put her face close to Jessamine in the dark and said, "Does nothing frighten you, Sister Jessamine?"

"I am not unafraid, Sister, but my wonder sometimes overpowers my fear."

"So it ever does," Sister Annie muttered as she peered past Jessamine to see if Sister Edna was hearing them.

With the retreat of the storm clouds and their eyes accustoming to the night, it was easy to see the shapes of the other sisters in the beds around them. A few had awakened but now were eager to pull sleep back over them before the bell rang to signal the beginning of their day. Sister Edna continued to snore in her sound sleep.

"We should go back to sleep." Jessamine turned away from her.

"Wait." Annie reached out to catch her arm before she could step away. "I saw Abigail go to your bed before she slipped away."

"She was telling me goodbye."

Sister Annie's eyes flashed disbelief in the waning darkness. "Sisters don't lie to one another."

"Forgive me, Sister. What I said was the truth, but not the complete truth. Sister Abigail did return to do more than bid me farewell. She asked me to rise and go with her."

"I thought as much. She wanted to pull you into her wickedness."

"I did not think her wicked." Although Jessamine's words made Sister Annie's frown darken, she didn't back away from her words. She didn't know why she felt compelled to defend Abigail, but she did. "She was only unhappy here in our village. You haven't been here as long as I have, but even so, you surely have seen yourself that many come to us who seem unable to set their feet firmly on our path and so leave for the world."

"Unable or unwilling? Sister Sophrena tells me the world is like a siren song to many." She hesitated a moment as her hand tightened on Jessamine's arm. "I am glad you didn't go with her. I held my breath that night unsure what I should do or say if you rose up to follow her."

"If one is determined to leave, there is no stopping her. Now the dawn is coming. I would not want Sister Edna to catch us whispering thus when the rising bell begins to toll."

Sister Annie dropped her hand from Jessamine's arm. "You will have to confess it. We both will."

"Yea, I have much to confess," Jessamine said before she went back to her bed. She kept a wary eye on Sister Edna and felt a good measure of relief when the woman's heavy breathing continued unabated. It was a gift to have one watching her who slept so heavily. It could be that on another night she might even be able to sneak out of the room to dare sit under the stars and allow their glitter to return some of the peace to her soul.

What was wrong with wondering? Was the world so evil?

She had lived the first years of her life in the world, albeit the world of the woods. Sister Annie would tell her that was not the real world, the world she knew from her father's tavern. Jessamine let out a whisper of a sigh. She thought of her own father. The prince who loved her mother. Her mother and father had shared the kind of love the Believers said was so wrong.

She had long wondered about such love between a man and a woman, but never before had her curiosity caused her discontent. Not until finding the stranger in the woods. He'd awakened feelings inside her that were nothing like the sisterly feelings she had for her brethren here in Harmony Hill. When he touched her face, her whole body had tingled down to her toes. She had wanted to reach her lips up to his. She had been ready, nay even eager, to embrace sin with no hesitation.

She pushed away memory of their moments in the trees and in the garden. She needed to push him from her mind altogether. She could think about her father. There was no danger in that. Every person who was born had a father. Even the Christ, the Son of God who was born of the Holy Spirit, was given Joseph for a worldly father. Fathers held places of honor in the Scripture. She remembered Bible stories told her by Granny. Stories of the Jewish patriarchs. That was another name for fathers.

Sister Sophrena said some of those stories revealed the stress and sin brought about by the individual family group. Brothers killing brothers. Brothers stealing from brothers. Even King David was betrayed by one of his own sons. Right living the Shaker way prevented such sin. Here there were no fathers and sons, mothers and daughters.

Some could abide by the Shakers' rules. Some could not. Jessamine wondered how she would feel if her father came into the village. Would she think of him differently than her other brothers? She would not know him even as well. She had no idea how he might look other than having the dark hair he mentioned in the letter. And that had been many years before. His hair could be graying now.

She looked toward the window where the sun was near enough to the horizon that it was elbowing past the clouds to push back the darkness. She wished she had thought to push up the window before she lay back down. The sleeping room was stuffy with her nine other sisters breathing in and out. She tried to match her breaths with Sister Annie who had fallen back to sleep in the bed across from her. In and out. In and out. Easy breathing. Easy thinking. No wondering about things that she shouldn't be wondering about.

She thought of praying. Not for answers, but for peace. For the discontent to leave her so she could go back to being Sister Jessamine with a heart of love for her sisters and no reaching for a love that would divide her forever from her family of Believers.

As she lay there waiting for the sound of the rising bell to release her from bed and allow her to so concentrate on working with her hands that she might be able to forget all else, a prayer did rise up inside her. A prayer with no words but that was filled with all the wonderings of her heart. She would lay it at the Lord's feet. Whatever answer he sent her, she would embrace it with trust.

The storms in the night left the gardens too wet for planting, but since the sun was shining now, she and Sister Edna were sent to the far edge of the pastures where the brethren had discovered the wild raspberries she and Sister Annie had been unable to find in the woods. Sister Edna was not happy with the duty and grumbled of how she would have been allowed to make bonnets or sew aprons if not for Jessamine.

"Instead we are sent out here to work among the snakes and bees," she complained as she reached to pull a berry from the vine. Two other sisters worked alongside them, but none near enough to hear Sister Edna.

"I like picking berries." Jessamine reached for a particularly plump berry and didn't wince when her hand encountered the thorny stems. She turned away from Sister Edna and pretended to put the berry in her bucket but instead sneaked it into her mouth. Then she quickly picked three other berries to drop into her picking pail to make up for the one she ate.

She could feel Sister Edna staring at her, suspecting her of wrongdoing, so she pretended great innocence as she turned back toward her.

"You may be able to hide wrongdoing from me, Sister Jessamine, but be assured you cannot do so from Mother Ann," Sister Edna said crossly as she swatted at a June bug.

"June bugs won't hurt you." Jessamine reached out to capture the bug. It buzzed angrily in her hands, beating its green iridescent wings furiously to be free. She was careful not to hurt it as she opened her hands to let it fly away. Free. How would it feel to be so free? Her mind trailed after the bug as a story began to awaken in her mind. Why was it that she was always dreaming up stories about bugs and animals? Why not people? Why not her sisters? Why not a prince? Her grandmother's stories had almost always had a prince.

"You cannot fill your pail if you are playing with bugs, Sister Jessamine. I would not want to have to report to the Ministry that you were neglectful in your duty this day."

"Nay, I would not like that either. I will work with more diligence."

Jessamine began picking again. To shut away Sister Edna's whining complaints, Jessamine thought of her father's letter. She could shut her eyes and see his flowing handwriting. She could imagine his voice. While a baby, he had talked to her. He had held her close. That memory was stored somewhere in her heart, even if she couldn't pull it forth.

As the morning passed, she let those words, those imagined memories, circle in her mind and managed to barely be aware of Sister Edna beside her. She didn't ignore her. She was careful to nod or murmur a yea whenever it seemed appropriate. She cared not what she might be agreeing to. As long as Sister Edna seemed satisfied. As long as she didn't report to the Ministry that Jessamine was not cooperating. As long as Jessamine could believe the constant supervision might soon be lifted.

By the time they heard the bell calling them in to the midday meal, Jessamine's skirt tail was damp, her hands scratched by many briars, and her fingers stained purple from the berries. But her pail was full and Sister Edna's was not. She wanted to ask who was being neglectful in attending to her duties, but she wisely bit her lip and remained silent. She had been constantly with Sister Edna for four and one half days and it seemed more like four and one half weeks.

But whether it was for days or weeks, what could she do but submit to the Ministry's orders? She knew nothing about what lay outside the village borders except the evil Sister Sophrena said lurked there. And in truth, while the stranger in the woods had not seemed evil, evil had been done to him. There was the gunfire that had so frightened Sister Annie. There was the very real path of a bullet through the man's hair.

Plus Sister Edna would say the man lying to the good doctor and claiming a fake name showed he was on familiar terms with the wickedness of the world. Lying was wrong. Jessamine couldn't deny that. But perhaps he'd had a reason for his untruth. What that could be, she could not imagine as she followed Sister Edna to their eating table. She kept her eyes on her plate and away from Sister Edna as she ate the thick stew and biscuits. The woman seemed to divine when Jessamine was allowing her thoughts to stray into imaginings that were not proper Believers' thoughts. Any thought of Tristan Cooper should be denied. He was the reason she was burdened with Sister Edna's constant companionship.

Nay, if she were honest, it was not he who was the reason, but she herself. Her own tumble from discipline and obedience. He had not sought her out. She had sought him. Enticed by her own wonderings about things she should have closed from her mind.

Sister Edna began complaining as soon as they went out the front door of the Gathering Family House and kept on with her harping all the way down the steps as if the complaints had piled up during the time of silence while they ate and now of necessity must come tumbling out.

"You know there are snakes down under those briars. Perhaps even copperheads. The brothers have seen such snakes in the woods toward the river. And the vines are so thick one can never reach the best berries. You can be assured we will be carrying home ticks and chiggers. No amount of raspberry jam is worth such. Ruining our dresses and aprons and all."

She looked over at Jessamine and went on. "Just look at your sleeves. You've caught them on the briars and pulled holes in them. You really should be more careful, Sister Jessamine. None of the rest of us have torn our sleeves."

"The tear is small," Jessamine said. "I will mend it myself during the quiet time before practice of our songs this evening."

"Nay, Sister. You will need every moment to meditate on your wrong actions then in order to move your spirit closer to the perfect way. Not do mending."

"I've seen Sister Sophrena mend during that time of rest," Jessamine insisted.

"But our good Sister Sophrena does not have the wrong attitudes and behavior to repent of that you do."

"Yea, it is as you say." Jessamine ducked her head.

"It is good that you recognize that truth. You have much to learn, my sister, and I am up to the task of seeing that you learn such."

Jessamine managed to keep her sigh inside. But she was much relieved when she heard Sister Sophrena call her name and hurry after them down the path with purpose.

"Wait up, Sister Edna. I have need to speak to Sister Jessamine." When she reached them, Sister Sophrena put her hands on her chest to catch her breath.

"What can be of such import that you must chase after us?" Sister Edna asked with a slight frown. "What has our sister done now to cause alarm?"

"Nay, nay, there have been no wrongs done." Sister Sophrena was still panting a bit as her eyes shifted from Sister Edna to Jessamine. She suddenly looked worried. "Eldress Frieda asked me to find you, Sister Jessamine. She says you have a visitor."

"From the world?" Jessamine did not try to hide her surprise. "But I know no one from the world other than the man I found in the woods. Tristan Cooper."

Sister Edna stared at Jessamine. "You should not even speak his name much less think the Ministry would allow him to visit after the lies he told."

"I agree, Sister Edna, so I am sure that it is not he," Sister Sophrena said. "But I do not know who it might be. All I know is that Eldress Frieda has summoned you and so you must go. If you do not want to see whoever awaits you at the Trustee's House, you can tell her and she will send your visitor away. You have that freedom, my sister."

Freedom. The word sounded strange to her ears with her wish for it all through the week while tied to Sister Edna. She had felt no breath of freedom.

"Come." Sister Sophrena held out her hand toward Jessamine. "The berries will wait."

Eldress Frieda was waiting for them inside the door at the Trustee's House. She wore the same worried frown that had settled on Sister Sophrena's face as they walked back through the village to meet her. Behind her the twin staircases rose up toward the upper floors with a graceful beauty that usually made Jessamine want to run up their winding steps with the feeling of climbing on air. But now she barely glanced at them. She had no curiosity about anything but the visitor who awaited her. If not Tristan Cooper, who? The prince who loved her mother? The father from her letter? Had she thought so intensely about his words that she had somehow been able to draw him across space and time to her?

Eldress Frieda looked from Sister Sophrena to Jessamine. "Did Sister Sophrena tell you that you do not have to see the visitor? There is upset enough in your way right now. You might be wise not to open yourself up to more disconcert."

"Yea, Eldress, you may be right, but my wondering would be so great about who seeks me here and why, that I would have no peace. If you thought I should not meet with whomever awaits, you should not have called me." She had to restrain her desire to peek past the eldress toward the room that opened off the hallway where a visitor might wait.

"Nay, my sister. We are apart from the world, but we do not prohibit visitors if they demonstrate no ill intent for our brethren or sisters. We are free by choice here."

Jessamine felt the eyes of the three sisters on her. Sister Edna would be looking with condemnation, but Sister Sophrena and Eldress Frieda would be looking with loving concern. Even so, she knew only one choice. If she was free to make it, she would. "I will see my visitor."

Eldress Frieda shut her eyes for a moment as she breathed in and out slowly. Jessamine could almost feel her unspoken prayers. When she opened her eyes, she said, "Very well, my sister. Follow me."

When both Sister Sophrena and Sister Edna started to walk behind them, the eldress turned to them. "You must wait here. The air is close in the small meeting room in the heat of the day. We would not want to crowd the room and make our visitor overly uncomfortable. I will be with our sister if she needs support."

The two of them walked on between the stairways rising to the upper floors. Wondrously and magically clinging to the sides of the wall with the handrails curling down through the air. But Jessamine didn't need the stairs to awaken her wonder now. It was already racing through her as to who might be waiting for her. The eldress opened a door and led the way into the small room.

"Our sister has agreed to see you, Mr. Brady." Eldress Frieda stepped to the side to allow Jessamine to see the man waiting for her.

He stood up and let his eyes sweep over her from her head to her toes and back again. His voice when he spoke was not much more than a whisper. "My Jessamine." Tears began to stream down his cheeks. He made no move to wipe them away nor did he show any sign of embarrassment because of his weeping. "You are even more beautiful than I imagined."

And Jessamine knew without anyone saying the words that this was the prince who had loved her mother. She brushed off Eldress Frieda's hand when she tried to stop her and walked straight across the room into her father's arms.

Journal Entry

Harmony Hill Village
Entered on this 21st day of June in the year 1849
by Sister Sophrena Prescott

There is much sorrow in our hearts this evening.
Yet another of our novitiate sisters has left our
village for the world. The other sister running toward
the world was not unexpected, but for our Sister
Jessamine to choose to leave us so quickly with no
more than a few tears and a slightly regretful look
back was much harder to bear or understand.

Perhaps we were wrong to have let her read the
letter. Perhaps that is what made her embrace the
man who was her father from the world with—
Eldress Frieda reports—no hesitation as if she had
known him forever instead of having no memory of
him at all. As she could not. But she reached for him
with eagerness. I fear we may have pushed her from
us by the order of constant supervision. These last
few days she has seemed to be struggling to hold
onto the joy of her spirit. But the Ministry knows best.
As Eldress Frieda says, if our sisters are tempted by
the world, then there is very little we can do to keep

them from running toward sin. We can only pray their journey out into the world will be short-lived and they will see the error of their way and return to us. If that happens with our Sister Jessamine, we will hold our arms out to welcome her home. She will have to make confession of her sins, but she will be restored to us as a loved and loving sister.

Eldress Frieda was attempting to comfort me for she saw how watching our former sister walk away and climb into the carriage with her father of the world was grieving me. But Sister Edna had no pity in her heart. For our former sister or for me. She was quite vocal in proclaiming how she knew the sister's waywardness would land her feet in a miry pit of sin. She kept saying to anyone who would listen how it was plain to be seen that when one stepped on the slippery slope of disobedience and sin, then one could expect to be overcome by disasters. Disasters of one's own making. Sister Edna looked very smug as she predicted various disasters. It was wrong of me to point out how she had been with her every minute for over four days and so it would seem she should have been able to encourage the sister to alter her path to destruction.

I will have to confess my sin of unkind words and for laying fault at another's feet when the fault should be laid at mine. For although Sister Edna had been with her for days, I had been guiding our sister for years. Many times over the years I have questioned in my mind what to do with our former sister. I did not labor hard enough or pray strongly enough to find the proper answer to help her see that life here is the better life. Why could I not get her to believe the love of her sisters and brothers would be strong enough to carry her through any trouble? Nay, not only believe, but to be so sure as to not let any worldly temptation lessen that love.

I shed tears as I followed her out of the house and down the steps. She turned back to me before she let her father of the world hand her up into the carriage. Tears filled her eyes as well when she clasped my hands. Behind us, Sister Edna was stomping and shouting woe as she pushed the sins and evil temptations of the world from her. Other sisters and brothers came from the house to do the same. Their noise seemed far away as I looked into my sister's eyes and asked her if she was sure this was what she should do.

Yea, she told me, looking very sorrowful but determined as she insisted she must go with the father who loves her. Those were her very words. "The father who loves me."

I reminded her of how such worldly love would do naught but disappoint her as I clutched her hands tightly. I spoke of how she was surrounded by love here and of how her salvation would be assured.

She brushed aside my words, claiming the Lord was with her before she came to live among us and that he would go with her from the village.

Then my sorrow increased because I knew she was not going to listen, but I pushed the truth toward her of how sin would separate her from the Lord and from us here, her beloved sisters and brothers. From me.

Our former sister's voice was very soft as she said she did love me, but that her heart desired a different kind of love. I knew she did not only mean the love of her worldly father. So I closed my eyes

and let my heart pray for her then. Without words,
for I knew not what words would be acceptable.
I have lived in the world, but I have never known
the sort of love her heart was seeking. That love that
brings strife and conflict.

This night I must confess there is conflict in my
heart as I sorrow her leaving. Eldress Frieda is right.
I sinned to allow our former sister to take up such a
large place of residence in my heart. I sinned.

I must remember Mother Ann's instructions to
labor to make the way of God my own. Let that be
my inheritance, my treasure, my occupation, my
daily calling.

On the morrow I will return to weaving bonnets.
On the morrow I will work with my hands and
honor God with my labor. I will look toward the
day of meeting and the joy of exercising the songs.
I will whirl the sin from my heart and seek the way
of God. And I will pray in my heart that all my sisters
do the same. Especially my former sister whom I
loved too much.

22

They went to the town first. Jessamine knew about towns and cities. Her granny had told her stories of exotic sounding cities across the ocean. Places where real princes lived. At the Shaker village, she'd seen maps in the schoolroom and had imagined how the towns indicated by those black dots might look. But since she had come straight from her granny's woods to the Shaker village, she had never actually been in a town.

One could encounter evil in towns. She did know that much, for it took much work and vigilance to keep Satan from the borders at Harmony Hill. So there was little doubt the old devil slipped around undetected in the towns, lying in wait for the unguarded.

That's how Jessamine felt as they rode into the town of Harrodsburg. Unguarded. Exposed to whatever evil might be lurking in the shadows. She thought it might be best if she kept her eyes downcast as she sat silent by her father, but she could not. Instead she grasped the edge of the carriage seat and leaned forward to take in every new sight. She eagerly read the signs on the stores crowded side by side close to the street. She had never thought to imagine the stores without yards like those surrounding their buildings in the village.

And the people. She could hardly believe what she saw. Men stood talking together or taking their ease on benches along the street as if they had no duties for the day. The women appeared to move with more purpose as they went in and out of the stores. Some wore bonnets but others had on jaunty hats. A few had no head covering at all. Their full skirts of figured material were held out in sweeping circles with what had to be an overabundance of petticoats. Most surprising of all, some of the men and women walked side by side with the men's hands under the women's elbow. Touching. Comfortable. With no sign of worry that sin might overtake them for practicing such familiarity.

Jessamine reminded herself she was no longer in Harmony Hill. If nothing else proved that, the commotion in the street did. In Harmony Hill there was noise, of a surety, but it was the sound of commerce. Tasks being done. Hammers pounding. Brooms sweeping. Kettles rattling. Oxen yokes creaking. At Harmony Hill she would never hear shouts for no cause other than to yell a greeting to someone across the street or see dogs barking at the carriage wheels.

"If you could only see your face, Jessamine. I don't believe your eyes can get any wider." Her father smiled over at her.

She sat back and lowered her gaze. He would think she had no knowledge of proper behavior. "Forgive me. I suppose I am too eager, but I have never before seen a town. At least none other than our Shaker village town."

He touched her arms softly. "Please, look. I am enjoying seeing the town afresh through your eyes. Although I can't imagine there's much to see in this little burg. Wait until you see the likes of New York City."

"Do you have a house there? Or here?" She had not once

considered where they might live. She had simply taken her father's hand and trusted him to show her the world.

"I have no house anywhere, but never fear, there are many places where a man and his daughter might reside," he said. "Places, I daresay, more accommodating than that where you have spent the last decade of your life. The eldress told me a preacher brought you to them when you were less than ten years old."

"He thought it best. He promised they would be good to me. And that I could go to school. Granny had taught me to read and write already, but he said there were many other things to learn. Things I could not learn living alone in the woods the way I wanted to do. I didn't want to leave Granny."

"But the eldress said Granny had passed on before you came to them." He frowned a little as he looked toward her.

"Yea, but I thought to tend her grave. I was very young and had little understanding of what it took to live, but the old preacher told me I couldn't stay in the woods. He was sorry for me, but he said winter would come and the snows and I would freeze or starve." She breathed out a small sigh. "I know now he was surely right. The Shakers took me in as a sister and did all the preacher promised they would do. I missed Granny and my trees, but the Shakers were exceedingly kind to me. They showed me much love."

Her heart still hurt at the sight of Sister Sophrena's tears when they spoke words in farewell. She understood her sister's worry. She shared some of that worry about the world. But how could she not go with her father? It seemed meant to be. First the letter and then him appearing in front of her eyes. Nay, more than appearing. Holding his arms out to her. Claiming her as his daughter. To Sister Sophrena, to the Believers, that was a worldly feeling to be shunned. But to her, it was a gift straight from the Lord in answer to prayers she hadn't even known to pray.

"Are you regretting your decision to come away with me?" He sounded concerned.

"Nay." She looked up at him. "I have ever wondered about the world. It has been a thorn in the flesh of dear Sister Sophrena for many years. My wondering and imagining about things I did not know. And in truth, I have fallen from grace among them many times. No times as badly as the last few days." She blinked to keep back tears. "Now I suppose I have fallen forever from their graces."

"If they truly care for you, they won't stop loving you simply because you are no longer one of their group."

She didn't answer because that would be exactly what happened. They, or at least Sister Sophrena and perhaps Sister Annie, might not stop caring about her, but they would consider her completely lost with no hope for redemption. They would not talk about her except to mourn her choice. Unless she turned from the world and went back among them. Sister Sophrena had held out that possibility to Jessamine.

"You can return, my sister. We will be here for you now as we were when you were but a child," she had whispered into Jessamine's ear.

Her father's voice brought her back to the present. "This looks to be the place."

He stopped the carriage in front of a house with a small sign in the window advertising dressmaking. When her father climbed down from the carriage, she had to grab the seat as the carriage bounced down and then leveled again. She had imagined riding in a carriage, but she had never imagined such bounces.

So much she didn't know. All at once she wanted to ask a dozen questions about where they would live and how long it would take to get there and why hadn't he come before. She bit the inside of her lip and held the questions in.

After he tied the horse to a hitching post in front of the

house, he held his hand up to her. "Come, my daughter. You can't go to White Oak Springs in a Shaker frock."

White Oak Springs. The place she had been so curious about the day she and Sister Annie were in the woods. The day they had heard the gunfire and found the stranger. Could he really be taking her there? And would Tristan Cooper be there? And what about Sister Abigail? It all seemed too impossible to believe. Perhaps she was merely dreaming it all.

She took a deep breath and smelled the horse's lather. She felt her father's hand holding hers. A man's hand in hers. Strong and capable but with slender fingers that did not show the calluses of labor she'd noted on the hands of her Shaker brothers when they held them up during the exercising of the dances. Of course, she'd never touched them. But she was touching her father's hand now. She was not dreaming. Her father was real.

He smiled at her as she climbed down out of the carriage. She had yet to call him by any name. She feared Father would sit oddly on her tongue even though she had welcomed him as such the moment he spoke her name at the Trustee's House. Nor did it seem right to speak aloud the name the eldress had used. Mr. Brady. All her life, she had thought of her father as the prince who loved her mother. The name her granny gave him. Jessamine could hardly call him that without him thinking the Believers had bent her mind in some unusual way when actually, it was her own unusual bending Sister Sophrena had done her best to unbend.

Edwina Browning met them at the door and ushered them into the house with quick movements that belied the thickness of her waist. Garments hung all about the walls in varying stages of completion. So many wonderful colors that Jessamine felt she was standing in the midst of a rainbow while her father talked to the woman about what she needed.

The woman eyed Jessamine and took in her dress and apron. "So you got smart enough to shake loose from those Shakers." She laughed, pleased with her own wit.

Jessamine's lips turned up in an uncertain smile that brought even more amusement to the woman's eyes.

"A real innocent, aren't you, dearie?" the woman said. "How long you been out there with those people?"

"Ten years," Jessamine said.

"Way too long. Time to shed that bonnet." She reached up and jerked off Jessamine's cap. "Look at that hair and those eyes. I've got the very piece of goods to make a fine dress that will get you plenty of notice. You'll catch a man quick as anything."

"That is not one of my concerns." Jessamine shot a look toward her father who had backed up to stand near the door as if needing an avenue of escape from so many articles of feminine clothing.

His smile was sympathetic, but he didn't appear upset by the woman's words. Perhaps in the world, such talk was common.

The woman tapped a fingertip covered with a silver thimble on Jessamine's cheek. "Your mouth says one thing, but I'm thinking those eyes will be saying something else soon enough. Especially after the gentlemen at the Springs see you in that dress I've got in mind to fashion for you. The midseason ball will be next week, but it could be I might be able to work it up in time. For a price." Mrs. Browning shot a look over at Jessamine's father.

"Any price for my daughter," he said. "But she needs some things ready to wear now. Perhaps two or three day frocks as well as something for the evening."

She narrowed her eyes on Jessamine again as she pursed her lips. Then without asking permission, she circled her hands around Jessamine's waist. "This slender with no corset. I should be so fortunate." She looked straight at Jessamine. "Do you ever wear a corset?"

Jessamine blushed. She knew a corset was an undergarment. She'd heard some of the sisters speak of their torture, as they told of how to be a true lady in the world, one had to wear the undergarment laced so tightly it was hard to draw breath.

"Nay." She stared down at the floor. Surely even in the world it wasn't proper to speak of underclothing with a man present.

The woman laughed and so did her father but with no sound of meanness. "Mrs. Browning, you're embarrassing my daughter. She is not very acquainted with the ways of the world, so I must ask you to be gentle with her."

"Right enough, sir. I'll watch my tongue." Mrs. Browning peered over at him. "Why don't you leave us alone to do the fittings? Me and your Jessamine will get along just fine."

He pushed away from the wall he was leaning against. "Very well. I'll trust her to you then while I see to my horse." He stopped and looked back before going out the door. "I'll pay double your price for anything she can carry away with her today."

After the door shut behind him, Mrs. Browning said, "Now aren't you the lucky one to have such a generous father? But how does it happen you were with those Shakers if that is true?"

"He knew not where I was," Jessamine said.

"Well, that I can understand. Those people hide away their women out there like as how they're doing something they're fearing regular folk to know about. Is that true? I mean, I've heard all manner of tales. For instance, do those old preacher men call on a different girl every night for their entertainment?" The woman winked at her. "If you know what I mean."

Jessamine did not know her meaning, but it was not hard

to guess her thoughts were of some sort of improper behavior. "Nay, our elders would never do anything to harm us," she said quickly.

"Nothing but keep you locked up away from the normal way of living. God's way or else he wouldn't have talked so much about begetting in the good book. How do your people get around that?"

"If you speak of marrying, there are many stories in the Scripture to demonstrate the sorrows one opens up one's spirit to with worldly love."

"Sounds like they got you believing their way." Edwina pulled a long cord out of her pocket and wrapped it around Jessamine's waist. Then she slipped it up under Jessamine's armpits. "Just a little measuring here. Don't get alarmed. I won't be hurting you. Just raise your arms a little."

Jessamine did as she was told. She was accustomed to obedience when the order was given with authority.

The woman slipped the cord off, holding her finger and thumb on a measuring place. She held the string from where she'd measured and found a piece of paper to jot down some numbers. "But what about babies? It seems to me it would be a sad old world without any sweet tiny babes. What about them?"

"There are children in the village," Jessamine said.

"Children with no loving mother watching out for them. The very thought of it makes my eyes prickly with tears, and I've heard tell the Shaker way of breaking apart families drives some of the females out there to madness." She stepped back to study Jessamine's shape. "As it would. Nothing natural about separating a mother and her children. Even wolves don't do that."

"The Shaker sisters loved me," Jessamine said. "Like a mother would."

"Oh, I ain't meaning to bad-mouth them to you." She

handed one end of the cord to Jessamine. "Hold that at your waist, dearie, so's I can see how long to make your skirt." Then as she bent down to the floor, she went on. "What with you not knowing any better all these years shut up there with them like that. But now you just let your sweet papa introduce you to the better way of the world. The natural way. The Lord intended there to be babies. He designed us to hanker after the loving between a man and a woman."

She straightened up and wrote more numbers on her paper. "You keep that in mind when you're out there at that White Oak Springs. Romance is ever in the air at the Springs and romance is just what old Edwina is ordering for you. And we're going to find you something to get that romantic air a stirring round about you."

More than an hour later, Jessamine went back out the dressmaker's door a different person than the one who had climbed down from the carriage with her father. She'd shed her Shaker clothes like a hen molting old feathers. She had on her new feathers, a rose-colored gingham dress with a square neckline trimmed in lace that showed a shocking amount of skin. Mrs. Browning claimed it very modest, but without the Shaker collar wrapped around her, Jessamine wanted to cross her arms over her chest to hide her exposed skin and the way the dress molded around her breasts.

Mrs. Browning had wanted to lace a corset around Jessamine's middle to make her waist fashionably slender, but Jessamine could not imagine wearing the thing with its stiff rods the woman claimed were bones from a whale.

"I don't believe I will need to be so fashionable," she told the dressmaker firmly.

Even with a mouth brimming with pins, Mrs. Browning had managed to cluck her tongue with some disapproval at Jessamine. She pulled the pins out to say, "You can get by in a day dress, but you will need the corset laced for the ball gown. Your waist is small, barely over twenty, but sixteen is so much more desirable for the ladies and would be easily managed for you."

Jessamine put her hands on her waist and stared at the corset hanging on a hook on the dressing room wall. "How would there be room for nourishment? Or breathing."

"You do have much to learn, dearie. A lady takes tiny bites and flutters her fan to push air to her nose." She laughed as she smoothed her hands down over her own generous waist. "Plenty are the times when I've been relieved not to be one of the fine ladies. I would have had to push away my plate much more than I have."

"I have never aspired to be a lady," Jessamine told the woman. But then she remembered her granny telling her to wait for her prince to come. A prince would expect a lady at the very least. It was all enough to make her head spin.

"Perhaps not, but I would not be surprised if your gentleman father may have different aspirations for you."

And so when she emerged from the dressmaker's house in her new dress over three starched petticoats and wearing a bonnet with a matching rose-colored ribbon and a fake silken rose, he did seem pleased with the change. Even her feet had been freed from the sturdy Shaker shoes and now wore shoes that would be of no use whatsoever in the garden or berry picking. Both evidently things a lady would not consider doing at any rate.

Mrs. Browning had declared Jessaminie's berry-stained fingernails and scratched hands a shameful blemish and insisted Jessamine don white gloves. It felt silly to wear gloves with the sun beating down on her head, but Mrs. Browning assured her such wasn't uncommon for ladies.

"You'll be gardening the soil of hearts now, dearie. And I'll wager you'll bring in a good harvest," Mrs. Browning said before she packed up three other dresses for Jessamine. One evening frock of silky lavender and two more dresses much like the one she was wearing. She had made the dresses for a girl who had failed to get her father to pay for them.

She picked up the Shaker dress and apron. "Sturdy cloth, this. I suppose I could cut it apart for a child's dress if you want to leave it with me."

"Nay," Jessamine said quickly. "I'll take it with me. I may have the opportunity to send it back to Harmony Hill for use by one of the other sisters. It is not good to be wasteful."

Mrs. Browning shook her head with a little chuckle. "Would that I could be one of the pins in your hair this evening to witness your introduction to the Springs. I do hope your father can find a lady's maid to help you dress and fix your hair."

Jessamine touched her hair. She was beginning to understand that the things she had wondered about the world were only a tiny drop in a perplexing sea of wonders.

The woman seemed quite pleased with the bills Jessamine's father handed over to her before she stashed them in a hidden pocket. Then as if noticing the sun beating down on her own uncovered head, she said, "Wait. One thing more is absolutely necessary. With those lovely blonde waves, our young lady should not have to wear a bonnet every minute at the Springs. But we must keep the sun off her nose. Freckles aren't at all to be desired."

As she rushed back into her shop, Jessamine's father laughed. "She's turned you into quite the young lady, but I can see you are more than bewildered by it all. Never fear, my beautiful daughter, you will enchant everyone you meet, just as you have Mrs. Browning."

In all her wondering about things of the world, she had never once thought to wonder what the world would think of her. That was because she never thought to actually be part of the world. Now here she was wearing a dress with ruffles and a bonnet festooned with ribbons. She wasn't sure how she could have lost the gift to be simple so completely, so quickly.

She smoothed her hand down over her skirt and thought of the petticoats under it. Even they had ruffles and lace. Such had to be sinful vanity, for what purpose could ruffles on a petticoat have? For that matter, what purpose could there be in wearing so many layers of petticoats that they sprang up in the way as she climbed into the carriage? She had to shove them down with energy to keep them in the seat.

She could only too well imagine Sister Sophrena's disapproving look and Sister Edna's harsh words of condemnation. And yet, even while she worried about sinful vanity, she did like the swish of the petticoats against her legs. She liked the way the lace on the bottom of her sleeves looked against her skin. She was surely being enticed by the devil to embrace so many worldly things with no resistance.

But Mrs. Browning didn't seem to have any of the devil in her. Nor did her father. They thought these clothes natural and normal. But would she ever feel the same? Perhaps it would be better for her to be at Harmony Hill, listening for the bell to signal the evening meal. Perhaps it would be better for her to continue to wonder about things of the world instead of experiencing them. If only the Lord would send her a sign, give her a message.

At that moment, Mrs. Browning came bustling back out of her front door. "A parasol, dearie." She pushed up on the rod she was carrying and blue material popped up. She twirled it a bit before closing it down and handing it up to Jessamine. "You will definitely have need of a parasol as you stroll around the lake at the Springs."

Jessamine took it and ran her fingers over it. "A parasol," she whispered, remembering leading Sister Annie through the woods in a vain quest to see this very thing of the world.

And now she held one in her hands. Now she was on her way to the Springs where perhaps she would see the stranger she had found in the woods that day. Her hands tightened on the parasol as her father flicked the reins to start the horse walking. She had asked for a sign, but how could she be sure the sign had come from the Lord?

23

Thursday afternoon Tristan once again watched Laura toss bread crumbs to the ducks as they strolled around the lake. They were more at ease with one another as if things had been, if not settled between them, at least begun. When they started toward a bench in the shade of a tall oak tree, he reached for her hand. He thought he should make some attempt at romance.

Her eyebrows lifted a bit as she looked down at his hand grasping hers, but she didn't pull away. Instead she said, "I daresay it's past time we talked about this, don't you?"

"You're a beautiful woman," he began.

She cut him off with a wave of the fan she held in her free hand. "We can dispense with the sweet words, Tristan. We both know why you took hold of my hand. My father and your mother. They've determined we make a good match. The Cleveland money. The Cooper name."

He didn't know what to say. He'd never been around a lady who spoke so plainly.

"I've shocked you." She whispered a sigh as she gently freed her hand from his and gingerly perched on the edge of the bench. After he sat down beside her, she peered over at his face intently and went on. "But don't you think it better to be at least somewhat honest if we are to form this required partnership?"

Tristan leaned back and considered his words carefully before he spoke. "I don't know that I would consider it a partnership exactly."

"But that is exactly what it would be. I'm not a shrinking violet of a girl as many see my mother. That's how you see her, isn't it? As completely overpowered by my father."

"She does seem somewhat reserved."

Laura laughed. "You are delightfully polite, Tristan. But right now the truth would tickle my ears much more than polite nonsense. In fact, my mother is a very determined woman. That is why it is so difficult for her when she is in company with my father and why we maintain a second residence in Boston to, as she says, keep her sane. What seems like nervous worry to those who do not know her is actually often pent-up irritation. She, like you, my good sir, feels the need to be socially correct and polite, but I will not be one whit surprised if she stands up in the dining room and lets everybody there know exactly what she thinks before we leave the Springs."

"About what?"

"About the servants. You are aware that many of them are slaves, aren't you? Purchased to do the bidding of Mr. Hargrove. Even the band that plays so charmingly. Slaves with no freedom. My mother comes from a long line of Boston abolitionists." She looked straight at him again. "I told Father that might be a problem in the merging of our families, since I'm sure you are accustomed to slaves attending your every whim. Of course, Father would be jubilant if he could make everyone his slave. He does expect to get his way. You should be forewarned of that."

"I am not always polite," Tristan said.

She blew out a long breath. "I'm relieved to hear it, but even so, my father can be difficult."

Tristan studied Laura as he considered his position. She looked lovely in a yellow striped dress with matching roses woven into her dark hair. He thought back through the days since they'd been introduced and couldn't remember seeing her in the same dress twice. Whatever she was saying about her father, it was obvious she wanted for nothing. Tristan could not possibly supply her with the same unless the father surrendered some of his fortune to them. He moved uncomfortably on the bench. If they married, Tristan would never be his own man again. He'd be bought and paid for. A name for his daughter.

"He seems to give you whatever you want," Tristan said.

"Things are not always as they seem," she said softly as she turned her eyes from him to stare out toward the lake. Her shoulders drooped and the smile slipped away from her face. "The thing I want most I cannot have."

She sounded so sad. He might not be moved with love for her, but that didn't mean he couldn't be moved by her obvious unhappiness. "And what is it that you cannot have?"

"Some things are better left unspoken." She shifted her gaze to her hands grasping the fan in her lap.

"I thought we had dispensed with politeness and were being brutally honest with one another."

"I don't know about brutally," she said. "But honest might be a good way to begin our relationship since a relationship we do seem to be fated to have."

"So tell me what you want that you cannot have."

She hesitated as color rose in her cheeks. Then she lifted her chin and stared straight at him. "The love of my heart."

"You love someone else?" Tristan didn't know why he was surprised. Wasn't he haunted by another as well? A girl he barely knew. He barely knew Laura either. She had to be near twenty. Plenty time enough to meet and fall in love with a man deemed unsuitable by her father. There was no doubt the blue-eyed beauty whose face would not fade from his memory would be considered more than unsuitable by his mother.

"If we are to start on an honest plain, I might as well admit the truth of that." She fluttered her fan in front of her face a moment before she dropped it to her lap and reached over to touch his arm. "You are very nice, Tristan. I like you. But this man, well, he is different. He took my heart practically from the first word I heard him speak. I met him long before I met you. I hope you aren't troubled by that."

"But he's unsuitable."

"My father would surely think so."

"You've never told your father you love this man?"

She sighed and picked up her fan again. She twirled it open and waved air toward her face. "As I said before, some things are better left unsaid. I know my father. He would never accept this man. Not only that, but he might do something to ruin him. That I could not bear."

Tristan took a considering breath and was silent for a moment before he said, "We don't have to do as our parents order. I will tell my mother we will have to find another way to keep her house in Atlanta."

"No, you mustn't do that." The color drained from her face as she grasped his sleeve.

"I don't understand." He looked at her with puzzlement.

She let go of his sleeve and shut her eyes a moment as she struggled to get her emotions under control. "You are not the only man who desires to marry me." A blush rose back into her cheeks as she began to fan her face furiously. "I mean that your mother wants to pair me with. I suppose I am being forward mentioning marriage when we've only talked of arrangements and plans."

"Marriage was implied," Tristan said. "But I still don't

understand why you can't tell your father you won't marry me if the idea is not one you favor."

"Calvin Green, that's why."

"I saw you dancing with him."

"The man is a cad." A frown chased across her face. "An absolute cad. He thinks he can finagle a way to force me to marry him. He fancied himself the frontrunner with my father until your mother came on the scene last summer with stories of her heroic son fighting for his country. And Father knew of the Whitley buggies. Father is harsh and often overbearing, but he does know business. If he thinks the buggy business will succeed under his tutelage, you can be assured the buggy business will succeed and your fortune will be restored."

"And everybody lives happily ever after," Tristan said drily.

She shifted on the bench, discomfited by his words. "Perhaps not totally happily, but certainly happier than I could ever be with Calvin Green. He makes my skin crawl."

"I can't believe your father would insist you marry a man repulsive to you."

"Father thinks love can be ordered up like three-minute eggs for breakfast." Her lips turned down with disgust at the thought.

"And you prefer something a bit more romantic," Tristan suggested. "What girl wouldn't."

"What I do not prefer is Calvin Green. I want to shrink away from his eyes every time he looks toward me. There is something . . . I don't know what. My mother says a woman has a sixth sense about some things." She shuddered and wrapped her arms around herself.

"And does your mother want you to marry for position or convenience?"

"Oh no." Laura pulled in a deep breath and began fanning herself again. "My mother claims such is overrated. That even money is overrated, although she enjoys all the benefits of my father's Midas touch with business. She abhors the south and would love nothing better than moving back to Boston permanently. Father thinks once we can make a climb in Georgia society, all will be well, but at times Father can be rather dense when it comes to personal affairs. Or to Mother."

"So you consider me to be the least abhorrent choice among those available." Honesty was freeing to the tongue.

She peered at him over the top of her fan, her eyes suddenly amused. "As I would hope you might consider me the better choice among those your mother might pick. I've been told I am attractive."

When he didn't jump in on cue to assure her that indeed she was very attractive, she folded up her fan and lightly tapped his arm with it. She twisted her mouth to the side to hide her smile. "Perhaps it would be better if you didn't abandon all your gentlemanly politeness. Even in a business deal, a smattering of flattery is not a bad thing."

"Do forgive me, Laura. You are very much better than merely attractive. You are quite lovely, and much the best choice my mother could have made."

"Good. Then it's done. You will propose in a gallantly romantic way in the gardens. Perhaps at the midsummer's ball next week. I will accept with shy gladness." She stood up and he rose quickly as a gentleman should. "If we cannot have love, friendship is the next best thing."

"But why can't we have love?" Tristan asked suddenly.

"Because my father is wrong. Love can't be ordered up. It is a serendipitous thing with wings that swoops here and there and sometimes lands on you when you least expect it. Or when you can ill afford to follow your heart." She looked away out across the lake and beyond. "But oh, how you desire to do so."

He followed her gaze and felt an answering longing rise inside him. To follow wherever love beckoned him. Whether back through a Shaker village or on an unknown as yet pathway. But instead duty to his mother, duty to his family name, kept his feet on this path.

Beside him, Laura let out a sad chuckle. "You're wishing you could follow your heart too. Who is it? The beautiful Shaker girl. Did she steal your heart so quickly?"

"No." He smiled to allay her suspicions. "I only talked to her twice. It would take more than that to know love."

"Perhaps," Laura murmured. "Perhaps not."

"Either way, I'll never see her again, so it little matters."

She was silent as they started back toward the hotel. It was easy walking with her with no pretensions between them.

He looked at her, lovely in the sunshine with purpose written on her face as though she had figured out a satisfactory answer to a dilemma. He couldn't keep from wondering if she had considered all the hidden angles. One he thought well to push toward her. "They will want children. We will want children."

"Yes. Yes, of course," she murmured as she stared down at the ground and kept walking. Her voice was too soft, nothing like her assured tone of moments ago. "But not tomorrow. There will be a time of engagement. Why don't we consider the, uh, potential awkwardness of producing children on another day?"

He wished his words back. Everyone knew young belles such as Laura led sheltered lives and knew little of the expectations of married life. She was right. It would be better to take things one step at a time. He hadn't even officially proposed yet. The deal had been made between them. More telling, it had been made between his mother and her father days ago, if not months before he and Laura had even met. There was no going back. No changing things. Love would have to wait. Perhaps forever.

His mother was jubilant when he reported progress had

been made in regard to his and Laura's relationship and a proposal was in the offing. She laughed out loud, something he hadn't heard her do in a natural way since he'd returned home after his father's death. Then she actually gave him a hug or as much of a hug as his bandaged arm would allow.

"Oh, Tristan, I knew you would captivate her with your charm. The two of you make such a lovely couple. I saw you strolling around the lake today. Perfectly matched. Absolutely perfectly matched."

"We're not a team of horses you're purchasing for your carriage, Mother."

Her smile disappeared as her eyes narrowed on him. "Don't be vulgar, Tristan."

"That's how business deals can be at times," he said bluntly.

"Honestly, you're trying to make this all sound so, so . . ." She searched for the right word.

"Arranged?" Tristan suggested with raised eyebrows.

"Perhaps, but all for your own good." She pretended not to see his irritation as she turned to the mirror to give her hair one last pat. "But speaking of arrangements, Mr. Ridenour arrived at the Springs today with paperwork to be signed."

"Mr. Ridenour?"

She met his eyes in the mirror. "Our lawyer. Please do try to pay at least a bit of attention to the necessary information about running our business. He will be dining at our table tonight. He is quite anxious to meet Laura."

"He probably wants to marry her too," Tristan said, his voice dry. "Everybody wants to marry Laura."

"Don't be foolish. Jackson is at least as old as I am."

"Jackson?" Tristan smiled widely. "So it's Jackson."

His mother actually blushed. "Now there's not the least need in you thinking up something that isn't true. Jackson is merely a dear friend. He was very helpful when your father passed away." She wiped away a convenient tear before she tapped his chest with her index finger. "I do expect you to be civil to him."

"When have I ever not been civil, Mother?"

"I know. You are a good son." She gave his cheek a pat before she picked up her gloves. "I hear there will be another surprise guest at our table. The rumor is going around about our writer—Mr. Brady—that he has brought a guest. I'm surprised Laura didn't tell you about it this afternoon. Mr. Brady seems to be an old friend of the family."

"He probably wants to marry Laura too." Tristan intended it to be a joke, but then he remembered the smoothness of their dance the evening before.

"For goodness' sake, Tristan, stop worrying about everybody else who wants to marry Laura. She is most desirable, but you are the one she is going to marry." She smiled up at him, obviously very pleased.

A few minutes later they were seated at the dining table, thankfully minus Mr. and Mrs. Floyd. Jackson Ridenour had taken one of their places. He was a tall, slim man with a face that looked more familiar with frowns than smiles, but the smile won out when he held the chair for Tristan's mother. Tristan wasn't sure whether it was his news of progress with Laura or the lawyer's attentiveness, but whatever the reason, it had been years since he'd seen his mother so animated.

Sheldon Brady was late to the table once more and the salads had been served before he appeared with his surprise guest in tow. All the way across the dining area, heads turned to watch them—the writer and the beautiful girl in the lilac gown with her blonde hair caught up on her head in a careless twist. She seemed to have no awareness of her beauty as she watched everything around her, her eyes gobbling it all up, embracing the newness of it.

He knew her at once. But at the same time he wasn't sure he could believe his eyes. The beautiful sister from the Shaker village. The sister whose blue eyes had stolen his heart. Jessamine. He'd thought never to see her again, and now he was standing up along with the other men at their table as Sheldon Brady presented her to them.

"Ladies and gentlemen, I'd like to present my daughter, Jessamine."

The young woman kept her eyes on Brady as he pulled back her chair to help her be seated. Color rose in her cheeks as she hesitated as though unsure of what to do before she gingerly sat down and stared down at her hands. Tristan and the other men settled back in their chairs too.

For a moment their table was an oasis of silence in the noisy dining room. Tristan willed the girl to look up at him, but when she didn't, he took a quick glance around the table in hopes one of the ladies might break the uneasy silence. Laura had a smile spread across her face that looked a shade too polite to be sincere. Tristan's mother made no effort to smile, politely or otherwise. Instead she looked as if she might have just swallowed something unpleasant as she touched her handkerchief to her lips. Viola Cleveland was watching the girl intently, but Tristan had no confidence she would speak up in spite of what Laura had told him that day out by the lake. He expected her to start fiddling with her silverware or napkin at any moment. Robert Cleveland, on the other hand, had only a passing acquaintance with politeness. He leaned forward to stare at Jessamine, who kept her gaze demurely downcast. Tristan thought she might be praying.

He searched for acceptable words to fill the silence before Cleveland could spout something brash, but it was Viola Cleveland who spoke first. "Good heavens, Tristan. You were right. She is exquisite."

"Tristan?" The girl looked up and straight across the table at him as a smile lit up her face. "It is you. I did so hope I would see you again, and here you are."

"Yes, here I am." Their eyes met and all he could think about was the last time he'd looked into her beautiful eyes in the Shaker doctor's garden. A profound desire rose within him to be in a garden now, alone with her. He forced himself to remember his manners. "It's good to see you again too, Jessamine. I've told my friends how you rescued me."

"Nay, not rescued. It was simply my duty to help you when you were in need."

Tristan knew he shouldn't keep staring at her, but he couldn't pull his eyes away from hers. She had been beautiful in her Shaker dress and cap, but she was a breathtaking princess in evening attire.

"Nay?" Tristan's mother said. "Is that some kind of Shaker talk?"

Jessamine looked down at her hands again and Tristan frowned at his mother, who merely glared back at him before she turned a smile toward Mr. Ridenour next to her. "Well, really, it would be clearer if everyone would just speak yes or no when asked a question, don't you think?"

"Dear Wyneta, I beg you to show a bit of patience for my daughter." Sheldon Brady smiled as he spoke up. He'd been sitting back watching the scene unfold as though taking mental notes for one of his romance stories. "The Shakers say yea and nay instead of yes and no as we do, and since my daughter has been with the Shakers for almost ten years, such habits of speech are not quickly broken."

Jessamine looked up at Tristan's mother. "My father speaks the truth. I know very little of the ways of the world."

"I'm sure you'll learn quickly," Laura said. "With your father to help you." She looked from Jessamine to Sheldon Brady, her polite smile firmly in place.

"And so you found your long lost daughter," Robert Cleveland boomed. "Good for you, Sheldon. She looks to be a fine asset." Then he picked up his spoon and banged it against his glass. "Where are those waiters? A man could starve at this place."

Jessamine watched him a few seconds before she picked up her spoon and hit it against her glass the same as he had. "Is this the way you begin dinners in the world? With much noise instead of silent prayer? That is much different than the Believers."

Everybody at the table stared at her. Even Sheldon Brady looked surprised, but then Viola Cleveland laughed and picked up her spoon and clanked it against her glass too. Brady's laughter joined hers as he followed suit.

Laura did the same as she poked Tristan with her elbow. "Come, come, Tristan. You do want dinner, don't you?"

So he picked up his spoon and joined in. Robert Cleveland seemed taken aback a moment, but then he let out a booming laugh. Even the serious Mr. Ridenour was smiling.

Tristan's mother was not as she stared at them as though they had all lost their minds. "For mercy's sake, they will ask us to leave if you all don't stop this outlandish behavior."

"Oh, don't get all in a stir, Wyneta," Robert Cleveland said before hitting his glass again. "Nobody's going to ask paying customers to leave. Not when we're just having a little fun. And look. Here comes our food." He pointed with his spoon toward two waiters hurrying toward their table with loaded trays. He smiled over toward Jessamine. "I guess we can put our spoons down now, Miss Brady."

She laid her spoon back beside her plate as she gave him a shy smile, aware the laughter had been because of her, but not appearing to be upset about it. "I do beg your forgiveness if I did something wrong. I have much to learn about the world."

"Don't worry about it, my dear." Viola reached across the table to touch Jessamine's hand. "Your innocence is quite charming."

"Quite," Laura echoed. "Enchantedly charming."

"Is that good?" Jessamine looked at Laura. "To be charming? It would not be considered so at Harmony Hill. There one is to think of her duties, not of how others might see her."

"You are no longer at Harmony Hill," Laura said.

Jessamine looked from Laura all around the room and then back down to her own dress. "Yea, that is a truth. I am no longer at Harmony Hill."

Tristan heard an echo of sadness in her words, but then she was smiling again and looking at everything as though she couldn't see enough. It was certainly true that Tristan couldn't see enough of her. Somehow before the night was over, he would have to steal a few moments alone with her. Somehow. Perhaps in a garden.

24

It was more, much more, than Jessamine had ever thought to imagine. Things of the world kept flying at her as though she were running through a strange meadow of wonders. Here a bright-colored flower, there a sharp stone. Then a bird taking wing in front of her or a snake in the grass to startle her. One minute she couldn't see enough. The next minute she was afraid to look.

But she couldn't keep her eyes from sliding to wherever Tristan Cooper was. He looked different here in this place of the world. Very different. Not the man needing help in the woods. Not someone she might seek out in a garden to talk to about his world. Her world too now, she supposed, although she felt very much like a visitor who wouldn't be able to stay.

Of course, she looked different too. Even more different than Tristan did. Much more. She had seen her reflection in a large oval mirror swinging free in a wooden frame back in the room her father had arranged for her. He had moved his things to the room adjacent to it so he would be close should she have need of something. The owner of the Springs, a Mr. Hargrove, had been very accommodating, but Jessamine was relieved to escape his eyes. He'd kept looking at her as though she were some sort of new specimen of female never before seen.

Her father laughed when she told him that. "You'd best get used to it, my daughter. There are going to be many eyes on you this night." Then he had left her to go get dressed for dinner.

Later when he came back to escort her downstairs to the dining room, the thought of more people of the world staring at her made her hesitant to go with him. Instead, she suggested, "Perhaps it would be best if I stayed in my room this evening. I'll be quite content here."

The room her father said was for her and her alone was lovelier than anything she had ever seen, with a bed as big as three of the beds back at Harmony Hill. When she first came into the room, she had stared at the bed in wonder and barely constrained the impulse to fall upon it to see if it was as soft as it looked. The white lace coverlet topping the bed seemed to have little purpose other than beauty. Pink and green scarves spread over the table and on top the bureau. Scarves that would surely make cleaning the tables much more difficult, especially with the glass bowls and vases scattered here and there on them. Morning chores would not be quick, with the way everything sat on the floor or the furniture with not even one peg on the wall to hang them out of the way of a dusting brush or broom.

"But you look so lovely in your new dress and I do so want my friends to meet you." He studied her a moment before going on. "I know this place is much different from what you knew at Harmony Hill, my dear, but you have nothing to fear. I will stay right beside you through dinner. However, if the thought of going down to dinner is too daunting, I can have our meals brought up here."

"Oh nay, I would not want you to miss dinner on my account," Jessamine said quickly.

"But, my dear," he said with a gentle smile. "I won't leave you alone while you're feeling lonely and afraid."

"I don't know that I'm afraid, but it is true the ways of the world are very strange to me. I won't know what to do."

Her eyes caught on her reflection in the mirror, and for a moment, it was as if a stranger was in the room with her. A person she did not know. A person she could not even imagine knowing. And yet her eyes stared out of the face.

"Just watch those around you," her father assured her as he put his arm around her to turn her toward the door. "It will come easily. The ways of the world are not difficult."

But she'd found out soon enough that worldly ways weren't simple like the Believers' ways. She had done as her father said and watched the others at the dining table. But it had been wrong when she had followed the lead of the man named Robert Cleveland, a stern man who might have made her think of hiding behind her father, except that he made her think of Elder Hobart who often wore the same unhappy glower but was forever kind. A person couldn't always judge by the looks of a face. Actions mattered more. And so she had tapped on her glass the same as Mr. Cleveland had and realized almost right away that such was not common behavior. The lady introduced as Tristan's natural mother was quite distressed by Jessamine's blunder. It seemed to upset her even more when the others at the table copied Jessamine with great amusement. Not because she was concerned for Jessamine's feelings, but because she feared being thought an embarrassment.

Jessamine had asked forgiveness with no hesitation. Confession of wrongs, especially such silly wrongs, was as natural as breathing to her. Oddly enough, that made her feel more comfortable in the strange dining room where nobody prayed, everybody talked, and much food was left on plates carried away by servers who didn't seem to notice, much less mind, that perfectly good food was being wasted.

She tried not to make any more mistakes at the table, but

she had to remove her odd summertime gloves in order to eat. She thought nothing of it until she noticed the young woman named Laura staring at her hands. Jessamine's nails were still stained with the berry juice from the morning, even though that seemed weeks ago now. And there were angry red scratches from her too enthusiastic pursuit of the berries. In contrast, Laura's creamy white hands had long slender fingers with oval-shaped nails that didn't look as if they had ever picked anything except perhaps a berry from a bowl placed before her. The way a princess would.

After that, Jessamine hid her hands as much as possible between bites. It was obvious putting on a dress of silk and ruffles wasn't enough to turn her into a princess as Cinderella had been in her granny's fairy tales. Perhaps the fairy godmother had magically transformed the poor girl's ashes-stained hands along with giving her the beautiful dress and glass slippers. But that was no more than a story. In real life, hands were not so easily transformed from the hands of a worker into those of a princess.

At any rate, it was almost impossible to properly eat with all the talk swirling around the table. And not only around the table where she sat, but around every table in the large dining room until the voices were a din of noise as loud as when the Believers stomped out the devil back at the meetinghouse. Jessamine wondered if they were thinking of places such as this when they were laboring to keep Satan from their hearts and minds. She had no problem imagining Sister Edna's woeful cries and stomps if she were there beside Jessamine. And perhaps Sister Sophrena's as well.

Before tears could climb into her eyes, she pushed away thoughts of Sister Sophrena and dug her fork into a piece of yellow cake that was so dry it made her wish for two glasses of water. But she diligently ate every bite even while thinking of the delicious raspberry pies her sisters and brothers would be enjoying back at Harmony Hill. It was a relief when her plate was empty, the meal was over, and Mr. Cleveland stood up and eased back his wife's chair for her to stand as well. Jessamine didn't follow his lead. She'd learned her lesson there, but then everybody else at the table did stand. The ways of the world were a puzzle.

Mr. and Mrs. Cleveland led the way out of the dining area followed by Tristan's mother and her dour-looking gentleman friend. Jessamine couldn't remember the man's name. In front of Jessamine and her father, Tristan escorted the princess. A prince and a princess. They split the air as they walked with no need to keep stumbling over all the wonders that kept drawing Jessamine's eyes.

None of it was a wonder to them, but the expected. Opulence. Food nibbled at and sent away. Roses in huge vases in every corner of the huge room her father called a ballroom for dancing. Women in every color of dress with skirts so wide they could surely sweep half the floor at a time with their skirt tails. Flowers carried in the women's hands for no purpose other than the sweet scent.

"This room can get very warm when the dances start up," her father warned her as he led her to a chair near a veranda door. "So if the air begins to feel too close for you, don't hesitate to step out into the gardens for a cooling break."

"Yea," she agreed. "But I know nothing of gardens of the world."

"Don't worry. Gardens everywhere are much the same. Although I'm sure it's very likely that the gardens here at the Springs are the setting for more marriage proposals than those at your Shaker village." He smiled at her. "I proposed to your mother in a garden where yellow jessamine bloomed. A beautiful flower. That's why your mother chose your name. She knew you were going to be a girl long before you were born."

312

"How could she know?"

Her father smiled with a tinge of sadness stealing into his eyes. "I asked her that myself. She said you talked to her. Spirit to spirit."

Jessamine closed her eyes and tried to bring forth her mother's spirit that she might have once communed with. Nothing was there in her imagination. She had no vision of the woman her father had loved enough to give a child. She opened her eyes and looked at the prince who had loved her mother. "I have no memory of her at all."

"The memory may be there, but buried by too many years."

"What did she look like?"

"That's easy." He looked around and then pointed toward the nearest mirror on the wall opposite them. "Just go look in a mirror and there is Issandra. You look very much like her."

"Now? Or this morning before I . . ." She hesitated and looked down at her dress. "Before I changed."

"You are still the same girl, Jessamine. Only the outward wrappings have changed." He leaned down to look directly into her face. "Remember that. Dresses aren't who you are. Who you are is inside. In your heart. Perhaps that is the way you are most like your beautiful mother. She had a very loving heart and I sense the same with you."

"Sister Sophrena has always told me there are many rooms within one's heart and that it is important to keep those rooms open and free of the clutter of sin or improper thought."

"Not bad advice," her father said. "But what of love? Are you supposed to keep a room open to love?"

"All rooms are to be full of love for one's sisters and brothers." She kept her voice soft. It didn't seem right to talk of the Believers' love in this room with music that was not for worship and men and women moving out to dance with arms wrapped around one another. The dances were nothing like that of the Believers. But even as she knew she could not do them, she wondered how it would feel to glide across a dance floor holding to a man.

Without thought, her eyes found Tristan Cooper on the other side of the room. He was not dancing, but instead seemed to be waiting for her to look his way.

Her father noted the direction of her eyes. "But perhaps you have saved some room for a forbidden love?"

She quickly whipped her eyes away from Tristan as a blush rose up in her cheeks. "Nay." She stared down at her hands with the stains hidden by the gloves once more.

Her father made a sound that might have been a laugh but it carried little levity. "And so the plot thickens."

She looked up at him, but he was staring across the room. Not toward Tristan as she expected, but toward the princess. Toward Laura. Her father's face was devoid of any expression as though he had purposely pulled a blank sheet over it.

"What do you mean?" she asked.

He looked back at her and laughed again. This time the kind of laugh she'd heard often since she'd ridden away from Harmony Hill with him. "It means that I am a writer and always looking down the path at what might happen next. To the end."

"Granny used to tell me stories," Jessamine said. "About princes and princesses. Fairy tales she called them."

"And they all lived happily ever after." Her father's smile was gentle on her.

She returned his smile. "They did. After they conquered their troubles and kissed. Such stories were not welcome at the Shaker village."

"But you remembered them anyway."

"I did."

"And now you have turned into a princess." He touched her hair softly.

She bit back the nay that wanted to escape her mouth.

Nor did she mention her granny's promise that someday her prince would come. That was all so long ago. Perhaps it was enough the prince who loved her mother had come and wanted to show her the world. But one thing was becoming clear to Jessamine. She could never be a princess. She was no longer even sure that she wanted to be a princess.

It seemed better to have a purpose, work to do, for surely one showed love for the Eternal Father by the use of the gifts one was given. A gift to be beautiful didn't seem to be enough. One should have a gift to be useful as well. Yet, the room was full of girls who seemed to have no more on their mind than how to attract the eyes of the men in the room. The world was a much stranger place than she had expected.

"Could I go back to my room, Father?" It was the first time she had used the word. It sat oddly on her tongue.

"Tired of being a princess already, my daughter?"

"It is much different than being a sister," she said.

"But both dance."

"I know no dances such as this." She motioned toward the dancers swirling past in individual circles of two.

"Worry not, my child. We all have a dance we know. It's just sometimes hearing the music." He let his hand drift down to squeeze her shoulder. "Simply give yourself more time to hear your song. To know your story. You don't have to dance right away."

"Do you hear your song? Know your dance?" she asked.

His smile faded. "I am not young like you, my dear. I have heard many songs, tried many dances." Then his smile was back, fuller than ever. "But I have never tired of dancing."

She knew he wasn't talking only of moving to the music the way the couples were doing on the dance floor, but she said anyway, "Then go dance. I will be fine sitting here watching and listening. And learning of the dances of the world."

"I did promise a couple of ladies a dance," he said hesitantly as he looked out at the dancers.

The music stopped and the men and women began moving back to the chairs around the dance floor, some still holding on to one another, flushed and laughing.

"Don't be concerned for me, Father. I am not afraid to sit here alone. There is much to entertain my eyes."

He looked back at her. "I doubt you'll be alone for long. I'll keep an eye out in case any of the men are too attentive."

She watched him go with something akin to relief. It was good to be alone for a moment, even if she was in a sea of noise as the music started up again. She watched her father speak to a lady she had not met and then escort her out on the dance floor. It was as crowded as the meetinghouse floor on a Sunday morning, but here there was no order to the dances. Here they seemed to move wherever they willed but amazingly didn't bang into one another. Occasionally her father would send her a smiling look. She made sure to have an answering smile at the ready.

And all the time she watched the dancers and let her eyes land on every ornate decoration in the gold-gilded room, she thought of the retiring bell ringing at Harmony Hill and of the tears that might be in Sister Sophrena's eyes as she wrote in her journal. She thought of her dear sister writing of her as a former sister and had to swallow back her own tears.

One dance went by. Her father brought her a cup of mixed juices, apple she thought, mixed with something else with a bit more tang. Then he went back out to dance with Laura who seemed to almost float above the floor, the very way a princess should dance. Jessamine's eyes sought Tristan Cooper to see how a prince danced, but he was standing to the side, watching as she was watching. He caught her eyes on him and smiled across the floor. Her heart began to beat faster and memories of the garden came to mind even as the heat in the room suddenly seemed oppressive.

The garden. Her father had sat her there by the doors to the garden so she could step outside if she needed a breath of fresh air. Other couples had been going past her and through the doors. Most returned after a short time as though unable to stay away from the music.

Jessamine stood up and slipped out through the doors. She sighed with relief as the night wrapped around her. She could still hear the music but it was muffled. Besides, it wasn't the music that had so banged against her ears but the talk and the laughter. She had caught snatches of conversation between people as they moved past her, but little of it made much sense to her.

It was better in the garden. Even if this garden was unlike any at Harmony Hill. In the moonlight she could see white benches scattered among the plantings. A place to sit with no purpose other than looking at the flowers, for one could not weed from the high benches or pick any of the blooms or dig the roots. But she knew from Sister Abigail that some people cultivated flowers for no reason other than enjoyment of their beauty. In this place with the ruffled dresses and soft hands of the princesses, she had no doubt that was the purpose of the gardens. Beauty. Pure and simple. Understanding the ways of the world was not going to be simple.

Behind her the door opened and closed again. She stepped into the shadow of an overhanging bush and waited for the couple to pass by her. But the person didn't walk past. The man stopped in a patch of moonlight on the path and spoke directly to her.

"And so we meet again in a garden, Jessamine."

25

Tristan stood in the moonlight and waited for Jessamine to speak. He'd been acutely aware of her across the dance floor all evening even when his eyes weren't on her. Others had come to engage him in conversation. He had taken Laura a glass of the punch, but he didn't try to dance with his awkward bandaged arm. More than once he started to cross the room to see if Jessamine might need something. To see if she might need him. But each time the thought of his mother's disapproval stopped him.

He was surprised his mother hadn't ordered him to sit with her so she could make sure he didn't do anything foolish. She did keep looking his way in spite of the distraction of the lawyer dancing attendance on her. Mr. Ridenour appeared to be interested in more than his mother's signature on the documents he'd brought to Kentucky for her perusal, and if the blush in her cheeks was any indication, she was more than a little flattered by his admiration. When the band began playing a slow song, she even allowed the man to lead her out to join the couples on the ballroom floor. Jessamine slipping out the veranda doors into the garden at the same instant seemed too good an opportunity to pass up.

The melody drifted out the windows to trail after him into the garden. The strains of music combined with the sweet scent of roses and honeysuckle spread an aura of romance in the air. But if Jessamine felt it, she didn't step from the shadows to welcome it. Or him.

"There are no spying eyes here, Jessamine. In this world, you can talk to me without fear of censure. So please come walk with me." He held his hand out toward her. "The garden is lovely in the moonlight."

At last she stepped out of the shadows into the moonlight beside him, but she didn't take his hand. "It is beautiful here." Her voice was low, barely audible as though she worried about, if not watching eyes, then listening ears.

"Yes, yes it is," he said without taking his eyes off her. She was what was beautiful. So much so he could barely breathe. "You look like a princess."

"Nay," she said with an impatient shake of her head. "I am not a princess." She jerked off one of her gloves and held her hand up toward his face. "See. This hand could never belong to a princess."

"Perhaps princess wasn't right. Perhaps what I thought might be true on my first sight of you remains the best. An angel. An amazing angel." He might have been slow to hold Laura's hand, but he had no such inhibitions with Jessamine. He caught her hand in his.

She drew in a sudden breath, but she didn't pull away. Instead she wrapped her fingers around his. "Is this a custom of the world?"

"It is." He kept his hold firm as he lowered their clasped hands down between them. "When two people walk in a garden."

He began to move along the path and she easily fell in step beside him. He wanted to get away from the veranda doors before his mother or Laura saw him there with Jessamine. He didn't really think Laura would care, but they had come to an agreement that afternoon. A man preparing to propose to one woman shouldn't be holding hands and strolling through a garden with another. But how could he turn loose of an angel?

"A princess, an angel," she was saying, a tinge of regret sounding in her voice. "I am not near to either one. I am no more and no less than I was this morn in my Shaker dress. Just someone who wonders about things that might be best left unimagined." She looked back over her shoulder toward the ballroom. "The girl at the table with us, Laura, she is the princess."

"She does have princess ways," Tristan agreed. "But it's a learned thing. A way she's been taught since a child. And something you could learn too."

When she didn't say anything, he went on. "If you want to."

"That's the question, isn't it? What I want." She let out a deep breath and looked up at the sky above them. A few stars were bright enough to show in the moonlight. "When my father came this morning, it seemed the only choice. But now the world seems too strange. Too different."

"How so?"

"Believers seek the simple life. Those of the Ministry pray and ask God and Mother Ann how things should be done and then they pass along the answers they hear. All is ordered and there is no need to think of one's path. It is laid out before you."

"But you wondered about paths into the world?"

"I don't know that I wondered of the paths, but I did wonder about many things. And about feelings that aren't a Believer's feelings. Sister Sophrena warned me such wondering could lead me into sin." Jessamine paused. When she went on, her voice had the seasoning of tears. "I'm sure she thinks it has. And perhaps she is right. I am here alone in a garden planted for nothing more than beauty, holding a man of the world's hand as if I found such an action as natural as breathing. She would not believe how quickly I have turned from the Shaker way and surrendered myself to the treacherous ways of the world."

"Would you rather I didn't hold your hand?"

"Oh, nay," she said quickly, tightening her fingers around his a bit. "I was saying what Sister Sophrena would think. Not my own thoughts." She looked down at their clasped hands and her voice was little more than a whisper as she went on. "I cannot deny that I like this worldly custom."

Tristan barely heard the music from the ballroom now. He wasn't sure if that was because they had walked that far into the garden or if the blood pulsing through him was blocking it out. He led Jessamine over to a bench under a tree beside a hedge of roses. Moonlight pushed through the leaves above their heads and dappled them with light. It would be the perfect place for a man to go down on his knee in front of a lady. A place for him to seal his arrangement with Laura.

He pushed the thought aside. That was a plan for another day, another time. Tonight he was with an angel, and if it was a good place for a proposal, it was an even better place for a stolen kiss. There would be no Shaker bell to break the spell over them this evening.

As if divining his thoughts, she turned her face toward his just as she had in the Shaker garden. The shadows were not so deep he couldn't see her eyes, so pure with an innocence that touched something deep within him. A spiritual place he thought had been lost forever on the Mexican battlefields. But now he felt, almost knew, that him being with this girl at this time was meant to be. Perhaps the Lord did really write love in the stars.

"Do you believe in God?" His words seemed to surprise her. In fact they surprised him. Talking about God was hardly the best way to lead into a kiss. And he did want to kiss her. So much so he could almost taste her lips against his.

"How could anyone not believe in God? He's everywhere. In everything."

"Is that what the Shakers taught you?"

"Nay." She seemed unaware of falling back into the Shaker speech. "Well, they did, but I have ever known it to be true. He has been with me always, ever since I can remember." She sounded perplexed as she stared at him. "Is he not with you?"

"My times have not been as innocent as yours. I have been witness to many things God would surely want no part of."

"I have been told there is much in the world such as that. Wars and battlegrounds. Thievery and killing. Such was shut from my life at Harmony Hill, but even before I was taken to the Shakers, my granny taught me the Lord would ever be with me."

"Even now?" he asked when she paused.

"Yea. Always."

She stared at him, expecting him to agree. He could see the depths of her faith in her eyes, the expectation that her truth would be his truth. She did not have his doubts. She had not seen his sights. But he had no desire to tear down her belief, so he kept silent.

"You think I shouldn't feel that way because I have turned my back on my sisters and brothers." Her voice quivered as she looked away from him toward the glow of light radiating from the ballroom at the other end of the garden.

He grasped her hand tighter. "No—" he started.

She jerked her hand away and interrupted him with fierce words. "He is with me even now. Even here. Even if I have let my feet stray on wrong paths where evil might pursue me. Granny showed me where in the Bible it says nothing can separate me from the love of God. Not death, not life. Not angels or powers or things present or to come. She said the only thing that could separate me from God's love was me. She said even then God would be there loving me, but I might refuse to see it."

He looked at her and didn't know what to say. Why in the world had he asked her if she believed in God when all he wanted was to feel her lips surrendering to his? Maybe he had lost his sense of romance. Along with his faith. He wanted to go back and change his words. Go back even farther to the day when his soul had emptied out of belief and somehow change that day. Cling to at least a modicum of the kind of faith Jessamine had.

But some things couldn't be changed. He told himself he should stand up, escort her back to the ballroom, turn his eyes from her to Laura. That was where his future lay. Where he had already promised his future. Not with the woman beside him. Not with the beautiful Jessamine. The empty place inside him yawned wider. He searched for something to say to break the uneasy silence between them, but every word that came to mind seemed foolish and wrong.

She did not appear to be as burdened by the silence as he was. Instead she seemed to be in deep thought as she turned to meet his eyes in the shadowy moonlight. She looked at him a long moment before she said softly, "Are you refusing to see it?"

"See what?" His voice was husky. He was seeing what his heart wanted to see. Her face only inches from his. He was feeling what he wanted to feel. Her breath intermingling with his.

"God's love," she whispered.

"I want to see it."

"Then you will." She raised her hand up toward his face before letting it hover there in the air as though afraid to allow her fingers to do the bidding of her heart.

He captured her hand once more. As though holding something of great treasure, he lifted her fingers to his lips and kissed her knuckles. He took her hand and rubbed his cheek with the backs of her fingers. He savored the feel of her skin against his.

Her eyes widened, but she didn't look away from him. He released her hand to run his fingers down her cheek to her lips just as he had in the Shaker garden. She kept her hand on his face, her fingertips as soft as eiderdown against his skin.

He slid his hand around to the back of her neck and dropped his head down to cover her lips with his. He had intended a mere brush of lips so as not to frighten her, but at the touch of her lips he forgot his noble intent. Her hand climbed away from his cheek up into his hair and he was lost. A man drowning with no desire to be saved.

Then on the other side of the roses, a twig snapped. A furtive sound somehow that was like a dash of cold water. Tristan lifted his head to see who was intruding on their moment. Nobody was visible, but it was as though the spying Shaker eyes might be on them still, even though they were miles from the Shaker village.

"Oh my!" Jessamine whispered as she dropped her hand back to her lap. "It is no wonder some of my sisters must struggle to forget such things of the world."

Then she noted his posture of listening. "What is it?" she asked. "Are there those who watch here the same as at Harmony Hill? Have we broken rules?"

"No, no." Tristan tried to push away his uneasy feeling. It could have been only a raccoon or an opossum looking for a dropped bit of food. Nobody would be spying on them in the garden. Nobody but perhaps his mother. "The gardens here at the Springs bloom with romance as abundantly as with roses. Romance and kisses. But it may be that I should not have kissed you."

"Why?" With no feminine wiles, her question was blunt and fair.

"Why indeed," he said as he fought the desire to pull her close again. But there was his mother. There was Laura. There was his promise. There was Jessamine's delightful innocence. "Because a lady has to guard her reputation in the world."

"So even though such contacts of the lips are not uncommon, they are not always good. Even in the world." She was silent a moment as if trying to understand what could not be understood. "As you guessed in our good doctor's garden at Harmony Hill, I have wondered about kissing and how it would feel."

She raised her hand up and soundly kissed the back of it. Tristan felt a consuming desire to replace her hand with his lips, but he made himself sit apart from her. Silent. Sadness welling up in him. He should have never followed her out into the garden. Some temptations were better avoided.

She appeared not to notice his silence as she held her hand toward him. "See, that was nothing but lips on skin. That's all I felt. Yet when it was your lips against mine, it was as if I stood in a whirlwind of feelings."

"What sort of feelings?" The words almost stuck in his throat.

"Good feelings. Apple blossoms and butterflies in the air and birds singing. Like I could spin in joy." She looked at him. "Perhaps wanton feelings. Sister Sophrena has often warned me that Satan can use such feelings to entice us into sin."

She looked at him with hope he might tell her something that could chase away her feelings of wrong. Hope that slipped away from her face when he didn't answer her quickly enough.

"You think it was wrong." Her voice was flat. Her smile gone.

"No, not wrong," he said at last, his words too late to be convincing. "Troublesome, but not wrong."

"Troublesome sounds very wrong." She stared down at her hands and sighed. "The world is indeed very troublesome for one such as I who oft leaps before I look. But I did look. As we left the eating area. And I did see. I simply didn't want to believe."

"Believe what?"

"You love the princess. As a prince should."

"Prince? Are you talking about a fairy tale?" He frowned a little, trying to understand.

"Nay, I'm talking about love," she said very softly as she looked up at him.

"Love," he echoed. He wanted to say more, but how could he claim love for this girl in front of him? He barely knew her, but there was little doubt he had lost his head and given her his heart. That was going to be very troublesome indeed.

"Sister Edna was right. I have put my feet on a very slippery slope with naught to keep me from falling into sin." She stood and stepped back from him up onto the path.

"Wait, Jessamine." He rose to his feet and reached for her, but she was as elusive as a moonbeam.

"Nay." She picked up her skirts and rushed away much the same way she had run from the Shaker doctor's garden.

"Wait." He started after her, but what could he say if he caught her? What could he promise that would be true? He could tell her it wasn't a princess he loved, but an angel. He thought of calling those words after her, but even if she heard him and believed what he said, the truth of that didn't make his situation one bit different. In a few days, at the midsummer ball, he was going to propose to Laura. She was going to accept, and they would both leave behind their true loves and begin their life together. For family honor, prestige, money. But was that enough?

The brush behind him rattled, and he jerked around to see someone moving away down the path. He took a couple of steps after the shadowy figure, but stopped himself. The garden was open to all. Other couples would be strolling in the moonlight. He had no reason to feel suspicious of a crackle of brush. None at all.

He tried to push the uneasy feeling out of his head. Perhaps that came from being shot in the woods. Was every rustle of brush going to set him on guard now? But nobody was going to shoot him in Dr. Hargrove's garden with ballroom music floating out to his ears.

Up ahead of him the veranda door opened and closed. She was gone from him. He had no right to chase after her even though she had taken his heart with her. He remembered Laura staring out over the lake earlier that day. Would their every day together be filled with such moments of regret?

He was almost back to the veranda when he saw his mother on the pathway in front of him. He looked around for the lawyer, hoping to see him there ready to stroll with his mother, but no, she was alone. Waiting for him. Even in the dim light, he had no trouble seeing how her mouth was twisted in an angry knot well before he reached her.

"What in the world do you think you are doing, Tristan?" she said in a fierce whisper when he reached her side. "Are you trying to ruin all our plans?"

"Calm yourself, Mother. Nothing has changed."

"So you think, but what if Laura noted your dalliance with that Shaker girl? What if she refuses to marry you now? We'll be ruined."

Tristan had no words to answer her. Inside he already felt ruined.

26

Jessamine was relieved when her father offered to escort her to her room. The music hadn't stopped. Couples continued to whirl about on the dance floor and also to slip past her into the garden. But Jessamine was ready to leave it behind. She needed time to figure out the world.

She couldn't think straight with so much new all around her. Mostly she couldn't think straight with Tristan Cooper there in front of her talking to the princess, Laura. Not while her own lips continued to burn from his kiss. A kiss that had meant nothing to him. Princes probably kissed a different girl every evening. But the kiss had exploded inside her like a shooting star that left a burnt streak across the sky. The trail of the kiss would evermore be on her heart.

Her father stood inside the door of her room and said he would find a maid to help her get ready for bed.

"Nay, there is no need," she said quickly. She had felt uncomfortable earlier with a woman she did not know helping her into the dress. And to call some person away from her nighttime rest so late into the night seemed altogether wrong.

"Are you sure?" He studied her face. "You might need assistance in undoing your buttons or taking down your hair. A maid can tend to your dress and lay out your nightclothes."

They had forgotten nightclothes when they were at Mrs. Browning's, but while they were at dinner, a frilly nightdress with pink ribbons and lace had appeared. It was folded on the bed waiting for her.

"I can surely do such myself," she told him. Then at the look on his face, she added, "Or is that against the rules here?"

He touched her shoulder. "No, no rules here. Not like at the Shaker village."

"I'm not so sure of that," she said as she hung her head. "I think I may have broken many of the world's rules this day. But it is so hard when the rules are such a mystery to me."

"Don't be concerned, my daughter. You charmed everyone just as I knew you would." He put his hand under her chin and lifted her face up to look at him. He was smiling. "Trust me. I know things are different for you here, but each new day will be easier. And I will be here to help you."

"Always?"

A look of distress flashed across his face before he said, "Some things can't be promised, and always is one of those. But I can promise to do everything in my power to help you find happiness in this new world."

"I was happy at Harmony Hill."

"Were you? In spite of your wondering?"

She sighed. "I did always wonder if there might not be more."

"And now you will know." Her father dropped his hand away from her chin. "You are going to find out there is much more. But if you think you can manage your buttons, I won't call a maid for you this evening. In the morning you will have your own personal maid. Dr. Hargrove says a young woman has just come to the Springs seeking such a position." He held up a hand before she could protest. "All ladies must have one."

"Is that a rule?"

He let out a funny short burst of air. "Perhaps it is. Perhaps there are more rules than I have considered before because I have taken such little notice of many of them."

"Sister Sophrena often accused me of the same at Harmony Hill. She said I only kept the rules if they didn't cause me bother. I had much need to confess my wrongs."

His smile was amused. "Here you can just laugh off your infractions. No need to dwell on them. Unless you want to write them down. Come morning I'll find you writing supplies."

"To record my sins?"

"My Jessamine, you are every bit as delightful as your mother." He laughed without reservation. "You can write anything you want. Sins. Blessings. Whatever. It would be good to have a record of your journey into the world."

"Anything?" Jessamine felt like twirling at the thought of a pen in her hand. A pen that would be free to write anything that came to mind. For a few seconds she forgot about her wanton actions in the garden and thought only of the promise of a blank page. "Does it have to be true?"

"So the Shakers didn't cure you of the writing bug. In the few letters that found me in my travels, our granny wrote of your fascination for words."

"I love the way some words sound in my ears and the look of their letters on a page. But the sisters who taught the school wanted only truth on their papers. Not the words that often took flight in my imagination with fanciful results."

"How about two books? One for truth and one for flights of fancy." He put his hands on her shoulders before he leaned down to kiss her forehead. "Now good night, my daughter. Tomorrow will be another day for you to conquer. I think with a pen in your hand you will do quite well at finding your path into this new world."

Then he was gone and she was completely alone. Wondrously alone. Dreadfully alone. A lamp had been lit on the table and the curtains pulled across the window by hands not her own. The same hands that must have brought the nightdress. Jessamine stared at the bed across the room. A white mound of pillows and ruffles that three, maybe even four sisters might have been able to sleep in. With that gown of ribbons and lace atop it waiting for her.

In spite of her assurances to her father, the buttons were not easy to undo. By the time she managed at last to reach that last button in the middle of her back, she was as out of breath as if she'd carried a heavy basket of folded sheets up to the top floor of the Gathering Family House. It would have been sensible to have someone unfasten the buttons for her, but it had sounded so odd. To think she couldn't ready herself for her night's rest.

Dressing like a princess had seemed so magical when she first dropped the silky dress over her head hours ago. The maid had been there to fasten the buttons then and to exclaim over the beauty of the dress. Jessamine had caught sight of her reflection in the mirror and been transfixed for a moment. With the silky lilac fabric glimmering in the lamplight and the lacy edges of the top against the pale skin of her neck, she had felt as changed as the caterpillar into a butterfly. But now with the dress no more than a heap of fabric on the floor, her earlier thoughts seemed but vanity. In every way it was surely better to be able to take one's dress on and off without such contortions and stretching. The way she could take on and off her simple Shaker dress.

With a sigh, she picked up the lilac dress and hung it in the wardrobe. Changing the dress on one's back didn't change the inside any more than kissing a prince changed her into a princess. She couldn't deny she had sought the kiss and even now thoughts of Tristan's lips touching hers made her heart beat faster. But it had meant nothing to him.

What had he told her? That kisses were common in the moonlight of the garden as though they were no more to be wondered about than the plentitude of dandelions blooming in the spring. A bright spot of yellow, pretty for the moment, but a weed nevertheless that needed to be plucked out of a garden. Perhaps that was what she should do. Pluck the kiss out of the garden of her heart and throw it away. But she couldn't. Sinful or not, it was implanted there and her desire was to nurture it and find the best soil for it to grow.

That was foolish. She knew that as she pulled the beribboned nightgown over her head. Very foolish. She had heard Tristan and his mother in the garden. Their words had been heated and intense. So much so they hadn't noticed when she had come back outside to search for the glove she had dropped on the path.

While she had not understood what his mother's words speaking of ruin might mean, she had perfectly understood what his words had meant. *Nothing has changed.* Their time in the garden, their touching of lips meant naught to him. The kiss had changed nothing for him even as it had torn through her, ripping open feelings so new and different she would never be the same again no matter which dress she chose to pull over her head come morning.

Jessamine lay awake long into the night. She felt very alone in the silent room. She had never before slept without hearing another's breathing. The empty silence brought to mind those hours after her granny stopped breathing and the knowledge of how terribly alone she was had filled her with panic. That day she'd picked up her granny's Bible and let it fall open wherever it willed and read passage after passage until it seemed as if her granny was sitting with her in the chair, guiding her hands and thoughts. Before dark, the old preacher man showed up. He'd known her granny had been having sinking spells so when the compulsion came upon him to ride into the woods to see about her, he had not put it aside. Once he looked at Granny on the bed, he said he figured Granny must have come by his house on her way up to glory land to nudge him so he would come be with Jessamine.

But this night in this room the aloneness was a different kind than that sad, mournful sorrow. Sadness was there with her for sure, mixed in with the strangeness of the silent room. She missed Sister Sophrena and the knowledge that come morning she could go confess her sins and be forgiven. Now the wrongs were simply piling up inside her until the weight of them seemed ready to mash her down into the bed until she felt near to disappearing into its softness. Swallowed up by worldly wrongs.

Come morning when she had pen and paper, she would write to Sister Sophrena. Not confessions. She couldn't confess her actions in the garden. But simply the thought of writing words for Sister Sophrena's eyes eased Jessamine's mind. She didn't know why. Any words she wrote about what had happened to her in the world would be sure to bring a frown to Sister Sophrena's face.

Still, the thought of her with her Shaker teachings on giving her heart to God and that of her granny's Bible telling her God so loved comforted her. John 3:16 was the very first verse she ever learned. She carried it in her heart with her to the Shaker village because she knew her granny had believed. Now she had carried it in her heart away from the Shaker village. For God so loved the world. All the world. He would continue to love her while she was in the world. She could whisper her wrongs into the dark air over her and be forgiven. Perhaps not by Sister Sophrena, but by the Lord.

She spoke the words, asking forgiveness for the hurt she caused Sister Sophrena by walking away from the Shakers. She asked forgiveness for her feelings of vanity when looking at her reflection before she'd gone down to dinner. She asked forgiveness for finding fault with the food and for every contrary thought she'd had throughout the day. She asked forgiveness for the indulgence of the too-soft bed.

Then she let her mind go to the garden. She was silent for a moment before she whispered, "If it was a sin, forgive me for kissing the man in the garden, Lord, but please don't let it be a sin here in this new world I am in. Even if it meant nothing to him, let me carry the memory of it in my heart without thinking it something that should be swept away. Please, Lord. At least for a little while."

She had no sure feeling of being forgiven, but her heart felt lighter as she said amen. She stretched out straight as she was taught to lie on the Shaker beds. Sleep didn't come. Instead, the day's events kept marching through her mind as she twisted and turned but found no comfort in that bed of frills. At last, she pulled a pillow and the top cover down on the floor. The cover folded over and made a perfectly fine mat to lie on. She was asleep almost the instant her head touched down on the pillow.

What seemed like minutes later, a knock on the door pulled her from sleep. Sunlight was streaming in the window, and for a few seconds Jessamine was confused. Why had she not heard the rising bell? The knock came again, this time more insistent, and Jessamine came fully awake. She jumped to her feet, grabbed the pillow and cover off the floor and threw them up on the bed. Her father would not understand her sleeping on the floor. If the knocker was her father.

Should she call out and ask who was knocking or should she open the door and peer out? What did people of the world do with no bells as signals for rising? Jessamine looked toward the window. At Harmony Hill, the morning meal would be over and duties beginning. She would be going out to the garden with Sister Edna to do useful work. Here, in the world she had no idea what she would be doing. Then she remembered the promise of pen and paper and almost ran to the door.

But it wasn't her father with his promised gifts. Before she could open it, a voice was speaking through the door. "Miss Jessamine, I am your new lady's maid. Your father has instructed me to find out if you are up."

Jessamine eased open the door to peer out. She stared at the girl standing there, not sure she could trust her eyes. "Is that really you, Sister Abigail?" She let the door swing open.

"You are even more surprised than I thought you would be." Abigail laughed. "Let me in before someone happens along the hallway and catches you in your nightdress. A lady would not want that to happen."

When Jessamine stepped back from the door, Abigail quickly came into the room and closed the door behind her. She looked at Jessamine with a smile clear across her face.

"What are you doing here?" Jessamine asked.

"Your father hired me to be your lady's maid."

"Nay, I mean here at the Springs, Sister Abigail?"

"You can't call me sister here. You'll have to say Abigail. Or Abby might be better for a maid. And it would be best to say yes and no instead of the Shaker talk."

"So I've been told."

"As to why I'm here, you remember how I told you I worked here last year. Well, after I left Harmony Hill, I came back here to see if Dr. Hargrove would give me a job. Then when your father needed someone for you, they both thought I'd be the perfect maid to help you figure out life here in the world. Trust me, Jessamine, it is better here in the world, but we don't have time to talk of that now." Abigail went to the pitcher of water on the table and poured some into the bowl. "If you don't hurry, you will miss breakfast and that might disappoint Mr. Brady."

"And me. It has to be hours past the morning meal at Harmony Hill."

"Forget Harmony Hill and wash your face." Abigail went

to the bureau and pulled out the cranberry-and-cream-striped dress Mrs. Browning had sold them. Before she shut the door, she ran her hand down the silky lilac dress Jessamine had hung there the night before. "It seems almost magical and right at the same time. A story come true just like those tales you whispered to me in the night while everyone slept at Harmony Hill. And now you have become the princess in the story."

"Nay," Jessamine said. Why did everyone think a dress could turn one into a princess? She couldn't even remember to say no in the world's way. She was that unchanged. "No. I am the same person I was yesterday. The dress is only a dress."

Then again, why had she stopped thinking about being that princess in her imagined stories? She was living her imagined dreams come true. Her father, the prince who loved her mother, had come to escort her into the world's ways. She had kissed a different prince in the garden. And that was where the story was going awry. The prince who loved another. A kiss that meant nothing.

Abigail was still stroking the lilac party dress. "Yes, but such a dress that two days ago would have been no more than a fanciful dream for you. One you had no thought of wearing and now you have a bureau of dresses with bows and ribbons." Abigail spread the striped dress across the chair and fingered the cream-colored ribbon threaded around the neckline before she looked up at Jessamine. "It is good that you escaped that nasty Sister Edna. Good that we both escaped."

"Escaped?" Jessamine echoed the other girl's word.

"To freedom. To life." She came over to start undoing the ribbons on Jessamine's gown, but Jessamine pushed her hands away and pulled them loose herself. Abigail laughed. "You will have to learn princess ways."

"And what ways are you having to learn?" Jessamine asked as she pulled the gown over her head. "To be a servant?"

"I was doing only the bidding of others at the Shaker town.

Now I still must do the bidding of others, but at least here I am paid. And at the end of the season Jimmy and I are going to marry. Between the two of us working here, we will have a bit of money for a start."

"So you found him."

"I found him." Abigail's face took on a happy glow. "He had not forgotten me."

"I'm glad for you. You might be the princess in the story instead of me."

"If love makes one a princess, you could be right." Abigail picked up the dress again and waltzed it over to Jessamine. Then she was all business. "But we must hurry and transform you into the actual princess before your father knocks on the door. I would not want him to be displeased with my service. You must let me help you into your dress."

So she held up her arms and let Abigail wrap petticoats around her waist and then drop the dress down over them. She stood like a post while the girl buttoned and tied and straightened. Her hair was hastily arranged and pinned away from her face. When Abigail worked some curls loose to let fall around her face, Jessamine lost patience.

"My Shaker cap was much easier and faster." She pushed Abigail's hands away from her head. "It is only hair and no reason for such vanity. I don't care how it looks."

"But your father does. That handsome man you dragged in from the woods might." Abigail grinned and raised her eyebrows as she reached back to shape another curl. "Here in the world women dress to please the eyes of the men in their lives."

"Even princesses?"

"Especially princesses. For what other duty can a princess have than the duty of being beautiful."

"But the beauty that matters most comes from having a beautiful soul. A loving heart. "

"That is every word true, but in the world, in a place like the Springs, what the eye sees matters too. That's why we have lace and ribbons and curling hair."

When Jessamine didn't say anything, Abigail turned loose of the strand of hair she held and leaned down to peer at her face. "Don't look so downhearted, my sister. You have the beauty both inside and out and the world is waiting for you."

A soft knock sounded on the door and then her father was calling her name. Abigail hurried over to open the door and Jessamine pulled on her shoes. A new day in the world awaited. And her father might have the promised pen and paper. That by itself was enough to make enduring the layers of petticoats and the scratch of prickly lace against her skin worth it. She thought fleetingly of the soft Shaker dress folded and stuck in the bottom of the bureau. Knowing it was there was a comfort to her, a connection to her sisters at Harmony Hill. To Sister Sophrena.

As she stood up to go to her father, she caught sight of her reflection in the mirror again. Sister Sophrena wouldn't recognize her. She barely recognized herself. She started to turn away quickly from this stranger staring back at her. Then she stopped as she heard Abigail greeting her father at the door. She stared straight at the girl in the mirror.

It was time she got to know her better. Maybe not a princess. She was right that a dress couldn't make a princess any more than one stolen kiss could make a prince fall in love with her. But she was in the world, and whether she decided to embrace it or not, she did want to see it. At least for a little while.

"You look lovely, Jessamine." Her father stepped up behind her and met her eyes in the mirror.

"Yea." She shook her head a tiny bit. "I mean yes. I've never worn such dresses or peered in such large mirrors."

"Nor wanted to from the look on your face."

"Mirrors are not one of the things I wondered about. The closest I had to this is a still pool of water on a sunny day and that reflection was most fun for the rock one could pitch to make it dissolve into ripples." Jessamine reached out and touched the mirror making it wobble a bit in its stand.

"Well, don't be throwing rocks at this mirror. Superstition claims a broken mirror leads to seven years' bad luck. Plus Dr. Hargrove would charge triple its worth to my account." Her father laughed and then held his hand up where she could see the pen and paper he held. "But I'll wager you have long wondered about these. Or at least wished for them."

She forgot the mirror and the strange girl staring out of it as she took the pen and paper from him. "Can I truly write anything I want?"

"Anything. Let the words spill out. Joy. Sorrow. Love. Hate. Truth. Lies. You get to choose every word, every feeling you want to write." He was smiling at her.

She hugged the book of paper to her and spun around in her happiness. She forgot her petticoats in the small room and Abigail had to grab the lamp before she jarred it from the table next to the chair.

Sister Sophrena Prescott
Harmony Hill Shaker Village
June 22, 1849

  Dear Sister Sophrena,
  The world is a surprising place. Yesterday morning
I rose from my Shaker bed with no expectations
other than those I had on any other day. To do my
duties for the good of the Society. This morn I woke
from my sleep with no idea of what to expect of
the day. It seems an almost opposite world where
each hour something unexpected jumps up to make
me wonder. I am nearly dizzy with the wondering.
I feel at sea, drifting with no familiar land in sight.
Of course, as you well know, my sister, that is
somewhere I have never been. On the sea. But my
father of the world says he will take me to see the
sea. And to see so many other wonders of the world.
Wonders I never even knew to ponder on.
  I do beg your forgiveness for the way I left
Harmony Hill. It surely seemed sudden and
impulsive. For years you have tried to cure me of
such impulsiveness. The sort of unrestrained curiosity

*that often ended with me in trouble and out of step
with my sisters.*

*I am truly out of step now here at White Oak
Springs. Worse than out of step. Fearful to take a step
for worry it will be in a wrong direction. My father
says I will learn more of the world's ways each day.
He says there are no rules, but I think he has been
such a part of the world that he has no vision of the
rules that seem to control every action of those here
at the Springs.*

*The man I found in the woods and brought back
to the village is here, but you need not be concerned
with him being a bother to me. Sister Abigail, who is
also here at the Springs, tells me that Tristan Cooper
is betrothed to a girl so rich she could be a princess.
Money seems to matter much in the world. At the
village all that mattered was doing our work faithfully
and loving the Lord and our brethren and sisters.
I do not see that sort of love here, or have not yet,
I should say. I haven't been in the world long and
surely there will be brotherly love here.*

*Everyone is being very kind to me. Especially my
father. He has bought me several new dresses, for he
says I cannot wear my Shaker dress here. You would
not recognize me on the outside, but I would hope
you would still recognize my heart that remembers
you with much sisterly love.*

*Your sister,
Jessamine*

Journal Entry

Harmony Hill Village
Entered on this 22nd day of June in the year 1849
by Sister Sophrena Prescott

Friday, a good day of faithfully performing our
duties here at Harmony Hill. I worked at preparing
the straw for more bonnets. Come Monday, my duty
will change to the sewing room since we have vital
need of new dresses and shirts for the converts who
have come among us in the last few weeks. I am glad
to be using my talents for the good of the Society for
from the time I was a child I have been able to make
fine, straight stitches that hold long in a seam.

During our time of contemplation after our
evening meal, Eldress Frieda brought me a letter.
I recognized the writing at once as that of our former
sister, Jessamine, and I cannot deny that my heart
grew light with joy. Eldress Frieda said the letter had
been carried here by Brother Hector who had been
out trading with the world on this day. The Ministry
read it at once and made the decision to allow me to
receive it so that I could correspond with our former

sister in hopes she will see the error of her ways and return to us.

Brother Hector reports he might have caught sight of our former sister, since he saw a lady conversing with the servant who asked Brother Hector to carry the letter here. He could not be sure it was her. He wisely does his best to keep his eyes away from those of the world as much as he can when he goes to White Oak Springs to deliver the rosewater and tonics and other items that are so in demand there. We are dutiful stewards of the blessings of the Lord and happy to make gain from the work of our hands. Brother Hector is glad to be of service by trading with the world, but he has no desire to be enticed into sin by the waywardness he sees there.

A waywardness that it seems, from the words of our former sister's letter, may be engulfing her. But upon reading her words, we—the Ministry, Eldress Frieda, and I—feel she may be somewhat regretting her decision and casting her eyes back toward Harmony Hill. If so, the Ministry is quite willing for me to convey our readiness to have her come home. We have given our former sister much of our time and training as well as much of our love. It would be good if she were to return. And in truth, she admits the world is a baffling place. Her words do sound a bit confused with first excitement and praise for the new world she is seeing and then worry as she wonders of the rules of the world that are so unknown to her.

I will write to her early in the morning. That way the Ministry can read it and decide if I should mail it from the Postal Office or let Brother Hector take it. When he next returns to the Springs, I am told that during their busy season, they require much from us—brooms and silk handkerchiefs and as much strawberry jam as we can spare for their morning tables. The jam is especially good this season, but we must supply our own tables first.

27

All day on Friday, Tristan had wavered between one minute wishing Jessamine had stayed at the Shaker village far from his eyes, and the next, wanting to haunt her shadow so he might be near enough to have the chance to touch her. To feel the magic of her lips under his yet one more time. The kiss they'd shared had shaken his world. He had told his mother when she confronted him in the garden that nothing had changed. He lied.

Everything was changed. Everything.

And yet he could change nothing. He had made a promise to Laura. He'd made a promise to his mother. His future was ordered. The beautiful Jessamine was not part of that future. He had felt the attraction at the Shaker village, but thought it no more than a dalliance. After all, the Shakers didn't believe in romantic love, and while Jessamine had not completely closed away the natural curiosity about love, she was a Shaker. So once he rode away from the village, he thought the temptation would end for both of them. He didn't deny he had wanted to turn his horse around to ride back to the village that Sunday to at least tell her goodbye, but he'd kept riding toward White Oak Springs. Kept doing what had to be done for the family name. The family fortune. Trade his future to keep his mother in jewels and feathers.

Then Jessamine had appeared no longer in her Shaker dress. So beautiful that his heart had leaped into his throat with his first sight of her. Something his mother noted right away. He had never been able to hide anything from her. She knew him the way she knew the back of her own hand. That's why she was waiting to confront him in the garden. To make sure he didn't do anything foolish. And so he'd told her nothing had changed.

His mother had believed him. Or perhaps more likely she knew he lied, but she believed he would do as she said. Hadn't he always? She accepted his lie, found her smile, and hurried back inside to entertain her lawyer friend before one of the other unattached women of a certain age latched onto him. Tristan followed her, steeling himself to practice more pretense when what he wanted to do was find Jessamine and beg her never to run away from him again.

She wasn't in her seat by the door. He didn't see her anywhere, and in spite of his lies to his mother, he might have turned back to the garden to be sure she hadn't lost her way if Laura hadn't slipped her arm through his to claim his attention. Laura was merely trying to keep Calvin Green at bay by claiming Tristan and giving credence to the rumors of their pending engagement.

Green obviously wasn't ready to accept that as he hovered in the background ready to pounce if Tristan happened to step away from Laura. She had no intention of letting that happen. What choice did Tristan have but to play the part of her admiring fiancé-to-be even after the beautiful Jessamine came in from the garden to reclaim her seat by the open doors? When other men approached her with a word of welcome, Tristan wanted to rush across the room and push them aside, but he could hardly shake off Laura's claiming hand. Not after the promises he'd made that very day. Not even if the only reason for her hold was her dislike of Calvin Green.

Tristan wished Laura was in love with Calvin Green. If so, he would have joined their hands together with gladness. But that wasn't the man Laura was pining after. Tristan had no idea who that man might be. Perhaps someone in Boston. Someone without the pretense of a socially acceptable name. Someone without pretense.

That's all he and Laura had. Pretense.

That afternoon as they strolled around the lake, he had thought of ridding himself of pretense. Ridding both of them. She could go chase her true love whoever he might be and he could go chase Jessamine. He'd seen Jessamine earlier on the veranda, her head bent over a pad of paper in front of her. Drawing or writing, he couldn't tell which.

She had taken no notice of him at all. Perhaps he had been nothing more than an answer to her curiosity of how a kiss would feel. If it had been more, she would surely glance his way. Allow him to capture her eyes if only for the brief flash of a second.

Now, here at the evening meal, when Tristan had thought their close proximity would mean she would have to notice him, she passed her eyes across his face quickly with a polite greeting as though they had never shared those garden moments. Perhaps the kiss had not lived up to her expectations. Perhaps she wanted simply to forget it ever happened.

He watched her covertly in hopes she would let down her guard and allow him at least a smile. She did not. She smiled at her father, easily and often. She smiled at Viola Cleveland as she copied her every move in eating her bread and salad and drinking her tea. Nobody clanged a spoon against a glass on this evening. Not even Robert Cleveland. He was too intent on being sure the lawyer from Atlanta knew the truth of things.

Mr. Ridenour had found his tongue during the day. The two men were ready to right the wrongs of the country, but the only thing they managed to agree on was that the country was in need of saving. While their words were civil, they were also loud enough to dominate the table conversation.

With eyes wide with fright or perhaps amazement, Jessamine watched them argue. The Shakers surely didn't have such disagreements, especially at the dinner table. Then he remembered Sister Lettie telling him they made no conversation at all as they tended to the serious business of supplying their bodies with the fuel for work. Pleasant or angry. The unaccustomed noise in the dining room had to be pounding against Jessamine's ears. She did seem distracted, perhaps overcome by all the differences of life away from the Shakers.

But then Laura seemed distracted too. She hardly spoke to Jessamine even though Mrs. Cleveland was continually offering the girl special kindness. He wondered if that was because she saw her own diffidence mirrored in Jessamine. But what was it Laura had told him? That most people misjudged her mother and mistook reserved politeness for timidity. He caught the woman watching him across the table a time or two after that, and wondered if perhaps his mother was mistaken about which of Laura's parents he needed most to impress.

Tristan let his gaze slide around the table. Was Viola Cleveland only pretending to kowtow to her husband's thinking? Was Robert Cleveland's bluster a noisy cover-up of his own insecurities? And what of Tristan's own mother with the blush coloring her cheeks while she pretended interest in the lawyer's political talk? Was the blush from worry that Cleveland would be offended by the other man's opposite views or was the warmth in her cheeks the result of Ridenour's obvious admiration? While Tristan had difficulty imagining his mother being swept away by romantic thoughts, when he really looked at her as a person other than his mother, he realized she was not too old to enjoy engaging in a bit of harmless flirtation at a place like White Oak Springs. And what of Sheldon Brady who made his livelihood penning romantic stories that were nothing but make-believe? Was he only pretending to be a devoted father because it was amusing him? Then again, who was Tristan to look down at anybody else's posturing? Heaven only knew, he and Laura were pretending to be what they were not. Perhaps the only person sitting at their table honest enough to simply be herself was Jessamine. What was it Sister Lettie had told him? That the Shakers valued the gift to be simple over all others.

The gift to be simple. To do what was right. To stop the pretense. But the Shakers pretended. If they believed they could conquer the need for love between a man and woman, they were fooling themselves, without doubt. But weren't he and Laura denying that same need? Denying romantic love the same as the Shakers. And so his thoughts went around until he felt as dizzy as one of those Shaker sisters he'd watched stagger and fall after being overtaken by a whirling ecstasy in their worship meeting.

Tristan was relieved when Laura claimed exhaustion and stated she planned to retire to her room after the evening meal. There was no dancing in the ballroom, but the band was playing on the piazza and luminaries traced the pathways around the lake.

Mosquitoes. There would be mosquitoes. Tristan made himself think of the whining pests so he could mash down the desire to be out there strolling around the lake with Jessamine. He leaned against one of the porch pillars and peered out at the ladies' light-colored gowns glimmering in the moonlight. One of them might be Jessamine keeping in step with another man and perhaps wondering about a kiss from lips other than Tristan's. The thought stabbed through him, and though he knew he had no right, he stepped off the porch to go find Jessamine. To see with his own eyes who she was with. To keep her from stepping into the shadows with the wrong man. Any man would be the wrong man.

"Looking for someone?" Calvin Green stepped up beside him. The man must have been in the shadows watching him. For what purpose, Tristan couldn't imagine.

"Simply enjoying the night air. How about you?" Tristan kept his voice cool. He hadn't liked the man from their first meeting when Green had bragged about perfecting his shooting eye by using his aunt's cats as targets.

Now Green had the look of a man with a secret up his sleeve he thought gave him a winning hand. "I've always got my eyes open. You never know what or who you might see. Things that might be interesting to others, if you know what I mean."

There was something vaguely threatening in the man's tone. Something that Tristan saw no reason to ignore. He stared straight at him as he spoke. "No, I don't know what you mean."

"Some people like living in the dark." The man made a sound that might have been a laugh as he slid his eyes away from Tristan and out toward the couples around the lake. "I don't think our Laura is one of those people."

Tristan could have told Green how in the dark he was if he thought Laura would ever look favorably on his courtship, but he kept back the words. He had no wish to goad the man into fisticuffs. Especially with his right arm still tethered in a sling. How long had Sister Lettie told him to leave it bandaged? Three weeks or was it four? It had been two. Two short weeks since he'd been shot and left for dead in the woods. Perhaps he owed his very breath to Jessamine.

"Our Laura?" Tristan kept his voice light. "I don't think either of us can claim ownership."

"Rumor has it you think you can, but you should know that I intend to marry Laura Cleveland. Whatever it takes." Green continued to look out toward the lake as though he were talking about nothing more important than how pleasant the night air felt after the heat of the day.

"Whatever it takes. Strong words," Tristan said.

"But words you can be sure I mean." The man slowly turned his eyes from the lake back to Tristan. "I'm a man who gets what he wants. And I want Laura Cleveland."

Tristan couldn't keep from smiling at the man's delusional thinking. "Don't you think Laura might have something to say about that?"

"Women." Green threw up his hand as though waving away the thought like a pesky mosquito. "They don't know what they want. Her father will decide for her and he had about made up his mind in my favor before your mother began talking you up like the second coming. As though riding off to fight in Mexico made you some kind of hero." His voice carried a tone of ridicule.

"No hero here," Tristan said evenly. "At least we can agree on that, but I think you'd better cast your eye in some direction other than Laura."

Green let a smile slip across his face. "Oh, you mean like that writer's daughter. The Shaker girl. She's a pretty little thing, isn't she? And so innocent any man probably could lead her down some interesting paths with a few fancy words."

Tristan curled his good hand up into a fist. The thought of this man even looking at Jessamine was enough to make him want to knock the smile off his face. The man's smile got wider. It was evident he was doing his best to goad Tristan, but if Tristan had learned nothing else in Mexico, he'd learned not to fight foolish men. Tristan pulled in a slow breath and straightened out his fingers one by one before he said, "I'm sure her father will watch after her."

"He wasn't paying much attention last night." The man's smile was more of a smirk now. "At least not as much attention as you were."

"What are you trying to say, Green?" Tristan had no intention of playing games with the man.

"It could be you and your sweet little Shaker girl weren't having as private a stroll through the garden last evening as you may have thought. And you can be sure I'm a man who doesn't mind using what he knows if it gets me what I want. If I were you, I'd keep in mind that people who get in Calvin Green's way tend to get knocked to the side." He leaned a bit closer to Tristan. "And maybe trampled down into the ground."

Tristan didn't back away from the man. "I've run straight into cannon fire, Green. So if you're trying to scare me, you've got to know it's not working."

Green laughed. "Survived cannon fire and then almost didn't survive a little ride in the woods." He poked Tristan's bandaged arm. "A man never knows when he might stumble into a hole he can't climb out of."

"What do you know about that?" Tristan narrowed his eyes on the man.

"I know that the next time there might not be any pretty little Shaker girls around to pull a man out of that hole."

The man started to turn away, but Tristan grabbed the front of his ruffled shirt in his good hand and yanked him back. "Are you saying you had something to do with shoving me in that hole?"

Green's eyes flashed open wider as if realizing he might have stumbled into a hole of his own making that was deeper than he expected.

"Gentlemen! Gentlemen!" Dr. Hargrove stepped up behind them. "I see you might be having some disagreement here, but we really can't allow fisticuffs on the veranda. We must consider the tender sensibilities of our ladies."

Tristan released his hold on the man reluctantly. Green stepped back and laughed a little, as though making Tristan angry had been his intent and he was pleased with his success.

He smoothed down his shirt as he said, "You're right, Doctor. Fact is, Mr. Cooper here was doubting the trueness of my aim. I'm sure you could settle that for us."

Dr. Hargrove smiled along with Green. "Well, I can attest that while Calvin may not be the sharpshooter I am, he does manage to hit the bull's eye more times than not." He turned to eye Tristan. "But I don't think we've seen you out at the shooting range, have we, Tristan?"

"I've been busy," Tristan said.

"So you have." The doctor laughed again. "In fact, I rather thought you'd be busy tonight. I just saw a beautiful lady slipping through the garden. Surprised me to see her so alone."

"Jessamine?" The name was out before Tristan could stop it.

A flicker of a frown chased across the doctor's face while Green's smile got wider. "No, no. I think our young Shaker sister is a bit overwhelmed by our world here at the Springs. I spotted her father escorting her back to her room some time ago. I was speaking of Laura."

Now it was Tristan's turn to frown. "Laura? She told me she was retiring early."

"Then perhaps I was mistaken," the doctor said. "I only caught a glimpse and it may have been another of our fair ladies slipping out to the garden to shake free of her chaperone. Could be I didn't see a thing." Dr. Hargrove was smiling again. "Yes, I think my eyesight must have been faulty. I didn't see a thing. Such a blind eye serves me well here at the Springs. You can be sure of that."

"That blind eye doesn't bother you when you're shooting?" Tristan said, hoping to change the direction of the conversation. He had no doubt the doctor had seen Laura in the garden. Perhaps just taking the air before she turned in for the night. Or perhaps her true love wasn't far away in Boston after all. But the last thing she needed was for Calvin Green to be tracking her down in the gardens.

"Not at all. A man doesn't need to see to hit the target. Just point." Dr. Hargrove slapped Tristan on the back and then squeezed Green's upper arm. "So we'll settle this dispute between the two of you soon enough out on the shooting range tomorrow. It will be a good amusement to fill the afternoon hours."

"I'm afraid I don't have a pistol. I brought my father's with me, but whoever waylaid me in the woods must have stolen it." Tristan stared straight at Green to see if he showed any sign of guilt.

The man didn't blink an eye as he said, "What a shame, but I'm sure Dr. Hargrove can supply you with a firearm if you're not too crippled up to give shooting a try."

"I have one good hand." Tristan held it up in hopes the man would remember that hand wrapped around his shirt.

"And a good thing to learn true aim with whichever hand is available, I would say. I'm sure you learned that well enough in Mexico, Tristan," Dr. Hargrove said.

"War can teach you many things. Some you'd rather not learn," Tristan said.

"True enough." Dr. Hargrove turned suddenly away from Tristan to stare out at the night sky. "Was that thunder I heard?"

Light flickered on the horizon followed by a distant rumble. Green looked from it to Tristan and the doctor. "A storm may be brewing."

If Dr. Hargrove caught the double meaning, he ignored it as he shook his head. "No need to worry about storms until they are over our heads, I don't suppose. And I'm still seeing stars up there now. So let's leave our worries behind, gentlemen, and enjoy the evening. Our ladies have come here eager for a little social interchange and we don't want to disappoint our ladies."

"I thought they came for the waters," Tristan said. "To cure whatever ailed them."

"To be sure, but that's mostly us older folks. You young ones are seeking a different tonic. The tonic of love." Dr. Hargrove lifted his eyebrows as he looked first at Tristan and then Green. "I'm wagering that's what the two of you are after, and it's a good chance you'll both be drinking deeply of that tonic before you leave here. Now come along. The servants are bringing out ice cream."

Dr. Hargrove hooked his arm around Green and turned him back toward the hotel. Lines were already forming to get a taste of the sweet treat frozen in churns using ice harvested last winter and preserved in icehouses dug into the ground. When Tristan thought about the heat of the day and the months since ice would have covered the lake, it seemed impossible. As impossible as him being able to drink of that tonic of love to enliven his heart.

Perhaps the Shakers were right to shut the temptations of love from their midst. To think only of giving their hearts to God. Hands to work. Hearts to God. That's what Sister Lettie had told him as if it were so simple anyone could do it. Simple. What else had she said? That it was a gift to be simple. The Shakers had sung a song with those words at their meeting. *'Tis the gift to be simple. 'Tis the gift to be free.*

But he wasn't free and nothing seemed simple. He'd turned his back on God in Mexico. Now he was turning his back on love.

Jessamine Brady
White Oak Springs
June 23, 1849

Dear Jessamine,

Oh, how I regret not being able to write, Sister Jessamine, but you gave up such an address when you went to the world. We can no longer claim you as our beloved sister, but we do so desire to continue to do so. We write this to you in hopes you will see the error of your ways and return to our family where you will be loved in a godly manner, in the way spoken of by the Christ, without the sin of matrimony and worldly family units that seems to be beckoning to you.

I know you were taught these truths for we often spoke of the reasons for our commitment to the peaceful life of living in brotherly and sisterly love. Think on the words of Jesus as written in Luke 20:34–35. "Jesus answering said unto them, The children of this world marry, and are given in marriage: but they which shall be accounted worthy to obtain that world, and the resurrection from the dead, neither marry, nor are given in marriage."

So, if we are to bring down heaven here into our village and attain the perfect life, we must embrace the ways of living that will be in the age to come for us. We have heaven here the same as heaven there. Such is the promised blessing of a committed and faithful Believer. The sort of Believer you were becoming before temptation led your feet astray.

But we are a forgiving people. Keep that truth close to your thoughts in the days ahead as you confront the dangers of the world. We will labor a dance for you, dear Jessamine, in hopes you will not be conquered by the world and that your feet will once more seek the way of truth and salvation and return you to our village. Be assured such a reunion would shower great joy down on all of us, your former sisters and brothers.

Eldress Frieda tells me also to relay the message from the Ministry that if you do return to us with a humble and loving spirit, they will end the order of constant supervision. They will know by your return that you have regretted your wrongs and are ready to step forward along the right way of discipline and duty to give your hands to work and your heart to God.

Your loving former sister,
Sophrena Prescott

28

Sister Sophrena's letter brought tears to Jessamine's eyes and doubts to her heart. Perhaps she had sinned by leaving Harmony Hill. Perhaps she had given up her sure salvation. It did seem the world was a hard place with many questions that had no answers.

"I can give you the answers you need," Abigail told Jessamine when she spoke that worry aloud on Monday afternoon. Abigail had brought her the letter from Sister Sophrena, delivered that morning by Brother Hector along with a few baskets of freshly picked cucumbers and a crate of strawberry jam. "You are free of those who would wrap you in chains and tell you what to believe. You need to stay free of those who would deny you happiness. And if you're worried about your soul, I can assure you the Bible does not only reveal answers to those Shakers. People got married plenty of times in the Bible and received the Lord's blessing."

Jessamine looked down at the letter in her hand as Abigail began arranging Jessamine's hair for the dance that night. Her father said it was the most elaborate dance of the season and all the ladies would be decked out in their finest. The promised ball gown from Mrs. Browning now hung on a hanger hooked over the top board of the wardrobe. A beautiful creation of blue silk and white lace and ribbons.

The same blue as her Shaker dress folded and hidden in the bottom of the wardrobe. Neither her father, Mrs. Browning, or Abigail seemed to note that truth. Instead they only spoke of the blue being the color of Jessamine's eyes, as though that remarkable occurrence gave the dress greater value. And yet the Shaker dress also was the color of Jessamine's eyes, and as far as she could remember no one had ever spoken of that. Not even the stranger from the world she had carried back to the village on his horse. Not even Tristan Cooper.

Jessamine held in a sigh. Why did her every thought circle around to Tristan Cooper? The prince who loved another. Even Abigail knew that to be true. That he was in love with the girl named Laura who knew how to be a princess. Who had been trained to walk right and sit right and eat with the proper fork. Things that Jessamine didn't know. Or even care to know. What was the need in a different fork for different foods? All went into the mouth and utensils were easily enough licked clean.

So much in this world seemed no more than foolishness. Even the parasols she had once so wondered about that she had led Sister Annie on a fools' errand into the woods. The frilly things barely afforded the first bit of shade and required a hand to hold them over one's head. Better to wear a bonnet to keep the sun off one's face so one's hands could be free to hold a pen and book of paper.

The pen and the paper. The free flow of ink. No foolishness there. She had been carried along on a river of words ever since her hand had taken hold of the pen and even now sitting there with Abigail combing and tugging on her hair, her hand itched to pick up the pen and take the stopper out of her pot of ink.

When her father had peeked over her shoulder at her many filled pages, he had laughed aloud, but he had not read them. Not yet. He said that in the beginning the words should be hers and hers alone. That was so she could write whatever came to mind without worrying about them being proper words acceptable to other eyes. Even his.

He understood the feel of words pent up inside and how holding a pen had broken open a dam inside her to allow out such a rush of ink. He understood, but Sister Sophrena would not. Jessamine stared down at the letter in her hand again. They had labored a dance for her at meeting in hopes she would return to them. Return to her salvation.

She shouldn't have written to Sister Sophrena. The sister knew her too well and had clearly seen the confusion of thought behind Jessamine's words. And yet, even with Sister Sophrena's letter pulling at her heart, she had no idea of turning from the world. She had so much more to see. So many more words to write. Plus her eyes longed for more sights of Tristan Cooper.

She had seen him strolling around the lake with the princess. She had seen him dancing attendance on Laura at the eating table. She knew there was no hope. Abigail had told her the gossip in the servants' quarters revealed a proposal was in the offing. Maybe this very evening.

When Jessamine was unable to hide the way those words stabbed her heart, Abigail had hugged her shoulders and said, "It won't be anything to do with you. The man could love you. He probably does love you, but marriages among the rich are made more often for money or position than love. Thank goodness, the same is not true for me. A poor girl like me and a poor boy like Jimmy can marry for love as they have nothing to lose and all to gain in their hearts."

"It doesn't matter to me what he does. I barely know the man." Jessamine tried to cover up her distress.

"Know him well or not, I'm thinking love has taken root in your heart for him." Abigail pushed the truth at her.

Jessamine was unable to deny the girl's words, but she did not have to give in to them. Instead she had lifted her chin and declared, "Then I will pluck it out like the useless weed it is."

But Jessamine had made no attempt to pull the weed of unrequited love from her heart, even though Abigail had confirmed her uneasy fears that she had been sinfully wayward to allow the man to kiss her. She had wondered about the feeling of forbidden love so long that she wanted to cling to it a bit longer even if the roots did grow and make the pulling out of it more painful.

She had at least been sensible enough to stay out of his path. She stayed buried in her book of paper during the days and only saw him at the dinner table because she couldn't reveal to her father any reason for avoiding the evening meals.

She would see Tristan again that night and her heart skipped a couple of beats at the thought. She did so wish the two of them might walk out into the garden again. The thought shamed her and she ran her eyes back over the words in Sister Sophrena's letter that spoke of the sin of worldly love. Then her eyes skimmed down to the offer of forgiveness. The sister was holding out a hand to beckon her home. Jessamine felt the pull of that hand, but the pull of the world remained stronger.

This time Jessamine didn't hide her sigh as she folded the letter to hide the sight of Sister Sophrena's handwriting.

Abigail stopped combing to peer at Jessamine's face in the mirror. "Now don't you let that ancient old sister's words spoil your night."

"She's not that old," Jessamine said. "Not even forty. Eldress Frieda, she has more claim to ancient."

"There are all kinds of ways of being old. A person can

be our age and be old in spirit. Those sisters over there try to make everybody old in spirit. What with their rules and duties." Abigail made a face.

"But shouldn't that be good? To be old in the spirit. To know what you believe." Jesamine looked away from Abigail's reflection in the mirror to stare down at the folded sheet of paper. She used to know what she believed.

Abigail poked Jesamine's shoulder with the comb. "You know what you believe. I'm not doubting for the first minute that you have the love of the Lord right there in your heart. Now, don't you?"

"Yea, I do love the Lord. I've never doubted that." Jesamine fingered the letter and thought of Sister Sophrena waiting to welcome her home. Home. That's what she no longer knew. Where was home?

"Then what are you doubting?" Abigail asked.

"My path. Where I belong. I am not sure I can learn the ways of the world."

When Jesamine kept her eyes downcast, Abigail scooted around to lean over and study Jesamine's face. After a moment, she said, "Ahh! It's not the sister's letter that has you sighing so much as Tristan Cooper."

Jesamine admitted the truth of that with yet another sigh. "The prince who loves another."

"Maybe. But I'm thinking from the gossip I hear among the servants that the mother has more to do with him court-ing that Laura than his heart." Abigail stood up and went back to arranging Jesamine's hair. "You are going to look so lovely tonight in your fairy-tale dream of a dress it could be he will forget his mother and follow his heart."

"But even if you're right, would that be the right thing to happen? Would I want it to happen?"

"Those are answers you must find on your own, Jessa-mine." Abigail pressed her lips into a firm line as she stared at Jessamine in the mirror a moment before going on. "But I do know this. You can't be afraid to look for those answers."

"I'm not afraid. I've never been afraid. Well, maybe except when Granny stopped breathing."

"And now." Abigail stuck another pin into the elaborate twist of hair on the back of Jessamine's head.

Jessamine watched Abigail's hands in the mirror as she kept her eyes away from her own face. She didn't want to see the stranger she'd become. Instead she fingered Sister Sophrena's letter and knew Abigail was right. She was afraid. Afraid to leap into the world and open her heart to pain. At Harmony Hill, she'd been like a little mouse sticking its nose out into the open to watch things of the world scurry past it but without leaving the safety of its burrow. Her curiosity about love as the world knew it had been no more than the memory of her grandmother's stories tiptoeing through her thoughts. It was fun to consider the prince her granny said would come for her, but it was never anything other than an echo of a fairy tale that she knew had little chance of ever coming true. Until she'd found the man in the woods. Until Tristan Cooper.

The prince who loved another. It didn't matter what Abigail said. Jessamine knew what he had told his mother. *Nothing has changed.*

Dinner that evening was a rushed affair, served early so the ladies could change into their party frocks. Many of the women didn't show up to eat at all, including Laura and Mrs. Cooper. Jessamine was relieved to see Mrs. Cleveland there so that she wasn't alone with the men at the table. Everything in the world was so upside down to how she had lived so many years with the Shakers. Talk and no prayer at mealtime. Sitting side by side with her father with no distance between to keep them from touching. At Harmony Hill many pains were taken to keep such touching from happening. Even from one's own natural father or brothers of the world. Such relationships were to be given up to walk the Shaker way.

A few words of a song she had often labored in meeting ran through her mind. *Love not flesh, nor fleshly kin.* The fleshly kin would be her father. The flesh would be Tristan Cooper. Her heart did a fast, skipping beat whenever she looked across the table at him. She tried to keep her gaze on her food or Mrs. Cleveland, but her eyes were drawn to him like a moth to the candle flame. And each time his eyes seemed to be waiting to capture hers. Something she feared Mrs. Cleveland and her father noticed. The lawyer and Mr. Cleveland noticed nothing except their fury of words.

She was relieved when the food had been eaten and she could excuse herself to return to her room. If not for the beautiful dress awaiting her there, she would have begged her father to allow her to stay in her room by the window to fill more pages with words. But he had gone to great trouble and expense to see that she had the proper attire for the dance. She could hardly refuse to wear it even if the princess dresses became less appealing each time Abigail buttoned her into one of them. They poked and squeezed and revealed entirely too much of her female shape.

Mrs. Cleveland excused herself as well and walked with Jessamine back toward the stairs that led to their rooms. "Last year when we were here, this midsummer dance was quite the event." She smiled over at Jessamine. "Laura has been trying on this or that dress all afternoon. She does want to look her best."

Jessamine managed a smile back. "I'm sure she will look like a princess."

"A princess." Mrs. Cleveland blew out a little puff of breath as if the word was disturbing. "Yes, well, I've always thought being a princess overrated."

"The prince always comes and they live happily ever after."

Mrs. Cleveland laughed. "So the stories go, but happily ever after is not so easily achieved on the other side of the kiss as the storytellers would have you believe. Have you always wanted to be a princess, my dear?"

"Nay." Jessamine shook her head a bit. "I mean no. But my grandmother used to tell me fairy tales before I went to live with the Shakers."

"And there you became a sister instead of a princess." They walked in silence for a moment before she went on. "They tell me in the Shaker villages a woman's abilities are respected and the sisters share posts of leadership with the brethren. Is that true?"

"Yea." This time Jessamine didn't bother to correct the Shaker word with the worldly word. "Mother Ann taught that all are equal in the eyes of Creator God. He does not distinguish blessings by sex or race."

"If only all would be so forward thinking. Not that I could accept all the teachings. The separation of families appears to go against the words I read in the Bible."

"There is Scripture that suggests the purity of life without the sin of marriage." Jessamine thought of the verses Sister Sophrena had written to her. "It is the hope of the Believers that they can live a perfect life in their villages apart from the world as the angels do in heaven."

"And what is your hope, my dear?" She put her hand on Jessamine's arm and stopped her beside a window in the lobby. "Do you want to be a princess seeking her prince or do you want to be a sister seeking a life of purity?"

When Jessamine just looked at her without an answer, Mrs. Cleveland smiled sadly and said, "Some questions require much thought to answer, and even then it is hard to know if the answer we find is the proper one."

"I lived long among the Believers and I must admit the world is very mystifying to me."

Again Mrs. Cleveland laughed. A short, intense sound before she said, "It mystifies me at times too, my girl."

As they turned toward the stairs, a rumble of thunder tickled the windowpanes behind them. "Oh, I do hope the storms hold off until after the gala. Rain would spoil the garden proposals. I hear there are to be several this evening."

"I have heard the same." Jessamine watched the tips of her shoes peek out from under her full skirt as she walked.

"And are you hoping for a proposal so soon into the world where such could be a possibility for you?" Mrs. Cleveland asked.

"Oh nay." Again she let the Shaker word stand. It didn't seem to matter to Mrs. Cleveland how she talked. "I have never even wondered of such a thing."

"But you have wondered of princes and love."

"Wondering does not seem to me to be a sin." Jessamine almost whispered the words.

"No indeed. Nor is love, but it can be troubling at times. Very troubling."

"Why is that?" Jessamine asked as they climbed the steps to the second floor of the hotel. She knew it was true, but she wanted to know why.

"People," Mrs. Cleveland said as though the answer was plain. "It's as simple as that. People."

"Simple," Jessamine echoed. "We sing a song at Harmony Hill that it's a gift to be simple. A gift to be free."

"And so it surely is," Mrs. Cleveland agreed. "But it is not a gift we often embrace. We twist and turn and complicate everything and especially love. I tell my Laura it would seem so much better to simply follow one's heart, but she does not." The woman sighed as she stopped at the door to her room. "Some things aren't as simple or as free as they seem, but it is this mother's wish for the simple gift of happiness to overtake my daughter and I wish the same for you, my dear."

Her words along with the echo of the Shaker song followed Jessamine to her room where Abigail was waiting to disguise Jessamine as a princess. And outside the window the thunder continued to rumble with no concern of spoiling the night.

29

Tristan readied himself for the dance without the assistance of a servant in spite of his mother's worries that not having a manservant would make him appear to be impoverished. He told her they were impoverished. Besides, he had managed to tend to his own needs in the dust and death of the Mexican battlefields. There the only things he'd worried about being clean were his gun and his feet. Both needed to be dry and in working order.

As he combed back his hair and tied his cravat, he thought again of his father's gun with regret. Dr. Hargrove had supplied him with a firearm Saturday at the shooting range. He had capably aimed and fired at the targets with his left hand. Calvin Green had not taken defeat gracefully, blaming the target, the sun in his eyes, the noise of the onlookers who broke his concentration. Tristan hadn't bothered to listen to the man after a while. He was no more than the irritating whine of a mosquito in his ear. Nothing of real concern.

No, the real concern was going down on his knee to speak his proposal to Laura that night as he had promised. Calvin Green's veiled threats wouldn't stop that from happening. Tristan wasn't through with the man. If Green knew anything about Tristan getting shot in the woods, he'd find out. Not that the man knowing Tristan was rescued by the Shaker sisters meant anything. Anybody at the Springs could know Jessamine and her friend had come to Tristan's aid. He'd told the story here. Stories got repeated. Often.

Green, by his own admission, was the kind of man ready to use whatever might fall in his lap to get what he wanted. He wanted Laura. He'd probably already told Laura about Tristan walking with Jessamine in the garden. More than walking with her. Kissing her.

The memory of the kiss stabbed through Tristan as thoughts of Jessamine filled his mind and pushed aside Green and his spying eyes. He wanted to take her arm and walk with her through the garden again. He wanted to go down on his knee in front of her instead of Laura. That's where the dream stopped and reality stepped in. A man kept his promises. He didn't throw over his duty for a girl he'd known a bare two weeks. No matter how much he wanted to.

It wouldn't matter to Laura what Green whispered in her ear. She wouldn't care who Tristan kissed. She was doing her duty every bit as reluctantly as he was. While love between them didn't seem likely, they would make a life. Jessamine would make a life too. Her father would show her the world. There would be another man in another garden. Another man to go down on his knee and beg her to be his.

Tristan stared at the mirror. He wanted to slam his hand into the glass and shatter the image of his face. He couldn't stand the sight of himself. He shut his eyes and with deliberate moves lay the comb down on the chest and moved away from the mirror. He had been a soldier. He knew discipline. He knew how to deny himself and do the things he must.

He stepped to the open window and peered out at the sky. The storm clouds were definitely sweeping closer. Already the wind was ruffling the leaves of the trees, promising rain.

Promising to spoil his garden proposal. His heart lifted at the thought. That would give him yet another night, another day to be free to look at Jessamine with hope.

At the dinner table, she had been so lovely he was unable to keep his eyes off her even with Laura's mother watching him much too closely. None of the three of them had paid the first bit of attention to the ongoing argument between Ridenour and Cleveland. Jessamine's father had also seemed preoccupied. So much so, he had actually apologized and blamed the story he was writing for failing to be a properly attentive dinner companion. That could perhaps be true, but Tristan had doubts a made-up story could make a man look to be wrestling with demons the same as Tristan was.

Demons. The word jarred in Tristan's thoughts. If he was wrestling with demons, they were of his own invention. He stared out at the horizon where streaks of lightning reached down for the ground. Still so distant that the thunder following the flashes was a mere rumble. But the sound made him think of the battlefield again. The guns on the shooting range had done the same. Was that a sound he would never get out of his head? A sound of death in the offing.

He had heard it on the battlefield while fear rose inside him as he waited for the order to charge forward. But the fear wasn't as bad as the overpowering regret that settled deep within him at the thought of not seeing another dawn. He wanted more days, more time. Time to love and be loved. To hold his firstborn child. He wanted to ride a horse across a field he owned and to feel a dog's wet tongue on his face again. He wanted to bite into an apple and hear the pop while apple juice sprayed his face.

Sometimes to take his mind off the very real possibility of dying, he drew pictures with a stick in the sandy dirt. Pictures that only lasted a few moments before a foot tromped through them or the wind shifted the dust. And he wondered if that was his life. Just a few moments of duty and discipline and then death.

But he had lived through the war. He had come home to do some of those things he'd imagined doing to keep from losing his sanity while fighting in Mexico. But he had not loved and been loved. At least not until now, and now he was refusing that chance. Embracing instead the duty and discipline.

Was this God's punishment on him for turning his back on belief? To put the opportunity for the love Tristan had always dreamed of right in front of him but to make it impossible for him to reach for the opportunity. *For with God all things are possible.* The Bible words slid through his mind. He'd heard them often from the men in the army who were more preachers than soldiers. Words meant to encourage the men when facing a charge into the face of cannons. Or when burning with fever with no hope for the morrow.

Hope, it was such a tenuous thing when mixed with the need for love. His mother said he didn't need love. Laura said they could marry without love. Robert Cleveland would laugh at his yearning for love. But what would Jessamine say?

A gust of air pushed through the window, carrying the hint of rain. Its cool touch on his cheek was like a caress. Perhaps from God. To his surprise, prayer words bubbled up inside him. He tried to shove them aside. God wouldn't help him. Why would he? Tristan had never done anything to deserve the Lord's favor. And yet standing there with the breeze wrapping around him, Tristan felt favored. A bit of another Scripture came to his mind. Something about God being a help in trouble.

Tristan couldn't deny he'd been helped in trouble. He'd come through the war, still breathing. Jessamine had found him in the woods. That had to be the Lord's providence. A gift. Jessamine was a gift. Even if Tristan was never able to declare his love for her, she was a gift who would live in his heart. He'd never forget their kiss. But was that enough? Couldn't he beg for the blessing of more? The need to pray rose inside him again, even though no proper words surfaced with it. Nothing but the thought of Jessamine.

But this time he didn't try to push it away. He just stared out at the storm moving closer and whispered, "Please, God!"

Then embarrassed by his weakness, he slammed the window down and turned toward the door to go face his future.

The rain did come dashing down before the band struck up the first song. Laura wasn't bothered by it. She claimed his arm as soon as he entered the ballroom and turned an amused smile on him when he worried the rain might make a problem with the promised proposal.

"Honestly, Tristan, I don't see the need of us going through that charade. We made our deal. We can let the world imagine the romantic words." Her smile disappeared and she looked suddenly weary as though she hadn't been sleeping well. "I think there's little need of that between us. We both know the reason for our union."

"But it seems so . . ." Tristan couldn't come up with the proper word.

"Businesslike. My father says marriage should be a business decision."

"And what does your mother say?" Tristan looked from Laura to her mother watching them from the other side of the room. She was not smiling.

"My mother does not always think with her head." Laura too looked toward her mother before she whispered a small sigh. "But never fear, Tristan. She likes you and she is quite happy to welcome you into our family. She says she can see your generous heart, and I think she rather looks forward to trying to be a northern influence on some of your southern thinking."

"My thoughts are as malleable as a ball of wet clay," Tristan said with a smile. "But she might have more of a challenge with Mother."

Laura narrowed her eyes on his face then. "It's only the outer edges of your thoughts that you reveal to anyone, Tristan. Your heart you keep secret."

A stir at the other end of the room kept him from having to come up with an answer as Jessamine was escorted into the room by her father. And while his heart might be a secret from Laura, it spilled every bit of its feelings out inside him. The sight of Jessamine grabbed his breath as though someone had slammed a fist into his midsection.

"There's your beautiful little Shaker friend," Laura said.

Tristan was glad Laura was watching Jessamine and her father so intently. Glad he had time to compose his face and shove his heart back down in his chest. Jessamine seemed to almost float across the floor to the chair she'd claimed as her spot at the last dance. She was a vision in a silky blue dress the color of her eyes. He wasn't near enough to see the blue of those eyes, but his memory had no problem bringing them up before him.

Even though she didn't look his way, he had the feeling she was aware of him standing there with Laura. Her father did look toward them and let his gaze linger a moment on them as a frown etched a deep line between his eyes. Jessamine was smiling, an uncertain smile as she carefully arranged her skirts. It was as though the storms brewing outside were coming into the ballroom to mash down on them all. Then the band struck up a new song.

Across the room, Ridenour took his mother's hand and led her out on the dance floor. She looked completely smitten. In fact, Tristan didn't remember her even glancing his way as if her infatuation with the lawyer had made her forget the object of their visit to the Springs. Or maybe she had been so reassured last week by his promise that nothing had changed that she no longer thought she needed to police his every moment.

He was turning to see if Laura wanted to try a dance, awkward though it was with his arm still in the sling, but Sheldon Brady had come up to them while Tristan's attention was on his mother to ask Laura for the dance.

"You don't mind, do you, Tristan?" Laura said with a quick glance toward him before she took Brady's hand. "We'll have so many years to dance. When your arm has healed."

He pushed a bland smile across his face as he watched them glide away to the music and wondered if he and Laura would ever be in perfect step like that. He watched all the couples spinning around the floor in front of him, his eyes going from one smiling face to another and knew there was only one face he wished to see smiling at him.

He looked toward the chair by the veranda doors but it was empty now. Jessamine must have stepped out into the garden in spite of the approaching storm. He imagined her standing there, the wind pushing against her skirt and undoing all the elaborate curls her maid had surely spent hours arranging. Turning away from the pretense of the ballroom and embracing the freedom of wind sweeping through the garden.

Without conscious thought, he took a step toward the doors, but a servant stepped up to hand him a folded bit of paper. He turned his back on the dancers and unfolded the note.

Meet me at the far end of the lake.

There was nothing to indicate who might have written the note. While the words were printed with no flair, the letters were so small and neat they had surely been written by a female hand. Who else could it be but Jessamine? She wouldn't put curls and frills on her letters. The Shakers would have taught her economy in writing as well as everything else she did. But why would she summon him with a note instead of moving across the room to speak to him face-to-face? What message did she have for him that she feared others overhearing?

He looked at her empty chair. A sudden flash of lightning lit up the garden followed a few seconds later by a booming crash of thunder. A few ladies let out startled shrieks, but the music continued.

She surely hadn't gone out into the threatening storm to wait for him, but she wasn't in her seat. She wasn't standing outside the doors in the garden. He would have spotted her there when the lightning flashed. He had to go after her. He had to be sure she was safe. It wouldn't change anything, but he owed her that much.

Across the room, Dr. Hargrove was signaling his musicians to keep playing as other servants scurried around pushing down windows. The party must go on. Tristan spotted his mother. From the look on her face, she had all but forgotten she was a mother. And Laura and Sheldon Brady were still gliding effortlessly to the music. No one would miss him.

30

"Jessamine. Jessamine!"

Jessamine looked around, but no one seemed to be paying the first bit of attention to her. No one calling her name. The silk and satin skirts of the dancers must have fooled her ears with their whispers as they whirled past her. Her father had escorted her to the same seat near the veranda doors. Then with an odd look, almost of guilt to be leaving her alone, he was off to dance with the princess. He had promised Laura a dance that morning at breakfast, and he claimed to be anxious to get the fulfillment of his promise out of the way in order to free the rest of the evening for Jessamine. To teach her some of the dance steps.

"You danced the Shaker dances. These steps will be simple compared to those," he said.

Then he left her attempting to contain the bothersome billowing skirts and petticoats as she sat down. Across the room, her father took Laura from Tristan's side.

Jessamine had spotted Tristan the very instant she came into the room. Just as she could not keep her thoughts from circling to him, so it was the same with her eyes. She was ever aware of his presence. Even after she shifted her gaze to the others in the room, she was still seeing only Tristan Cooper. Now he stood stiffly watching her father and the princess gliding away from him as though they were on ice. She tried to read his thoughts. Was he angry at her father for stealing away the princess? Or simply envious his broken arm kept him from being the one to whirl his love around the floor?

Jessamine had no envy of the dancers or resentment for her father abandoning her so soon. She was rather relieved to be quietly sitting. She had not the least desire to step into the rush of dancers, who as far as she could tell moved with little discipline. While she had always enjoyed laboring the dances at Harmony Hill, there she knew the other dancers would march in order. At least until some Believers began receiving whirling or shaking gifts.

She had never received a whirling gift. Not during meeting, anyway. She had known plenty of times when she did a few twirls simply for the pure joy of movement. The joy of life in the sun. Or in the garden.

As her eyes slid back over toward Tristan, she remembered how he had looked watching the Shaker dances last Sunday. Now their situations were reversed. She was the one watching the world's dance. Not a dance with any thought of worship, to be sure. Here at this place everything was pointed toward romance. Jessamine knew as little about the ways of romance as Tristan had about the ways of the Believers.

She'd seen him watching her that day at meeting. Before he'd been caught in his lie by the visitor from the world. If he could lie so easily about who he was, then there could be much else about which he might not tell the truth. Like a kiss in the garden. That had not felt like a lie, but it surely was. When a man was in love and ready to marry, he should not slip off in a garden with another and encourage a wayward kiss. Even in the world that could not be right. For a certainty, it was not right for a Believer. The kiss she'd given to Tristan, whatever the reason, whatever the motive, was a sin of the first order. If she went back to Harmony Hill, she would have to confess as much.

The thought of confession brought Sister Sophrena to mind. What would the good sister think of her sitting there in a gown of silk with her neck bare and her bosom squeezed and pushed up by the tight bodice of the dress? And with curls lapping down beside her ears and tickling her neck. What would she think of Jessamine's heart leaping at the sight of Tristan Cooper? Jessamine had told Sister Sophrena in her letter that the man was no temptation to her. She had not told the truth. It mattered not that he loved another. That didn't change who she loved.

"Jessamine!"

The dancers were still swirling by her, but the skirts weren't what was whispering her name. A pebble slid across the floor from the veranda door and landed against her skirt. Pitched to get her attention. Jessamine looked around to see if anyone else noticed, but all eyes were on the dancers. No one was paying the first bit of mind to her even after she stood up and moved toward the doors. The music continued on.

Outside the air carried the feel of rain. Abigail would be very unhappy with her if her elaborate curls drooped. And who knew what would happen to such a frothy dress if rain dampened it? Abigail, who had been trying to instruct her in the worldly rules of proper ladylike behavior, would be bound to tell her a lady didn't rush out into a storm. For any cause.

A hand grabbed her arm and jerked her out of the light spilling from the door back against the side of the building.

"Shh," a voice hissed in her ear. "Dr. Hargrove sees me, I'll get sent packing."

"Abigail!" Jessamine was unable to see the girl clearly in

the shadows, but she didn't need to see her face to know something was wrong. "Whatever is the matter? Have I done something wrong?"

"No, no. But I had to come warn you. So you could warn him." She stopped and pulled in a shaky breath as she squeezed Jessamine's arm harder. "I've got to try to make sense even if none of it makes sense. But I knew you'd want to help him. Since you love him."

"Who? Tristan?" She started to lean out to peer around the open door to see if she could see him, but Abigail jerked her back.

"Yes, Tristan. Who else?" Abigail's whisper came out with force. "Jimmy heard two men talking behind the barn about arranging an accident to befall him."

"An accident?" Jessamine couldn't take in the words. Lightning flashed and the garden was filled with gray shadows. Seconds later a jarring boom rattled the windows behind her. The storm had arrived. "You mean to hurt him? Who would want to do that?"

"I don't know. Jimmy didn't see their faces or recognize their voices." Abigail brushed her damp hair back out of her eyes. "He didn't want me to come tell you. He doesn't think they meant it. He says the gentlemen here are always going on with this or that foolishness and this is probably only some kind of joke that will do nothing but get us fired if we raise a stink. But your young man getting shot out in the woods was no laughing matter. I think you should warn him whether it turns out to be a real danger to him or not."

Lightning flashed again and revealed Abigail's distraught face for just a moment. That even more than her words made Jessamine's heart begin to pound. "What did they say they were going to do?" She had to know what to tell him.

"Something about an unfortunate accident down by the lake." Abigail gave Jessamine a little shove back toward the door. "Now go. He can tell Dr. Hargrove. If I get fired, I'll just get fired."

Jessamine's heart was beating so fast she could hardly breathe as she stepped back into the ballroom. The musicians continued to feverishly play their fiddles and guitars as if in hopes of covering up the thunder outside. It seemed to be working, for the dancers who whirled past her were intent on their pleasure and giving little notice to the storm blowing their way.

Her father and the princess swept by. His eyes were on Laura's face, and he gave absolutely no sign of seeing Jessamine. She jerked her skirts back and worked her way around the edge of the dance floor past those waiting their turn with a partner when the music stopped. Tristan was no longer among them. She scanned the room but couldn't catch sight of him anywhere. Not among the dancers or the watchers.

The music throbbed in her ears matching the panic growing inside her. Why would he have left the dance with the evening just starting? He had to be there somewhere.

A touch on her arm stopped her. "My dear, what's wrong? Are you frightened by the storm?" The lady leaned close to speak directly into Jessamine's ear so she could hear over the music.

"Oh, Mrs. Cleveland, I didn't notice you there."

"I know. You were looking quite frantic. No reason to be ashamed though." The woman smiled at her. "I've always thought it shows a healthy respect for nature to be worried when lightning starts flashing, but we should be quite safe inside here. Dr. Hargrove's hotel is built very sturdily."

"Oh yea, I'm sure you're right." Jessamine looked toward the window as if only just remembering the storm.

Mrs. Cleveland frowned a little. "If not the storm, what has you so concerned?"

"I need to find Tristan." Jessamine wanted to spill out the

whole story Abigail had told her, but if Tristan was actually in danger, she'd already wasted too much time talking.

The lady's frown grew deeper and Jessamine decided it might not be any more proper in the world to chase after a man than it was in the Shaker village. So she tried to swallow her panic and pretend a calm she didn't feel as she said, "I had a message to give him from a friend."

The frown eased out from between Mrs. Cleveland's eyes, but she kept studying Jessamine as though unsure of whether to believe her or not. "How odd. You wanting to give him a message when he just got a message delivered by one of the servants." Her eyes sharpened on Jessamine. "To be quite frank I thought the message might be from you."

Now it was Jessamine's turn to frown. "Why would you think that? Sister Abi—" Jessamine stopped and bit off Abigail's name. "I mean my maid told me he plans to propose to Laura this night."

"So I've also been told, but if that is his plan, things are not going very smoothly with Laura dancing with your father and Tristan taking off out the front like he's on a mission."

Jessamine looked toward the front. The lake was in front of the hotel. *An unfortunate accident by the lake.* Abigail's words stabbed through Jessamine's mind. "Perhaps I can catch him," she said as she turned away from Mrs. Cleveland.

"Wait, Jessamine."

The woman tried to hold Jessamine's arm, but Jessamine pulled away from her. There was no time. Even now, she might be too late. "I'll explain later," Jessamine called over her shoulder. She was relieved when the woman didn't take a step to follow her.

Outside a dash of rain swept across the porch and sprayed Jessamine. She paid it little mind as she rushed down the steps and found the path toward the lake. Lightning crackled through the air and nearly blinded her as the thunder following it was almost instantaneous. Only a fool would be out in this storm. But she couldn't turn back.

The lightning kept flickering like a lamp buffeted by the wind, its flame never completely extinguished. The thunder rumbled over her head as she braced herself for another ear-shattering boom. The rain began in earnest and she couldn't see a thing. She knew she had started off on the path to the lake, but grass was under her feet now instead of the sandy path. She stopped and brushed her wet hair back from her face to peer through the rain when the lightning flickered.

A prayer rose up inside her that she mouthed aloud into the rain and wind. "Dear Lord, put my feet on the right path. Help me find him, please. I promise to listen better and not be wayward if only you'll help me find him in time to warn him."

She felt a stab of guilt for her prayer. It wasn't proper to attempt to make bargains with the Eternal Father. He already owned everything, and other than a perfect life, a person had nothing to offer him. And nobody could live a perfect life. Certainly not Jessamine. But then what about King Hezekiah in the Bible who was given more years to live? Or King Solomon who was given wisdom. Perhaps not exactly a deal, but a gift. A gift. That's what she needed. Just the gift of a point in the right direction. *Please, Lord.*

The rain slackened a little even as the wind picked up and blew her skirts and bothersome petticoats against her legs. How was a person supposed to run with all that cloth wrapping around her? She grabbed handfuls of her sodden skirt and the top layer of petticoats and lifted it up so she wouldn't trip as she took a couple of hesitant steps in what she hoped was the right direction.

The storm was like a live thing poking at her from all sides trying to keep her from catching up with Tristan. She'd been wrong to rush out on her own. She should have grabbed her father off the dance floor and asked for his help, but instead she'd run directly into the storm without proper thought. How many times had Sister Sophrena taken her to task for the very same thing? Not thinking things through. But this time it might be a matter of life and death.

She shut her eyes and prayed with her whole spirit, the way she'd seen some of the Believers in meeting surrendering every bit of themselves to the Lord as they lifted their hands and began to shake. The way Sister Sophrena could do even with no visible sign of shaking as she prayed for Jessamine, but with her spirit open and believing. The way she'd heard her granny and the old preacher talk about how prayers could be when the Holy Spirit took over and made intercession with the Lord in groanings that could not be uttered.

And then whispering through her thoughts was Sister Sophrena's voice. *Engaged in thy duty, fear no danger.* Was she engaged in her duty or was she so out of step her prayers would never be heard? *Pray believing.* This time it wasn't Sister Sophrena's voice in her head. It was Granny's. *When the way gets dark, that's when you reach up for the good Lord's hand. He'll be there, reaching down for you, showing you the way.*

The rain and wind didn't let up, but the calm came inside her as she began to move forward again. The storm kept attacking her on all sides, but she was no longer trembling. Then as the lightning continued to flicker, she caught sight of the glint of water and a man moving toward it.

"Tristan," she called, but the wind jerked his name out of the air and carried it in the wrong direction. She couldn't even be sure the man in front of her was Tristan. But she grabbed up her skirts again and began to run.

Tristan thought he heard a voice, but with the wind he couldn't tell from where. The wind was rising, pushing against his ears, no doubt fooling him. Jessamine wouldn't have come out in this storm. She would be far too sensible for that. He should have been too sensible himself. Running out into a crashing thunderstorm with no more that a few scribbled words to lead him.

But what if she was there in the storm waiting for him? His mother would be furious because there was no way he could go back to the dance in his sodden clothes even if he was on a fool's errand here. If she noticed. She'd seemed very happy in the lawyer's arms dancing past him. As happy as Laura had looked in Sheldon Brady's arms. They'd made their deal. He and Laura. A promise that required no romance but that would keep everybody happy. Everybody but him. Even Jessamine had seemed happy enough as she sat by the veranda doors, but then she was not there. Then he had the words on the note stuffed in his pocket.

Meet me at the far end of the lake. Why would she want to meet by the lake? They had never strolled around the lake together. Why not in the garden?

Something wasn't right about all this. Something he should have stopped and considered before rushing out in the storm. Just as he had rushed out into the woods a couple of weeks ago. Even if he couldn't remember the reason why he'd ridden into the woods, the end result had been near disaster.

Wet as it was, the hair raised up off the back of his neck. A feeling he had learned to note in the war. A feeling that had kept him alive on more than one occasion.

In the lightning he caught sight of a figure in a cloak up ahead, the hood pulled up over the woman's head. He pushed aside his caution and hurried forward. He was almost to the figure in the cloak when he realized it was not a woman. His foreboding was warranted.

"What do you want?" he said, but the man didn't answer as he threw off the cloak that had been hiding some sort of club. Tristan looked around to see how best to escape the man if he came toward him. He took a step back when someone sprang from behind a tree. Tristan stepped to the side, but he was trapped between them. He did the only thing left to do. He spun on his feet, lowered his head and charged straight at the man behind him. He could hear the other man running toward him.

The club caught him a glancing blow on the back of the head. As he fell, he thought he heard his name on the wind again before he sank into blackness.

31

The storm was moving away. With the lightning dimming to a distant flicker away to the east, the black of the night wrapped around Jessamine like a thick, wet blanket. She slowed her steps until her eyes began to adjust to the darkness and she could once more see the glint of the lake water. All at once two figures emerged from the shadows to attack the man she'd been following. Tristan. She hadn't found him in time to warn him.

Yelling his name again, she ran toward them. She had no idea what she thought she could do. She wasn't thinking at all. Desperation was moving her feet as Tristan crumpled to his knees and then fell. The men grabbed his shoulders and feet and carried him toward the water. She tried to run faster, but she tripped over her wretched petticoats and fell flat. As she scrambled to her feet, she heard a loud splash.

A scream ripped out of her. Abigail had been right. This was no gentlemen's prank.

Both the men looked up at the same time. Their hats pulled down low on their foreheads hid their faces, but she knew neither was Tristan. He was nowhere to be seen.

The splash. She looked toward the lake and prayed for

more lightning to show the lake surface. But only the wind remained, turning Jessamine's full skirts into sails that were trying to push her back instead of letting her go forward to where she'd last seen Tristan. A tree limb crashed down behind her as one of the men started toward her.

She stopped in her tracks as frozen as a frightened rabbit caught too far from cover. It would do little good to run. The man would catch her easily. So she stood her ground waiting. The storm seemed to be waiting too as the rain became no more than a spattering of drops. The wind whistled past her, chasing after the thunder and lightning in the distance. Then it was quiet. Too quiet. The air pressed down on her. The storm was not over. That was as plain as the threat of the man coming after her.

Her breath caught in her throat. She stood as tall as she could. She would defy him. While the Shakers had taught her peaceful ways, this man was from the world. He had nothing about peace on his mind.

The other man came after him and Jessamine feared he was going to attack her too. But then he grabbed the first man's arm and yanked him back.

"We gotta get out of here." His words were plain in the still air. "We done what we was paid to do."

"But—"

"I been in storms like this. We're fixing to have a big blow." He turned away from his accomplice and began to run away from the lake.

The man hesitated. Jessamine stared straight at the dim outline of his face under his hat and spoke with as much confidence as she could muster up. "Dr. Hargrove is following me. As soon as he gets his gun." It was a complete fabrication, but she felt no guilt for the lie.

She wasn't sure the man believed her, but his head did turn away from her toward the hotel. The other man yelled at him again, and with one last glance at her, he turned and took off after the other man.

Jessamine gave the men no more thought as she rushed toward the lake. She couldn't see Tristan. Not on the bank near where he'd fallen. Not floating in the water. Panic grabbed her throat and she was barely able to squeak out his name. The heavy stillness pushed in against her skin even as the air grew darker. He had to be in the lake.

She had no idea how deep the water was. While her granny had taught her to swim in the deeper pools of the creek practically as soon as she could walk, that was years ago. She hadn't been in the water since she'd come to the Shaker village. And never in a broad, deep lake like this. Even so, she didn't hesitate. She kicked off her shoes and waded into the water.

Before she'd taken four steps, the water was up to her waist. Her silky skirt rose up to float on top the water, but the hindering petticoats soaked up the water and made every step a struggle. Her feet sank down into the soft mud, but she pushed deeper into the lake, trusting the Lord to guide her. Praying fervently for the Lord to guide her to Tristan.

The Lord is an ever present help in times of trouble. The verse ran through her head as she looked up toward the sky that seemed to be boiling with dark clouds.

"Help me!" she almost demanded as she stopped moving. She didn't know which way to go. Tears spilled out of her eyes as despair soaked through her. Her voice softened and she begged with a broken spirit. "Oh dear heavenly Father, please help me. I can't find him. Please, help me. I promise . . ."

But what could she promise? Her best was naught but filthy rags to the Lord. And yet, his love was in her heart. He wanted good for her. He wanted her to find Tristan. She knew he did. *Reach out your hand.*

The words whispered through her mind. She swirled her hand through the water around her and touched nothing. But she couldn't give up. She wouldn't give up. She stepped deeper into the water. Tristan was there. She might need to take only one more step to find him. The Lord would show her. She just had to trust.

A song they sang sometimes in meeting rose in her mind and she began singing the words under her breath for courage.

> Search ye your camps,
> yea, read and understand,
> for the Lord God of Hosts
> holds the Lamp in His hand.

The darkness didn't matter. The Lord held the lamp. The Lord could show her where Tristan was. The water lapped up against her, almost to her shoulders. The next step might slide her into depths over her head, but hadn't Sister Sophrena always told her she didn't possess a hesitant spirit? No sooner had the thought crossed her mind than a rock turned sideways under her foot and she went down. The water closed over her head, entombing her in absolute silence for a few brief seconds before she began floundering to get her footing. She got her head above the water only to get entangled in the wretched petticoats. With a gasp for air, she went under again, flailing her arms uselessly against the water.

Her hand hit something. Cloth. Not the silky feel of her own skirts. Purpose stilled her panic, and she jerked up her skirts to free her feet to find the bottom again. Her head broke above the surface and she coughed out lake water and pulled in a raspy breath. She wasn't over her head. All she had to do was keep her balance. And feel back through the water for the cloth her hand had touched in her panic.

Her hand touched hair. Tristan's hair. She wrapped her fingers in it and pulled him toward her to lift his head out of the water. His face felt cold to her hand and she couldn't tell if he was breathing. She tried to think how many minutes he might have been in the water. How long since she'd heard the splash. Three, four, five minutes? Too many minutes? With her own breath loud in her ears, she wrapped her arm around his chest and held him against her while she pulled him through the water toward the shore.

It seemed an eternity before she was finally tugging him up out of the shallow water, tripping over her skirts and falling. At last she felt grass under her feet. She dug her heels into the soft bank, grabbed Tristan under his arms, and pulled as hard as she could. She kept hold of him as she fell backward and managed to jerk Tristan out of the water on top of her legs.

She pushed him over on his side to free her legs. Water spilled out of his mouth. If only Dr. Hargrove had really been following her. He'd know what to do, but she couldn't leave Tristan to go after him. She thought she heard a gurgling and put her ear against his chest to listen for a heartbeat. She wanted to believe she heard a faint flutter, but he wasn't breathing. Why would the Lord let her find Tristan in the lake only to take him after she had him out of the water?

Anger swept through her as she shook Tristan's shoulder and then began pounding on his back. He had to breathe. He wasn't supposed to give up and not even try to breathe.

She looked up at the sky and shouted, "I wish you had never let me find him that first time out in the woods."

Before the words were out of her mouth, she knew there was no truth in them. Even with the pain, even with the loss of everything familiar in her life, even as a stranger in this odd world, she did not regret finding this man in the woods and knowing the gift of worldly love. But why was it being stolen from her so soon? Had Tristan died because of her waywardness? It was true that Sister Sophrena had often warned her of how sin brought its own punishment.

She leaned down to put her cheek against his. "I'm sorry," she whispered. "I'm so very sorry." Her tears mixed with the lake water wetting his face.

All at once his head jerked under her as he let out a strangled cough and began gasping for air. He was alive. Such joy exploded inside Jessamine that she wanted to stand up and whirl. But there would be time for twirling later. Now she needed to help Tristan grab for his breath by lifting up his head and holding him while he tried to rid his lungs of the lake water.

For a few seconds, she didn't pay any notice to the roar. Nothing mattered except Tristan pulling in breath. But the roar got louder like a million bumblebees swarming toward her. She looked up. A black mass of clouds was heading toward them swallowing up trees in its path.

A feeling of peace enveloped Tristan as he floated toward a bright light. He was dying. He knew that, but he couldn't fight it. He had no power to save himself. He wasn't even in the body floating in the water. He was above the water, watching in a detached way. It was out of his control.

Would angels come for him? He felt profound regret that he hadn't taken the time to figure out what he believed about God while he could do something about it. He had turned his back on God during the war, but he longed to embrace the light now. Now when it might be too late. A dozen prayers raced through his thoughts. Prayers he should have said yesterday and the day before yesterday. Prayers he knew mattered. Now when it was too late.

He saw Jessamine wading into the water toward his body and he opened his mouth to warn her to go back. But his voice was silenced by the water.

He remembered wondering if she was an angel when he

opened his eyes and saw her for the first time in the woods. And here she was again, trying to save him. He could almost feel her prayers rising up around him, buffeting him as they reached toward God. He added his own prayers. Not for himself. He knew it was too late for that, but for her.

She went under the water. Tristan reached for her with everything he had, and the light that had been so bright faded away to be replaced by a dark swirling hole that sucked him down.

The next thing he knew he was on the ground, coughing up lake water with Jessamine's tears falling on his face. He wanted to reach up and brush those tears away, but it was taking every bit of his strength to pull in a breath and then another.

At first he thought the roar might only be in his ears, but then Jessamine went stiff and looked away from him toward the sky. The noise surrounded them as loud as a hundred artillery shells exploding all at the same time.

He grabbed her and yanked her down beside him. With every bit of strength he could summon up, he threw himself over top her. Then he mashed his body down against hers as he shouted in her ear, "Pray."

He didn't know if she heard him or not, but she would be praying. He doubted any person could be in the middle of a tornado without a prayer rising up inside him. But he'd been in the middle of a war storm and refused to call for mercy. Why were the prayers rising so desperately within him now?

So many reasons. Jessamine with the joy of living radiating from her. Jessamine with her tears of love falling on his cheeks. Beautiful Jessamine. But even more than Jessamine, he didn't want to see the light fade the next time death came to claim him. If he had escaped drowning only to be jerked away from living by the tornado, this time he wanted to belong in the light. The same as Jessamine did.

The roar was deafening as it passed over them, pelting him with debris and then water as the wind sucked up the lake and spit it back out. He turned his head to look. Waterspouts were rising into the air as the twister headed across it straight toward the hotel. Then as if Dr. Hargrove were standing outside, daring the tornado to destroy his southern Saratoga, the wind lifted back up into the sky and roared over the building and on toward the river.

In moments, it was gone, but the silence that followed its passing seemed almost as deafening as its roar.

Beneath him, Jessamine whispered, "Is it over?"

"It's over." Tristan slowly moved off her. He felt bereft when he was no longer touching her.

"And we're alive. Thank God, we're alive!" She sat up beside him and grabbed his hand. "I thought those men had killed you."

He tried to remember what had happened, but it was all a blur. "I don't remember," he said.

"The way you didn't remember before?" Her voice changed, got quieter.

"No, not like that." He had to cough again before he was able to go on in a weak voice. "I remember being in the water and drifting toward a bright light, but not how I got into the water. It was strange. Like I was out of my body. That's how I could see you." He reached over and took her hand. "And I was afraid. Not for me, but for you. Then everything went dark and the next thing I knew I was here fighting to breathe." He pulled her hand up to his mouth and kissed it. "Because of you."

She drew in a quick breath as he scooted closer to her to touch his lips to her cheek before tipping her face around toward him and capturing her lips. She surrendered her lips to his and twined her arms around his neck, and this time the whirlwind was sweeping through his heart.

When he thought he could bear no more joy, he raised his head and whispered into her wet hair. "I love you, my beautiful Jessamine."

She pulled away and stared at him. "But you love the princess."

"Only if the princess is you." He reached for her again.

She didn't scoot away from him, but she resisted his embrace as she stared at him. "Nay, Laura is the princess."

His promises to Laura and his mother came crashing down around him. "I don't love her. I love you," he said. But she must have heard the echo of sorrow in his voice.

"But you're going to marry the princess."

"I have made that promise," he admitted.

"A person should keep his promises whether to man or God."

Jessamine spoke in a voice so low he had to strain to hear her words even as they poked his conscience. He had made promises to God too. He couldn't so soon slide back into living a life where his vows meant nothing.

The moon edged out from behind the clouds and shone down on the destruction around them with unmerciful light. Downed trees had been tossed willy-nilly like a game of pickup sticks. The same destruction lay within his heart. The destruction of his happiness. How could he turn her loose and return to his life as though nothing had happened?

"I can't—"

"Shh." She put her fingers over his lips. "Let's give thanks to the Lord that we are still alive this night. That and nothing more. Tomorrow will be soon enough to think of what must or must not be done. The men are coming from the ballroom."

She was right. People were streaming out of the hotel toward them. And he regretted that he wouldn't be able to pull her to him for another kiss to celebrate breathing. He tried to stand but his legs wouldn't hold him up. He tried again and this time Jessamine put her arm around his waist to lend him her strength. He leaned against her and wished with everything in his heart that he belonged there by her side forever instead of only until other hands could hold him up.

32

The next morning, the sun came up on the devastation on the far side of the lake in front of the hotel. The day before the trees reached leafy branches toward the sun and supplied shade for the couples strolling around the lake. Now they were nothing but firewood waiting for the crosscut saw.

Jessamine could not look out her window without tears spilling out of her eyes. She hated the tears, but she felt as scattered and broken as those trees. She'd already soaked two handkerchiefs. It had been years since she'd had the need to do more than brush aside a stray tear. Not since her granny died and the old preacher had taken her to the Shakers. Those first months in the Children's House, everything had been so strange with so many rules she couldn't keep in her head that she cried herself to sleep every night. She missed not only the love of her granny but the freedom of the woods.

But the sisters were kind, and one morning she'd risen from her Shaker bed determined to be one of them. To remember to step up on the stairs with the right foot every time. To follow the rules. To pray on her knees at assigned times instead of simply grabbing hold of the Lord's hand in the morning and talking to him all through the day the way her granny had taught her to do.

At the Shaker village, she had to keep her mind on her lessons or her assigned duties. She had to ask forgiveness over and over again when she forgot one of the rules, but the forgiveness was always forthcoming. She was encouraged and admonished to continue down the Believers' pathway with the goal to do better on the next day. So her tears dried up. She had no reason for tears. What had happened could not be changed. Her granny was in heaven and the woods the same as lost to her except in her memory.

She had no reason to cry now. Nobody had died. Not Tristan in the lake. Not any of the guests in the storm. The hotel had been spared by the tornado. Trees about the grounds had not fared as well, but as much as she regretted the beauty of the trees being ripped away by the wind, her tears weren't for the trees.

Nor could she blame her sorrow on her narrow escape from the lake and the storm the night before. That wasn't reason for tears. That was reason for rejoicing.

Exhaustion and lack of sleep. That's what Abigail blamed the tears on as she fussed over her and the excuse she used to turn away the people who came to inquire after Jessamine.

They had both been questioned by the sheriff early that morning. Dr. Hargrove had sent for him after he heard hers and Tristan's story. The two men by the lake were nowhere to be found and another guest had disappeared before the sheriff arrived. A man suspected of conspiring to hurt Tristan. Why he had wanted to do so wasn't clear to Jessamine, but Abigail said Jimmy heard it had to do with Laura Cleveland. A jealous suitor.

After the sheriff asked his questions and left them alone, Abigail had gone to the kitchen for tea and come back full of information. A good number of the guests, unnerved by the storm, were packing to leave. Dr. Hargrove seemed to be everywhere at once as he confidently assured his guests of their complete safety in his hotel while announcing a new round of parties to encourage them to stay. He promised his workers would have the fallen trees cleared away in a couple of days and that such severe winds were a rarity.

"If anybody can get them to stay, Dr. Hargrove can," Abigail said as she poured a cup of the tea for Jessamine. "He's a wonder. The piazza is already cleared off and he's got his band out there playing their cheeriest tunes to discourage the guests from stepping up into their carriages."

She handed Jessamine the cup and then picked up one of the sodden handkerchiefs. "It appears we could use some of that cheering music in here."

Jessamine took a sip of her tea and reminded herself again that she had no reason to cry. She swallowed hard before she asked, "Is it working? The cheerful music?"

"On some," Abigail said with a glance out the window. "More carriages appear to be arriving than leaving. The dining tables will be full again tonight. My guess is that the storm and all will bring in more people. Curiosity seekers once the word goes around."

Jessamine stared down at the notebook in her lap. The page was empty. Her father had encouraged her to write it all down. He had been nigh to distraught the night before as he helped her back to her room from the lake. She hadn't cried then. She'd been so drained she could barely talk. Mrs. Cleveland had followed them to her room where Abigail was waiting.

After her father stepped out of the room to allow her to change, Mrs. Cleveland said, "Oh, my dear child, I should have followed you out of the ballroom."

Without a bit of concern about getting her own party dress wet, she put her arms around Jessamine and held her close for a long moment before she gave her over to Abigail's care. Abigail sniffled now and again as she helped Jessamine strip out of her sodden dress and petticoats, but neither she nor Mrs. Cleveland pushed her to talk.

Once she was dry and wrapped in a dressing gown, Dr. Hargrove came into the room to make sure she wasn't injured. While Jessamine's father hovered anxiously in the background, the doctor gently questioned her about how she was feeling and what had happened.

So she forced out the words to tell him about Abigail's warning. She admitted her foolishness in chasing out of the ballroom after Tristan. She tried to describe the men she'd seen at the lake, but they had been little more than shadows in the night. When the doctor patted her hand and told her how brave she was to pull Tristan from the lake, her father came over to touch her hair with a tearful smile.

She hadn't told them of her desperate prayers promising God whatever she had to offer if only he would lead her to Tristan in the water. She hadn't spoken about Tristan kissing her or his words of love as they sat at the edge of the lake in the midst of nature's destruction. She would never tell anyone that. Nor was there any reason to speak of the promises Tristan had given others that were the reason for the tears of the morning.

Promises. At the very thought of those promises now, new tears slid out of her eyes and down her cheeks.

Abigail kept talking as she straightened the coverlet on the bed. "They say Tristan is fine. A nasty bump on the head and the bandage on his arm had to be replaced. Jimmy says no one has seen him except Dr. Hargrove since the sheriff left. Tristan doesn't have a manservant and that maid of his mother's isn't likely to carry any stories from their rooms down to the servants' quarters. She's a tight-lipped one."

Abigail turned back to Jessamine, and noting her fresh

tears, she fetched a dry handkerchief. "There, there, my sister, don't spend all your tears. He is alive. There may yet be hope for the two of you."

"Nay, he has made promises he must keep. The same as I must keep the promises I have made." Jessamine pulled in a breath and wiped the tears off her face. The Lord had answered her prayers. The Lord had helped her pull Tristan out of the lake. The Lord had covered them with his hand as the storm passed over top them. The Lord had allowed them a treasured kiss. She had every reason to be thankful and none to be tearful.

She loved Tristan Cooper. He had claimed to love her. She had the gift of those words in her heart. And she would keep her promises to the Lord. Promises that had not had words but that had meant faithful obedience to his will for her life. Whether that was here with her father or not, she did not yet know, but she had assurance the Lord would reveal a path to her.

She would not let herself dissolve into tears again. She took a sip of the tea Abigail handed her and peered up at the girl. She looked ready to drop as she stood watching Jessamine with concern. "You must be as tired as I am, Abigail. You should rest."

Abigail hesitated. "But you need someone with you."

"Nay, I do not. I simply need time to think things through." When Abigail continued to look doubtful, she added, "But if I do need someone, my father has promised to be close by."

"True. He came to his door when I went to get your tea. He is very worried about you. It was hard for him to see you so upset this morning. Tears injure some men more than stones."

"I know. I should have controlled my weeping, but I could not."

"And have you now?" Abigail peered at her.

"I have." Jessamine blew out a breath. "Go tell my father I am fine and then rest awhile. I will do the same. While it seems sinful to sleep in the afternoon when one is not sick, perhaps that is what we both need to do this day." What was one more wayward sin to add to her growing number?

"I am so thankful you weren't hurt last night." Abigail leaned down to touch her cheek to Jessamine's in a quick embrace. "You feel more like a sister to me now than you ever did while they were forcing sisterly love down on us at Harmony Hill."

Harmony. After Abigail went out the door, the word circled in Jessamine's thoughts. That was what she was lacking. Harmony. Perhaps such wasn't possible in the world when the wrong kind of love sprouted in one's heart.

She set her teacup down on the table beside the chair and picked up her pen. The nib had dried, but she didn't dip it into the ink. Just as she had no more tears to cry, she had no words to write. She was still staring at the blank page when she heard a soft knock on the door.

Before she could rise from her chair, her father eased open the door and stepped inside. "Abigail said you might be up to having a visitor."

"Yea, I mean yes. I have recovered," Jessamine said.

Her father pulled the dressing table stool over in front of her and sat down. He looked at her for a long moment. "I promised you adventures, but I had no plans for any of them to be a danger to you."

"I am not hurt."

"Or cause you sadness."

"I'm no longer tearful." Jessamine looked away from her father's face down at the notebook in her lap.

"No tears on the outside," he said as he reached out to touch her cheek with his fingertips. "Floods of tears on the inside."

401

She looked up without saying anything. How could she deny his words without adding to her sins?

"My dear child, you may think it was wrong of me to come find you at the Shaker village and bring you out into the world where there can be such pain. At the village, you might never have known these feelings since you would have stayed closed off to the love that can take you to the heights or drop you to the depths. But even in the depths, love is worth it. I know for I have been in both places."

Jessamine studied his face, so concerned, so familiar even if she had only actually known him for a few days. He was familiar in her very being. "Granny called you the prince who loved my mother."

"I wasn't much of a prince." He smiled a little but the echo of sorrow was in his voice. "But I did love your mother. With her I knew the heights and then when she died, the depths."

"The elders and eldresses say such love is sinful. That those who marry will fight and know no peace."

"There are many kinds of peace, Jessamine. Your elders and eldresses have found their peace by shutting away the temptations of the world. That is not wrong for them, but for you . . ." He paused and smiled into her eyes. "For you it would be as much a sin to deny the joy of love as to stomp on a beautiful butterfly."

"But he loves another."

"You don't believe that."

Jessamine managed to hold in a sigh. "Whether I believe it or not, I do believe he made a promise he must keep."

"At least one he thinks he must keep," her father said. "Some promises are ill made."

"Even promises made to God?"

"I've made a few of those. I did when your mother was birthing you."

"Did you keep them?"

"The ones the Lord wanted me to keep," he said.

"And how did you know which ones they were?" She peered at him, anxious to know his answer.

"The Lord showed me." He was quiet for a moment before he said, "Have you made promises to God?"

"Yea." She didn't bother changing the Shaker word. "Do you think he will show me?"

"I not only think it, I'm sure of it. The Lord gives us many gifts. Your quest for life is one. A longing for love is another. But so is happiness. I believe the Lord wants us to seek those gifts. He wants to give us the desires of our heart and sometimes the desire of our heart is to love another person more than we love ourselves."

"Is that how you loved my mother?"

"It is, but the heart can hold many loves. That's what the Lord showed me. For a long time after your mother died, I refused to open my heart to the possibility of love again. But then the Lord put a woman in my path. I didn't love her as I loved your mother. Each love we invite into our hearts is different, but I did fall in love with her. I do love her even now."

"Will you marry her?" Jessamine looked at him with some curiosity.

"She is young in experience even as you are and does not understand the worth of love, but I have hope of convincing her before it is too late."

"Too late?"

"Too late for all of us."

She bent her head down to stare at the pen she held. It was already too late. It had been too late before she even stumbled over Tristan in the woods. Such sad words. Too late.

He put his fingers under her chin and lifted her face up until she met his eyes. Dark eyes full of concern for her sadness. "Don't fret, my little girl. You had a terrifying night.

It's only natural for you to feel unsettled. So rest today and tomorrow wake with the sun and be ready to begin the rest of your life." He smiled at her. "Trust me on this. I do believe the morning to come will be a gift to you."

He left her then, after she promised to lie down and rest. That was a promise she could keep. So she lay in the too soft bed and listened to the thud of axes and the scraping sound of saws outside as the workers cleared away the downed trees. So much broken and torn away in such a few moments. And yet when she had looked out that morning, some trees were still standing. Trees that had been outside the path of the storm.

A good place to be. Outside the storm. Protected and spared. That's how she'd been at Harmony Hill. Protected and spared from the winds of the world. Was her father right that no matter the destruction, it was better to have known the wind?

And what could he mean by the morning being a gift to her? The morning would change nothing. But come morning, perhaps the Lord would show her the way, show her how to keep the promises she'd made. She would not see Tristan again. It was enough that she knew he was well. He would marry the princess and keep his promises. And she would pray for a sign.

There are many kinds of love. Her father's words echoed in her head. Then Sister Sophrena's words were there. *The love of the Eternal Father and that of your sisters and brothers will forever be the same.* But over them all were Tristan's words. *I love you, my beautiful Jessamine.*

Was that gift enough? Hearing those words of love even if there would never be more. She stared up at the ceiling and prayed that her way would come clear. She prayed for gifts to shower down on them all. She gave thanks for the trees out of the path of the storm. She gave thanks for the

Lord's hand protecting her. Protecting Tristan. More gifts of grace.

She had so many reasons to be thankful. It was wrong to want more gifts. Hadn't Sister Sophrena always told her it was a gift to be simple? To do her duty and receive what the Lord gave. A song she had sung in meeting hundreds of times began playing through her mind.

> 'Tis the gift to be simple
> 'Tis the gift to be free,
> 'Tis the gift to come down
> Where we ought to be.

Where she ought to be. That was what she needed the Lord to show her. That was what the morning would bring her. That sign.

Jessamine woke before daylight and listened for some sound that might give a hint of the time. No noise came to her ears except the whine of a mosquito. She slapped at it as she sat up and stared toward the window. Her father had promised she would be ready to welcome the morning. That she might know her way then, but all she felt was very alone.

No, not alone. Never alone. Her granny's words whispered through her memory. *You don't ever have to feel alone, my sweet Jessamine. I'm here with you and even if something were to happen to me, you can be sure the good Lord will still be right here beside you. He won't let you be bewildered or frightened too long. He'll send you light in the dark, answers in the day, and joy for your heart. That you can depend on.*

Jessamine had depended on that and the Lord had been an ever-present presence with her, as close as a prayer the same as he had been when she was stumbling around in the lake.

She got out of bed and went to the window. The morning was coming. The eastern horizon was uncurling fingers of pink. In her head, she heard the echo of the Shaker bell that would be ringing to signal the time to rise and begin work. She missed the sound of the bell. It had been such a rhythm of her life. Keeping her in order. Letting her know when it was time to rise or time to eat or time to worship.

The world had no bells to keep order. She could sleep all day and no one would ring a bell to wake her. They did ring a bell to signal the evening meal here at White Oak Springs, but it didn't bring about order. Instead the people pushed against one another, talking and yelling as they rushed for their tables.

She looked toward her pad of paper and pen and ink on the table and wished for more light so that she could write down her contrary thinking. While at Harmony Hill she often chafed against the rules, but now here in this garden of indulgence, she reached for rules.

Something white caught her eye over by the door. An envelope slipped under her door while she slept. Dare she believe it might be from Tristan? Her heart was beating up into her ears as she leaned over to pick up the note. There was no writing on the envelope. She pulled the letter out and unfolded the thin sheet of paper, but the light was too dim for her to read the words. She carried it over to the window where dawn was beginning to lighten the air.

The handwriting was familiar, changed somewhat from the letter she'd read only days ago, but still her father's.

My dear Jessamine,
The morning has come and with it your new
beginning. You may not be able to understand
what I am doing or forgive it. But I assure you
I am not deserting you now any more than I

did when you were a baby. I carried you with me through the years in my heart. I will always carry you in my heart, my beautiful daughter.

That said, there is something very important that I must do. As much for you as for me. Perhaps even more for you. And so I have left. But not for long this time. That is a promise I make without hesitation.

But this brief separation is necessary for the happiness of us both. I saw your tears and though I could not wipe them away, I must do whatever I can to eliminate the reason for your sadness. Love is worth it. Whatever the sacrifice, love is definitely worth it. For me as well as for you. Now you must trust and wait for that love.

Your room is paid here at White Oak Springs until the end of the season. I will always see that you are cared for, but I am confident what I do today will open up other opportunities to you. Do not be afraid to seize those opportunities. Especially if that is what your heart is telling you to do. Do not doubt your heart. Never doubt your heart.

You are every bit as beautiful as I always imagined you would be, my Jessamine. You share my blood and you share my gift. Embrace the gift of words. It will bring you joy and sorrow. But be confident that the joy will always overshadow the sorrow.

So I beg you to trust me and remember my promise to return. Meanwhile this is the best way. Seize your chance for love.

Your loving father

She looked up from the letter. He claimed to love her. He promised to be part of her life. To be her father. She believed him, but the fact remained underneath his words that he was gone beyond her reach. First Tristan and now her father. Both loving her. Both leaving her to find her own way.

She glanced down at the words again in the gray light coming in the window. He was right. She did not understand. How could she trust what she did not understand? He'd left her alone in this strange world.

Sister Sophrena's words echoed in her mind. *Worldly love will disappoint you, Sister Jessamine. You can be assured of that, but the love of your sisters and brothers will forever be strong.*

Her father had told her that with the morning her answer would come. She would know her path, but she didn't know when she'd ever felt more unsure. She shut her eyes, bent her head, and spoke her prayer aloud. "Please, Lord, I don't know what to do."

When she looked up, the sun was peeking over the eastern horizon, and there, riding toward the hotel was Brother Hector making a delivery to the kitchens. He was getting an early start to his duties on this day.

She went to the wardrobe and reached down under all Mrs. Browning's lovely dresses to pull out the neatly folded Shaker dress. She had her sign. 'Tis the gift to be simple. 'Tis the gift to be free. Free from heartache. She had run to the world, ready to embrace its gifts, and found them wrapped in nothing but sadness.

As she pulled the familiar dress over her head, her father's written words whispered through her thoughts. *Now you must trust and wait for that love. Never doubt your heart.* But she would not wait to see Tristan marry the princess. She had her sign.

She touched the pen and notebook. She so wanted to carry

them with her. But they would not be allowed at Harmony Hill. There were rules to follow. Rules to give order to one's life. She dipped the pen in ink and wrote Abigail a note giving her the dresses. Then she laid the pen on the book, turned, and went out the door, leaving the world behind her.

Journal Entry

Harmony Hill Village
Entered on this 27th day of June in the year 1849
by Sister Sophrena Prescott

What a joyous day for us here at Harmony Hill! Our
sister has returned to the fold. Brother Hector brought
her back to us before the midday meal this day. I
could hardly believe my eyes when Eldress Frieda
summoned me to the Trustee's House. But there was
our Sister Jessamine standing with the eldress, in the
Shaker dress she wore away from here only days ago.

She kept her eyes downcast, shamed by her falling
away, as she begged my forgiveness. I gave it readily,
for I was so very relieved to see her back within our
safe borders. I expected her to look up and smile then
as she has done so many times over the years after I
have forgiven her some slight, and she did. But it was
not the same smile as in past years. Her lips did turn
up, but the sorrow in her eyes took away any thought
that her smile might come from her heart. She looked
bone weary as if she'd been harvesting beans all
through the day without the proper rest breaks to
keep her body strong.

The world has mistreated our sister. She has been wounded in some sorrowful way, but we will love her back into communion with us as Believers. We will stand between her and whatever tries to separate her from this, her family. Here she will once again find peace. Here she will once more dance and laugh and receive our mother's love. The love of her sisters and brethren will heal the bruises of the world in time.

Time Eldress Frieda says the Ministry has granted her. She will not be pressured to give her confession until she is ready. Such is our way. While the sins must be confessed and such confession is the beginning of healing, we do not force such words from our sisters. Those words repenting of whatever sins led her away from us must rise from within her and not be put into her mouth by my eagerness to have her as a loving and forgiven sister again.

What wonderful words to say once more? What will we do with Sister Jessamine? Tomorrow she will be allowed to rest if she so chooses, but she indicates she would rather be given a duty. "Idle hands are a temptation to the devil," she said when the rest was offered. So Eldress Frieda gave her a duty in the gardens. There is much work to do there right now. Beans to pick. Corn to gather for roasting ears. Peppers and onions. Our tables will be weighted down with the product of our hands.

Hands to work. Hearts to God. That truth is circling my head on this evening as the sun sinks in the west. Our beloved sister has come home. My feet will be light when we labor our songs at meeting on Sunday.

33

Tristan had no idea what day it was when he awoke to sunlight streaming in his window. Dr. Hargrove had dosed him with something to make him sleep. First the Shaker doctor. Now Dr. Hargrove. When Tristan had protested, Dr. Hargrove told him knocks on the heads were nothing to mess with and a man who had narrowly escaped with his life twice in less than a month should be more than ready to rest awhile before chasing after time three.

Tristan had no argument for that. He had been flirting with death a little too often. If he wanted to think back to his time in Mexico, he'd already cheated death more than those three times Dr. Hargrove was warning him about. In wartime, death could catch up with a man on the battlefield at any time and lurked continually in the sick camps. It wasn't as expected at a watering spot where healing and romance were supposed to be the orders of the day.

Not that anyone expected there to be a third time here on this side of the war. This side of the storm. Not Dr. Hargrove, not the sheriff with the thick eyebrows over tired eyes who had asked questions Tristan couldn't answer. He had no idea why Calvin Green would arrange for him to drown any more than he knew why he'd been shot in the woods.

This time he did remember. He knew he'd gotten the message he thought might be from Jessamine. He'd rushed outside with the storm rising. The men had come at him from the shadows and clubbed him in the head. He remembered the feeling of floating above the lake and looking down at his body and Jessamine. Then sadness and darkness had engulfed him and wiped away his knowing until he came to, coughing up water and struggling to breathe. Before the tornado.

That he had not forgotten in spite of his thumping head. Nor had he forgotten the words he'd spoken so truthfully to Jessamine. Words of love. Words of regret. Those words had chased through his head all the while he slept. Had she really told him she loved him too or were those simply words that had risen out of his desire? Perhaps he hadn't remembered as clearly as he thought he did.

Now he pushed open his eyes and wondered how long Dr. Hargrove's powders had kept him asleep. A night? Through a day? Or more? He tried to move, but while his mind was awake and ready, his body continued to sleep. His arms and legs felt as though an elephant was sitting on them, and for a panicked moment he worried he might be paralyzed. But he'd walked to the hotel from the lake. With help, but he'd walked on his own feet. He had sat in the chair and talked to the sheriff. He would arise from the lethargy wrapping around him. The residue of the doctor's drugs. He'd felt some the same at the Shaker village, but Sister Lettie had given him an energizing draught to help him up on his feet.

Maybe he should have listened with more attentive ears to Sister Lettie's talk about being a Shaker. At least then he wouldn't be marrying the wrong woman. He wouldn't be marrying at all. He pushed aside marrying thoughts and concentrated on raising his left arm up so he could see it. He hoped the good doctor hadn't found more broken bones after his powders put Tristan to sleep.

Sister Lettie's hard bandage was gone. In its place were strips of cloth wrapped tightly around his arm, but he could bend his elbow now. He moved his arm back and forth a few times to savor the movement even though the joint complained. With effort he pushed himself up to a sitting position. It was time to awake and decide his future.

He'd told Jessamine it was decided. That he'd made promises he had to keep, but now doubts were creeping in. Whether it was the hours of sleep or the bright sunlight forcing him to open his eyes, he was ready to stare down the truth. Jessamine's face would never fade from his thoughts. He loved her. He could not deny that love for a house. Not even for his mother. He could not sentence Laura to life with a man who could never love her. He could not live a lie. Love was worth pursuing.

His head thumped when he stood up, and his leg muscles complained but didn't give way. He was alone in his room, but someone had brought water in the pitcher for washing and a tankard of water for drinking. He sipped the water, remembering Sister Lettie's warning not to drink too greedily when he awoke at the Shaker village. The cool water he poured from the pitcher into the bowl and splashed on his face brought him fully awake.

He practiced what he would say to his mother as he dressed and combed his hair. His words rose out of him like a prayer for understanding until he wasn't sure who he was trying to convince the most. His mother or himself. Or perhaps the Lord. He raked the comb across the knot on the side of his head and winced. Without Jessamine following him from the ballroom and wading into the lake after him, he'd be on to his final reward.

He dropped his hands down to his sides and stared at himself in the mirror. Would the light have pulled him into it or would he have been released to the darkness? He shuddered as he remembered the light fading and the black surrounding him.

"Dear Lord," he whispered. "Forgive me. Whatever happens, help me never to again lose sight of your light."

There was a tap on the door between his room and his mother's. She opened the door a few inches and peeked around it, almost fearfully. Then she was smiling. "Oh Tristan, I am so relieved to see you up and dressed."

"Come in, Mother, or would you rather I come into your room?"

She pushed the door the rest of the way open and beckoned him toward her. When he was near she laid her hand on his cheek. "You've given me such a fright. I prayed daily protection down on you while you were in that horrible war in Mexico, but I had no idea danger would stalk you here. But you don't have to worry now. That Green man is long gone." She took his hand and pulled him toward the two chairs in the sitting area of her room.

"The sheriff didn't catch him then?" Tristan asked as he sat down in one of the small chairs. It supplied little comfort in spite of its upholstered seat.

"No, no." His mother perched on the other chair. She fingered her skirt and wouldn't meet his eyes. "We felt it enough that he was gone."

"We?" Tristan frowned at her. His head was thumping again, but not so much that he couldn't think.

"Dr. Hargrove, Jackson, and I." She rushed on before he could say anything. "I told them I was sure you would agree."

"Jackson?" Tristan stared at her bent head.

"Yes, it was great good fortune Mr. Ridenour was here to be of help to me. You will have to thank him," she murmured as she continued to fold and unfold a pleat on her skirt. At last she looked up at him, her eyes a bit wary, before she went on. "You have to understand that Dr. Hargrove is quite concerned of how news of the attack on you might do damage to his establishment here. You must admit the dear man does work so hard to give his guests a lovely experience. A time of healing and good times, not danger."

"They tried to kill me." He didn't mince words as he stared straight at her. "I'd be dead even now if not for Jessamine."

"And I will forever be grateful to that girl for her bravery in following you into the storm. I could not have borne it if you had drowned, Tristan." She reached over to grasp his hands in hers. "But you are alive. And since no permanent harm was done to you or the young woman, it seemed only reasonable to allow Dr. Hargrove to keep the reputation of his establishment clear. He has offered to wipe our charges off the books this year and even offered a free return visit next season. Jackson thinks that very fair."

Jackson again. Tristan swallowed down his irritation. "What of justice? Doesn't your Jackson believe in justice? Green tried to kill me. Twice."

"You don't really want to be embroiled in such a scandal." She turned loose of his hands and sat back in her chair to eye him as her sympathy drained away. This was the mother he knew. The one who expected him to listen to her and do as she said. "It is not only our family you must consider, but also the Clevelands. It is said that man, Green, was pushed over the edge by his love for our dear Laura."

Laura. The name brought Tristan back to his practiced words. Perhaps she was right. It didn't matter about Green. It just mattered about Jessamine. "Mother, there are some things I need to tell you."

"I'm sure, but first, you must listen to me."

He opened his mouth to protest, but she held up a hand to stop him. "Wait. You may not realize that you have slept around the clock and then some. Much has happened that you do not know."

"I know that I love Jessamine Brady."

She shut her eyes and breathed out a sigh that he wasn't sure sounded more irritated or sad. "My dear son, some things are not easy."

"I'll find a way to help you keep the house. I don't know how, but I'll find a way. It would not be fair to Laura or to me for us to go through with this sham of a marriage. No matter what you say. Love does matter."

"Yes, it does."

Tristan looked at her as though he might not have heard her right.

She smiled and repeated her words. "Yes, it does. Jackson has asked permission to seek my favor with the intent of asking me to marry him. I know that news might be upsetting to you since your father was so very dear to you as, of course, he was to me too. But life goes on."

Tristan couldn't think of the first thing to say as she kept talking.

"He is going to help unravel your father's investments and has worked out a deal with Robert Cleveland in regard to our company. While it is very true that Robert was much in favor of a match between you and Laura, as was I, he says our business relationship did not necessarily hinge upon your alliance. Especially since it seems he had very little control over Laura at any rate. Viola's northern ways must have had more of an impression. That woman is quite radical in her thinking."

Tristan's head was beginning to spin. Whether from his mother's convoluted words or the knot on it, he wasn't sure. "What in the world are you trying to tell me?"

She blew out a puff of air as though she'd been holding her breath waiting for his reaction. Then she leaned toward him with sympathy in her eyes. "It seems our dear Laura cared little for her father's plans. She and Sheldon Brady have run off together. I thought they looked entirely too familiar out on the dance floor." She lifted her head with a sniff before she sat back and reached in her pocket for a handkerchief to delicately dab against her nose. "Robert is quite beside himself, but Viola acts as if it was the very best thing that could have happened."

Tristan wished his head would stop pounding. That might make things easier to understand. His mother and Ridenour. Laura and Sheldon Brady. Then his heart lifted. Prayers he hadn't even thought to utter had been answered. He was free. Free of his promises to his mother and to Laura. A smile pushed out on his face and he wanted to jump up and go in search of Jessamine.

His mother must have guessed his thinking. She put her hand on his arm to keep him from standing. "She's gone." She looked genuinely sorry to say the words.

He knew who she meant, but he asked anyway. "Who's gone?"

"That young Shaker girl. Jessamine. Her maid told Dr. Hargrove she returned to her people. Those who shut away the world and live lives we cannot understand. Dr. Hargrove says they are peaceful and good people, but it all sounds very odd if you ask me. Dancing for worship and wearing those odd clothes. All looking so the same. I can't imagine."

"How long has she been gone?"

"The maid found a note in her room when she went in yesterday morning and now this day is more than half spent." She squeezed his arm with compassion as she said softly, "I am so sorry, Tristan."

He pulled away from her. He had to go after Jessamine. But when he stood up and started toward the door, his head went round and round and his stomach rolled over. He staggered against the wall and his mother rushed to his side to steady him.

"Let me help you back to your bed. Dr. Hargrove says you need rest."

"I don't want to lie down."

"It's either lie down or fall down." His mother pushed the truth at him as she guided him through the open door back toward his bed. "Besides, even if you were able, she made her choice. Don't you think you should honor that?"

He let her help him into the bed then. Her words stabbed through him. *Made her choice.* Jessamine had retreated from the world. She was gone. The pain in his head thumped and the bed kept spinning. Nothing was making sense. He wasn't sure anything would ever make sense again. Not without Jessamine.

Journal Entry

Harmony Hill Village
Entered on this 28th day of June in the year 1849
by Sister Sophrena Prescott

The temperature is reaching toward 90 today.
Very warm for June, but we have been continually
blessed with sufficient rain for our gardens and
crops. It looks to be a bountiful summer with much
reward for our labors.

The sisters who were assigned duty in the sewing
rooms have been brought to the preserving houses
in order to put up our bountiful vegetable harvest
in a timely manner. We have many bushels of string
beans that must be prepared for canning or drying.
It is not a bad chore as we are able to carry the
beans out under our shade trees and work there.
Those in the canning house have a more tiresome
duty and the eldresses are rotating the duty by the
hour so that none of our sisters will overheat in the
kitchens.

Our Sister Jessamine has stepped back into our
ways willingly. She is not the same sister who left us

last week. She came to me early this morn and asked forgiveness for her waywardness, but she seemed reluctant to list her sins. She named pride and vanity, which are so abundant in the world. She spoke of her yearnings to write down the frivolous words that run through her mind. She did not speak of the man from the woods until I asked her about him.

It is obvious she carries some worldly feelings for him in her heart, but I did not try to pry them out. Perhaps I erred in not doing so. If she had shown me a splinter embedded in her finger, I would have insisted it be removed before it festered. So why did I not do the same when I noted this splinter of worldly sin buried deep in her heart? Until it is removed, she will not heal. I must pray for the wisdom and fortitude of purpose to do whatever is best for her.

But her sadness is so deep that my own heart hurts when I look at her. And I wonder. I should strike out those last words. I should not wonder about the feelings of the world. I have been here surrounded by the love of my sisters and brethren too long. I know the peace of a true Believer. But our Sister Jessamine does not. She is longing for something she left behind in the world.

I fear she may never be the sister I knew and loved before she found the stranger in the woods. I seem to be mourning with her even though I know not what I mourn. Eldress Frieda will take me to task for these errant feelings and I will ask forgiveness. Such forgiveness will be needed. I must turn from these feelings and separate myself from our sister's sadness. Only she can shrug that heavy burden off her shoulders and step back onto the proper path

*that will bring her happiness. She has put her feet
on that path, but she yet looks over her shoulder
toward the world. While that is something I will
never do, I do seem to be wondering about what it
is that draws her gaze.*

34

Tristan woke early on Sunday morning. When he sat up, the dizziness and thumping were finally gone from his head. And again, as he had every waking hour since his mother had told him Jessamine had gone back to the Shaker village, he wanted to go after her. But each time his mother's words stopped him. *She made her choice.*

He surely had only dreamed those words of love after the storm swept over them. He hadn't dreamed his words. He knew he had spoken of his love to her. But he must have only wished like words spoken back to him. She had run from him. From the world. If only he could talk to her one more time. Kiss her lips once more. Then perhaps she'd make a different choice.

The thought went round and round in his head, but as much as he wanted to brush aside his mother's words, he could not. He did need to honor Jessamine's choice. She knew her father had left. Her maid told Dr. Hargrove that. So she was aware that Tristan had been freed from his promises and yet she had still run back the Shaker village. Perhaps she felt bound by promises he knew nothing about.

He pulled his bag out from under the bed. He couldn't keep hiding out in this room, his mind in a fog, not wanting to face the truth. It was time to move on. The lawyer would see to his mother's welfare. Tristan had been relieved of that duty. In time he might even appreciate that, but now sadness set too heavily on him. He felt adrift. Last week he was ready to give up his own dreams and marry a woman he didn't love to satisfy his mother's need for security. To be a dutiful son and gentleman. And why? Out of a sense of duty.

Duty. That was what Jessamine had said about the Shakers. That they had duties. Had she returned to them out of her sense of duty?

He pushed the thought aside as he began laying clothes in his bag. She made her choice. Whatever the reason.

He had to make some choices of his own. He was free to go west now the way he'd planned before his mother interfered. "Strike it rich" stories were still coming in from California. It would be good to be in the wild, seeing new territory, putting out of his mind everything about White Oak Springs. The first day of July would be a good time to begin over. He'd simply wipe away the last few weeks. Forget love.

She had chosen. So he would do the same. Choose to begin again. He would not forget his beautiful Jessamine. She would go with him in his memory and in his heart. He would remember how she'd looked, searching for him in the water while he was drowning. He'd seen her with more than his eyes as he'd floated above the water. Perhaps that was when he'd imagined the words of love because he'd felt that love. It was her love that had pulled him back to life when the light had faded and darkness had wanted to take him.

He would remember that love and the light. Scraps of Bible verses surfaced from some deep well of memory. *I am come a light into the world. And the light shineth in the darkness.* He would not step back into that darkness ever again.

He was about to fasten his case when he heard a soft knock on his door. When he didn't answer right away, the knock came again. This time stronger and more determined. Not his mother, for she would not knock from the hallway. Perhaps the lawyer or Dr. Hargrove. That would be good. He would be spared the chore of finding suitable words to pen a note to his mother.

When he opened the door, Viola Cleveland had her hand up ready to knock yet again. "Oh good. I was concerned you might be too deeply asleep to hear me and I did so want to speak to you before we left."

"You're leaving?"

Tristan could not imagine why she had come to talk to him. It certainly wouldn't be proper to invite her in. But she didn't appear to be worried about her reputation as she stepped past him and into the room.

"Please shut the door," she said. "Unless you are worried about propriety."

"I think that is your worry, madam, and not mine."

When she waved a hand in dismissal, Tristan shut the door and offered her the only chair in the room. As she perched on the chair, he awkwardly leaned back against the bed and waited for her to reveal the purpose of her visit. Laura had been right about her mother. She was far from the timid creature he had assumed she might be on their first meeting. Sitting there with her eyes leveled on him, she reminded him of his mother but without the pose of Southern charm.

She didn't bother with polite chitchat as her eyes went to his open case on the bed. "You are going after her?" It was half inquiry, half command.

"After who? Laura?" He shifted uneasily against the bed. Surely she didn't expect that.

"No, of course not. Laura finally came to her senses. Thank goodness. Saved me a good deal of grief in going against Robert." She pierced him with a steady stare. "I am quite aware you had little interest in Laura. The two of you were making

425

a deal as if love were no more than a piece of cloth that could be measured and bought and made into a serviceable coat."

"I liked Laura."

"More reason than ever not to deny her a chance to be loved." She got to her feet and stepped over in front of Tristan to poke her finger into his chest. "Jessamine. I'm talking about Jessamine. Any fool could see the two of you were in love. Don't run from that. Grab it with both hands. It's not a gift given to every person."

"She made her choice to return to the Shakers. I have to honor that." The words seemed even sadder when spoken aloud.

"Men. Southern men in particular." She blew out an irritated breath of air. "Gentlemen to the core but with such blinders on you can only see straight ahead to what you've been told is your duty to family, God, and country. Injustice can bubble and boil all around you, but if it's the way it's always been, then you can't see it."

He looked at her with a puzzled frown. "I did no injustice to Jessamine."

"Do forgive me. I do not do well in the South. Being in such familiar contact with the institution of slavery upsets me greatly." She shut her eyes a brief moment as she pulled in a calming breath. "And you could be right that you have done no injustice to Jessamine and then again, you may be very wrong."

"She is the one who left. Not me."

"She left because she thought you were marrying Laura. I spoke with her maid. It was very evident to her that Jessamine is much in love with you and in deep sadness at the thought of you marrying another." Her eyes narrowed on him. "I heard Jessamine speak those words myself and saw the sorrow they brought her. The thought of you wedding Laura."

"I did tell her that," Tristan said. "But I was going to tell her differently. Even before I knew Laura left, I was going to tell her differently."

"She had no way of knowing that."

"She knew her father left with Laura."

"That is where you are wrong." Mrs. Cleveland pinned him with her eyes. "She did not. She left before the morning meal. She only had her father's letter. The maid showed it to me. The silly man wrapped his leaving in such pretty words, his note told her nothing other than that she should trust him and wait for love to come grab her. I'm sure that is what he thought would happen when he spirited Laura away in the night. Poor Sheldon. He has written so many romantic novels he must have forgotten the art of clear communication. I fear he will be distraught when he finds his words sent Jessamine running back to the Shakers."

Tristan didn't know what to say.

The woman's face softened and her eyes were suddenly sad. "As distraught as you were. As you are."

"I love her." The simple words rose from deep inside him.

"I know you do." She touched his arm. "Go after her. It's not too late. It is never too late for love. Even your mother is discovering that."

"Do you love Mr. Cleveland?" He didn't know why he asked the question, but he did want to know her answer.

"I do. It surprises me every time I realize it." She laughed. "I can't live with him every day of the year, but I do love him. It's good we have two houses."

Tristan stared at her as hope began to awaken inside him. "I don't know what to say."

"I am not the one who needs to hear your words." She reached into the pocket of her dress and pulled out a tight roll of bills. "Here, you may need this."

"I couldn't." Tristan pulled back his hand.

"Consider it a loan from a friend." She reached around him

and shoved the money into the case on the bed. "I was quite taken with Jessamine. Make her happy, Tristan. Do that for me." She tiptoed up and brushed her lips against his cheek before she turned on her heel and pulled open the door. She looked back at him before she closed the door behind her. "Don't delay. Go after her."

When the bell tolled for meeting Sunday morning, Jessamine lined up with her sisters to march to the meetinghouse. On the outside it looked as if she had never left, that she was one with her sisters. On the inside it was a different matter. On the inside she could not stop weeping.

Tears that didn't show, but that her father had seen. And yet he had left her alone in the world. She could not make her way in the world alone. But here in the village she was not alone. Sister Sophrena had welcomed her back with open arms and heart. Eldress Frieda had greeted her with a smile when she had climbed down from Brother Hector's vegetable delivering wagon. Her waywardness had been forgiven. At least the waywardness she had confessed. It had been easy to shed some of the sins of the world. She did not miss the lacy dresses, the soft bed, or the noisy dinner tables. She felt comfort in the familiar clothes and surroundings and was more than ready once again to embrace the simple gift of silence.

Sister Sophrena warned her that the improper silence of not speaking sins was as wrong as the clanging noise of words spoken merely to tickle the ears of those listening. Even so, Jessamine had not confessed her sin of clinging to the memory of worldly love. She could not bear the thought of purging her heart and mind of Tristan completely, as she knew Sister Sophrena would tell her she must. That she would be unable to do. He was there in her mind, a glowing ember that the memory of his words of love kept bright.

In time, she would have to confess that sin. She would have to pick up her cross of denial and block memories of him from her mind in order to regain the proper communion with her fellow believers. But not yet. For a bit longer, she wanted to cherish thoughts of him. To treasure his words of love and hide them in her heart. She had more than a year before she would turn twenty-one and be expected to sign the Covenant of Belief. Time enough for the Lord to help her stop looking back toward the world with regret and find a gift of peace. Time for the Lord to show her that this place among her sisters and brothers was where she ought to be.

In the meetinghouse, it was the same as any other Sunday. The Believers sang and marched, whirled and trembled. Jessamine marched with the others and hoped she would appear to be in harmony with her sisters even though she was not. Her every movement felt wrong.

Upon her return to the village, she had gone to the gardens willingly to pick the beans. There during the busy daylight hours, she felt useful and part of the Believers' family. At night the sound of her sisters breathing in the beds around her cushioned her with familiarity. But singing of love falling down on them and going forth to exercise the songs that were to show her love for the Lord seemed to tear away her pretense.

She had promised the Lord she would live for him. He would not want a sad sham of belief. He deserved joy. A verse her granny taught her years ago came to mind. *Now the God of hope fill you with all joy and peace in believing, that ye may abound in hope.*

She did not stop dancing. She continued to move her feet through the well-known exercises even as a prayer rose up inside her. For another sign. She felt like Gideon in the Old Testament who had put out his fleece once, and even though he got his answer, he nevertheless put it out again. The Lord had not denied Gideon that sign. He would not deny her the sign she needed.

The singers suddenly changed from their marching song to one about chasing away the devil. The dancers began stomping and pushing down with their hands. Jessamine stopped moving in their very midst and looked around to see what had brought on the warring dance. And there in the doorway was Tristan. Her love. Her sign. Her gift.

He was watching her, waiting for her to see him. When she looked his way, he held out his hand toward her. A simple gesture, but one that made her heart leap with joy. Her prince had come.

Shouts of woe began sounding around her, but she paid them no mind as she moved toward him as though drawn by some unseen force. Her sisters grabbed her arms and dress, but she shook them off and kept walking. Her feet seemed to almost be floating above the floor.

She put her hand in his and the woes grew louder, but in spite of the noise, his words were clear in her ears. "Will you come with me?"

"I will."

Joy flooded through her, burning away even the memory of her tears as she followed him out of the meetinghouse. Whatever happened, her father was right. Love was worth it.

Sister Sophrena caught up with them before they reached Tristan's horse out by the road.

"You don't have to listen to her," Tristan said.

Before Jessamine could say anything, Sister Sophrena glanced at Tristan and then settled her eyes on Jessamine as she spoke. "Worry not, my brother. My words will not take her from you."

"I must go with him." Jessamine appealed to Sister Sophrena for understanding. She did not want their parting words to be woeful.

"I know." Tears shone in Sister Sophrena's eyes as she reached out to pull Jessamine close. Her words were a whisper in Jessamine's ear that none around them could hear. "I love you, Jessamine. As a mother loves her daughter, I love you. Go and find happiness."

She stepped back from Jessamine and smiled. A smile that buried itself in Jessamine's heart and one she returned in kind.

Tristan mounted the horse and then pulled Jessamine up in front of him and wrapped his arm around her. The sound of singing followed them as they rode out of the village. The woes had stopped to be replaced by the song Jessamine had hoped they would sing that morning in meeting.

> 'Tis the gift to be simple,
> 'Tis the gift to be free,
> 'Tis the gift to come down
> Where we ought to be.

Jessamine did not look back. She did not need to. She was carrying away with her everything she needed.

The sound of the song faded away behind them as they rode out of the village. When they could no longer hear even an echo of the Shaker song, Tristan leaned down close to speak into her ear. "Will you marry me, Jessamine Brady?"

"Yea." She started to change the Shaker word, but then she didn't. The Shakers were part of her just as her granny was and also her father. And now Tristan was part of her too. A wondrous, joyous part. She turned her face up toward his and said, "Yea, I will."

He bent his head down to touch his lips to hers even as the horse kept walking, taking them toward their future.

Journal Entry

Harmony Hill Village
Entered on this 1st day of July in the year 1849
by Sister Sophrena Prescott

Sunday—a day of rest and worship. I should be sad this night, but I am not. Our Sister Jessamine left us again. This time, barring a tragedy in her life, I do not believe she will ever be back. I feel no sorrow for that truth. Instead it brings me peace.

The stranger from the woods came for her. Caused a disturbance during our morning meeting as he stood at the door and beckoned to her. Before he came, I was watching her, mourning her deadened movements as she went forth to pretend an exercise of worship. She was not the sister I knew and loved, and my heart was as heavy as her feet. I lifted my hands up in the air and silently asked our Eternal Father what could be done about Sister Jessamine. I beseeched him to restore her joy.

The words no sooner went from my mind toward heaven than the man appeared in the doorway, his shadow falling across me where I stood. While my prayer was not answered as I had expected, it was

*answered when Sister Jessamine turned toward him.
A brother—Brother Andrew, I think it might have
been—began a warring-against-the-flesh song at the
sight of the man from the woods. Woes and stomping
began to shake our meetinghouse.*

*But there was no woe on Sister Jessamine. The
heavy cloud of sorrow that had enveloped her every
moment of the day since she returned to us vanished
like mist in the heat of summer sunlight. Joy lit up her
face and the sister I loved, that I do even now love,
was back.*

*And I was glad. I ran after her to give her my
blessing. I did not want her to look back with sorrow
on her time with us, but to remember the times of joy
she knew here at Harmony Hill.*

*Eldress Frieda will think I sinned. Perhaps I did.
I fear every word I write here adds to my sin. With
that in mind, in a moment I will hold the corner of
this paper to the flame of my lamp. These words are
not for others' eyes, but I had need to write them.
After I brush away the ashes, I will turn to a fresh
page in my journal and report without emotion the
leaving of our sister. I will write of the songs we
sang, how her brethren and sisters tried to keep
her among us. Then I will write of the duties of the
morrow. I will not record how it gladdened my heart
when she took the hand of the man from the world
and found joy.*

It was as it was meant to be. All cannot be Shakers.

Acknowledgments

As an author, each story I am given is a gift, but once the story is written and I'm ready to share my story gift, then it takes many other hands to wrap it in the best possible package to present to readers. I am blessed with a wonderful editor, Lonnie Hull DuPont, who reads my stories with enthusiasm but also with her editor's eyes wide open to see ways to make the finished story stronger. I can always count on Barb Barnes to show me places to polish and smooth to help make my words disappear and the story shine.

A book needs a great cover, and I'm grateful to Cheryl Van Andel and all those who work to make my book covers bright, colorful, and so appealing to the eye. I also appreciate the marketing and publicity teams who find ways to get my books before readers.

I am always thankful for each and every one of you readers who pick up my books and give my stories a chance. It takes both our imaginations—mine while writing and yours while reading—to make my characters fully come to life and live their stories.

I very much appreciate my agent, Wendy Lawton, for her encouragement and help as she guides me through the business side of writing and keeps me thinking about the stories to come.

I am mightily blessed with a wonderful family, and I treasure their loving support. I especially appreciate my husband who puts up with me disappearing into the past for hours every day while I'm writing.

Most of all, I thank the Lord for giving me the gift of one more story to tell. His story is the greatest story ever told, and I feel blessed beyond measure each time a bit of his story shines out of my books.

Ann H. Gabhart and her husband live on a farm just over the hill from where she grew up in central Kentucky. She enjoys reading, being a grandmother, and taking walks with her dogs. Ann is the author of more than twenty novels for adults and young adults. Her first Shaker novel, *The Outsider*, was a finalist for the 2009 Christian Book Awards in the fiction category. *Angel Sister* was a nominee for inspirational novel of 2011 by RT Book Reviews Magazine.

Visit Ann's website at www.annhgabhart.com.

Meet ANN H. GABHART at
WWW.ANNHGABHART.COM

Learn about New Books, Read Her Blog,
and Sign Up for Her Newsletter

CONNECT WITH ANN AT
Ann H Gabhart
AnnHGabhart

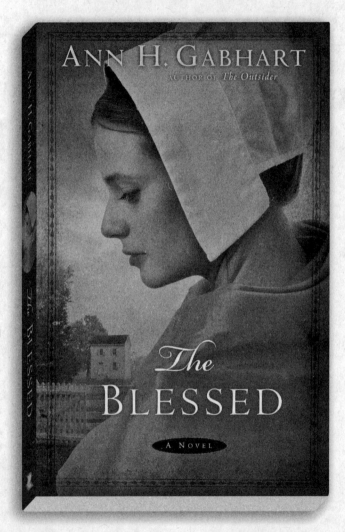

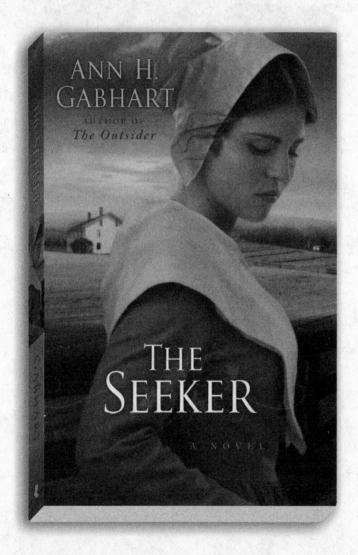

THEY LIVE IN A COMMUNITY WHERE LOVE IS FORBIDDEN,

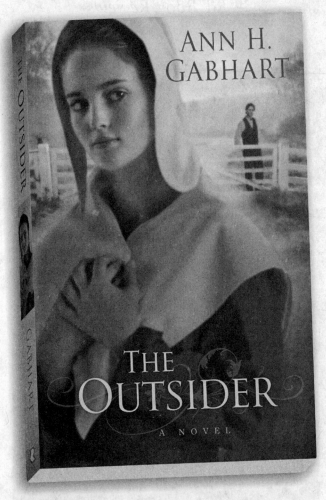

Gabrielle thought she was content—until a love from
the outside world turned her world upside down.

BUT WILL THAT STOP
THE PASSION IN THEIR HEARTS?

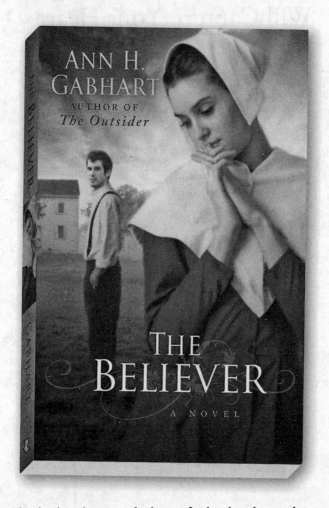

Elizabeth only wanted a home for her brother and sister.
Will her forbidden love separate her from her family?
Or will Ethan's love for her change their lives forever?

A New Novel by Bestselling Author
ANN H. GABHART
Will Capture Your Heart

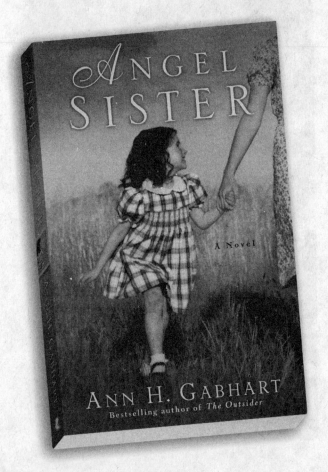

In this richly textured novel, award-winning author Ann H. Gabhart reveals the power of true love, the freedom of forgiveness, and the strength to persevere through troubled times.

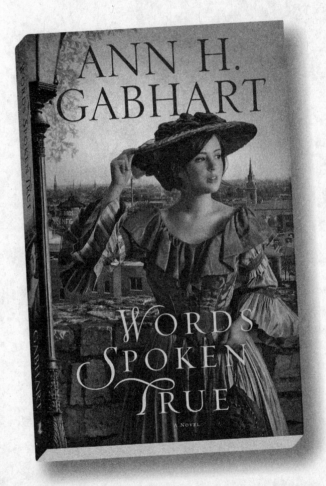